continued . . .

Ace Books by Chris Marie Green

NIGHT RISING
MIDNIGHT REIGN
BREAK OF DAWN
A DROP OF RED

Anthologies

FIRST BLOOD
(with Susan Sizemore, Erin McCarthy, and Meljean Brook)

A DROP OF RED

VAMPIRE BABYLON
BOOK FOUR

Chris Marie Green

ACE BOOKS, NEW YORK

THE BERKLEY PUBLISHING GROUP
Published by the Penguin Group
Penguin Group (USA) Inc.
375 Hudson Street, New York, New York 10014, USA
Penguin Group (Canada), 90 Eglinton Avenue East, Suite 700, Toronto, Ontario M4P 2Y3, Canada
(a division of Pearson Penguin Canada Inc.)
Penguin Books Ltd., 80 Strand, London WC2R 0RL, England
Penguin Group Ireland, 25 St. Stephen's Green, Dublin 2, Ireland (a division of Penguin Books Ltd.)
Penguin Group (Australia), 250 Camberwell Road, Camberwell, Victoria 3124, Australia
(a division of Pearson Australia Group Pty. Ltd.)
Penguin Books India Pvt. Ltd., 11 Community Centre, Panchsheel Park, New Delhi—110 017, India
Penguin Group (NZ), 67 Apollo Drive, Rosedale, North Shore 0632, New Zealand
(a division of Pearson New Zealand Ltd.)
Penguin Books (South Africa) (Pty.) Ltd., 24 Sturdee Avenue, Rosebank, Johannesburg 2196,
South Africa

Penguin Books Ltd., Registered Offices: 80 Strand, London WC2R 0RL, England

This is an original publication of The Berkley Publishing Group.

This is a work of fiction. Names, characters, places, and incidents either are the product of the author's imagination or are used fictitiously, and any resemblance to actual persons, living or dead, business establishments, events, or locales is entirely coincidental. The publisher does not have any control over and does not assume any responsibility for author or third-party websites or their content.

PRINTING HISTORY
Ace trade paperback edition / March 2009

Library of Congress Cataloging-in-Publication Data

Green, Chris Marie.
    A drop of red / Chris Marie Green.—1st ed.
        p. cm.—(Vampire Babylon; bk. 4)
    ISBN 978-0-441-01681-5
    1. Madison, Dawn (Fictitious character)—Fiction.   2. Women stunt performers—Fiction.
    3. Vampires—Fiction.   4. Hollywood (Los Angeles, Calif.)—Fiction.   I. Title.

    PS3607.R4326D76 2009
    813'.6—dc22
                                                                        2008049490

PRINTED IN THE UNITED STATES OF AMERICA

10   9   8   7   6   5   4   3   2   1

To Sajen, Torrey, and Morgan.
I'll love you forever.

While writing this next batch of books, I had lots of help, and I'd like to thank everyone who so kindly offered aid. First, there's my "Kingswood crew": Claire Ross from London Walks, who served as guide and driver; Alexander Ockwell, my student guide; Philippa Watts, who arranged my tour of Kingswood; Sally Cunliffe and David Hughes from the Kingswood English department and Darryl Harding from the drama department; and Angela Snelling, the welcoming receptionist. Thank you also to Dee Lim from Royal High School for her tour and her time. To each of you—I'm so lucky to have met you and learned from your store of knowledge. Also, thank you to "C. S." for the use of what just might be his land around the fictional Queenshill.

I'd additionally like to extend my appreciation to the authors of the books that lent insight into this world, particularly Jack Zipes for editing *The Trials & Tribulations of Little Red Riding Hood* and Raymond T. McNally and Radu Florescu for *In Search of Dracula*. Thank you to Wally Lind and Paul from Thames Valley on the *crimescenewriter* web loop, as well as Ginjer Buchanan, Cameron Dufty, and the Ace staff, plus the Knight Agency. As always, I also owe a lot to Sheree Whitefeather and Judy Duarte, my incredible critique partners.

I've taken advantage of fictional license in some locations and historical details for the benefit of telling this story, and I claim any errors as my own.

Now, on to the hunt . . .

ONE

When You Stray . . .

İt was a night Kate Lansing would've ended up regretting.

If she had only survived to regret it.

At the moment, she was taking a numbing sip from her third cosmopolitan, her legs tucked under her on an Italian leather settee in a flat just outside of London's financial district. Inadvertently mocking the last minutes of her life, which were ticking, ticking to an end, she tapped her fingers against the cocktail glass while an Amy Winehouse song played.

The raspberry taste in her mouth sent a giddy wave through her, and she dizzily smiled at a dancing redheaded girl across the lounge. Nearby, a second female—plump, quiet, with frizzy russet hair—sat in a chair, content to merely watch.

These were just two of the quick friends Kate had met tonight in a Brixton club, several tube stops away.

At the foot of Kate's settee, two more of her new mates sat on the luxurious carpet while stretching their knee-high-booted legs out from under their identical long skirts. Like the other girls, their matching slender red ties were askew, their faces fashionably pale, their own cosmos untouched on a marbled table.

A fifth girl had gone to the loo and would return shortly.

They were all from the same exclusive school, they'd revealed under the throb and humidity of the dance lights after they'd used fake IDs to buy Kate and her friend Harry drinks. Then, as if a part of their club now, Kate and Harry had agreed to carry on the party here, where they said one of their cousins lived when he wasn't traveling on business. Where they had let flow the liquor and turned the music on high. Where Harry had already gone upstairs to zonk out in a bedroom.

Where, even now, Kate didn't have much longer to live.

"So tell us, Katie-luv," said the girl with the long, sleek sable hair and vivid eyes that resembled her name. Violet. "With Harry cozy and warm upstairs, we girls can really chat."

Kate nodded, her eyelids fighting a battle to stay open. Why did she seem so rat-arsed on alcohol while the rest of the group was as sober as judges?

Violet continued, voice all sweetness and light as she glanced at the curved stairway that led to the next floor, where Harry rested. "How's the old boy in the shagging department?"

Kate coughed, and the abrupt gesture tilted her cosmo in her hand. As she righted the cocktail, she caught a warped view of Violet and the second girl—whatshername?—through the glass.

Kate shuddered at the bent vision, at their twisted smiles and piercing irises. She lowered the beverage, splashing it on her low-cut jumper in her clumsiness.

"Me and Harry?" she said in carefully enunciated drunk-speak while brushing at the wet stain on her chest. "We're . . . chums. That's all. No naughty involved."

"Brilliant news," Violet said. "He's quite yummy, you know. You wouldn't mind if I . . . ?"

The second girl, with her chopped-to-the-chin strawberry blond hair and a smattering of freckles, took up where the playful Violet had left off. "Vi, you wouldn't dare keep all the fresh meat to yourself."

They both giggled now, and Kate blinked, knowing she should join them. After all, Harry might welcome a bit of sport with a female who was actually interested. Kate had meant it when she said they were merely chums—even if Harry often pushed for more.

So why wasn't she laughing, as well?

"Well then, Katie," Violet said, leaning forward, her long hair spilling over a delicate shoulder. "How about other boys? Do you have any spicy stories there?"

Kate felt her skin heat, and at the telltale sign, Violet covered her mouth with a hand, pseudo-scandalized as she half hid another giggle.

"I believe the answer is no," Whatshername said in a voice that belonged more on a grassy hockey field than in a posh flat. "Could we actually have genuine purity in our midst?"

"Please," Violet said, cutting the coyness. "You could smell it on her at the club."

Kate blinked at that, then decided it was only a turn of phrase.

"I just want to hear her say it," Whatshername said. "Especially since she gave us that bad-girl story about having skipped away from Mummy and Daddy's home only to take up with good old Harry. Doesn't sound so innocent to me."

Violet raised her brow, daring Kate to contradict them.

But Kate was still back at the part about her father. Earlier, when she had first become warm and pleasantly filled with drink, she had told her new mates that he'd died last year. Kate rarely saw any old friends now that school was done, so talking had been a relief.

Yet now, it was almost as if these girls had brought her father up because, somehow, they'd known it would hurt.

Perhaps it was in the way Violet and the other girl were watching her, their chins lowered. And when Violet's eyes narrowed so that she reminded Kate of a cat—a purring little thing ready to pounce—the thought only gained credence.

"Oh, yes," Violet said. "I remember now. Katie told us that Daddy's passed on. Mummy, too."

"She's got a stepmum," Whatshername said.

"Ah, the mean woman back home who kicked our Kate out because she's become a touch too hard to handle lately. Nice mothering, that. But luckily, there was Harry to turn to."

"Good old Harry," the strawberry blonde echoed.

A cloud seemed to be closing over Kate—a hazy weight from the buzz of her cocktails pressing down on her chest, her head, her vision.

She didn't want to be here with these girls anymore. They'd been amusing enough back at the club, but now?

Something had changed, making Kate feel mousy and cornered.

Something unnameable but there all the same. . . .

A great smashing sound rent the air, and Kate flinched, once again blinking at what she saw.

Across the room, the dancing redhead—wasn't her name Noreen?—had . . .

Kate refocused her gaze. Noreen was swinging from a chandelier over seven meters off the floor, whooping and laughing as her quiet friend looked on with blasé interest.

How . . . ?

Kate swallowed. How had Noreen jumped that high? A chair? A table?

With one look round, Kate didn't discover anything sufficient to have provided such a launch.

Both Violet and the strawberry blonde stood and ran to the action. And when Whatshername crouched, then zinged up to the other side of the chandelier herself, Kate's jaw dropped.

The girl had jumped from the floor.

·The room seemed to dip and sway as Kate grappled with explanations. Just how drunk *was* she?

Crystals banged together in demented chaos, and all of the schoolgirls clapped and urged their mates on.

Violet turned to Kate. "Join us, Katie? Come now!"

Kate couldn't answer, couldn't move.

The friendly smile Violet had been wearing melted.

Then, just as Kate's heartbeat started filling her head, dampening it in cottony, far-removed throbs, she spotted something descending the stairs.

The fifth new friend, Blanche. Her normally alabaster skin was pink against her waist-long raven hair as she wiped her hand over her deep red lips.

It occurred to Kate that Blanche had been gone awhile. Had she been with Harry . . . ?

When Violet saw Blanche, the room went silent except for the music. The chandelier-swinging girls even dropped to the floor with shocking ease, then straightened, cool as the fog that kept muddling Kate's mind.

But Violet's bristling posture was far easier to understand as she stalked toward the staircase.

The chandelier kept clanking and rocking.

"Tell me you didn't, you slag," Violet said, her voice different, more of a vibration than real words.

A rain of shivers attacked Kate. Go. She should just get Harry and go.

Now.

She edged toward the end of the settee, hoping no one would notice.

Blanche paused near the bottom of the stairs. "I was only visiting the lav, Vi. No need to get excited."

Violet circled to the front of the stairs until her back was to Kate, her face hidden. All the girls' eyes widened at what they must have seen in their leader's expression.

But Blanche? She merely rolled her eyes and descended the rest of the way, sauntering across the floor and toward the bar, with all its opened, loitering bottles.

"Vi," she added, "it's hardly fair that you should always go first. After Wolfie, I mean."

When the black-haired girl offered a challenging smile to Violet, her teeth were sharp, gleaming.

Bloody hell.

Lurching to a wobbling stand, Kate forgot subtlety and headed for the stairs, intent on fetching Harry.

Fangs. Kate had only been imagining them . . . at least that was what she kept repeating.

She stumbled up the first step, falling to her hands and knees as her balance betrayed her. The music seemed to get louder as the girls lost interest in each other and laughed at her, cruel jabs of mirth knocking at Kate's skull.

"Oh, Katie-luv," Violet said, coming over to stand at the lip of the staircase.

Her tone was calm now, as if she had set aside her anger with Blanche. "Don't mind us. We fight; we kiss and make up; we go to the next party. No reason to fret."

The rest of the group—even Blanche—meandered closer, flanking Violet.

A pack, Kate thought as she pulled herself to the next stair, her heartbeat shredding her chest into slivers.

"We tend to celebrate a bit madly when we're away from the school and its silly rules," Violet added. "And we're always on the lookout for girls like us. That's why we brought you here."

Whatshername placed a hand on Violet's shoulder, then rested her chin there. "We thought *you* might be open to running at our pace."

"Yet it seems you're not an ideal candidate after all." Violet addressed the girls: "Is she?"

"No," the lot of them said in the same disappointed tone.

"From all appearances," Violet added, "I would venture that you're only on track to give binge drinking a terrible name, Katie-luv."

Then, as one, they all tilted their heads at Kate.

Fear spiked in her, and that was even before their gazes started to glow.

Now that Kate thought of it, hadn't their eyes done the same back at the club when she'd first met them and before she'd dismissed it as a trick of the flashing dance lights?

Grasping for something to hold—a stair, carpeting—Kate tried to suck in oxygen. But her lungs were too tight.

She grappled, finally clutching the edge of a step, pulling herself up, but she was too weak, the room spinning too wildly. . . .

Violet's voice poked into her consciousness, a hollow, faraway sound.

But not far enough.

"So it appears we've come to that time of night," Violet said with a sigh. "Pity you didn't work out."

More adrenaline consumed Kate as she tried to crawl just a centimeter more—

Then she heard a whoosh from the bottom of the stairs, felt a pair of hands on her as her body left the ground and she was lifted, *forced*, to the top of the landing, where—

WHEN Kate next opened her eyes, gradually making her way out of a mental blank, she was slumped on the lower portion of a massive, white-duvet-covered bed, resting peacefully with a swathed Harry at the other end. Paintings, with their bold, dark strokes, loomed from the pale walls, and a heating vent blew air at the sheer drapery ghosting the night-hushed windows.

She took a moment to regain her bearings, then remembered.

Jumping to a chandelier . . . *fangs* . . .

But now there was only peace. Thank goodness, just peace.

Pulse smoothing out, Kate thought, *Maybe it was only a nightmare.*

Had she got utterly pissed, then blacked out and fallen asleep only to have bad dreams?

Mortified, baffled, relieved that she wasn't truly crawling up a staircase or trying to get away from sharp teeth—what had been in those drinks anyway?—Kate moved farther up the mattress, toward the shape huddled under the duvet.

"Harry?" she asked.

"Mmmm." A deep, almost growly sleepy sound.

His form rose and fell in a rhythm that comforted her. She had never been so happy to see Harry in her life.

She exhaled, so tired now that she was safe. "You should've been in my head earlier. It was Daliesque."

Moving even closer to him, she lay down, then put her hand against his rising and falling back.

His breathing picked up, and she took her hand away. She never meant to get him going, but somehow she always did.

Hollow, heavy gasps . . . Yet there was also a trace of primal urgency underneath it all.

Kate turned away, preparing to get out of bed and take him with her. Time to get back to his much-less-impressive—yet far-more-welcoming—flat.

But that was when she saw it in the front corner of the room.

It.

Her mouth opened, but the only thing that came out was a croaking excuse for a scream.

Drip . . .

A thick glob of blood fell from the gaped mouth of the dead man impaled through the stomach on what looked to be a spike embedded in the floor. The body's eyes—Harry's eyes? *Harry's?*—bugged out of their sockets as Kate tried to scream again.

But just as she had on the stairs, as she had in every childhood nightmare, she couldn't make a sound.

The form behind her rolled over in the bed, its weight making the mattress dip and shift.

That breathing—excited, ragged . . .

She felt a touch on her back, fingers . . . *claws* . . . snagging her jumper as the nails dragged downward, lower, lower. Her spine arched away, stabbed by chills.

Get out of bed, she told herself. *Just go*, go . . .

But before she could, a paw swiped her back to the mattress, and the thing behind her loomed over her now.

Feral eyes—

Fur—

Teeth.

Rows upon rows of white daggers fronted by two prominent fangs and stitched together by saliva as the creature opened its mouth to take the bite it had obviously been waiting for.

TWO

✝HE FEEDinG

Nearly One Night Later

Dusk closed over the Southwark borough of London like a falling gravestone, casting a November pall that Dawn Madison couldn't lift.

Maybe it was because a whole year away from the California sunshine had deprived her of verve, she thought while turning away from the window with its parted velvet-curtain view.

Or maybe she was just feeling the weight of her second vampire Underground hunt bearing down on her.

After sitting in a Queen Anne chair near her four-poster bed, she flicked a cigarette lighter to flame, held it under a sharp sewing needle. Then, with the tool sterilized, she deftly threaded it and hitched up the skirt of her nightgown so she could unwind the bandage she'd wrapped around her lower thigh.

Even though she'd already cleaned her gaping cut, she wiped it with an ethanol pad from her kit, clenching her teeth at the sting.

A girl could never be too careful.

"You used to at least wince," Costin said from the shaded corner near the head of the bed, where the creamy, diaphanous draping hid most of him from view. His voice was deep, scraped, hinting
at a foreign inflection that betrayed his roots in a dark country
while also revealing a centuries-long weariness.

Dawn smiled tightly, damned if she was going to give in to any
pain. "Accidents happen. I didn't lose much blood because you
began healing me pretty quickly. No skin off my back."

"No, merely layers of skin off your leg. I'm sorry, Dawn."

"Sorry for what? Needing blood to survive?"

Or sorry she was the reason he was a vampire who, even after a
year, was still finding his way?

He sighed. "Specifically, I'm sorry I was not able to heal this
injury as well as I manage to erase a typical bite wound."

This—and other recent nips—was deeper than a normal bite.
He'd been getting carried away lately.

"You tried to close the injury up," she said, "and you came
pretty close this time. You even helped me to bring it to a point
where I could take care of it myself, but you just need more years
on you as a vamp to be a more efficient healer." She kept sterilizing.
"Right now, dealing with something way deeper than a regular bite
takes more of your power than your age and inexperience allow.
The older you get, the better you'll be."

The minute Dawn stopped talking, she realized that maybe she
was sounding too mentorlike.

Was she acting like the cornered hunter who'd once used
Benedikte, the most dominant creature in the Hollywood Underground, to become a vampire, herself? Of course, she'd wielded her
new powers to save Costin's fading existence by turning *him* into a
vampire and, in unwitting return, become *his* creator. Yet that's the
last thing she wanted to be. His master.

It didn't matter that she'd killed Benedikte, her own maker, and
that the act had directly restored her humanity. But it'd done nothing for Costin, and she'd promised that she would never come off

like she was in charge of him, even if a power trip could make up for all the betrayals he'd put her through for his quest.

She heard Costin move away from the wall, probably to offer help with what she needed to do next with her injury—a process she'd already perfected.

"I've got it," she said, working quickly to pinch together the parted flesh of her wound, then slide the needle through the cut's middle.

Sh-iiiittt.

She schooled herself to show no pain.

Stitch, knot, snip the thread.

Damn it, damn it. . . .

Stitch, knot, snip.

When she finished, she tried not to act as if she'd been holding her breath. But Costin wasn't fooled.

A shadow slanted over the top half of his face as he lingered at the bedpost, dressed in a silken black shirt and pants, his arms loosely crossed over his chest, as if to counter the long-suffering sorrow in the topaz eyes that burned out of the near-darkness. Where he used to have scars marking his sculpted face, he now had smooth, pale skin, which contrasted with the dark, lustrous hair that fell just past his neck.

I took away those scars by making him this way, she thought. *But I gave him injuries that go so much deeper.*

Her chest constricted, yet she didn't know what else to do to assure him that she was a big girl, that she could handle another night of making things up to him.

"Getting excited while you're feeding is par for the course," she said casually, hoping it would get them out of this funk. On the wound, she dabbed a smudge of healing wonder gel that a team member had developed once upon a time, then secured a fresh bandage over it. "It happens to all of us."

"Yes, *all* of us."

She caught the emphasis on the word "all," and she knew he was referring to Jonah—the covetous owner of the body Costin had once "rented" so he might carry out his crusade against the Underground vampires. Since Costin was a soul traveler, he had required the aid of a healthy host, but the arrangement had backfired in this bargain with Jonah—the body Dawn had trapped him in when she had made the choice to save him.

Thing was, Jonah's consciousness was now enclosed inside this vampiric form, too, suppressed by Costin, but every once in a while, the original owner managed to emerge for a short time before Costin tamed him again.

But even from inside, Jonah urged Costin's hunger, more and more.

"Stop thinking about him." Dawn eased her nightgown over her bandaged injury, which throbbed with the cadence of a stilted apology. "You've managed to keep Jonah at bay for a while. He didn't crash in on tonight's feeding."

"There are reasons other than Jonah for losing control, Dawn. The sensing I felt last night . . . It's still enough to stimulate, to make me overly excited."

She glanced up to find a fervent glimmer in his gaze. So that's what had pushed him overboard—the perceptive twinge that assured him an Underground was active somewhere nearby. He wouldn't have begun to constantly sense this master unless a rival blood brother was running around above the earth in the London area and the other vampire wasn't bothering to shield his powers, either.

"Or," Dawn added hopefully, fishing for more information, "there was that phone message you accessed after waking up?"

"There was that, as well."

"What was it about?"

He hesitated, still so unused to sharing information with her, even after so much time had passed.

A whole year after that terrible night.

Flashes of seeing Costin crumpled on the floor of Benedikte's quarters, his borrowed body—Jonah's body—slick with blood, his soul shut away by the strange bargain he'd made with a higher power so Costin might find a state of grace after erasing each and every Underground in existence.

A soldier with a mission to win back his own soul.

She stood, going to him. It was as if there was a magnetic pull, a link between a master gone human and her progeny.

A force neither of them could fight.

She got so close that heat vibrated between their bodies. Trembles cascaded down her length, melting her under the skin until need pooled low in her belly, pulsing.

Hungering.

Always hungering . . .

She folded her arms over her midsection, as if to contain her constant desire for him. "When I tricked the Master into making me a vampire so I could exchange with you and save you, I really thought it was the only way."

"I know." He touched her hair, which she had worn long and loose tonight, just the way he liked it.

Leaning into his palm, she felt his preternaturally soft skin hiding a harder layer beneath.

She closed her eyes. Sometimes it was hard to see Jonah's face with Costin peering out from behind the facade.

"It sounds like you're okay with the way things are," she said, "but remember, we've got Awareness—or whatever it is that can open your mind to mine now. Don't bother sugarcoating."

He drifted his fingers from her hair to her face, to the cheek where she used to have a blazing scar from a fight with the vampire Robby Pennybaker. But becoming a vampire herself, even for a short time, had healed all the outer wounds except for the ones she'd gotten recently.

Yet the so-called healing had also left behind a stain in her returned soul, a heaviness.

She almost gave in to the slump of it when Costin used their Awareness to come in to her. He was light, drifting through her head like a brushstroke of bright color.

The old Dawn would've closed him off, just for the sake of defending what remained of herself, so she fought the instinct.

As he continued easing into her—now a shimmer, now an invisible spark—her muscles went liquid. Yet this wasn't anything like the times in L.A. when he'd entered her for sexual gratification, when he'd fed and rooted off of her very humanity. The welcome invasion wasn't as carnal now. It was . . .

What? More intimate?

It couldn't be. She wasn't built for intimacy, and she'd spent a long time proving it to herself.

As he went deeper, her heartbeat escalated, pushing at her from the inside out.

"Are you still hungry?" she asked. "You didn't get much blood earlier."

Usually when he bit her, he took only a little, just enough to satisfy. Then he'd move on to one of the blood bags he quietly secured from a blood-bank contact.

But Dawn's own blood did something for him that the others didn't—he liked the taste, the immediacy.

Maybe even the intimacy.

His fingers skimmed to her eyebrow, where she'd once proudly worn a scar from a stunt gag. A badge from what seemed like another lifetime.

"You are generous for a woman who had to fend off a starving creature less than a half hour ago," he said.

"I know that you won't always have to feed so regularly. It's just another thing we'll have to trip through."

He trailed his fingers down to her lips, and she automatically reached up to place her hand over the back of his.

Cool skin, she thought, knowing how she could heat it up. Desperate to do it.

An ache drilled between her legs. His appetite was her appetite.

"I say we try again," Dawn murmured against his fingertips.

He started to draw his hand away, but she grabbed his wrist, keeping him where she wanted him.

With every hammering beat of her pulse, memory stamped her, formed from the moment she'd felt him awaken beside her in bed tonight.

As she had slowly stretched to consciousness, he'd checked messages on a cell phone registered to Jonah. Afterward, more excited than usual, he'd kissed her neck, then gone lower, over her chest, dragging up her nightgown along the way. His fangs hadn't emerged yet, so she'd helped him rev up by squirming under his mouth as he'd tasted the skin of her stomach, her belly, then the slickness of her sex.

Shuddering, she'd encouraged him by parting her legs, her heartbeat thudding so loudly that it had blocked—or maybe welcomed—the danger of having him in such a vulnerable place.

Normally she was good about guiding him to slow satiation, but tonight, he'd gotten more quickly stimulated than usual.

The phone message, she'd thought. It had to have played a part. . . .

Before she'd been ready, he'd reared back his head, revealing fangs fully primed and aimed at her femoral artery.

But it was the silver fierceness in his eyes that had warned her to dodge out from under him, leaving her with a deep gouge from his fang on her lower thigh.

She hadn't recognized this level of wildness in him before, even though they'd both been concerned about his appetite getting to this point. That's why they kept a crucifix under the bed, among other easy-access places around the room. As a newer vampire who was slightly more powerful than one of the lower Groupies from the Hollywood Underground, Costin had found through controlled experimentation that he was susceptible to a holy-item stunning, and it had put the kibosh on this particular feeding.

Now she whispered against his fingers. "Just take a drink. I'll be okay."

His body tensed, resisting like he always did. "What if—"

"We'll deal. But we've got too much to do for you to be at low power. Those twinges you had last night are stronger than ever now that we've narrowed down a London location. And heck knows that Kiko's visions—when he gets them—haven't panned out lately."

Even though the process of isolating this new Underground was taking forever, she knew that a search usually lasted much longer for Costin. After he'd gotten his first twinge for this Underground—this master must've been visiting the U.S., outside his regular area—they had followed the vibes eastward, combing their way from L.A. to the Midwest to New York to Ireland, Scotland, and finally, south to London. Now that they had homed in on this city, the vibes were more solid than he'd experienced with many other Undergrounds. It made them wonder if this one might be relatively careless.

Or if this community might be even stronger than the others.

"You're sick of waiting, are you?" he asked. "You're eager for a fight?"

She grabbed his shirt, bringing him closer to her as she leaned back against the bedpost. Its baroque etchings dug into her back, but she couldn't have cared less—not with his heady presence searing into her.

His mouth was a breath away from hers, and when she spoke, the moist heat of her deflected words made her lips tingle.

"I'm on pins and needles to get this started," she said, raising her mouth so that her lower lip touched his.

She rubbed it against his mouth as his eyes misted with a hint of the silver he'd inherited from her—from the Hollywood line of vampires.

"Then what are your pugilistic plans for the night?" he asked, slipping one of his hands to her waist.

Lust.

Need.

The contact branded her skin, even with the linen of her gown between them. Her sex throbbed, damp and ready.

"The usual," she said. "See if Kiko's mind is clear enough to guide us through a psychic stroll down an alley we haven't combed before. Maybe get in some physical training. Troll the Internet for more possible subterranean havens."

"That's assuming Kiko hasn't indulged."

The reminder of how their team's psychic had gradually gone back to a reliance on pain pills, in spite of all his best efforts, pinched at Dawn.

Costin sensed her distress, then soothed her with a caress of mental warmth.

Let us not worry about Kiko. He silently spoke via their Awareness. *Not right now.*

Wave upon wave of his shared thoughts flowed into Dawn, weakening and strengthening her at the same time, tearing her apart with the agony of wanting him.

When he rested his forehead against hers, she clung to his shirt all the tighter. "I wish I could stop worrying."

"Tonight you will."

His slow smile made her slide down the bedpost an inch.

"Why?" she asked.

"The message left for me on the phone."

He was ready to tell her now, and the knowledge heated her. But if she got too greedy and tried to search his mind for more, he would only block her.

Blood coming to a simmer, she twisted his shirt.

He leaned his forehead against hers. "The caller was a woman who claims to know where the bodies of some vampire victims have been buried."

She inhaled sharply, then asked, "Underground vamps?"

"Not necessarily."

Still. "I knew your excitement during the feeding had to be something out of the ordinary."

"Always picking up on the clues." He was stroking her neck now. "Your detective work is most worthy."

"How did this woman know to contact us? We don't exactly advertise our paranormal leanings. We haven't even put out a shingle telling people we're Limpet and Associates. Not that we ever settled on any plans to open up shop . . ."

"Limpet and Associates was a guise that worked well in L.A. I am not in a hurry to repeat the operation so soon. There are other, unofficial modes of investigating." He rested his thumb against her jugular. "And we shall find out how this caller knows of us tonight when we meet her."

" 'Meet'? You trust her enough to—"

"Dawn."

In his clearly building eagerness, he gripped her waist, and something spiraled inside of her. She buried her fingers in his hair then dragged him down to her, needing to feel his mouth, needing to feed as much as he did.

As their lips touched, their thoughts mixed together: a dreamscape of melded colors, textured and separated like thin swirls of paint before spinning together and disappearing into one deep shade that existed only when she was near Costin.

Dizzy, she inhaled the scent of his clothes—those spices from ages gone by, from lands she had only recently started to visit.

Weak, she thought. He made her so weak.

But there was also strength in knowing that she was his constant sustenance. That it was partly her blood that kept him from needing to hunt in the night.

That it was her availability that controlled the vampire within him—the creature he'd fought and despised for centuries.

Costin sucked her lower lip, ending the kiss, but still cupping her neck with one palm, his thumb nestling against the center of her throat.

As his fangs thrust out one stimulated bit more, he pressed her throat, and she gasped, then cuffed his hand away.

They stared at each other, blood pounding, the rhythm of it shared in body and mind.

His gaze seemed to explode as he cupped her neck again, squeezing ever so slightly once more.

This time she allowed it, taking her punishment, believing it made her even stronger. Besides, after what had happened back in L.A., she could take anything.

His fangs grew a little more, and he inhaled, closing his eyes in his resistance.

"I can take it," she said, reaching up to his hand, twining her fingers with his until they were both gripping her neck. "Accept what we both are now."

But what exactly that was, she didn't know.

As far as vampires went, the team had started to think that their preternatural states of being were more about being spiritually dead rather than physically. Costin definitely wasn't human, but with the blood exchange that had created what he was now, he and the others were *beyond* human. They had powers that blew her mind, but at the same time, on a basic level, they couldn't reproduce except through the exchange.

They had lost their souls, leaving behind personalities instead, and the new blood had altered the makeup of their bodies.

What were they?

That was the million-dollar question.

Opening his eyes, his gaze back to a familiar hue of passionate self-hatred, Costin disentangled his hand from hers.

"Why do you keep pushing me?" he asked.

She had no answer.

Both of their chests were rising and falling as he held his fingertips to her collarbone, then skimmed his hand down her chest, as if wishing to slow the pace. Her own hand followed his, but she stopped to untie her gown's closures along the way.

The material parted, huffing air over her flesh, her breasts.

"Why can it not be *this* way?" he asked.

Her nipples peaked as he insinuated his fingers into the open gown, slipping upward, over a breast. He circled his thumb over her, tenderly exploring.

The turnabout threw Dawn off balance. She arched against him, feeling the bulge under his thin pants.

"Faster is more our speed," she said, panting.

He closed his eyes again, his hand still on her breast as he kept fighting himself. A shudder wracked him, and she reached out, ripping at his shirt to get it open.

But his words kept punching at her. *Why do you keep pushing me?*

She didn't know. And maybe she didn't want to.

He was shaking now, his eyes silvering again as he fought the vampire within.

"You want this, Costin. . . ." she whispered. "Admit it."

At the mention of his name, he jerked his head back, like something had shifted inside of him.

And her instincts told her that it wasn't a change of heart.

Wary, Dawn watched him. His previous attack in bed had been brutal, and this was too prolonged. She had an idea about what might be ailing him now.

Even without going into his head, Dawn freakin' knew.

In the next breath, he had righted his posture, and when he opened his eyes again, they were still silver, but Dawn knew they'd be blue under any other circumstances.

Damn it, just what they needed. Costin must've really been worn down by fighting his hunger to allow this to happen.

"Just because we talked about you doesn't mean we want you around," she said, bracing her hands against his chest. "Get out of here, Jonah."

Costin's deeper, more eloquent voice gave way to Jonah's younger, brasher American one.

"Is that how to welcome me back?" he asked.

Dawn glared at him, but he didn't seem to mind.

No, he was too busy taking in the view from this newly dominant position in his vampire body, absorbing the warm air from the heating vent on his skin, enjoying the smell of lavender from a vase on an end table. All his senses would be heightened, and he was obviously reveling in them firsthand.

When he was done, he looked down at Dawn, at his hand on her bare breast.

Lifting his eyebrow in amusement, and maybe in wry apology, he removed his touch, even while keeping his other arm around her.

"Don't ever tell me I'm not a gentleman," he said.

"Oh, you're a keeper, all right."

He laughed softly. "Last time I saw you up close and personal like this, we were moving into this place. Just like Costin to pick a fixer-upper to nest in, isn't it?"

Maybe Dawn should've been stunned by his casual attitude, as if him showing up and taking over happened all the time. But at this point in her life, even Jimmy Hoffa crashing through the roof and smashing onto her bed wouldn't have seemed strange.

"Yeah," she said, "it's been a while. But you might also recall how, at your last visit, Costin pressed you right back into the depths of this body, where you belong. Why don't you leave before he has to bother again?"

"That would mean going back to my jail cell, and I like to get out into the yard every once in a while."

She continued glaring. "You need to let go of me."

"And ruin a fantasy?"

But, surprisingly, he did loosen his hold. After a pause, he even exhaled and shook his head, then used one hand to close the gape of her nightgown, although that didn't do much to chase the goose bumps from her skin.

She tried to pull away from his other hand, but he still had a grip on her arm.

I need a crucifix, she thought. But the nearest and most available one was way on the other side of the bed, where she'd dropped it earlier after calming Costin.

There weren't any other weapons within reach—not even a vial of holy water to flick at him.

So she geared her mind for an attack, hoping that all the telekinetic training she'd done would pay off.

Jonah read her body language. "I can guess what's coming next. Remember, what Costin knows, I know. You and I are linked just as surely as you and the boss man are."

She shut her mind against him. That way, if she could catch him by surprise, she might have a chance at thrusting him across the room with the force of her will. Maybe it'd even jar Costin back into control.

Calling upon each and every *acting!* skill she'd learned from Hollywood, she relaxed. But that only made Jonah suspicious.

Great.

He finished giving her an endlessly long look, then turned his attention to perusing her new, improved, postvampire complexion. Another grin followed. Dawn wasn't used to that mouth smiling so comfortably, and she found herself glancing at it with a little too much interest.

"I miss your scars," he said, cocking his head, taking to the vampire habit with all the ease of someone who was way too comfortable being a creature of the night. "On you and me, both. They added a lot of character."

"In your case, they added an early alert system. Any guy who'd take a razor to his face just to spite someone else doesn't have character—they have a psychosis."

He laughed at that. Yeah—laughed. Probably because he knew that Dawn had found the scars on her mysterious boss's body to be disturbingly hot—at least before she'd found out how they'd gotten there.

"So . . ." he said, changing the subject. "What about that bite you offered earlier?"

Dawn just gave him a you've-got-to-be-joking look.

It didn't deter him. "Didn't you say that this body needed to feed? And you and I both know I'd be much more willing to enjoy the process than Costin."

He had her there. But . . . "If you think I won't get a crucifix just because it'll affect Costin, too, you're wrong. He's probably urging me to do something with you right now and I just can't hear him because you're suppressing him."

"He's having a fit." Hardly caring, Jonah instead touched the tip of his tongue to a fang, as if wallowing in the sensation of experiencing it firsthand. "But I'm going to stay longer, if you don't mind."

His refusal made her angry enough to summon energy and shape it into something like a fist. She reared it back, then pushed out at Jonah.

Bam—

He reacted a split second too late, one of his hands coming up to block the attack. After stumbling backward, he finally found his balance.

"You realize I can do a lot more than just give a loathe tap," Dawn said, advancing a step forward.

His hair covered half his face as his shoulders bristled into a hunch.

Then his mouth shaped into another smile, fangs gleaming.

Definitely up for this, Dawn borrowed from all the pent-up rage she carried around.

Benedikte . . . all the betrayals . . .

The rancor bunched together, and she rammed at Jonah again.

He jerked with the jab, then smiled as if this was a game of slap and tickle. That made her even angrier, especially when Jonah got to a crouch, ready to spring.

But then he went taut.

"No," he choked.

He fell to all fours, hair shrouding his entire expression. "Not yet—"

Convulsing, he tumbled the rest of the way to the floor and curled into a ball.

Dawn felt Costin's emerging consciousness connecting with hers. *Again,* he silently said. *Punch him again.*

She fisted her hands, tendons straining as she thought of L.A. once more.

Push—

This time, she did something she'd never done before.

Her energy forced Jonah's arms over his head, just like he'd been shackled.

She heaved in a breath and he broke the restraints, obviously stunned at what his body had been forced to do.

Yet with another punch, she put him flat on his back, his hands gripping the carpet as he fought an inner battle with Costin.

"Not this time," Jonah's voice said. But it sounded cracked, like glass separating. "I won't let you overcome me this—"

With a gurgling choke, he stopped, then wrestled for breath, staring at the ceiling while letting go of the carpet.

Dawn realized she was still clenching her own hands, and she relaxed. Yet the dark stain deep inside of her still remained. The heaviness.

"Costin?" she asked.

She could feel his presence in her head. So why wasn't he responding?

Ignoring the wound on her leg, she ran to him, dropping to his side. His eyes were closed, but he managed to speak.

"Dawn," he said in his dark, skin-heating voice.

Costin.

"Thank goodness," she said. "I was—"

Before she could utter another word, he opened his silver eyes, opened his mouth, exposing fully sprung fangs.

He reached up and pulled her down, his mouth to her neck.

With a tight pop, he broke her skin, entering her jugular, sucking, drawing, drinking just enough. . . .

All Dawn could do was grip him, gasping with pleasured pain as the blood ebbed from her body during this latest desperate attempt to fill each other back up again.

THREE
The Mysterious Woman

After feeding on Dawn, plus a bag of stored blood, a renewed Costin had healed Dawn's neck, just like always. Then he'd checked to see if she was okay after their bang-up start to the night.

But there was no time for dwelling on emotional stuff, so she'd assured him that it was time for business as usual and sent him off to his study where he could privately contact the woman who'd called, then arrange the quickest meeting possible.

Dawn knew he'd be initiating a background check, too, using one of the many discreet contacts Jonah's wealth could buy. As a reclusive heir, Jonah had access to a huge medical supply fortune—one of the many things that had swayed Costin to choose this particular human's body as a host over any other.

Of course, that had been way before Jonah had shown his true I-want-what-Costin-has colors, Dawn thought as she went to a minifridge in her walk-in closet and extracted a small bottle of supplement juice that had also been created by a team member. The vitamin-laden concoction gave her some verve, so she drank up, also snacking on a couple of "biscuits"—or cookies as they were called back in America. Then she bathed, taking care not to disturb her dressed thigh wound.

All the while, she wondered just how strong Jonah was getting and if he would prove to be a problem from this point on. But who the hell knew, since Costin plus Jonah equaled a vampire unlike any the team had ever encountered or studied?

After her bath, she made fast work of drying her dark brown hair and slinging it into a braid that trailed down her back to her shoulder blades. But she didn't stay at the mirror long enough to slap on makeup over paled skin. At twenty-five, she didn't have wrinkles to cover; besides, there was no amount of cosmetics that would make her Angelina Jolie anyway.

Even more important, she wanted to be ready when this mystery woman showed up. So she pulled on some thin, silk thermal long johns, black pants, a long-sleeved turtleneck, and thick-soled dark boots that would lend proper traction if she needed it.

As a final touch, she donned a silver crucifix necklace that boasted needled points at the ends. She secured it beneath the turtleneck, where she could feel the pendant's sharpness, even through the thermal shirt.

A reminder of what she needed to do.

A penance.

During her descent down the winding, claustrophobic stairwell, she passed stark walls lined with portraits of gorgeous, ethnically diverse women—most looking like boudoir honeys with their shoulder-baring robes and serene, satisfied expressions.

These were the Friends: former team members who had agreed to stay on with Costin's mission even after their deaths. They were in spirit form now, which allowed them to aid the present hunters with surveillance and defense.

And it all *still* might be a real kooky concept to Dawn if one of her good pals wasn't among their number.

As she entered a first-floor hallway—in the States, they would've called it the second floor—she passed by a bedroom. There, she found Breisi resting in her own portrait, safe and sound amidst the painted background of the L.A. lab where she had done her best work before dying and going all spirity. Her dark, twenties-siren bob framed a strong yet somehow delicate Latina face, striking a homesick chord in Dawn as she stood in the doorway, unable to look away.

But her reverie ended at the sound of a bearish voice from the other side of the small room.

"Just can't get used to getting up at this time. Is it just me, or does it get darker way earlier here?"

She glanced at the single bed where her father, Frank Madison, was sitting and tying the laces of his black combat boots. Like her, he was dressed for action, his bulky muscles covered by a night-blending sweatshirt and jeans, his receded dark hair hidden by a knit cap.

Not that he needed to warm his head if they ended up going outside. As a vampire, he wouldn't react so much to mild changes in the weather. Probably he just liked the way the cap muffled his heightened hearing.

"Just waking up?" she asked. Both Frank and Costin had taken to resting during the day, when their powers were at their weakest. They saved their strength for nighttime, although Frank had to be careful about being vampy in the open even then.

Her dad nodded. "Word is, something's going down. You know what that might be, Dawnie?"

"I'll bet I don't know much more than you do." She entered the barely furnished room, which was dominated by a table covered with the half-formed hunting weapons he and Breisi were devising together. He acted as the spirit's hands because she couldn't use them to shape the finer details of her inventions anymore.

Frank rose from the bed to his full height. "And here I thought you had the boss's ear."

And a lot more than that, Dawn thought. But talking about

domestic issues with Dad, vamp or not, squicked both of them out.

"All I heard," she said, "was that some lady left a message about a vampire burial place, and Costin's arranging a meeting with her."

"Our first informant."

"Or our first contact with an Underground spy."

Frank's hazel eyes went darker. Like her, he'd been in the middle of the last hunt. Eva, his ex-wife and Dawn's mother, had drawn him into it, turning him into her vampire child. Of course, with the termination of Benedikte, Eva's own maker, *she* was human now, but the Master's death hadn't directly affected Frank, her own progeny. Nope, he was still a reluctant night creature who fought the type of vamps who'd messed up his life.

"You think this caller is with an Underground?" Frank asked.

"I wouldn't put it past them to send her to us if we've made a blip on their radar. The last Underground had an impressive spy network, and they used it aggressively. Even their master did his share of aboveground subterfuge."

"Benedikte," Frank muttered.

The name said it all: how the Master had shifted into the form of a fellow PI/vampire hunter—a supposed ally—to sneakily try to win Dawn to their side.

She hadn't trusted anyone since. Not that she'd ever been awesome at that anyway.

Frank began to look about as doubtful as she was. "When're we meeting this informant?"

"It could be an hour from now, it could be tomorrow. But I'm sure Costin used hypnosis to persuade her to hurry it up."

He could even utilize the talents he'd been given as a soul traveler over the phone, which was a positive sign that turning into a vamp hadn't destroyed his chances to get his soul back. But Dawn didn't like how he would have to go to an open window or unprotected place to make the call, since headquarters' walls shielded his powers as well as secured all of them.

She jerked her chin toward the door. "Want to grab something from the kitchen before we do our thing?"

In answer, Frank got up from the bed. But he made a detour over to Breisi's portrait, kissing his fingers and touching her painted cheek. Since she was in sleep mode, she didn't stir, as the Friends were sometimes prone to do when they awakened. Dawn had seen their shifts in energy before.

As her dad headed for the door, Dawn reached up to the picture, too, bumping her knuckles against Breisi's before she followed Frank.

After going down the rest of the stairs, they came to the ground-level kitchen, which had been gussied up with stainless steel and white tile during the renovation Costin had undertaken once he'd decided this would be their headquarters. He had rituals for each Underground hunt, and one of them included preparing a secure domain so he could hole up before launching a final attack against the Underground once the team had uncovered its location.

As their ultimate weapon, he was always the one who attacked the lair in the end, and surprise was invaluable. Having a master detect Costin beforehand would ruin that, so he laid low, sequestering himself in the thick of a hunt.

Frank opened the refrigerator, taking out some roast beef sandwich fixings for Dawn and then a packet of blood for himself. Like Costin, Frank used bags to supplement a main nutrition source whose blood tasted better and provided more pleasure than an anonymous donor's seemed to.

As she set to work on her meal, Frank opened the IV bag, then blew out a breath before downing the contents.

She shook her head as she spread mustard on her whole wheat bread.

Frank finished drinking, then stared at her. "What?"

"You. It's been a year, and you still haven't found a better way to get your nourishment?"

"Oh. Maybe I should hit the streets for food. That'd really be the ticket to hiding our presence." He wiped a hand over his mouth. "Dawn, this is the only way to go for me."

"Don't get me wrong—I'm not saying you're taking advantage of Eva's donations, but . . ." Dawn dealt a few slices of meat onto her bread. "I guess it bothers me that she traveled over here with us because she thinks your taste for her blood somehow means you'll come around to her again one day."

"She knows I love Breisi. That's been clear since all the dust settled in L.A."

"Yet you still didn't say no when Eva offered to be your main supplier."

"We're still friends, Dawn. I'm not forcing her to do this."

Dawn pushed her sandwich together. "You're right, I know you are. But every time I see her, I can't help thinking that she's . . . confused, I suppose. She's not doing much else with her life after losing what identity she had with the Underground."

Her dad didn't look at her. "Kiko's helping Eva there."

"What, with getting her a new identity?"

Kik had been in charge of supplying Eva with a makeover as well as with expertly falsified documents before they'd even left the States. After all, Eva Claremont, legendary actress, was supposed to have been murdered decades ago.

It's true that, as a vampire, she'd taken on a new life, a new acting career, but that had been under another name—one she couldn't keep using because she was too famous as Jacqueline Ashley also.

Frank retrieved a waste disposal bag from a cupboard, then stuffed the IV bag into it. "I'm not really talking about her new identity. I mean to say that Kiko's helping Eva develop interests over here."

"So that's why he's at her place as we speak, taking her blood for your next meal and not teaching her macramé or something." Dawn appealed to her dad with a look.

He turned away, hiding his expression. A year ago, she had

been naïve enough to think that a vampire couldn't look guilty—or show any emotion at all, for that matter, even if they did appear pretty human when they wanted to. But her dad's frown went a long way in reminding her she was wrong.

"Sorry for bringing it up," she said, going to the fridge to see if any supplement juice was in stock.

Frank finished disposing of his trash, then stood behind Dawn, resting a meaty hand on her shoulder as she shut the door, juice bottle in hand.

"You've been trying real hard with Eva," he said, turning her around to face him. "Everyone sees that."

"I couldn't leave her behind, by herself. Not after what happened."

Her dad dropped his hand to his side. He knew there was nothing he could say to persuade Dawn that Eva didn't resent her. Everyone on the team never failed to tell Dawn that she'd made the right decision by killing Benedikte, but suffering all the consequences seemed endless.

"Hey." Frank lifted her chin with his index finger so she could see how his face had its own wrinkles—age imperfections he'd brought with him into vampirism. "Even though she's got little crow's feet under the cosmetics and graying hair under the dye now, Eva loves you. She loves you so much that she went overboard to provide for you with that resurrected career the Underground gave her. She was never into all that Hollywood crap anyway. No big loss to her, because she's got you now. That's all she ever wanted."

Dawn bit a response back. *She wanted you, too, Dad.*

Instead, she said, "I know, but it's what she doesn't say that bothers me. With every month that goes by, I think she misses the adoration, the fame, the youth. . . ."

Frank opened his mouth to add something else, but their discussion was cut off by a voice over an intercom.

Costin's dead-of-night tone.

"I hate to interrupt," he said, clearly having heard at least the

tail end of their conversation, "but our guest will be here momen-
tarily. On the phone, she gave me an estimated time of arrival,
which should be minutes away."

"Arriving . . . here?" Dawn asked. "At our place?"

Frank added, "You'd let her in here when it's pretty suspicious
that she's coming to *us* with information?"

"We had a long discussion on the phone." That was Costin-speak
for "I tested her and measured her up as well as I could without
her being present."

"Now you want to feel her out in person," Dawn said.

Costin's tone remained mild. "Actually, I told her that we have
a position open on the team, and she is interested."

"What?" Dawn and Frank stereoed.

"Our guest has been searching for work in this city. Desperately,
I might add." The speaker hummed. "In this new location, with a
new Underground, I would like a fresh perspective, and I believe
she could be of great benefit to us."

"And if she ends up bein' a stinker?" Frank asked.

Costin laughed. "Are you implying she is out for harm?"

"Yeah," Dawn said.

"I will definitively know if she is a good match for our purposes
when she arrives, but I've detected no dark agendas in her."

Dawn held up a finger. "It was real chancy to let down your
guard to test her."

"Better to take that initial risk at a distance."

Okay, true enough. And since Costin had a talent for recruiting
the kind of true-blue people with high senses of justice—the types
who'd fight for good because they couldn't tolerate the bad—she
clammed up for now.

But she would also remember how Benedikte had blindsided
her.

"So," Dawn said, "you're telling us that your discussion with
this girl went from her having information to your offering her a
job?"

"I have not officially offered it yet. I look at this as the final phase of an interview."

"If I know anything about how *I* started out with this gig, she'll be knee deep in para-dung before the night's out."

Conversation done, she picked up her sandwich and took a quick swig of the bottled juice before putting it away again. Then she headed toward the kitchen exit while eating her meal, Frank right behind her.

They came to a common area that gave Dawn the willies. But what was new? The Los Angeles house had been gothic creepy.

Yet this one took the cake.

Dark paneling gave the area an ominous pressure, especially with the wood bas-reliefs of medieval friars decorating the ceiling. A simple, golden chandelier hung down from one figure's outstretched hand, like he was providing dim illumination over the high-hung mirrors framed by carvings of angels' faces.

But the most chilling part of all was something that had traveled here with the team: the portrait of Kalin, the Fire Woman Friend with her flaming cape, which still had a place of honor over the gutted shell of a fireplace.

Dawn ignored the one spirit who couldn't stand her and finished her sandwich instead. Still, the redheaded Friend stared out at the room with her usual withering glee.

Unaffected by any of it, Frank took a seat in a deep leather chair near the doorway, leaning back his head and closing his eyes.

By the time Dawn finished her food, Costin had come back on the intercom. "Dawn."

"Still waiting for our visitor."

"Yes. Well, she seems to have been . . . sidetracked. Outside."

"I'll get her." Dawn started for the door, then backtracked. "You're *sure* about this?"

"I am as sure as I am able to be. Besides, I am well hidden at the moment."

His meaning was clear: he was going to talk to this girl via the speaker—just as he had done with Dawn when he'd used her as vampire bait back in L.A.

Slowly, she glanced up at where his speaker was ensconced in one of the angel carvings. Even though Costin had stayed hidden in all their hotels and rented rooms, he'd truly gone back to being The Voice now—the enigmatic question mark who sheltered himself in secret spaces.

And, the thing was, he sounded so in his element. . . .

Going to the doorway, she opened a panel in a wall, grabbed a silver-bladed dagger from a rack, and slid it in a back pocket. She also prepared herself for a visiting creature who might be vulnerable to holy items by strapping on a bracelet that shot holy water from a sack when she flipped her wrist. Totally Spider-Man-licious.

"Hey, Cujo," she said to her reclining dad after she'd prepped herself.

He opened one eye.

She cracked open the heavy door. "Stay frosty, just in case this lady gives me grief?"

Frank grunted, then got out of his chair. He'd be watching from the entrance, taking up Dawn's back without intimidating the caller unless required.

Ready for a hunt—shit, she hoped this was finally the start of it—Dawn stepped outside.

The cold air instantly sucked up to her as she descended the few stairs that led to the pavement. Streetlamps gave weak assurance while a train slowly rumbled by on its raised track to the left of the brick structure where the team resided. Music from the vintner next door mumbled in the night as Dawn focused across the street.

There, in front of the iron gates of the Cross Bones Graveyard, stood a woman packed into a heavy red wool coat and scarf. A breeze toyed with her shoulder-length, ultra-curly black hair while she perused the ribbons, cards, and mementos tied to the cemetery gates.

They were gifts from locals and visitors who'd dropped by to respect the dead. A group had even been here on Halloween with their candles and sympathy, and Dawn had watched them out the window, her hand on the cold glass.

Now, she walked closer to the graveyard, which wasn't actually much more than a cement slab beyond the gates. Still, in the quiet wind, she could hear the ribbons stirring, as if restless.

Hand on the dagger in her back pocket, she cleared her throat.

The woman turned around, and right before she smiled, Dawn saw that she had the plushest, deepest-pink lips ever. Blow-job lips, one of the stunt guys on a movie set might've called them. And even in the deepening night, the visitor's dark eyes sparkled—but not with anything preternatural, necessarily.

Although you never could be sure.

She also wore a poppy in her hair, right above an ear, but Dawn thought that might be because of the approaching Remembrance Day, which was like Memorial Day in the U.S.

"Hello," the informant said in slightly accented English.

Good God, she talked a little like Costin.

"Hi." Dawn kept ahold of that dagger. "Are you the caller?"

"Yes." The girl—on closer inspection, she couldn't have been older than her early twenties—took her gloved hand out of her coat pocket to shake Dawn's free hand. "I'm Natalia Petri."

Dawn greeted her, then took a couple of steps back, keeping her distance as she introduced herself, too.

The other girl narrowed her eyes, as if inspecting Dawn and finding something . . . off. But then she was back to glancing at the graveyard again.

"They're loud here."

Was she talking about the music from the vintner's?

As a shiver traveled Dawn's skin, she thought that might not be it at all. . . .

"This place," the girl said. "Do you know much about it?"

"A bit." Dawn had read the plaque on the gate, and she'd even done research since Costin had been so drawn to the building across from these grounds. "When they built the Jubilee tube line at the end of the twentieth century, they found layers and layers of the dead here. It's a community grave starting from medieval times, unconsecrated ground filled with prostitutes and then paupers before it was closed in the mid–eighteen hundreds. This whole area was a real piece of work until they tidied it up. You can read about it in any Dickens book. I guess there's talk of turning the grounds into office buildings or something, but the people around here are up in arms about it."

"As they should be." Natalia sent the train tracks—the representative of progress, Dawn supposed—a harsh glance. "Why hurt the dead even more?"

"Why indeed." Dawn reluctantly motioned toward headquarters. "Should we get out of the cold?"

The woman looked at the graveyard again, and for a moment, Dawn thought maybe she wasn't going to go anywhere. But then Natalia furrowed her brow, like she was concentrating.

Listening.

Dawn waited until Natalia touched a glove to a photocopied picture of a skull tied to the gate, then backed away.

After walking across the street, which hardly suffered from traffic in Dawn's experience, they entered the building, escorted by watchdog Frank.

Natalia's eyes brightened even more as she surveyed the gloom and doom of the common area. She even flashed dimples as Frank introduced himself and vice versa.

"You . . ." she started to say to Frank before Costin's speaker came to life.

"You made it safely, Ms. Petri," he said.

The girl seemed confused at a man's low voice coming from high in the room, seemingly from one of the angels' mouths. But she still answered as if she were in a normal conversation. "Yes, Mr. Limpet, thank you."

Okay, time to get down to it. "Natalia, when you called, you mentioned vampire victims?"

She nodded. "I—"

"A moment, please," Costin interrupted again. "I'm sorry, Ms. Petri, but would you like any refreshments? Tea perhaps?"

Hey, Dawn thought. When she'd first come to Limpet and Associates, there'd been no tea at all. Just an attitudinal Kiko and a good mind-diddling from Costin's hypnotic sway; it'd been his way of feeling her out to see if he could trust her.

"No, I'm fine, Mr. Limpet," Natalia said. "But I appreciate your offer."

Frank led her to a chair, and she doffed her coat to reveal a not-so-fashionable tweed dress worn over thick tights and practical shoes. She looked like what most people in L.A. would call a "healthy girl," but that didn't mean she was overweight. Hollywood was just too full of women who ate a leaf of lettuce and called it a feast.

As Frank took position by the fireplace, arms crossed over his massive chest, Natalia sat, folding her coat on her lap, even after Frank offered to hang it up for her.

"As I was asking," Dawn said, hoping Costin wouldn't cut in again to offer anything like scones and clotted cream, "you had information about some bodies?"

"An unmarked place of the dead," Natalia said, refreshingly forthcoming. Or maybe as forthcoming as a spy? "On Billiter Street, in the Square Mile. I was walking past what's said to be an abandoned construction site on my way to a job interview this morning, and I heard them."

They're loud here.

"Do you hear dead people?" Dawn asked.

Natalia seemed relieved at the question. "Yes. It's almost as if I can read their vocal imprints, which means it's more like I'm overhearing whatever they care to say. However, I can't have conversations with them."

"And what did they say to you this morning?"

"Precious little. A female voice cried out, asking for help, as if she was summoning anyone who might hear her. 'Here,' she kept saying. 'Over here.' Then a male . . . He repeated the word 'vampires' over and over again. Other voices mingled, too, unclear, jumbled. But I did understand that the creatures who put the dead there had discarded them after feedings."

Interesting story. But it didn't mean Dawn accepted that Natalia was telling the truth, even if Costin already felt secure in their guest. Dawn wondered if Frank was even thinking of tapping into the girl's mind to measure her up.

"Did the victims also tell you to contact us?" Dawn asked.

"No. The name 'Jonah Limpet' . . ." Natalia smiled like she was conjuring some kind of warm memory. "I saw the name in my mind—a detective, I thought—shortly after I left the site, and I knew I should contact him."

Costin's voice filtered through the air. "Natalia has precognitive talents, as well."

Had his background check yielded that? Or had it come up during their nice little chat on the phone?

Dawn didn't access his mind to seek an answer; they respected each other's thoughts and didn't abuse the privilege of entering. Besides, now wasn't the time for personal issues.

Natalia was focusing on the angel speaker near the ceiling. "Why do I keep feeling . . . something . . . at the edges of my mind?"

"It is only me," Costin said.

Dawn stiffened, because he was mentally gauging Natalia. With her permission, he would use his powers to go deeper into her—the most personal of all interviews.

He'd done the same exact thing with Dawn when she'd first come on board. . . .

She pushed back any jealousy. Natalia wasn't the new Dawn.

"Forgive my curiosity, Ms. Petri," Costin said, "but in our business, we wish to know up front if our contacts are valid. From the first, I did not sense anything deceptive about you, but this is only a superficial conclusion."

"I have nothing to hide," Natalia said. "My visions have never led me wrong before. I trust them more than *anything*."

There were shadows in her gaze, and Dawn recognized them. Didn't this girl trust anything else? Why?

"Then," Costin said, "would you mind if I . . . ?"

"I do not mind."

But as the psychic closed her eyes, Dawn found that *she* minded.

Natalia's not the new Dawn, she kept telling herself. *Repeat, repeat, repeat.*

It didn't take but a few minutes for the girl to open her eyes, no doubt because her permission had made the testing easy for Costin. Grrrr.

Yet at least it didn't seem like Natalia had enjoyed a Costin moment as much as Dawn had always . . . well, *enjoyed* them.

"And?" Dawn asked, trying not to sound peeved.

But Costin seemed to know that she wasn't happy anyway. She could sense it—an apology via their Awareness.

"We need Ms. Petri," he said. "And I would appreciate your discussing our situation with her before we visit Billiter Street tonight. Perhaps we might obtain readings from the graves or find a fortunate telltale clue."

"Wait." Dawn faced the angel's head, her hands on her hips. The carving had chubby cheeks and a blank, innocent look about it. Faker. "You want us to tell her everything? I mean, I know you've been in her head, and all, but . . . seriously?"

You're going to trust her when it took you forever and a day to trust me? she finally thought to him.

She tried to use their Awareness to understand what he was thinking, but he had blocked her out.

Her. His creator. His supposed intimate . . .

His tone was remorseful as he spoke. "Please give Ms. Petri

every last detail. I am certain she will understand all of it. She comes to us with a great deal of paranormal experience."

Then the intercom clicked off, leaving Dawn reeling with the return of The Voice—the stranger who had already begun the ritual of fully sequestering himself for the endgame of this particular hunt.

Even from her.

Not for long though—not if she had anything to say about it. After they took care of business tonight, she would talk to him, see if she was wrong, because things *had* changed between them since L.A., right?

Right?

In her seat, cuddly as could be with her coat in her lap, Natalia smiled again. "A job. I knew I would find one today, even if it wasn't at my interview this morning."

The abrupt, metallic sound of keys clanging to the wood floor made them all look toward the darkened hallway, where Kiko stood in his little leather jacket, cargo pants, and oversized boots, his eyes wide and reddened from his meds.

"Don't mind me asking," he said, "but who's this quack, and why do we need her around when we've already got a psychic?"

FOUR

THE UNWELCOME

FRANK was smart, because he excused himself right away and went to prepare coffee or tea or *anything*. Thankfully, he also asked Natalia to join him.

Which, proving to be a smart girl herself, Natalia did.

But Dawn? She had the pleasure of staying behind to calm Kiko down and fill him in on current events.

Simmering, he took it all in while perched in a chair on the opposite side of the fireplace from Natalia's empty seat, his short legs hanging off the edge as he gripped the armrests. His cheeks were nipped by the weather, but he sure wasn't as pink and jolly as his complexion hinted.

And why not, if he was being replaced with a shinier version who might've gotten a reading on the new Underground?

Dawn sat on the floor near his chair, knowing she'd have to handle this diplomatically—diplomacy being a quality she didn't really have in spades. Kiko's pride and ego revolved around his psychometric, telepathic, and precognitive talents, and Costin was even training him in hypnosis, but the pills weren't helping with any of it. Not lately, since Kiko's back had been acting up.

A back that had been broken by a vampire.

In frustration, he ruffled his blond hair. He'd shaved off the soul patch beneath his lower lip, and the lack of facial derring-do lent him a lost boyishness.

"Maybe I'm just being paranoid," he said. "But the boss has used new teams for every hunt all these hundreds of years, so how can I even think of job security?"

"Not a bad point."

At her bluntness, Kiko shifted in his chair. "You think this is his first step in weeding me out?"

"I don't know. Costin always liked to work with new hunters because he feared too much knowledge would corrupt the team's willingness to obey directives."

"That is, if any team members were left standing at the end of the battle."

"But, last time, we *were* left standing, and in way different circumstances than ever before. Costin's a vampire now. He's been trying to work around that, but I'm thinking it's worth the risk to have a trusted crew around to help while he gets used to it."

Even though Costin could still hypnotize, he didn't seem to be able to use the extent of his master-slaying powers—something he used to access full force by going out of body during a final attack. Nowadays, ever since having been locked into his vampire body, he couldn't even *get* outside, and there were times when Dawn wondered just how the hell he was going to destroy another master.

"So I shouldn't worry about my job." Kiko grinned.

Dawn resisted the guy's charm, bracing herself to say what needed to be said.

"Did you maybe stop to think that Costin's not getting rid of all of us?"

Kiko's grin died. After a few seconds, somewhere in the room, the heating kicked on, a low hush expanding the tension.

But he didn't argue. His own doctor back in the States had told him to get out of his med habit, and Dawn had gone the extra mile to help him this past year while on the road: intervention, visits to more doctors and therapists. Kiko had worked to get clean, but he was too hooked.

She locked gazes with him, damned if she'd be the first to glance away.

"I hate to see you like this," she said, "but if getting knocked off the team is what's going to put you in gear, Kik, then I'm not going to go against Costin if he's brought in someone to take your place. I'm tired of trying everything *I* can think of."

Kiko shrugged, but it didn't fool Dawn. Back in L.A., he'd been a "little person" thespian, and even though he could *act!* like hell, his career had failed along with his back.

"It's easy for you to be okay with that job security, ain't it?" He redirected his glare to the deadened, charred fireplace. "You're so key that the boss is never going to let you go."

She didn't answer, because Frank was walking back into the room bearing a tray of beverages. Natalia trailed him.

As Psychic Number Two sat in her chair, sans coat this time, Frank poured her a cup of coffee. The aroma of roasted nuts should've smelled comforting. Should've.

Frank gave Kiko a steaming cup, too, which Kik didn't drink.

Her dad didn't remark on that, merely handing Dawn a glass of supplement juice and winking at her. He'd no doubt caught her entire conversation with Kiko from the kitchen with his vamp hearing, muffled or not.

Man, it was hard to live with these guys.

"You two were talking about the whole 'key' thing?" Frank asked, refraining from a drink of his own as he confirmed Dawn's suspicions about overhearing. "Is that where we want to start with Natalia?"

"I'm not sure *where* to start," Dawn said.

Kiko fixed his gaze on the new girl across the way. "I was just saying to Dawn that none of us can be too cozy when the boss hires us. Not unless you're key."

Backup Psychic sipped from her delicate cup, listening intently, withstanding Kiko's stare like a pro.

Impressed, Dawn gave her a few brownie points. But just a few. Costin might've looked into the girl's head, yet what if she was better than any other type of vamp at shielding? What if this new Underground didn't give off any preter vibes at all?

"What Kiko means," Frank said, assuming his place by the fireplace mantel, "is that Dawn is key to the team. Once upon a time, he had a vision about how important she'd be to bringing down this whole bad-vamp house of fangs."

Kiko added, "And that vision came true. Or, at least, it's on its way to being fulfilled."

Frank gave the floor to Confident Kiko. "Then maybe you should explain and we'll take it from there."

"Eh, I'm not so on board with dumping all my intel on some poppy-wearing gift who walks in off the street. Or maybe Ms. *Putri* has already sensed what she needs to know by now?"

Dawn cringed at Kiko's implied challenge as Natalia gently laid down her cup on a saucer, then transferred the set to a nearby end table.

"I think both you and I know that we don't divine anything and everything, Koo-Koo." The new girl put on a sweet smile. "It comes when it wishes—we cannot turn it on and off. So unless you've already sensed everything about *me*, I would be more than happy to make you comfortable with my background."

Latching on to the girl's obvious eagerness to land this job, Dawn settled in for a good listen. It was weird that Natalia was so desperate, even if she had said she trusted her visions more than anything else.

Then again, maybe that made total sense in their world.

At any rate, "Koo-Koo" seemed focused on the fact that Natalia wasn't telling him to go to hell yet.

"What Kik is saying," Dawn offered, "is that your hiring is pretty sudden. We're used to depending on each other and not really anyone else."

"I understand," Natalia said.

When she saw how the group was waiting for her to start the background talk, she added, "So I should perhaps tell you about myself first?"

"Enlighten away," Kiko said, spreading out an arm, just like he was the prince of sarcasm lounging on a throne.

Natalia didn't react. "Then I'll begin by saying that I arrived in London from Bucharest two months ago."

The accent. Dawn's untrained ear had been right about vaguely linking it with Costin's; he hailed from the Wallachian region.

"Romania joined the European Union recently," Natalia continued, "and we can freely come to places such as England now. So I did. I'm a legal immigrant, with university education in business. But I'm not Roma."

Her smile grew strained, as if she were ready for a barrage of insults.

"Roma?" Frank asked. "You mean 'gypsies'?"

"'Roma' is probably more politically correct," Dawn said, hardly believing she was up on what was "in" and "out" in polite society.

Natalia's smile remained in place. "No matter what name is used, popular opinion holds that crime rates have been on the rise in this area since more Roma immigrated here."

"I guess," Dawn said, "'Roma' equals trouble to a lot of people, and that's why you're telling us outright that you're not one of them?"

"Yes." Natalia absently toyed with a plastic button on her dress. It looked loose. "Many of them have taken to begging, trading on the street, doing odd jobs. Some resort to petty crime like picking pockets, and a great deal of the public thinks that any Romanian is Romani."

Kiko had inched back in his chair. He knew when to play "bad cop" and when to cool it. But he still looked like he was biding his time.

Frank asked, "What brought *you* over here?"

Her shoulders lost some of their defensive stiffness. "I have distant family in Slough. Besides, the London I read about in books always appealed to me: the museums, the history, the opportunity. I felt the same lure for America, and I once spent a time in New York, caring for an old aunt. But she passed on, and there's no one there for me now."

"That's why you know English real good," Frank added.

Natalia smiled at his affable tone, probably knowing he was trying hard to balance out Kiko's vinegar.

"Yes, thank you, Mr. Frank."

"Just Frank." He motioned toward the team. "Same with all of us—first names only. Right, Kiko?"

"Oh, she already has a pet name for me, Frank. Or didn't you notice?"

Ignoring him, Natalia's body language seemed more fluid and relaxed now.

That is, until Kiko asked, "So did you suddenly become psychic one day or what?"

"No." She fiddled with her dress button again. "As long as I can recall, I've heard the dead. But I learned to filter the input. The same applies to my precognitive visions."

"You've always had those, too?" Dawn asked.

"Actually, the visions first came when I was an adolescent. But my parents told me never to speak of my gifts. They didn't want me to be 'different.' They thought my talents were 'Romani,' and they didn't want me to be looked upon or treated in the same way the group is treated in Romania . . . or anywhere else, really." Natalia frowned. "In private, I still listened to the whispers and watched the visions. The first time I heard one of them, it was from behind a door in my apartment building. A neighbor had died, and she told me her husband . . ."

Natalia looked around at the team, then laughed when she no doubt realized she couldn't shock them with this story. Hell, they had a boss who spoke from a carved angel's mouth.

She continued. "My neighbor told me that her recently departed husband had come back as a revenant. Evidently, he blamed her for his heart attack. She never said why."

"Revenants," Kiko muttered. "Is that what you call a vampire?"

"From what my neighbor said," Natalia answered, "he was more a zombie."

"Got it," Frank said.

"Of course," Natalia added, "I reported her passing to the authorities. I told them my family had a copy of her apartment key and she was sick, so I was bringing soup when I discovered her body. The authorities never suspected what truly happened. Her husband was never seen in the area, and my parents told me to leave it at that. I was young, so I did. And once she was properly buried, her voice disappeared from my hearing."

Frank said, "Too bad you couldn't ask her questions."

"That'd be helpful in our line of work," Kiko added.

"The dead can be very focused." Natalia didn't even acknowledge Kiko's slight dig. "I find that they're normally seeking peace or righting a wrong."

"You ever actually see a revenant?" Dawn asked. "Or a ghost or a vampire?"

Natalia shook her head.

Kiko took the cue. "There's a big difference between eavesdropping on 'em and actually coming face-to-face, which we do all the time."

The new girl raised her eyebrows a little.

Even though Dawn was skeptical about Natalia, she liked the effect the second psychic was having on Kiko. Maybe, with his beloved job at stake, he'd get off those pills.

"What about now," Frank asked, "since you moved away from your parents, Natalia? Do you tell people about your talents?"

"Not generally, but I do what the dead ask of me in my own discreet way. The voices I heard this morning . . . They needed me to come to you, and I've never turned my back on them." Her smile grew wistful. "They led me to you, and they're giving me what I most need."

"A job?" Dawn asked.

"A job," Natalia repeated. "I came to London to use my university degree and work for an honest wage, then send money home. Yet finding employment hasn't been as simple as I had hoped. I've been living on savings, and they're almost depleted. Before now, I thought revealing my gifts might give future employers the impression that my sixth sense made me a 'gypsy'—a criminal. An outcast even here."

For some reason, Dawn related to her situation: being earmarked as something you weren't and trying to make up for it.

Natalia addressed Kiko, her expression hopeful. "We have a lot in common, yes? Perhaps we can share stories someday."

He didn't say anything, just focused his reddened eyes on the empty, ash-scarred fireplace.

Although Natalia only smiled at Frank, just like she was signaling that she was fine with Kiko, Dawn knew she'd been stung by the blow off.

But Frank did his best to soften the injury. "I suppose I should add that I have a few psychic stories to tell, myself."

"Ah," Natalia said. "I knew there was something about you. With Dawn, as well. You both seem . . . different. And I should know the very definition." She smiled, as if she'd finally found good company.

"You mean we don't resemble anything close to normal?" Dawn asked.

Kiko leaned toward Natalia. "You can *read* Frank?"

Not even Sober Kiko could read Frank. Something to do with vampires lacking souls.

But the other psychic shook her head, and Kiko's knuckles got a little less white.

"I cannot read Frank exactly," she said. "Yet when he's near, I can . . . hear . . . something I've never heard before. Not a whispering like the dead. Just . . . This will sound odd, but it's as if he is an empty room."

Stunned, Dawn could only widen her eyes.

But Kiko was all over it. "So you do have vamp radar."

Natalia froze. "He's a . . . vampire?"

"So's Dawn," Kiko said, taking great pleasure in it.

"I'm not a vamp," Dawn said. "I just *used* to be."

"I . . . see." Natalia sat there, hands in her lap, looking like maybe she wanted to scram after all.

When she didn't, Kiko's curiosity got the best of him. "What did you hear in Dawn? Does she sound hollow, too?"

"No, it wasn't a sound so much as something I saw superimposed over her when we first met outside."

"And what was that?" Dawn asked.

"Only a flash. Like that old song . . . 'There's a little black spot on the sun today.'"

Kiko humphed. "'King of Pain.'"

There were no words, because Dawn had felt that dark mark on her, and nothing she did could wash it away.

"A black spot, huh?" Frank said. "Dawn reclaimed her soul, but I suppose I sound hollow because I'm a full-on beastie."

At Natalia's next speechless moment, he added, "See, I'd have to kill my ex-wife—my master—to get *my* soul back. It's . . . complicated."

"You think?" Dawn said.

He went on to explain about how he, a no-account bar bouncer, and movie-star Eva had defied her managers and married. How they'd given birth to Dawn just before Eva was "murdered."

"She'd been recruited into a vampire Underground," Dawn

tacked on after Frank did his part. "The Master took major celebrities while they were still in their prime, staged sensational deaths that would guarantee infamy, gave them shelter belowground while their legends grew, and then performed plastic surgery on these Elite creatures before they appeared Above again, where they'd use their Allure to make humans think they had the same star quality as the old model."

"When Dawn killed their master," Frank said, "most of the humanized Elites committed suicide. Some disappeared. Eva reformed herself."

Feeling that they were getting too personal—why did this new girl have to know *everything?*—Dawn stuck to the technicalities.

"Basically," she said, "the Hollywood Underground had a stratified class system. There were human Servants who took care of dirty work Above and served as food. There were Guards— freaky-ass Nosferatu things that defended the higher beings. Then came the Groupies—pet vampires who didn't have as much power as the Elites. The Master even had a lieutenant of sorts. Sorin." Dawn took a breath. "If I had stayed a vampire, I would've had his power."

"But you didn't stay a vampire," Natalia said.

"Didn't want to." Liar. "Besides, the Master needed to be put down, and my turning human was the result. Anyway, what I'm getting at here is even though we know the details of the Hollywood Underground, we can't be sure about this new one we're hunting—" Dawn stopped. "You figured out we're hunting vamps, right?"

"It is beginning to . . . click." Natalia swallowed again.

This was where they'd really lose her, no matter how much the girl wanted to help the dead or how vividly her visions told her she was making the right move by coming here tonight.

Full steam ahead anyway. "What I was saying is that we can't be sure about what to expect from this Underground that might have created the burial ground you passed."

"This is a real tough job, Natalia," Frank added. "Lots of curve balls."

Kiko obviously saw an opening to cut every last tie keeping his competition here. "Since all the Undergrounds the boss has destroyed were different, we never know things like how exactly we can defend ourselves at first. The masters are all blood brothers, but over the centuries, they developed diverse talents based on individual strengths."

"And to make things more interesting," Frank said, "the masters have a history of merging Undergrounds, and even going after one another to capture each other's communities."

Mouth dry, Dawn took a swig from her juice, then said, "I was exposed to the last master's knowledge, including his memories, when he turned me, and he experienced one of those takeovers firsthand."

"Tell her how Benedikte betrayed you by pretending to be your pal," Kiko said. "Oh, and tell her how she shouldn't expect total truth from the boss, either."

Natalia sent Dawn a don't-do-this-to-me glance.

"Just don't trust anybody," Dawn said, still unwilling to open herself up to an emotional autopsy. "Every creature involved is bent on survival." She gestured with her glass toward the angel carving. "Even the boss."

In the mist of her mind, all of his apologies threaded together. *The good of the many outweighs the good of the few. I had to do what was necessary. . . .*

Yeah, Dawn knew Costin would still choose his soul over her if it came right down to it, and she couldn't blame him, either, because she'd lost her soul once and . . .

And she'd *liked* what she'd been. For the first time, she'd felt accepted. Complete.

Blocking that out—damn it, she couldn't help the ingrained habit—Dawn started talking again, hoping the sound would chase away the truth.

"Even though we have a few answers from Benedikte—none of which probably apply to the new Underground—there's another question that's been bugging us since we came here. It seems that London's been the center of a lot of Underground activity, and we don't know why."

Natalia asked, "It's as if these vampires were drawn here?"

"Yeah, looks like the blood brothers keep coming back." Dawn finally acknowledged the painting above the fireplace. Kalin. "See this girl? She was part of a team that hunted a master and some vamps around this area in the early fifteen hundreds, even though there weren't established Undergrounds at that point. Then, after Undergrounds started to form, there was one in some abandoned tube areas. It was the Hollywood master's first community, but it was destroyed by another blood brother."

Frank said, "Then there appears to be *this* Underground."

"So why do they keep coming here?" Dawn finished. "It's something we need to find out, along with the usual junk."

Natalia volunteered a theory. "Why are there so many hauntings here, as well? There's much spiritual activity."

"Enough to even draw what's referred to as 'the dragon,' " Kiko added, probably because if this part didn't get the other psychic out the door, nothing would.

Natalia had leaned toward him, her dark curls tumbling forward. "The dragon?"

Kiko chuckled softly, the terror.

But Natalia surprised the tar out of Dawn when she sucked it up and smiled right back at him. It was a bring-it-on gesture if there ever was one.

Kiko slid out of his chair, folding his hands behind his back in preparation for his doom speech.

"Oh, yeesh," Dawn said at the drama.

He forged on anyway. "Our boss—the guy you're about to sign on with? Well, a long time ago, he got caught up in some real hairy stuff with some real hairy men. I ain't naming names, but the boss exchanged blood with a guy who made a bargain with the devil. And that guy was freakin' brutal. A warrior who turned all his closest men into master vampires and eventually told them to secretly create powerful, individual armies that would all gather one day to take over the world once this guy woke up from a loooooong sleep."

"This is the dragon," Natalia said.

It looked like Kiko's story had bitten a chunk out of her second-wind courage.

But Dawn watched carefully for any signs of deception. If she'd done the same with Matt Lonigan, aka Benedikte, back in L.A., she would've saved them all a lot of trouble.

Kiko hammered on. "In my vision—we call it the 'key vision'—I saw Dawn bathed in a vampire's blood, victorious. At first, the boss interpreted it to mean she would find the L.A. master and somehow be the key to besting him. And she was."

"But . . ." Natalia said.

"*But* we think there's more—that Dawn's going to be key in the destruction of the dragon, too."

"Or maybe you're being optimistic." Dawn took another drink of juice, basically to cover how her pulse had just tried to jolt its way out of her chest.

"Or maybe I'm right," Kiko said.

She didn't mention that *maybe* he was holding onto the glory days when his visions had been on the ball.

Dawn drained the rest of her glass and turned to Natalia. "I'd make a guess that you're familiar with the history of Vlad Tepes and how he inspired Bram Stoker."

Swallowing *really* hard now, Natalia nodded.

A few moments passed, and Kiko seemed to be loving every one of them.

"Am I to understand," the second psychic said, her voice thin, "that Mr. Limpet is one of those masters?"

"Sort of." Frank stood away from the fireplace. "But he's not using us to take over his blood brothers' Undergrounds. He's fighting them."

"Tell her the rest, Dawn," Kiko said, as if she were the only one who could.

And maybe she was, even if Costin was showing signs of going all secretive Voice on her again. . . .

Although Natalia looked like she half didn't want to hear it, Dawn complied. Last year, she wished *she'd* known everything.

"Our boss regretted exchanging blood with the dragon," she said. "He even began seeing himself as a monster. But then some higher being—Mr. Limpet doesn't even know exactly what it was—made him an offer."

"The being in question was like magic," Kiko said.

"Whatever he was, he told the boss he could rent back his soul and someday bring it to peace if he agreed to kill the dragon before its rising. But Mr. Limpet would also have to terminate every last master, too."

"And there's a catch," Kiko added. "One of the masters is hiding the dragon while he sleeps and gathers his power. We could find him at any time, and we when do . . ."

He paused, stretching out the horrific possibilities.

Natalia cleared her throat, then asked, "What if Mr. Limpet isn't successful in killing all these masters and the dragon?"

The room went still, wind moaning through old creaks and crevices that hadn't been shored up.

"His soul becomes damned for good," Dawn said softly.

As the reality sank in, Natalia grew pensive, disturbed.

Kiko pursued. "You think that's a bummer? Well, the boss abandoned his vampire body and became this 'soul traveler' who borrowed pure human bodies so he could carry on this fight throughout the centuries. And that's caused some issues."

Both Kiko and Frank peered at Dawn again.

"I suppose I'd be a big part of those issues," she said.

The guys averted their eyes as Dawn sighed, then gave Natalia the basics about Jonah, the willing host whose vampire body was trapping Costin.

"Since the boss and Jonah have a symbiotic relationship," she said, "they feed off of each other. During the big throw down with the Hollywood master, the boss came out of his host's body so he could use all his powers, pure and undiluted. Thing is, he would gradually lose energy when he left his host, and the fight battered him, so he had to go back to Jonah and anchor inside of him to revitalize. He wouldn't have survived outside at that point."

Kiko added, "The boss used to feed off human energy, but now it's all about blood."

"So he couldn't come out of Jonah's body until he was healed?" Natalia asked.

Dawn nodded. "Jonah was severely wounded, too. He was dying and the boss couldn't get out—he was trapped by his need to root on what was left of Jonah's humanity. If Jonah had died, it would've been just like a cave-in of dead matter, and the boss would've never been able to escape. I think he might've even perished there from lack of sustenance."

She stilled her pulse, trying not to show how upset she was getting. "So, as a vampire, I exchanged with Jonah, thinking that would set the boss free. But even though I reanimated Jonah, his body altered in the process. I only made him *undead*. I didn't actually realize it at the time, but his matter still ended up trapping the boss's soul."

"So he can't leave now," Natalia said.

"Right. But his powers make him dominant . . . most of the time. He's done everything to escape over the past year, but it hasn't worked. Besides, Jonah doesn't want to let him go."

The wind kept howling, and finally, the weight of all the eyes in the room got to Dawn.

And when Frank hitched in a breath, she realized that there were more gazes on her than just the team's or the eyes from Kalin's portrait.

The scent of jasmine had filled the room, and Dawn lifted her head as the invisible Friends entered, no doubt summoned awake by Costin. Several of them surrounded her, whispering encouragement, just as they did night after night. Even Kalin gave her a mean nudge, just to say her version of "Hi, bitch."

Above the fireplace, her portrait stood empty as the room brimmed with life.

Dawn glanced over to Frank, who had raised his face to the invisible Breisi. He was smiling, languishing under the greeting of his girlfriend. Kiko was nearby, standing alone, seeming so defeated that Dawn started walking over to him.

On the way, she focused on Natalia again, finding the new girl . . . at home?

Her hands were outspread in the presence of the spirits, her face glowing while she took in the Friends' voices. They would be encouraging her, too, Dawn knew.

Whispers from the dead, she thought. Maybe Natalia really was meant to be here.

But was that because of some kind of Underground-designed plan? Or was Dawn giving the enemy way too much credit?

Hell, they'd find out soon enough once the team got to those bodies on Billiter Street.

FIVE

The Whispering Ground

THIS is it?" Frank asked Natalia as he leaned on the handle of the shovel he'd brought with them to the Square Mile, which housed the financial district.

They'd hauled themselves and their equipment over here in a modified black Kia Sedona, noting the deserted streets at this witching hour, when most everyone was safe at home in their beds outside of the City's core.

"This is where I heard them," Natalia said, lacing her gloved fingers through the chain-link fence separating them from the small, clearly dormant construction site. Like Dawn and Kiko, she'd strapped on a lighted headset that shone over the rotted cement bags and old dustbins littering the dirt. Frank had such good vamp sight that he'd gone without.

Nose and cheeks stinging because of the cold, Dawn glanced around while the air hummed with the hush of night. They were enclosed by lights-out banks and empty structures "to let"—which meant they were for rent, in American. In the near distance, the

Gherkin building loomed, coming off like the kind of shattered black and silver Easter egg a Goth child might create.

For Dawn, overseas had a removed tinge—a "BBC gray" with the colors and surroundings filtered and subdued, less vivid than what her eyes were used to back in the California sun. But that was probably homesickness at work.

Just homesickness.

Kiko's voice tugged at the edges of her perception.

"You hearing any voices now?" he asked Natalia.

According to Costin's most recent instructions, aired over their earpieces while driving here, Kiko's duty was to keep watch over the new girl. Right now, Natalia was propping her forehead against the fence, concentrating as her headset cast crisscrossed shadows over the buildings.

"One young woman keeps asking for help," the second psychic said. "Just like a traumatized child who hears a rescuer outside a room where she's been tied up all night."

In spite of Dawn's thigh wound, which was tingling with that healing goo she'd spread over it earlier, she prepared to climb the fence, a shovel in her hand.

Either the new girl was priming them as sitting ducks, stalling until an attack could be launched, or she was telling the truth. Sitting around wasn't going to change whatever was about to happen.

But Kiko took hold of Dawn's jacket. "Hold up. We don't have the go-ahead yet."

Damn. The Friends were still clouding security cameras around the area, distracting anyone who wandered too close, and taking a general look around to see if the team was safe.

"Frank," Dawn asked, "do you sense anything?"

"Best keep to our plan, Dawnie. Wait a few minutes."

But her father was scanning the rooftops, just like he was doing his own reconnaissance. He had distracted creases lining his forehead.

"Is there something . . . ?" Dawn asked.

He hesitated, then went back to leaning on his shovel handle. "Nah."

A whoosh of jasmine swept around them, and they all stood a little straighter.

It was Breisi; Dawn could tell from the way her Friend gently brushed against her braid in greeting.

"All clear," her wispy voice said.

As she flew by Frank, he lifted his hand, like he was sifting through the spirit while she flowed past him on her way back to sentry duty.

For a second, Dawn took in the glow of him: an inner light that had nothing to do with vampire stuff. Right now, he was just a creature who'd found the one soul who could possibly replace the loss of his own.

Dawn grasped the chain link, then hefted herself up and up, scampering over the hard netting and tossing her shovel over the top. The tool landed with a *thunk* on the other side.

Balancing for only a moment, she swiveled over the fence, airborne until she landed in a crouch, then stood.

Much to her chagrin, she grunted as her thigh wound reminded her it was there.

Frank followed Dawn over, but he was way more graceful, even with his muscled bulk.

Kiko flanked Natalia on the other side, staying put. He kept one hand in his jacket pocket, where he'd stuffed a small silver stake. Just in case.

When Dawn and Frank chose their spots and dug into the dirt, Natalia hitched in a breath.

They stopped.

"Something wrong?" Kiko asked.

"You . . . didn't sense it?" Natalia held her hand over her chest.

"No . . ."

Dawn came to the rescue of Kiko's professional pride. "Sense what exactly?"

The new girl fisted her coat. "Maybe it was a groan. Or two of them . . . three . . . maybe more?"

"Did they change their minds about us being here?" Kiko asked. "Are they trying to tell us to leave?"

"I don't think so." Natalia looked down, listening. Then she made a defeated sound. "I wish Mr. Limpet could be here. Perhaps he would recognize what they're trying to communicate better than I."

Kiko coughed, reminding her that it wasn't a good idea to talk about Costin in the open. On the way over, they'd told Natalia why the boss had remained behind, how he'd be their ultimate weapon once the vampires were targeted.

Natalia should've known better.

Or was she just too nervous to remember?

Thinking about other, darker explanations for the girl's lapse, Dawn went back to digging. As for Frank, he was glancing at the rooftops again.

"That's the second time you've taken a gander there," she said.

"Okay, there's something, but I'm not sure what." He met Dawn's gaze, his eyes light green as Dawn's headset caught them. "Maybe that's what the dead are groaning about?"

Warning fluttered down Dawn's spine as she halted in mid-dig, looking behind her at the rooftops, too.

Out of the corner of her eye, she saw Kiko put his other hand inside his jacket, where his shoulder holster would be. He was the only team member who was packing an illegally obtained revolver with silver bullets. If he was caught with it here in England, where not even the cops routinely carried guns, Costin and his connections would have a fine time clearing him. It'd been enough to secure the team visas, for God's sake.

But Kik thought his notoriously great aim was worth the gamble.

Frank exhaled. "It's gone now."

"Whatever it was," Dawn said, "the Friends are bound to find it."

"Maybe we should leave," Natalia said.

Dawn hoped Costin was getting all this through the earpieces. She only wore one herself because she couldn't access their Awareness out here: too distant, too risky. But the earpiece robbed her of any sensory connection with him, and she wished she knew what he thought of Natalia now.

"You hear that, Dawn?" Kiko asked, shooting her a conspiring glance. "The newbie wants to leave."

"*Shouldn't* we leave?" Natalia repeated.

Kiko chuffed. "Not unless *you* just want to heel it out of here because you know something we don't."

"I'm . . ." She took a step back from him. "What do you mean?"

"Bad guys." Kiko pointed at the rooftops. "You didn't happen to bring any here with you, did you?"

"Oh, Kik," Dawn said.

"You were thinking it, too. I'm just saying it out loud."

Natalia turned to the fence again, blinding Dawn with her headlight. But before that, just for a split second, Dawn had sworn she'd seen a hint of mortification on her face.

When the other girl spoke, her shaking words only proved Dawn's suspicion. "One of the voices I heard this morning . . . She was like me. Like any of us. A girl who was going about life until it ended so suddenly."

Like any of us?

Dawn gripped her shovel handle, because she wasn't like Natalia or this other victim at all.

"I only wanted to see that she found peace," Natalia continued, "along with any others here."

Surprisingly, Kiko seemed to lay off as he said, "To do that, we'll have to stay. Can you handle it?"

Natalia's bobbing headset light indicated her answer, and Frank grumbled under his breath, then started to dig, destroying the embarrassing pause that followed. After offering Natalia a look that said she was sorry about this situation, Dawn followed her dad's example.

But she was sorry about a whole lot more, too, like how she still couldn't believe in Costin's newest recruit. Like how they'd brought Natalia here with them in the first place.

They dug, Frank shoveling dirt in normal time, because he only used his powers in the open when absolutely necessary, and Dawn keeping up pace. Then, after what seemed like minutes later, the new team member sucked in another sharp breath.

And that was even before Frank stopped digging, falling to his knees and dropping his shovel as he inspected what he'd found under the dirt.

Dawn tossed her shovel away, too, and darted to his side.

Breathless, she aimed her headlight on the face of a pale corpse, its mouth twisted in a frozen scream. Holy shit.

"What do you have?" Kiko asked.

"Female," Dawn said. *Oxygen in, oxygen out. Come on.* "Very late teens, maybe? The body's real fresh, but there's dried blood caked around her mouth. And, crap . . . her neck."

"What about it?" Kiko asked.

Dawn looked closer, her stomach lurching.

"The rest of her body's not covered by the dirt. We've only got a head here."

A rattle of the fence made her and Frank look over to find Kiko hovering over a collapsed Natalia, who was mumbling.

"What's going on?" Dawn asked.

"She's talking." Kiko bent his head closer to the other psychic, then relayed what she was whispering. "Her name's Kate, and she's a local English girl. She should've known better than to go off with the others. . . . She should've stayed a good girl and listened to all the lessons her parents tried to teach her when she was younger. Somewhere, she forgot most of those lessons. God forgive her. . . ."

Frank flinched, and Dawn grabbed his arm, but shamefully, it was more of out of excitement than extended comfort.

Her mind whirred with the beginning of the hunt. Costin would be back at headquarters right now, already initiating a data search for missing persons named "Kate" or any variation thereof. He would also try to hit up an identified paranormal-friendly detective in London to wrangle up the names of known runaways, people who weren't closely cared for.

By now, Natalia had gone speechless, her head lolling forward as she began to weep. Kiko reached out, as if he were about to touch her shoulder.

But then he seemed to remember she was his competition, and he turned to Dawn instead. "Sounds like that's all we're going to get from her."

Dawn stood. "It might be enough for a lead."

Kiko got to his feet, too, shoving his hands in his pockets as Frank took up his shovel, lifting more dirt from the ground.

"Hey," Dawn said to Kik, thinking she should try to make him feel valuable. Tough love was hard. Besides, it'd go a long way in stoking his motivation. "Want to come in here? I know you've never gotten touch readings from corpses, but if the rest of the body's around, maybe there's clothing on it, and you can get something from that. Or the dirt, itself."

Frank had halted his labor again. "I'm thinking you won't get any clothing here."

Dawn turned to find him pointing to a hole he'd made. His finger was shaking, reminding her of how he got when he saw something like a shaving cut on Kiko's face before they got any healing goo on it.

"Disembodied, bare limbs and a couple of skulls," Frank said. "Some still have flesh on them—I can smell it. But most are stripped to the bone, like something was *real* hungry."

For the second time that night, Dawn's stomach dipped. "Have you ever heard of a . . . *client*"—she didn't want to say "vampire" out loud—"eating flesh like that?"

Dawn's earpiece came to life, and Costin's voice followed.

"Not any client I've seen before. But we cannot assume this was the result of a ravenous creature. Perhaps there is a ritual involved."

A moan sounded from the other side of the fence. Natalia.

She'd gotten to her knees by now, hunched over. Kiko even had his hand on her back.

"Shit," Dawn said under her breath, reaching into her jacket for her cell phone.

As Frank backed away and tried to get himself together, she took pictures of Kate's head, then the limbs, which she would forward to Costin ASAP. At the same time, she accessed her earpiece to communicate directly with him.

"Frank's tempted to fall off the wagon," she said. "Also? Our new girl's coming apart."

"She is only human."

At his brusque answer, Dawn went back to taking her photos. Even though she and Costin were technically connected on many levels, they didn't understand each other at all. He had no idea how he'd just pierced her, reminding her that, unlike Natalia, Dawn had gone beyond being repulsed by a dead body.

Meanwhile, Frank had taken out a kerchief and covered his lower face while using his own phone to take pictures. Flashes cut each night-dark moment into strobed blocks.

A whiff of familiar jasmine interrupted Dawn just as she was about to take a closer picture of Kate's head.

Breisi.

"Hey," Dawn said, "aren't you supposed to be guarding—?"

The spirit moved around her so fast that the motion whipped Dawn's face to the right.

Where something red gleamed from a rooftop.

Something like eyes.

Dawn's mind slashed to an image from the past. Red eyes.

Guards—soldiers from the Hollywood Underground. Machete tails, iron fangs, spit that burned.

The first vampire she'd ever fought.

Adrenaline surging, Dawn didn't think. She reacted, dropping her phone as she took a running leap at the fence.

Get it alive. Ask it questions. Put an end to all this—

"Dawn!" Frank yelled, just before she heard him tell Kiko to stow his gun away.

But she'd already scaled the chain link and dropped to the other side, her body filled with rushing ice, her breath stabbing her lungs.

Save Costin . . .

She sprinted ahead, following the eyes as they began to streak toward the right.

Get it!

Jasmine surrounded her. Friends.

But they were pushing her back, not forward.

"What're you doing?" Dawn swung her fists at them, keeping the red eyes in sight while they zipped over the rooftops, moving from one building to the other.

Farther away from her.

Farther.

As Dawn struggled to get free, the spirits pressed against her, binding her arms to her sides. But Breisi's thready voice circled Dawn's head, as if her friend was trying to make the others back off.

"Let her go."

Another Friend's voice—a thick Brazilian accent—trumped Breisi's.

"Capture . . . That thing had a capture box. An Elite vial!"

"If you're afraid that the intruder might know how to capture you like the Elites in L.A. did," Dawn said, levering her weight away from them as they held her, "don't. If that *thing* wanted you, it would have you by now."

"It's running away," another Friend said in Japanese-accented English. *"The boss would want you to leave it, Dawn. . . ."*

"Too dangerous," said another.

"Release me!" Dawn shouted, knowing they'd have to obey as long as the command didn't fly in the face of one of Costin's directives or result in his harm.

The pressure immediately lifted off, and she ran full steam ahead. But jasmine still pushed her, and she knew Breisi was helping, propelling her and protecting her while leaving the others to guard the site.

Pumping her arms for more speed, Dawn delved into the maze of streets around the construction area. Something—ivy?—from a flowered window box slapped her face as her headlight paved the way. A garbage bag nearly tripped her as she barged past the end of the chain-link fence.

Damn it—she couldn't see the eyes anymore; she'd been running blindly, hoping to catch up.

She slowed to a walk, panting, getting her bearings, the cold catching up to scratch her cheeks. A pain poked at her thigh.

But unwilling to give up, she speed walked ahead, toward a building that boasted pipes on its facade, almost as if it'd been turned wrong side out to show off its innards.

"Where'd you go?" she whispered to herself. "How could you have just disappeared?"

Like a dervish, Breisi gushed past. *"Look around!"*

But before she could, she felt something approaching from behind her.

Preparing herself, she took a fighter's stance, knees bent as she yanked her silver-coated throwing blades out of a jacket pocket, then spun around to fire one off.

"Whoa!" said a low, familiar voice.

Pulling back, she found Frank standing there, hands in the air. He'd caught up, yet he didn't seem winded in the least.

"Dad," she said, annoyed as she continued scanning the area, her blade primed.

"Do you have some kind of death wish, Dawn?"

A . . . death wish?

Her headlight blinked off, out of juice, shading Frank in darkness.

But her mind was far more illuminated. If she should die, Costin and Jonah would be free of their master and turn human again. Was she trying to make that happen without even knowing it?

Shaking off the notion, she forced her heartbeat to a calm thud, molding herself into ice. If anything, she needed more self-discipline, and she should've known that after Hollywood.

Maybe running off alone hadn't been so smart.

Done with Dawn, Frank turned to Breisi. "And you—why're *you* on this hysteria wagon?"

The air stirred as the spirit flew to him, around him.

"*Red eyes . . .*" she said.

Frank made a rough, disbelieving sound. "You think this group is going to have Guards, just like in L.A.? Well, how about this— what if these *clients* have the power to know what gets to us, and they whip up illusions, and this particular one was luring Dawn somewhere?"

Dawn caught her breath, poising her *shuriken* blade for an attack she was still expecting. Breisi stilled herself, as if realizing she'd gone overboard.

"You're way smarter than that, Breez," he added. "But you're stir crazy, so I get why you were gung ho."

Dawn extracted a locator from another pocket. Recently, Breisi and Frank had adjusted the small device so it could be thrown from up to a hundred feet away and attach to an object. "I could've at least bugged whatever it was we saw. It would've been handy to know where the red-eyed thing ended up."

"Let it go, Dawn," he said. "We—"

Then he stopped cold, bristling, just as he had earlier when he'd watched the rooftops.

Fear creeping over her skin, Dawn saw the red eyes come to light several yards above his head, from the utter darkness of the inside-out building's tubes.

Before Dawn could yell out a warning, a tiny explosion parted the air, a whizzing sound sang over their heads, then a thud capped the glass building across the street.

The red eyes zipped upward on a wire, toward that building, one hand holding something away from its body and toward the team.

The capture box the Friends had been talking about?

Oh, God—

Undeterred, Breisi zoomed toward the shadow figure, hell-bent for leather. At the same time, Dawn winged the locator at it, but it was flying up the wire so quickly that she didn't know if the device even attached.

But as the figure raised its hand—with the box?—Breisi's spirit voice screamed, and Frank roared, jumping after the intruder, his fingers outstretched like claws.

He was protecting his girlfriend, maybe because he hadn't been able to save her when she'd died.

High above Dawn, Frank caught the shadow figure in midswipe, and both of them fell from the wire—Frank controlled, coming to a solid landing on his feet.

The shadow figure waving its arms and splatting to the ground.

Pulling out a silver stake from another jacket pocket, Dawn ran over to the intruder, but Frank was already arched over it like a famished animal, sniffing at the blood pooled around the body.

"Dad?"

He looked up at her, his fangs flashing, his eyes burning through the night.

"Frank!" she yelled. "Back off! We can take it with us while it's still alive. We can give it medical aid, then question it."

Too late.

Even with Breisi doing her part to push Frank away from the body, her vamp dad reared back his head, then bit the intruder's neck.

The shadow figure didn't even fight back, its red eyes glowing as it convulsed. It let go of the boxlike device it'd been holding, the object tumbling over the ground until it came to a stop.

Dawn realized that the figure's fall from the wire had pretty much done it in, but she got out a pocket-bound crucifix anyway and thrust the item under Frank's face. He'd have to exchange blood to turn the figure into a vamp, but even just a bite was a bad precedent to set.

Her father yelped as he backed away, his hands raised to ward off the holy sight. As a lower vampire, it worked on him, just as it did with Costin.

Time seemed to drag as they looked at each other, as Frank's eyes dimmed and he touched the blood around his lips. She could see the dark of the liquid, even in the moonlight, and the sight tore at her.

Her dad . . . Gone . . .

"Not vampire," he said, like he was talking around what had just happened. He'd done that a lot back when he'd been stuck raising her and she'd nursed his booze benders.

And like the girl she'd been, Dawn fell back into the same pattern. It hurt less that way.

"The blood isn't a vampire's?" she asked.

"No." He lowered his hand and rested his head against the air, where Breisi was hovering, probably surrounding him and comforting him. "But it's not really human, either."

As Dawn absorbed that, she tried to shut out what Frank had done, but she couldn't. So she allowed the horror, the rage at life, to gather inside, where she could use it later.

She hid her trembling by fisting her hands, hid her emotions by bending down to the shadow figure's body, which looked human enough in its tight, dark clothing.

Then, as she unmasked it, she dissolved into shaky, terrified laughter.

Because those red eyes?

The faint moonlight told her that they hadn't been anything more than night-vision goggles strapped to a teenaged boy's face.

SIX

LONDON BABYLON

The Next Day

CHAQUE dimanche, avant la guerre . . ."

As another student stood in front of the classroom and recited her English-to-French translation of *Deux Amis*, Della rested her cheek in her palm while leaning on the desk table. Her lackadaisical pose made her eyelids heavy, and she imagined the reader's voice as light spilling through a window.

Melinda Springfield, Della thought, watching through her lashes as her classmate's lips formed around Guy de Maupassant's words.

Melinda, her idol.

Where the human's hair was rain straight and silver blond, Della's was frizzy and cursed with the hue of a potato's skin. Melinda's eyes were china blue while Della's were muddy green. Even their bodies were at different ends of the spectrum, Melinda's legs long, endless and Della's limbs slightly padded, seemingly half the length.

Yet perhaps she wouldn't have noticed to such an awful degree if Violet wasn't always there to reflect on Della's potato hair or stumpy legs.

"*Morissot partait dès l'aurore,*" Melinda continued, lulling Della.

Someone coughed delicately from the table facing her, and she knew who it was without even glimpsing.

She looked anyway, catching a smirking Violet, her cat eyes gleaming as she mind-spoke to Della.

How adorable.

Melinda finished her reading, and Della sat up in her chair, wishing she could tell Violet to sod off. Yet, as always, she kept quiet, merely pasting her attention on Mademoiselle, who sat at her desk with her Grace Kelly neck and smile while leading the applause.

"*Merci beaucoup,*" their teacher said as Melinda returned to her table.

All the upper-sixth-form girls round her stirred as she sank into her seat, easy, confident, so comfortable in her skin.

In French, Mademoiselle made small talk, winding down the last minutes of class. "Everyone who remains behind during Remembrance Day weekend will attend Melinda's basketball match, yes? Unless, of course, you are traveling home and not staying in the boarding houses."

"*Oui, Mademoiselle,*" the class of thirteen said in unison.

Violet crossed her eyes and jarred an elbow at Polly, who sat next to her, winding her bobbed strawberry blond hair around a finger as she stared at the clock.

Polly jabbed Violet in return, but they quieted when Mademoiselle cast them a stern glance, then excused the class.

As the students rose from their seats, Melinda sailed past Della, who managed to find her voice.

"Your pronunciation," Della said. "It's . . . perfect."

She began heading for the door before Violet could see her talking to the human.

"Cheers, Del," the object of her admiration said, genuinely pleased at the compliment. "See you at the match then?"

Della didn't dare say yes as she blended in with her mates and squeezed out the door.

While traveling, they were a swarm of the long brown skirts, knee-high boots, white shirts, and thin red ties they wore to distinguish themselves from the rest of the students. During these last two years of school, the sixth-form girls had earned the privilege of going without the basic plaid-skirt-and-blue-jumper uniforms, but Violet's group would always have their own exclusive marks.

They made their way down the musty halls lined with cases bearing pictures of prefects and lists of club announcements, then settled into the art room to complete their hour of extracurricular activity.

Afterward, they moved as a unit again and, out of the main building, with its dark brick, gothic windows and chimeras poised at roof's edge, the darkening sky rolled with clouds. In the distance, the city of St. Albans laid itself before them, a church bell marking the hour.

But none of the other students would be able to hear it from this far off. Only them.

Only the five vampires.

"Ill weather on its way," Violet remarked.

They all knew precisely what she meant because, this morning, the media had trumpeted news of the burial patch on Billiter Street. They would have to find a new place to do away with the scraps from their feedings with Wolfie, who often urged them to overkill.

Most nights the girls merely sipped from their victims then cleaned up the physical and mental aftermaths. Yet, recently, Wolfie had been goading them to build their appetites to a point where they needed more than blood.

Della hugged her books. She, more than any of the girls, expected punishment. . . .

They followed the stone path past the tiny chapel that most of the other Queenshill students used for peaceful reflection, the trail taking them beyond the new technology wing, the football field, the theater, and toward the art deco boarding houses that had been added long after Thomas Gatenby had donated land for the school back in the late eighteen hundreds.

Ultimately, they entered their house's lobby, the smell of bricked-up air and girls' perfume hitting Della's sharp senses. Students leaned on the counter of the main office as their parents signed them out to sweep them off for the weekend.

None of the humans looked at the passing pack, perhaps because the five girls didn't enjoy house competitions and activities as the others did.

Or perhaps because they intuitively knew the five were different.

"I'll tell you," Polly said as they entered the empty stairwell that led to the eldest students' rooms. "You wouldn't catch me dead at Melinda Springfield's match."

Blanche, with a red headband pushing back her dark hair, broke away as she took the stairs first. "You'd be caught *undead*, you git!"

She giggled and leaped to the next step, but Violet reached out in a blur and gripped Blanche round the neck, yanking her back so they were face-to-face.

The group halted, surrounding Violet so no one else would see, should interlopers come upon them.

"We've been rather tolerant of your cheekiness recently, Blanche," Violet said between her teeth.

The other girl chopped Violet's hands away from her neck and gracefully gained her feet. Then, unruffled, she continued climbing, a bounce to her gait, just as if nothing had transpired.

"I'm finally exhausted with you, Vi," she said.

"Is that so?"

"Yes, and the next time you touch me like so, I'll rip you to shreds, no matter what Wolfie might think. I don't recall anyone crowning you our sovereign."

Violet's eyes began to sizzle to light purple, her shoulders hunched, her low hiss dragging over the air.

Blanche continued on her way.

Throughout it all, the rest of the girls tried to blend in with the white walls. In particular, Della kept her mind clear. If she didn't have any thoughts for Violet to read, she wouldn't be singled out. . . .

Violet sniffed and the others did the same.

Humans.

A door opened at the top of the stairs, and the voices of other students intruded.

Violet straightened her back and resumed the look of a human again. And it was just in time, because two lower-sixth-form girls rounded the corner and spied the group.

The younger students grew silent, then rushed past Violet, Polly, Noreen, and Della, then out the bottom door.

Adjusting her skirt, Violet sauntered the rest of the way up. Noreen and Polly trailed in her wake.

Della brought up the rear, and soon they came to the first-floor hallway, where Blanche had been lounging against a wall, having paused until Violet arrived. She gave the brunette a saucy glance as Violet passed, then took up pace with Della.

Wasn't that brilliant? the other girl asked mind-to-mind. *It feels wonderful to put Violet in her place. I've wanted to do it for the last year now.*

Be careful, Della thought, trying hard to keep the others out of their link. If she had still been human, she would have been sweating, but she only felt the memory of panic all over her skin.

Careful? Blanche asked. *Violet's no stronger or better than you or I.*

Della shot a subtle glance to her friend. *Briana thought the same before she left us last year. And so did Sharon just after she deserted us, as well.*

Blanche halted. *What are you saying, Della?*

But she merely traveled on, shutting her mind altogether.

Even so, the recollection of the old group members' names surrounded Della as she caught up to the rest of the crowd. Aside from the fact that Briana had run away after the death of her guardian sister and Sharon had been taken out of school by her parents, no one knew what had become of either girl. Sharon had promised to e-mail from her new school in the north of Scotland where she had found another vampire group who had taken her in, but the communication had recently dwindled to nothing. And Briana? She had turned her back on them altogether.

Losing them had pained Della, but that wasn't the only reason their absences disturbed her.

It was only that, every time their names surfaced, Violet would get that little feline smile on her face, as if she knew the reason Sharon had stopped writing and Briana had truly run away from school. However, she had locked the answers away in her own mind, out of the reach of the others.

As the group passed an open door marked, "Housematron," they called out to the woman who sat at her desk, her dull hair latched into a bun at her nape, her skin sallow, her body frail.

"Hello, Mrs. Jones."

"Feeling chipper today, Mrs. Jones?"

"We do hope you improve, Mrs. Jones."

"You do seem better, Mrs. Jones."

The housematron shuffled her paperwork but didn't glance up as she spoke in a voice that seemed husky with a constant cold. "Off to concentrate on your prep time? There'll be no tutors today since most students are going home this weekend."

Blanche had joined them by now. "Certainly, Mrs. Jones. We have our A-levels to contend with, after all."

Shortly after the mention of the advanced-level exams, they separated, stopping in their single rooms only long enough to fetch their books and materials. Then they strolled to the common room, which truly was empty for the weekend.

They seemed to be the only ones who hadn't been called home by their distant parents, who traveled for business or took holidays overseas or went about their everyday human lives while never knowing what their daughters had become.

They completed their studies, returning to their rooms only after they had finished. Terribly hungry by now, they left notes on their doors for Mrs. Jones's sake in particular: "Taking a snack in town."

Then, on alert for anyone who might catch them, they dashed outside, skimming the grass, combing over a green hill, down its slope. Farther, into the darkening woods, where under a cushion of crimson and gold leaves, they stopped at a chained door.

Once they lifted the bindings off, they entered the hole, secured the hatch behind them, then zipped through the tunnel until they arrived at a fall of red and orange beads marking the entrance to their very own underground common room.

Parting the barrier, they headed for their own plush fur divans, then plopped to the cushions in this hidden place where Thomas Gatenby, the school's long-dead benefactor, had kept his . . .

Well, Della supposed they might have been called "household staff," but the leftover iron chains and shackles on the walls hinted at something more.

The beads parted again, and the girls watched quietly as a thin gray cat slunk inside, then crept to a corner. There, it curled itself over a nest of blankets near a lava lamp that Polly had nicked from her aunt's house.

When the cat closed its eyes, the girls relaxed. Violet even rubbed her face against the zebra-striped pillows positioned beneath a framed poster of Orlando Bloom. He, and other heartthrobs, decorated the rock walls, which were connected by strings of fairy lights that beckoned like far-off stars.

"Where shall we hunt tonight?" Violet asked.

Next to her, Polly reclined on the divan's cushions while leaning against Violet. "I don't want to go anywhere in St. Albans, even if it is the closest. It's such a tired spot. I prefer the thick of London, where the runaways are easy to find."

"I prefer it, as, well," Violet said, "and it was time for a change anyway. The same routine was stultifying."

Noreen was in front of a mirror, arranging her red hair into a Nicole Kidman–type style, even though she had more of a Sarah Ferguson face and figure. However, whenever she danced, she did it like Ann-Margret, as she had proven the other night while Della had watched and wondered if she should join.

"We could try that new club in Soho," Noreen said, turning this way and that to take in her reflection. Hardly pleased, she allowed her layered hair to whisk back down to her neck.

From Blanche's spot in the corner, where she was reclining on a netted hammock, she said, "No ideas of your own, Vi? I was quite looking forward to being ordered about some more."

Nothing in the room moved.

Not unless one counted the shooting daggers from Violet's gaze.

She'd been waiting, Della knew. Measuring out the moments until she could get revenge on Blanche for poaching that young man, Harry, the other night. No one took the first sip after Wolfie but Violet; the rest of them always waited to feed on what was left. It'd been their unspoken rule ever since being turned just over a year ago: the most dominant went first, the weakest went last.

It was a wonder Della survived on leftovers, just like the head and arm she'd been given with Kate after they'd lured her to Wolfie's flat. Unbeknownst to the others, she'd packed away the head in the tote she'd been carrying, thinking to save her spoils for later. She'd been working up the bravery to defy them for the last couple of months, but that night, she'd lost her courage and disposed of the head at the dumping ground instead. There, she'd made certain no one else saw that she hadn't picked it clean, fearing what might happen if she were to be caught squirreling away food.

She glanced at the cat, seeing that it was sleeping deeply, and Noreen broke the tension by adopting a chuffed tone.

"I don't much mind where we dine tonight. I'm famished."

"We're always famished by this point," Polly said. "I'm completely knackered from daylight."

Violet stroked Polly's neck. "We're fortunate to walk in the light."

"No complaints." Polly sighed and closed her eyes, anticipating what was bound to come next with Violet.

Della couldn't stop watching. She was only happy she wasn't Vi's favorite.

As Noreen crawled onto the divan next to Della, she said, "No complaints here, either." She put on a smile, knowing her every word and movement was being monitored. "I certainly don't mind our routine, even if it destroys the weekends because we have to rest."

Among their talents was the ability to play hard, then binge rest on the weekends plus the few hours they had before class began and after they had got in from their nightcrawls. Della enjoyed rest—it allowed her not to think.

A pleasured-pained sigh came from the other side of the room as Violet bit into Polly's neck.

It was just an appetizer since Polly had taken most of that girl's blood the other night, sharing Kate with Violet only after Wolfie had finished dining.

"Let's leave for some fun now," Blanche said, standing, the hammock swinging behind her. She gave a pointed glance toward the feeding Violet, then headed for the bead-covered tunnel.

Creak, creak went the hammock's boltings in the walls as no one moved to follow her.

Polly moaned as Violet continued sucking.

Blanche blew out a breath, then changed direction, walking over to the stereo system, where she plucked out a CD from the wall holder and stared at the song list.

In the meantime, Violet fed, her fingers slipping to Polly's breast.

As Violet caressed it, the other girl shifted her hips, biting her lip until a squiggle of blood trailed down her chin.

Della's belly went tight at the scent of the blood.

Hungry, so hungry. But she never went first. Always last. Always.

At another of Polly's moans, Blanche put the CD into the player, cranking the volume. A thundering techno beat covered the feeding noises.

Unable to resist a good rhythm, Noreen stood and immediately swayed into a dance.

In its corner, the cat blinked awake, then hefted out a sigh and put its head back down.

Della came to focus on the ceiling, the fairy lights sharpening to white points in her gaze. But the whiteness pained her, so she looked away to see Blanche joining Noreen.

They danced away as Violet raised her blood-soaked mouth from Polly's neck, her fangs shaded red.

"Mind the volume," Violet said, her command vibrating over the music.

Mocking the beat, Blanche shook her head.

In a brutal flash, Violet sprang out of her seat, flying across the room, crashing into Blanche with enough force to smash the black-haired girl against the rock wall.

In response, Blanche's fangs shot from her gums while Violet hissed in her face.

Noreen dashed over to turn the stereo off, glancing toward the cat, her fingers fidgeting into a tangle. Then she looked at Della.

What should we do? she asked.

Nothing. We shouldn't interfere. . . .

Violet's voice shivered the fairy lights. "Why can't you obey?"

Shadows jittered over the walls.

Blanche's eyes slanted, then went an electric blue, her hair receding back into her head, making her bare and ugly. Yet even as her face changed into something feral and catlike, her ears extended to points, like a wolf's.

Not to be outdone, Violet altered into the same full vampire form, as well. Then, opening her mouth all the way and brandishing her long fangs, she swiped at Blanche's face with fingers that had extended into claws, leaving deep, bloody gouges in the other girl's cheek.

Della's stomach tumbled. *Hungry.*

Scared.

The black-haired girl fought back, raising her foot to lever against Violet's stomach. The force lifted the brunette off her feet, and she landed on her bum with a grunt, then bounced right back up, her spine arched, claws outstretched as her hiss lowered to a screeching growl.

The blood, the frenzy . . . Della couldn't take any more.

"Don't!" she yelled.

As the two fighting creatures whipped their gazes over to her, she pressed her lips together.

She should've stayed quiet. Why hadn't she?

When a louder, angrier hiss filled the room, they all froze.

For against the rock wall behind Blanche and Violet, a shadow was growing, expanding, finally settling into the form of a human-like being.

Della felt as if needles were being shoved under her skin, and she cowered.

"You fight even as our carelessness causes trouble above-ground?" the shadow's owner said from its former sleeping spot behind Della. Its voice sounded like steam rising through the cracks of hell. "I was waiting to see if you appreciated the reprieve I was extending."

Violet and Blanche both cringed, their fangs receding and their eyes going dull as they lowered their gazes. They should have known punishment was coming. They had all known.

On the wall, Della could see the shadow crooking a finger at the two girls.

Summoning them for an even worse scolding.

SEVEN

The Misplaced Heart

Earlier the Same Day

At sunrise, Dawn had met Costin in their bedroom.

She was already in her nightgown—he liked the elegance of them, he'd always said—when he entered and shut the door behind him. The curtains were closed, and a sanguine light suffused the room from a lampshade decorated with red velvet swirls, just like blood curling in water.

"You showed," she said, getting under the sheets and quilt. "I almost thought you might stay locked up tight from now on."

Costin stood by the walk-in closet, shedding his roomy white shirt. Dawn couldn't help lingering over the streamlined beauty of muscles under pale skin.

Then she remembered that this was really Jonah's form, not Costin's. That she would never get to touch her lover's original body. Ever.

He left his torso bare, coming to stand at the side of the bed in his loose black trousers. She could see his topaz eyes shining through the sheer draping.

"You are concerned that I will be distancing myself?" he asked, his voice like a scratching caress over her skin.

Her belly heated. "It did cross my mind."

He leaned down, hands on the mattress. "It is nice to see that you care."

The last word rattled her. She'd never allowed herself to care about anyone, and when she'd let down her guard enough to try, she'd been burned. By "Matt." Even by Costin.

She didn't like where this conversation was headed, so she diverted it. "If you think I'm not going to grill you about what you've been doing for the last several hours since the team returned, you're wrong. Coming over here with your shirt off will do no good."

A low laugh acknowledged her directness.

And her emotional dodging.

"Thanks to the miracle of the Internet, plus our databases," he said, obliging her, "I have been able to construct a list of every missing 'Kate' or 'Katherine' or other variations in the area. It is not a long roll call since crime over here is nothing compared to what we are used to in America. Plus, we know Kate was a British local, so that has narrowed down our names, as well."

She wanted to ask about the night-vision boy who'd tracked them at the dumping ground, but first things first. "Sounds like the Scotland Yard cops didn't give you any help."

"Since this burial site was within what they call 'the City,' I contacted an old acquaintance in the City of London police. I have an . . . understanding . . . with Detective Inspector Norton. He's discreet, passionate, and very open to alternative explanations for unexplainable crimes. However, he is protective about open cases and will not share details."

"Can a Friend be assigned to look over his shoulder?"

"Done. However, our lot is not made easier by the fact that the press has already gotten ahold of the Billiter story. The police do not have many details, but if our Underground vampires are indeed responsible for this burial ground, then we can expect them to be less careless from now on."

"Do you think they could've been warned by that boy who was hanging around Billiter even before the press came into it?"

"That is a distinct possibility, as well."

Goody. "So are the cops going to give us any help?"

"We shall see. A Friend told me that Norton personally went to the burial site an hour or two ago. *He* already seems committed to the victims." Costin sat on the mattress. "Yet even though he may be open to strange explanations for a crime, the rest of his department might not be so inclined."

"So the dumping ground is a crime scene now," she said. "Do you think we can try to send Natalia back there, just to see if she hears anything else?"

"We can. I will also see if Norton will at least chat with the city coroner. If Natalia could be near the bodies again, she might discern any last whispers there, as well. However, as I said, Norton will most likely prefer to keep us out of an investigation."

"I can understand why. He probably doesn't want to come off like the department whack job. But maybe his keeping us out of it is for the best. More secretive that way, and we can continue doing our own thing."

In spite of the topic, Dawn's blood seemed thick in her veins. If she scooted over a couple of inches, Costin would be close enough to touch.

"Are you going to *persuade* the cops or the coroner to cooperate?" Dawn asked.

"That's chancy. They have to answer to many more people than a private citizen such as Natalia does."

"Right." Dawn was losing steam, but she wanted to know more. "What else is up?"

"After you returned, and while you were calming Natalia, I assigned Kiko the task of researching our list of Kates. He is prioritizing based upon the information Natalia was able to hear and from what we were able to see of Kate's corpse. We will arrange interviews with any acquaintances and possible family based on his recommendations."

The heater kicked on, and Dawn huddled under the quilt. "He'll do a decent job?"

"Kiko is suddenly very motivated."

She laughed. "Anyone ever tell you how sly you are?"

"You never fail."

His compelling gaze lured her, but she wouldn't rest until her questions had been smoothed under the weight of answers.

"And the boy?" she asked.

Costin's chin went up a defensive notch, and Dawn sensed that he was about to block her out.

"Don't you dare," she said.

He held up a hand. "Instinct."

She tried not to take it personally, because he'd lived hundreds of years waging his own private war.

"Costin." She reached out from under the quilt, but didn't touch him.

He waited one more second, then finally said, "After you brought the boy here, Breisi joined me in the lab."

On the ride back over, they'd wrapped the kid in a tarp since he actually hadn't been all the way dead—he'd still had a faint pulse, and Dawn had thought Costin and Frank might be able to do something if they both tried to vamp-heal him. Frank, who'd walked to headquarters on foot instead of being tempted by all that blood, hadn't been powerful enough to help the boy at the site, and even the usual healing goo had been useless for the kid's extensive injuries.

He'd died minutes into the ride, but instead of returning him, they'd decided to "question" him through other means.

"What did you find?" she asked. "Why did Frank think the kid wasn't quite a vampire or even human?"

A glow lit Costin's eyes. "His blood. Breisi and I found an unidentifiable element in it beyond any of our experiences, and Breisi is well versed in science. And his heart . . ."

Costin met her gaze, his own flaring with so much more than basic hunger. It was the craving to win this war.

"His heart," he said, "was oriented on the right side of his body."

It took a few seconds for her to absorb this. "Are you sure? I mean, how? Why?"

"Breisi tells me that there is a condition—dextrocardia—in which the heart may be flipped. But then again, there is the matter of his blood. We cannot identify that abnormality yet.

"And then there is this: we had brought Kiko into the lab to see if he could perhaps get a reading from the boy's clothing. Even though Kiko did not sense anything we did not already know, he had an interesting observation. One of his comic book connections."

"A . . . comic book connection." Detecting at its best.

"He maintains that in a graphic novel entitled *JLA: Earth-2*, a plane crashed. It was filled with deceased passengers whose hearts were in the same location as this boy's. In the course of the story, we find that these people were from an antimatter planet—a parallel Earth where everything is the same, yet different from what we know."

Dawn stared at Costin. "So this kid is part of the DC Comics multiverse?"

"Dawn." He sighed and lay back on the bed.

Even from a few feet away, she pulsed with his proximity.

"I'm just wondering what sort of conclusions we can draw from that," she said. "Are these alien vamps? Because that's a whole other ball of wax."

"Unless a blood brother exchanged with an extraterrestrial, it's unlikely. We were all quite human when we started."

"You never know." She pulled the covers up higher. "At least

Kiko's mind is churning. Maybe there'll be some kind of beneficial vision that comes out of it next."

"I only hope."

He folded his hands behind his head, and Dawn stopped herself from touching him—his chest, up and under his arms.

God.

She got it together. "I'm assuming you'll have Natalia try to listen to the boy's corpse after she wakes up?"

"We will try."

"And how about the box the kid was holding? Did Breisi and Frank tool around with that?"

"Frank easily found that it was a flash grenade the boy might have used to blind you and the others as he escaped."

"So it wasn't some kind of Friend capture box? They were freaked out that it might be."

"They recall being contained by the Elites."

Once bitten, twice shy, Dawn thought. She knew the story.

"Was it ultraviolet?" she asked.

"No. Aside from the boy being at the burial ground, there was nothing to indicate he was a vampire fighter . . . or even a protector."

Things weren't ever straightforward in this biz. "Where is he now? I can't imagine you turning him over to the authorities with all that exploratory stuff you must've done on him."

Costin kept his gaze on the bed's canopy. "We have put him to temporary rest in the lab's refrigerator/freezer. Even so, I am hoping his fingerprints will be of use, though they did not register in our database. I've sent them to a contact in Interpol who has helped me in the past."

"Should I ask if you also sent a sample of the kid's blood for possible ID?"

"I refrained from that. I would like to see what the prints reveal first."

Good move, Dawn thought. If the boy's blood was that strange, there'd be questions to deal with, secrecy to risk.

"Then we gear another search to a missing boy with sandy hair, green eyes, and terrible judgment," she said.

"The sooner we find his identity, the better. Among other matters, I would like to offer him a proper resting place." Costin still didn't look at Dawn as *he* started firing off questions now. "So tell me—how is Natalia?"

Dawn bristled. He sensed it and frowned, so she assumed the usual who-gives-a-fig demeanor.

"Aside from seeing her first disembodied head tonight?" she asked. "Natalia's fine. She took a while to come down from her wig out. When we got back, I had to sit there in the extra bedroom with her while she tried to sleep, but then a Friend came in and lulled her. That did the trick."

"Her family in Slough knows she is somewhere safe?"

"Yeah, I called them." The light bled over his profile: the straight nose, the full lips. *Control, Dawn, control.* "Natalia agreed to go home today to pick up clothes and necessities. We'll see if she comes back here."

"She will."

"You're pretty cocky." Dawn leaned on her elbow. "I know you've seen into her psyche and all, but what if she surprises you by deserting? What happens to the information we gave her?"

"Dawn, she is going to stay. None of my hunters have ever chosen to leave."

"But how many of them really knew what was going on?"

"A few." Costin finally faced her, removing one of his hands from behind his head to catch a strand of her hair between his fingers. He tested it, just like he was feeling the texture for the first time. "In the past, I have dispensed information merely on a need-to-know basis. I felt it necessary to withhold information so you would stay on board with me. But there is no need with Natalia. She is here for those voices because their pain disturbs her more pro-

foundly than you will ever know. All her life she has wondered if
there was a way to save them, and now there is. Have faith in that."

She hesitated, then nodded, even while noting that his hand emanated coolness where there should've been warmth. In Hollywood,
Benedikte, when he'd been disguised as Matt, had had the ability
to give off the perception of normal skin. But Costin wasn't as
strong as a master, wasn't as powerful.

He brushed his fingertips over her jaw, and she shivered, her
skin tingling.

She almost asked him the next question mind-to-mind, but didn't
want to open herself up. "Costin?"

"Yes?"

"I can't help thinking that maybe she's your new . . . whatever."

"Who, Natalia?" He dropped his hand to the mattress.

Dawn wasn't going to throw around accusations; she only
wanted to be clear. "Just give me the facts, without me having to
dig. What are your intentions toward this girl?"

Costin wiped his hands down and up his face, planting his fingers in his hair, and if Dawn didn't know better, she would've said
it was a very human male gesture of frustration.

"I forget," he said, "that you are unlike any other hunter I have
had before. And exponentially more maddening."

"Good to know that I stand apart from the rest of the harem."

That's one thing he'd always been honest about—his relations
with the Friends. He was, like, hundreds of years old, so Dawn didn't
begrudge him the need for intimacy over the centuries—and his
former need to root to humanity for sustenance.

"Is Natalia going to be 'one of those' Friends?" she asked, referring to some of the favorites he'd pleasured before Dawn had
shown up last year.

"Jealousy does not become you."

"Ex . . . *cuse* me?"

She sat up, and Costin groaned.

"All I'm asking," she said, "is for a little clarification. I'm your blood pump, you know? That entitles me to what you call 'jealousy,' I think."

Oh, man, total verbal vomit. Good going.

"For a woman who says she does not care," he said, "you are certainly adamant *about* caring."

"I can be adamant about a lot of things."

Now Costin was sitting up. "I have told you—you are unlike any other. Why can't you bring yourself to believe that?"

Because . . .

Hell, because it was way more comfortable to pick a fight than to put herself out there again. Giving him blood was fine because she could always regenerate it. Giving him her life was good because she had earned the need to sacrifice that, too.

But giving him everything else?

She slipped out of bed. "You know, I'm not all that tired yet, and there's a ton to do. You rest, and I'll be back in time for your wake-up nip."

Knowing from experience not to rile her, Costin leaned his forearms against his bent legs. "If that is what you require."

"I'm just doing this because the hunt's on." She headed toward the closet. "Besides, I need an hour or two later for personal reasons, and I want to get as much done as I can now."

"Why is that?"

She stripped her gown over her head, her words muffled. "I've got dinner with Eva at her place."

A fissure rumbled the atmosphere apart, and when Dawn looked at him, she could see why.

Costin's eyes were burning as he took in her naked body.

Even though it was cruel, she stood there and let him look. But the power of his desire made her cells collide and explode, made her sex go wet and swollen.

"Dawn," he whispered, his voice raw.

She snapped out of it, despising that she didn't know how to handle intimacy any way but this way. That she couldn't stand the thought of knowing that he needed her so badly.

She went into the closet and put on some jeans and a baggy sweater, covering herself, removing temptation.

Still, his longing thudded at her, and she stayed removed until his palpable hunger faded with the coming of sunrise.

By the time she came out, rest had overtaken Costin. Undead to the world, he lay back against his pillow, his eyes shut, his mind a blank wall she couldn't bypass, no matter how hard she might've wanted to try.

Only then she went to him, reaching out to touch his temple, to slide her fingertips down to his jaw with all the yearning she couldn't bring herself to show when he was awake.

EIGHT

THE DUELING PSYCHICS

Dawn took the stairs to the first floor, where she could hear the hum of the computer room even from down the hall.

Upon a first look, the place might've seemed like a generic class-room, with maps and readouts posted on the walls. But the televisions, virtual reality stations, and wide plasma computer screens topped by cameras testified that a whole lot of quid had been invested in *this* particular educational program.

She camped her butt at a computer terminal and logged on just as Kiko entered with a mug of coffee in hand.

"You the cavalry?" he asked, sitting in front of a screen colored with doctored pictures of the great Kiko surrounded by bikini-clad starlets on a deserted island.

"Sure," Dawn said. "What do you need me to do?"

"Take a couple names from my list. I've been doing thorough checks, and it's taking forever." He ripped a strip off of a printout and gave it to her. "The new psychic girl sure didn't give us many specifics to go on with Kate."

"But we saw the decapitated head at the site, so you're weeding out all the Kates based on our best guess at her age and her appearance, right?" Dawn didn't add that the police might also be able to glean something from the dumping ground's skulls and bones.

"Sure, I've been using Kate's physical description," Kiko said, "but so far, there're no decent matches. I'm wondering if anyone reported Kate MIA yet, and it makes me a little depressed that there're people out there who aren't missed for a while. What kind of family and friends wouldn't know she's gone?"

With a leaden conscience, Dawn thought of how she hadn't even known her estranged dad had gone missing last year until four days into his disappearance.

Kiko faced his computer, moving the mouse and making the screen turn into an endless scroll of links. "So what're you still doing up?"

"You know me—four hours of sleep, and I'm steel."

"I'm good to go, too. Damn, it's been a while." He rubbed his hands together. "There's nothing like a hunt, huh?"

She glanced at the names he'd given to her. "Sure. Nothing like it."

He must've noticed the serious note in her voice, because he started to say something else, then clammed up. But that was fine, because now they could get down to work, chatting aside. Kiko wasn't so great at listening to her romantic woes about Costin anyway. Not that she'd ever volunteered much.

They delved into their search and, after a couple of hours, they'd narrowed their list down to two possible Kates: a Katrina Smythe and a Katherine Darby. Both came close to the head's physical description and age, and both had also been missing for a while—two and a half years and six months, respectively.

Thing was, the head from the dumping ground had been much fresher than that . . . unless the vamps had done something to it.

Keeping that in mind, they went on to research names of possible contacts—anyone who might be able to tell them why Kate had been involved with vampires. Then they worked the phones for interview appointments.

When they'd secured a few for tonight, Kiko headed to his room. But Dawn decided to check in on Natalia before she grabbed her own shut-eye.

She found the new girl still sleeping, hugging a pillow to her chest under the blankets, the quilt bunched around her neck.

Good. Maybe the psychic would turn out to be a decent hunter after all if she wasn't tossing and turning with real nightmares by now.

Yawning, Dawn went to her bedroom and crashed next to Costin. Yet she had a tough time forgetting everything, and for a minute, she found herself wishing that she were like him—blankly at rest.

She'd almost had that once, after Benedikte had exchanged with her. . . .

The thought seemed to push her down into the troubled black of sleep, but all too soon, she was awakened by the rustle of sheets.

Dawn turned over to find Costin on his side, facing her, his gaze turning an even deeper silver than a Groupie's used to back in L.A.

Without a word, she offered her neck, which he fed off of until her arms and legs got heavy, yet so light.

Her mind a white canvas except for the whirled colors etching deep and low, where she never allowed anything else to enter . . .

As she clung to him, his inner voice tangled with the rapturous flow of the feeding, the tightening of her veins and the twisting in her belly.

I am sorry to hurt you time and again, he whispered in her mind, sending the words pumping through her body.

Pumping, pushing, building . . .

After he sipped to a climax that ripped through both of them, he drew away from her, his fangs receding as he laid his fingers on her wound. Breathing hard, Dawn kept cupping the back of his head, her fingers lost in his dark hair.

"No apologies," she whispered out loud. "I wouldn't be here if I didn't want to be."

Or was it if she didn't *have* to be?

She stiffened at the notion, blocking herself off from him. Thank God she hadn't allowed him to be in her mind to hear.

But maybe her body language told him everything anyway, because he sighed, his breath cool on her arm.

For several moments, they stayed like this while he healed her. And as his energy pounded into her, mending her, she tried not to allow him in again mentally.

Not more than she already had.

Soon, he finished, and she slowly sat up, light-headed, pushing the covers away, her neck wound nothing more than a tingling ache now. "I'm off to Eva's, but after I get back, Kiko and I will take Frank and Natalia out for some Kate interviews. Maybe we can even escort our newbie back to the burial ground for that listening session, if she's up to it."

Costin got out of bed, stretching his arms above his head. Dawn paused to appreciate the ripple of muscles before he eased to the bathroom to prepare himself for the coming night.

"When Kiko awakens," he said, "perhaps he can catch Natalia more up to speed, as you would say. I will also see if we can arrange that late, quiet visit to the coroner's."

"Kiko's gonna love training his replacement."

"When did I say he was being replaced?"

"I just assumed that's what was happening. A changing of the guard." Dawn inched up her gown to check her thigh wound and decided it was scarring nicely with the help of the goo.

She ripped off the rest of the bandage.

"Kiko will not have to go if Natalia can bring his gifts back." Costin smiled, then entered the washroom.

"Sneaky bastard," Dawn murmured, getting up and going to the closet fridge for her post-feeding snack.

"I heard that," he said.

She grinned wryly. "I knew you would."

JUST for Eva's sake, Dawn ended up choosing a decent pair of black pants and a fancy crocheted sweater that her mother had given to her last Christmas. It itched, and even though it was kind of pretty, Dawn couldn't wait to change into something more comfortable when she got back.

At any rate, she basically ruined any "pretty" when she armed herself with some antivamp weapons, like the holy water bracelet and a crucifix that made her pants pocket bulge.

Hell, safety *was* the height of fashion.

Costin had already sequestered himself, so she made good time down the stairs. Then she passed her dad's door.

Breisi was still slumbering in her portrait, but Frank was messing around with the box that the right-sided-heart boy had been wielding.

"Don't tell me," Dawn said. "You and the Breez are designing something like that for us."

"With UV light." He set the box down and raised an eyebrow at her lovely sweater. "You off to some ritzy nightclub?"

Self-conscious, Dawn pulled the material away from her chest. "Is it that bad?"

"Naw. It's just very . . . Eva."

"Cut it out. I'm not even in her galaxy." In spite of her denial, Dawn felt herself blushing, oddly happy with the comparison. She'd grown up hating and loving her mom, all the while knowing she was only a bleak reflection of the beautiful star. "Anyway, I'm going to her flat for dinner."

He turned back to the box. "Have fun."

His passive response struck her, flinting a spark of frustration.

"You haven't seen her for a while, Frank. Why don't you come along?"

Looking over his shoulder, he said, "Not a good idea."

"Sure it is." Dawn gestured toward Breisi's picture. "Breez would be fine with it."

"So why screw up her goodwill by going to Eva's?"

"I don't know—maybe because we're a family?"

The ridiculousness of that statement seemed to hang in the air for a second, then drop to the ground, shattering like a spent bulb. In the shards, she could see all the hopes that her mom's resurrection had encouraged, like the family Dawn had never had or the happy mom and dad who could prove that maybe love didn't suck. Or . . .

Yeah, whatever.

She backed away from the door, but not before Frank caught all the emotions that'd probably been flashing over her face like a slew of never-coming attractions.

Dawn jerked her thumb in the direction of the stairs. "I'll see you in a couple hours when we all hit the streets for Kate."

"Dawn . . ."

"Hey, I'm not guilt-tripping you. Don't think another thought about it."

Yet as she walked away, she heard Frank's footsteps behind her, and that spark of frustration turned to one of hope, even if he *was* grumbling under his breath.

She couldn't help grinning. Sure, she was on "Team Frank and Breisi" all the way, but Eva would be happy to see him.

By the time they'd descended the stairs, Frank had curbed his muttering, but he did stop by the front door to leave a note on an entry table's message pad.

"In case Breisi wakes up and wonders where I am," he said.

They put on jackets and went outside, where the sky was mean and rumbly, then headed toward Eva's.

"You're such a trouper, Pops," Dawn said as they rounded the corner. "Seriously."

Frank grunted and forged on through the biting night.

They came to the Bull and Cock, where a weathered sign boasted a crazy-eyed man with a rooster's comb on his head and steam coming out of his nostrils.

One day, Dawn wouldn't be surprised to meet a creature who looked just like him.

Inside, the pub was warm, thanks to a fire in the grate and the conversation from an after-work crowd drinking ale. Mahogany lent the room a dimness, and ivy crept out of brass planters while the elevated TV played what they called a "football" game around here.

Dawn and Frank avoided the flames and circled around to the back room, where a set of stairs hid behind a closed door.

They opened it, ascended, then knocked at a second door.

While the faint din echoed from below, Dawn gauged Frank. He was bothered, all right. She could tell because his jaw was as taut as a primed crossbow.

He nodded toward the door. "She called for us to come in."

Of course he would've heard it over the background noise.

Dawn took out her extra key—a long brass thing that reminded her of ghoulie stories—and unlocked Eva's door, then pushed it open.

"Hi," she said, sticking her head in. "Frank's with me."

Her dad shuffled his boots as Dawn entered a quaint room that was heavy with the soothing aroma of butter, rosemary, and thyme for the Cornish hens Eva was making. Like the pub downstairs, the area was laden with dark wood, but her mom had made it a real home, with sage damask curtains draped over golden rods. Modern art from a shopping trip with Kiko also hung on the walls—textured messes that looked like some child had barfed dark rainbows. But Eva had also used a history dabbler's touch to decorate, with a large carved oak bed fit for royalty in one corner and a medieval-style dining set on the opposite side, near the tiny kitchen.

Altogether, the place had the feel of a work in progress, of a resident who wasn't sure where she belonged.

Eva had been washing vegetables in the sink, and she turned off the faucet, then wiped her hands on a dish towel before approaching. Although paler than she'd been back in L.A., she looked as stunning as always, in a milky cashmere sweater dress she had belted below the waist, plus matching suede boots. With her sunny blond hair waving over her shoulders, she didn't look to be on the downside of her forties, thanks to makeup and the recent cosmetic surgery that made her seem like a slightly different person altogether.

But, as she stopped in front of Dawn, a closer view revealed something missing—a freshness that indicated real youth. When Dawn had killed Benedikte, she'd turned her mother human again, giving her the gift of her true age, and it broke Dawn's heart until Eva laid her doe gaze on Frank.

There it was again, Dawn thought. Hope.

She couldn't blame Eva for nursing it, especially because of last year, when her mom had kidnapped Frank. He'd strung her along by making her think that they'd be a family, and maybe he'd even believed it at the time, because once he'd loved Eva beyond words. But she'd destroyed that with her fake murder.

And then he'd met Breisi. . . .

"Sorry I'm running late with the appetizers," Eva said, folding her hands in front of her. She seemed to change her mind about that and smoothed down her skirt. Then she changed her mind again and embraced Dawn.

It was like her mom didn't know how to act with Frank here.

Dawn wasn't so great at hugging, but she tried. It helped that her mom's summery perfume smelled good.

"How're you doing?" she asked Eva while disengaging.

"Fine. You?"

"Great. I asked Frank to come along, if that's okay."

Eva's gaze found her ex-husband again. "I think I can manage to set an extra place at the table."

She smiled, and it was blinding.

For a moment, Dawn saw the movie star, the hint of what had made millions of fans love her as both Eva Claremont and Jacqueline Ashley.

But as soon as Frank closed the door behind him and opened his mouth, the magic disappeared.

"I can't stay long, Eva." He'd taken off his knit cap and was holding it in both hands.

"Oh." Her mom played down her disappointment, but Dawn could tell she'd just taken a kick to the gut.

Eva went back to the kitchen and resumed vegetable duty. "I imagine Breisi will wake up soon. You need to get back to her *and* your work."

"Things are busy." Frank stayed at the door.

Dawn wanted to kick herself for creating this slow-motion train wreck. "Can I help with anything, Mom?"

"Not unless you want to pour yourself something to drink. The other day, Kiko took me to a wine bar, and I bought a great Pinot Noir."

"Even your recommendation can't bring me over to the wine side." Dawn took off her jacket, tossed it on a chaise longue, then leaned on the tiled kitchen counter. "I'll just grab some bubbly water in a second, if it's all the same."

Eva smiled at Dawn and turned the faucet back on. "Frank, I suppose I don't have to ask if you want anything."

Whether it had been some kind of reminder that she supplied him with blood or if it had just been a comment, Dawn wasn't sure. At any rate, her dad kicked around some more and glanced at the window.

Sigh.

Well, this was *so* much more fun than Dawn had anticipated.

She reached for a plate of cheese and plucked off a chunk of what she hoped was smoked Gouda. Popping it into her mouth, she gave it a taste-drive.

"Good stuff," she said, then swallowed.

Frank took a step. "What have you been up to, Eva?"

Her mom turned off the water, putting some cut carrots on a paper towel to dry. "I took an organized walking tour today that Kiko recommended. Up in Hampstead."

"Really?" Dawn asked. Until now, Eva hadn't taken the initiative. "That's great. I heard Hampstead is swank."

Her mom laughed softly. "It was funny, seeing the village from the point of view of 'Mia Scott,' regular citizen, the 'new me.' A lifetime ago, a Realtor almost talked me into buying property there, even though I'd never seen it before."

Her smile waned and she went back to the vegetables.

Remorse scratched at Dawn, and as silly as it was, she wished that Eva could've stayed perfect, rich, and forever twenty-three. She'd seemed much happier then, even though Dawn had literally wanted to kill her.

A sound, like rapping on the window, made Dawn turn around. Instinctively, she flicked her wrist upward and aimed her holy water bracelet at the glass.

No need.

"Well, look who's here," Frank said, going to the window.

Even though there was nothing to see, Dawn lowered her wrist. Breisi had no doubt woken up.

Eva tore celery from its stalk and transferred each piece to the cutting board for trimming. "I can set a place for Breisi, too, Frank."

It wasn't sarcasm, just a resigned half joke, and Dawn went over to the window, hoping Frank wasn't thinking of opening it and letting his girlfriend in. The freak-in-love expression on his face told her it was a distinct possibility.

Breisi knocked again, not with any kind of spiritual fist, but as if she were exerting pressure against the glass with her entire essence.

Frank grew serious. "I think she wants to talk to us, but the glass is too thick."

He waited, yet there was no more knocking.

"I think she left," he said.

Dawn went to the door. "Tell me she's not coming up here."

All the while, Eva chopped at the celery.

Just as Dawn was about to turn the knob—she had to get to the bottom of the stairs to tell Breisi that Frank hadn't wanted to come here in the first place and this situation was all Dawn's fault—a more emphatic pounding rattled the door.

It sounded like an actual fist.

"Frank?" Dawn said.

"I'm here," he said, at her back.

Eva's chopping suspended.

Just as Dawn heard a raised voice beyond the wood, her dad sniffed the air, trying to catch an identifying scent through the herbs from the meal.

More urgent knocking.

Her phone rang.

She checked the ID screen and her blood pressure fell to a series of relieved bumps.

"Unbelievable," she said, opening the door to reveal the last people she'd been expecting to show up for dinner.

Kiko and Natalia.

He had his phone to his ear, and both of them weren't wearing coats. Both of them were also breathing hard, as if they'd just burst out of the Limpet house and run on over.

"Dawn," Natalia said, "I had a vision, but Kiko—"

Shoving his phone into a cargo-pants pocket, he stepped in front of the new girl, cutting her off, his blue eyes feverish.

"*I* had a vision about some cemetery," he said, "and we've got to chase it down now!"

"You saw something?" Dawn asked, overjoyed that Kick-Ass Kiko was back.

"Yes!"

She beat her emotions into smoothness. *A vision. A lead . . .*

"What did you see? Where? And why aren't you online researching which cemetery it is while you called me on the cell phone instead of freakin' running over here like morons?"

"I was excited!" Kiko said, raising his fists in the air.

Natalia looked embarrassed. "He ran out the door to tell you, and I . . ." She frowned. "I really don't know why I ran, too."

Kiko pointed his index fingers, assuming the internationally known "I'm number one" sign. "You ran over here with me because you've already won over the boss and now you're working on Dawn, brownnoser."

His eyes seemed bright as he addressed Dawn now. "After Natalia finally drug her caboose out of bed, we had . . . I suppose you could say we had a lively discussion about vamps and visions, blahblahblah. We were both touching dirt from Billiter in a sample dish—"

"He wanted it for a psychometric reading and I wanted it to see if listening to it might help at all," Natalia interrupted.

"—when BLAMO! It just happened. I saw a cemetery with black gates in front of a pinkish metal gatehouse. Then a grave that looked like a boxed garden with a burning glass lantern."

Natalia kept her cool, even though it looked like the poppy she'd been wearing ever since Dawn had met her had been shoved into her curls. "I believe my own vision is from the same cemetery with the pink building. But I saw a different grave. Near a sign that read 'five,' and marked by a Celtic cross."

Dawn's heart rate picked up. "You guys really had competing visions."

They nodded.

Find this cemetery, go go go—

Dawn dashed to the chaise longue to grab her jacket, hoping like hell that Kiko wasn't doing something pathetic like making up a similar vision to Natalia's just to compensate.

But he wouldn't do that. Kiko had been too good a psychic. And he still could be, if this lead paid off.

"Eva, I'm really sorry about this," she said on the way back to the door. "Rain check for later?"

Her mother nodded, taking the vegetable plate over to the dinner table, like she was going to eat alone.

Hating the sight, Dawn went to give her mom a hug. She sort of accomplished an awkward version of one, then followed Frank into the hall as he waved to Eva.

As Dawn closed the door, she caught a glimpse of her mother striking a match and lighting a candle, illuminating the emptiness of the table she'd set for company.

Illuminating the vacancy in her gaze, too.

NINE

THE HIGHGATE DILEMMA

MORNING peeked its way through a threat of rain while Dawn, Kiko, and Natalia stood in front of the black iron gates of eastern Highgate Cemetery—the location of the psychics' visions.

While they waited for this section to open, Dawn knew what was behind her without even glancing: a former chapel with arched windows like staring eyes that never looked away from the mist-slicked lane that divided the east and west graveyards. The building, which reminded her of a place where some governess might run around with a flickering candle while chasing down a ghost, served as the entrance to the western section, but it was closed, only open to those who had arranged a tour.

The Web site had posted an opening time for the east side of 11:00 AM on Saturdays. But Kiko, who was on fire to get going, had suggested that they sneak in last night. Needless to say, Dawn had talked him down, refusing to stir any shit.

"The biggest urgency is your ego," she'd told him. "And

Highgate's dealt with too much vandalism in the past to be low profile, so we're going to wait until everything's kosher."

Yet she'd known how to use their resources, and after the team had cyberidentified eastern Highgate as the location of the visions, they'd sent a few Friends there. As expected, the spirits had pinpointed the graves in question while the team itself had gone with this promising lead, rescheduling all Kate-contact appointments and, instead, putting their efforts into finding out everything they could about the cemetery.

However, for the Friends, Highgate had been too dark to make out fine details, like names or dates, on the stones. So this necessitated a team visit come morning, when they would be able to see the graves up close and personal while Kiko attempted touch readings and Natalia listened for voices.

For the rest of the night, they'd researched, pushing back a second visit to the Billiter burial ground for Natalia to catch more possible chatter. They didn't even get to go to the coroner's so she could listen there, because an appointment had never come through.

They did have enough time to take Natalia to the right-sided-heart boy in the lab fridge/freezer though. But just as Costin had surmised, she wasn't able to hear anything from him, probably because she'd looked like all she wanted to do was run from a corpse with stitches and ice dusting its skin.

Around then, sunrise had broken, and Costin and Frank had retreated to their dark beds, leaving the humans to nap and then strike out for Highgate.

Now, Dawn blew out a smoke-warmed breath, holding back a shudder at the oppressive creepiness weaving through the trees and bushes beyond the eastern gates. Kiko, Natalia, and even the Friends who were with them had noted it, too. The new girl had even said something about an "uncomfortable hollowness" the second they'd emerged from the tube stop down the hill.

Kiko checked his watch for the umpteenth time, the brim of his black baseball cap pulled low as mist spangled it.

"Five 'til eleven," he said, glaring at the closed gates. Breisi and a couple Friends were inside right now, just to check things out, and he kept anticipating their return.

Natalia was pacing, one hand stuffed in her red coat pocket, the other holding a closed plaid umbrella. There were bags under her eyes.

As she passed, Dawn could tell she was still tuned in to whatever they were feeling around here.

The other girl turned around and paced toward Dawn again, then stopped in front of her. "I can't help dwelling on what we read. About the Highgate Vampire?"

"Don't dwell." Dawn rubbed her bare, mist-clammy hands together, then shoved them into one of many pockets in her long black rain jacket. Normally, she would remind Natalia that they shouldn't talk loudly about vampires in the open, but since this particular one was a big part of the Highgate Cemetery's mystique, it wouldn't be out of line for some random tourists—like they were pretending to be—to mention it here.

"What if the stories are true?" Natalia added.

Her other concerns went unsaid. What if the Underground vampires tied in with this legend of the one at Highgate? The fact that both psychics had gotten readings from this cemetery had to be significant to their hunt.

"From our pamphlets," Dawn said, playing the part of a tourist to the hilt, "we know that most activity was in the nineteen sixties and seventies. A lot of people"—such as Costin, who'd studied the Highgate Vampire in the past—"think this story's just a case of legend tripping. So don't worry."

Natalia didn't seem so sure, even though Costin had explained "legend tripping" last night. It was a sociological thing where thrill seekers gathered at notoriously scary spots to drink, drug it up, screw, and prove their courage to the opposite sex. Based on his experiences, he believed the Highgate Vampire was a good example of how humans tended to use the paranormal to entertain themselves, not to look deeper at what might lie beneath their very streets.

"And what about the rumors of black magic?" Natalia asked.

"Okay, those are real." Their documents said that there'd been mutilated animals on the premises and evidence of vandalism indicative of rituals. "But that would probably be from human activity."

"It's only . . ." The second psychic glanced at the daunting gates, then shivered. "This cemetery is not as peaceful as most are for me."

Dawn followed Natalia's gaze. Somewhere back in her overactive imagination, she expected to find a tall, dark, looming figure—one that might look perfectly at home among the houses of the dead.

She leaned toward Natalia so she could whisper, "What else has you on edge? Are you hearing voices?"

"Distant murmuring." She lowered her tone. "Most who are buried here are resting nicely. *Most.*"

Dawn shrugged into her jacket, telling herself it was because she was cold.

Kiko strode up to the gate, where he could get a better view of an elderly man who was moving around inside the pink-tinted gatehouse. The psychic tapped his toe and stared at him, as if that would do anything but tick him off and make him lollygag some more.

"Dawn?" Natalia asked, her voice still low. "I have been wondering. . . . There seem to be different types of vampires in our . . . travel literature. Good ones and bad. I thought they were all bad, except in movies and romance books."

Yeah, Dawn had thought so, too.

So how did a person explain the difference? Especially when that person didn't really even understand the distinction herself, what with having a fanged father who was way better than he'd ever been when she'd known him as a human, and a sort-of boyfriend who was a vamp bent on saving the world.

And *especially* not when she'd felt so good being one of the bad guys for a short while, too.

Dawn wished the gates would just open. But . . . no luck.

"My best explanation," she said, knowing she'd have to answer sometime, "would be that maybe it's in how a creature reacts to what's taken them over. Like 'the Force,' you know? It could be that some vamps use it for the dark side and others use it to redeem what needs redeeming." Sounded pretty persuasive.

"But," Natalia responded, "it's said that vampires have no souls. How can the loss of one result in any good?"

Besides Costin and Frank, Dawn thought of how Eva had risked everything back in L.A., defying the Master so that she might save her daughter.

Dawn tamped down a swell of emotion. No need for it now.

"I read"—no, she *knew*—"that vampires are left with a conscience. A personality, really. They still have memories and longings, and I guess each creature deals differently. Some leave the past behind and dive into a whole new party existence, like they've gotten a chance to do everything they couldn't do before, and there's nothing to stop them now. Some just wish they could go back to what they used to have."

Natalia took that in, looking like she half believed the explanations and half didn't. It reminded Dawn of something the girl had asked the night before last as she'd fallen asleep.

"All these years and Costin has never written a book or gone on the telly to reveal the truth about vampires. Why?"

The answer had been easy.

"Because even though the world likes their scary stories, they'd never believe it," Dawn had said. "Most of us really don't want to acknowledge that there might be anything so close by as bad as what we've imagined, so we need our fantasies to keep it underground."

If they'd only stayed there.

She also hadn't added that Costin wasn't crazy about the notion of having the public—and hence unsympathetic authorities—in his business, either. He'd be persecuted like any vampire, no matter whose side he was on.

By the gates, Dawn heard Kiko say a "Yessss," under his breath as the elderly man came out of the small house. Number One Psychic shifted from one foot to the other, then calmed down when the gatekeeper gave him a curious look as he opened the gate and retreated back to his pinkish dwelling.

"Breisi?" Dawn asked. But it was really more of a command for the nearby Friends to return to them so they could get a move on.

After a few seconds, a burst of jasmine whooshed by.

"All clear," Breisi said in her spirit voice as her pals hung back.

Natalia exhaled and glanced around as they all went to the little window in the gatehouse and paid a few pounds each for the entrance fee. The man gave them an I'm-watching-you look before they sauntered away.

Kiko had a bounce to his own walk as they scanned the ornate headstones and mausoleums flanked by rhododendron bushes, tulip and oak trees. There were also simple markers, wooden crosses where flowers like lilies and yellow roses kept vigil.

Then there were the marble angels that sadly looked down upon them as the rain started to fall. One of them had a broken finger, and it seemed to point right at Dawn.

She pulled up her hood while Natalia opened her umbrella.

"Feel that?" Kiko asked, turning around like a compass needle searching for a place to point. "My grave's close. Breisi, do you wanna take us there first?"

But their Friend had already flown in a straight line up the blacktop, where crowded, cracked gravestones tottered on slight hills. Ivy crept up the markers' sides, just like the vines were clawing out of the ground to keep the stones there.

Raindrops popped on Dawn's hood. Otherwise, there was nothing. No activity.

Just a sense of waiting . . .

She shivered as she felt a tingle at the back of her neck, like long nails only an inch away from touching her.

Turning around, she only saw the graves, trees, and the pink house in front of the gates, then the old chapel.

"Breisi?" Kiko said as Dawn faced them again, her hand touching the silver throwing blades in one of her pockets.

Their Friend's voice wound through the rain. *"We're all feeling a pull to Natalia's grave. Let's go there first."*

As the new girl followed Breisi's voice, Kiko looked like he was going to order their Friends to see to *his* vision.

But then he clenched his jaw, too proud to force them.

"Kik?" Dawn said.

He shrugged. "They feel a pull. But *I* do, too."

Before anyone could respond, he took the path to the right, speed walking, then halted and glanced back at Dawn as if he'd expected her to be right behind him.

Natalia had stopped and was watching Dawn, too, a hopeful lift to her brows.

A niggle in the back of Dawn's mind testified that she should put her money on the new psychic, that maybe when they got to Natalia's headstone, she might have another vision that would lead to a break in the hunt.

But when Kiko got that same beat-down expression he wore whenever he disappointed her by taking those pills, she didn't know what to do.

"Are you coming?" Kiko asked, his tone indicating that he knew how little faith she had in his ability these days.

And . . . game over.

Dawn addressed Breisi as she moved toward Kiko. "I'll keep an eye on this one."

Natalia lowered her gaze, drowning in that big coat of hers while Breisi circled around Dawn and the other spirits divided themselves between the two psychics.

"We should stay together," Breisi said in a warped version of

the voice she always used to adopt when leading a hunt as a human. She'd been totally kick-ass then, too.

"We're in public," Dawn said. "If our 'clients' survived this long, they did it through some secrecy. We'll be okay."

Breisi sighed, but she didn't argue while she flew to Natalia again, her voice fading as she said, *"Follow your Friends by taking the path on the right, then going a hundred and fifty feet. The grave will be on the left side."*

"Thanks, Breez."

Dawn raised her hand to say bye to Natalia, but the girl was already following her own spirits, her hands stuffed into her pockets.

But why would Natalia give a hoot about Dawn's support? Didn't she know it wasn't worth a three-dollar bill?

When she got to Kiko, he broke into a smile, and her chest squeezed into itself, just like it was trying to wring every last drop out of her damn heart.

"Knew you'd pick me," he said, then spun around and dashed down the path.

Rolling her eyes, she nonetheless backed him up, flanked by Friends and recalling Breisi's instructions as well as the details of Kiko's vision: on the left, a boxed garden with a burning glass lantern. . . .

They passed slabs laid out like flat, marbled resting beds.

Newer dates. Older dates. Graves with Asian symbols. Crosses. More angels.

"Kiko," she asked when they'd gone the required length, "maybe we already passed it."

"Nope."

He sounded utterly confident, and when he came to a halt several yards in front of Dawn, the goofy grin on his face told her that she'd made the right choice by being with him.

When she caught up, she rested a hand on his shoulder.

They stood there like that for some seconds, the movement of

Friends swirling around them while they looked at a cross surrounded by blood-hued leaves. Someone obviously cared enough to visit often, because it really did seem like a small well-tended garden. Red roses and ferns guarded the foot of the grave, where a flame danced in a protective glass box that held a mirror in the back of it, reflecting their faces back at them if they bent low enough.

The rain had grayed to a drizzle, moistening Dawn's face as she slipped off her hood.

"I wonder if a family member comes every day," she said.

"Maybe a son or a daughter." Kiko motioned toward the gravestone dates. The deceased had been in her early forties, but the Friends hadn't been able to see that clearly last night with the lantern tucked beneath the shadow of foliage.

Dawn had already reached into her jacket pocket, ignoring the throwing blades and silver crucifix to pluck out a small PDA that included a recording option. Accessing it, she dictated her impressions, then the information on the gravestone, including the name: Colleen Abberline.

When she was done, she said, "Maybe an interview with Colleen's family and friends will give us some clue as to why you saw her grave in a vision."

"Or maybe the flame, the garden . . . Could these be symbols that are trying to tell me something else?"

Kiko had bent down to the grave, touching everything while Dawn was recording. But when he ran his fingertips over some fallen rose petals near the lantern, his spine stiffened.

Adrenaline shot through her. *He's got something.*

After a minute, he stood, laughing, fully energized.

"You got a clear reading?" she asked.

His smile was so wide it stretched his face. "H-yeah. I saw a guy's face in the mirror of that lantern box." Kiko pointed toward the constant flame. "This flower was touched by a young male in his twenties with dark hair and greenish eyes. He looked like the tall, thin type."

"How tall?"

"I'm not sure, 'cos I just have that mirror to go by. It was near dusk, and he was kneeling in front of the grave and setting the flowers down, so I didn't have anything to scale him against. Maybe he comes here to take care of Colleen."

Two words had lodged in Dawn's brain: tall. Thin.

Descriptions of what had once been witnessed beyond the gates of this cemetery in the dead of night.

But the Highgate Vampire was supposed to be *abnormally* tall with red eyes, and Kiko's vision didn't necessarily indicate either. . . .

She shook her head. Her imagination was wonky. Still, she couldn't forget those hollow vibrations Natalia kept noticing around here.

Was there something more than just an urban legend at work?

Her mouth was dry as she asked, "Kiko, do you think there's any reason you might've tuned in to this grave in particular?"

And the tall, thin guy who visited it?

"I don't know yet," Kiko said, "but you can bet we're gonna find him and have us a nice talk. Before that though, what do you say we track down Natalia and the wrong grave?"

He took up a cock-of-the-walk stride and whistled down the path, away from the flickering lantern and the garden grave.

As the Friends followed him, Dawn bent down to pick up a rose petal. Another tingle slid down her spine, and she glanced behind her, toward the north.

Nothing.

Hardly trusting in that, she stood and walked after Kiko, taking out a throwing blade and daring any Highgate lurkers to come out and play.

TEN

London Babylon

Later the Same Day

WHEN darkness arrived, the girls awakened from their binge resting, then gathered in Violet's room to wait until they sensed sleep from the rest of the students in the house.

"Last night wasn't fair at all," Noreen said as she sat on the floor and leaned back against the frilly bed.

Vi and Polly were up on the mattress, lying on their stomachs with their ankles crossed and lifted. Across from the bed, Blanche was slowly spinning in an office chair, just as distant from the conversation as Della, who reclined at the base of the accompanying desk.

"Most certainly unfair," Polly said. "Banning us from leaving the grounds for the weekend until all this media blather dies down was brutal enough. And *then* having us drink rodent blood instead of allowing us to go out for a true feeding? Such bad form."

"Infighting is bad form, as well," Violet said, glaring at Blanche.

The black-haired girl seemed to care less about listening to their self-appointed leader, so Violet went a step further and used a communal mind link.

Am I correct, Blanche? she said with such force that Della's skull buzzed. *We'll not do anything more to deserve such punishment again?*

The other girl stopped circling in her chair. "I agree," she said out loud, so carelessly that Della admired her for it.

Yet she hid her approval well.

Blanche began to spin again, and Violet sat up, lazily tracing her manicured fingernails over the flowered duvet and watching Blanche as if she were to be her next meal.

"No need to despair." Noreen sprang up to a stand. "We do have the run of the house tonight, y'know."

"I fancy the idea of avoiding more rats," Polly said. "When was the last time we sampled the wares round *here?*"

"Months ago when we were last punished," Violet added, still staring at Blanche. "But mind this: as we did back then, we would have to be careful to keep ourselves to a short, sweet drink and nothing more tonight."

Della leaned her head against the desk. A drink would suffice to keep them nicely nourished, but it wouldn't fill the appetites to which Wolfie had introduced them. Not entirely.

Blanche used the desk's edge to stop her chair from spinning altogether. She seemed exceedingly serious when she turned back toward the others.

"Let's think for a moment about what we're proposing," she said. "We truly wish to poach on the territory of the very one who meted out our punishment last night?"

"We weren't left with much of an option," Violet said. "And we were never told to starve ourselves tonight."

"We'll only visit the younger girls anyway," Polly added.

Della refrained from saying her own piece. Yet why should she when Blanche was doing it for her?

"Consider this from a human's point of view," she said. "Twice a week, there's a different girl in the house who takes ill. Both seem pale and listless, yet both quickly recover with bed rest and proper nutrition. We five are the only students who know what is actually occurring, yet none of us speak of it, because we know our keeper enjoys feeding here. But the other adults and students? They say the illness is due to stress. Only stress. Yet soon, there's another sickly girl. Then another later in the week."

"Your point?" Polly asked.

"As of now, we've been fortunate they haven't put the pieces of the puzzle together." Blanche didn't even blink. "Won't multiple cases over the weekend change that?"

Noreen crossed her arms over her stomach. "We've managed to hide a quick drink the other times we were told to stay on the grounds—"

Violet held her hand up and everyone fell to silence.

"Perhaps," she said softly, "we *should* consider Blanche's argument."

It had taken quite a bit for Violet to agree with Blanche, but Della knew just how much none of them wished to get caught. How they treasured this existence.

Truth be told, all of them fancied it beyond measure, because Queenshill was more of a home than any of them had ever possessed. Yes, they were well-bred and well-off, but all they had ever known since an early age was boarding school.

And, in school, they had come to find each other.

In fact, when the invitation to join in this exclusive class had come along, not a one of them had thought to refuse, for where else did they have to go? To whom did they have to go?

"Violet?" Noreen said, her fingers entangled. "I'm *so* ravenous."

"We all need better sustenance," Polly added, "especially after last night."

Della's veins grumbled in agreement.

Violet laid a hand on Polly's head and smoothed back her hair. Then she eased off of the bed.

"I wonder if providing the campus with something to chat about in the morning rather than ill little girls would be the answer," she ruminated out loud.

"Yes," Polly and Noreen said, excited to see that there was hope. Even Della whispered her own "yes."

Blanche merely folded one leg over the other. Even though she had argued, she was hungry, also.

Polly rolled off of the mattress to her feet. "Mrs. Jones should be out with Mademoiselle at the usual Saturday-night art cinema. That leaves Miss Fairchild in charge."

"The bumbling assistant on duty who's no doubt sleeping in front of the telly." Violet went to the lace-curtained window and peered at the night. "I'm able to work with that."

And work she did while the girls waited to see what she had in her blocked mind.

Restless, Della changed position on the ground. Polly shifted her weight from one foot to the other.

Noreen began to talk, as was her habit when anxious. "It *is* good to see Mademoiselle out and about, isn't it? Mrs. Jones seems to be the only one who can drag her away from that classroom, or even the latest campus project that's keeping her here until all hours."

"Oh, belt up, would you?" Polly moved toward the door, then put her ear to the wood. "I can hear Miss Fairchild snoring." She imitated it. *Snorrrrrrt-snort-snort-snorrrrrrt.*

Noreen giggled, but her laugh was interrupted by a mental fluttering that carved into all of their minds.

Then . . . a cawing.

As one, they all looked toward the window, where Violet was grasping the curtain.

"Vi?" Polly asked.

She still had her back to them, but the question had been rhetorical anyway. Della shrank into herself as the caws became louder in their heads.

Blanche got out of the chair, clearly unimpressed as she moved to the door. "Vi's securing our diversion, yet she's getting her rocks off, too. Two birds with one stone, eh, Vi?"

At the notion of finally eating again, Della's veins seemed to wrap around themselves, and she got to her feet as Violet turned away from the window.

She was grinning, her eyes flaring purple as she opened her mind to them. *Time to leave.*

Like one sleek, stalking entity, they moved into the quiet, fluorescent-paled hall, the lights stuttering above them, responding to the suddenly bristling energy that emanated from the group.

Violet slid toward the front, but Blanche crowded her. Then Polly nudged the black-haired girl back a position and took up her best friend's shoulder.

Mouth tight, Blanche didn't fight.

She was too hungry, too anxious for real human blood again. All of them were, even if they were bound for certain punishment if they should be caught.

Creeping along, they were as silent as a drawn-out gasp, edging through the upper-sixth-form floor, then to the next wing, where the younger girls stayed, three to a room.

Just from passing each door, they could smell how many students were in-house. The lack of overwhelming human aroma—musky, tangy, tempting—indicated that this section was relatively deserted for the weekend, the chances of getting caught slim.

Della noticed a particular scent in the air that seemed wonderfully familiar. Sunshine?

They came to a door that held a white board with neon-markered names—Yuki, Kristine, Annie—and in block letters "WELCOME TO THE FUNHOUSE! Come in unless you see a ribbon tied to the knob, hah-hah."

Yes, hah-hah, Violet communally thought while she reached for the knob, then gently opened the door, which always remained unlocked so the housematron or another adult could enter.

In the back of their minds, they heard the *caw, caw.*

Louder.

Louder.

As they filtered into the room, the scent of human washed into Della. Sunshine. Why did she keep smelling it . . . ?

A digital clock flashed the hour. 11:32. Moonlight leered through the window, silhouetting the warped branches of an oak and canting over the three girls who cuddled under their duvets.

When Della saw her idol, Melinda Springfield, in one of the beds, her heart kicked.

What is she doing in the younger section . . . ?

Sensing her unchecked reaction, the group turned their gazes on Della, and Violet bared her teeth in a smile.

Of course. Della hadn't known it, but Violet had no doubt heard that Yuki was away for the weekend and Melinda had come to the little girls' wing to be with her younger sister Annie. . . .

Caw . . . caw . . .

A black shadow blocked a portion of the window's moonlight, and Violet made an emphatic gesture toward Melinda's bed, then Kristine's, then Annie's, twisting her wrist as if she were locking something.

Then, overcome by the heady human scent, by the assurance of food, all five fell to their hands and knees, excitement dancing over their spines and making them arch.

Even Della couldn't stop herself as her hands hit the carpeted floor and saliva flooded her mouth, stinging her jaws. The cawing seemed to pull at her, even as the hair receded back into her body, leaving every inch of skin bare as her ears were shaping into points, her eyes slanting, her fangs sharpening and growing.

Caw—

Then a

Crash!

The window darkened as a mass of ravens flew into it, their cries abrading the night while they scratched and banged to get in.

Little Annie, a small model of her platinum sister, sprang up in bed, and she would've screamed if her clamped mouth and frozen vocal chords already hadn't been charmed by Violet.

As the second roommate, Kristine, awakened in terror, her hands clawed the air, attempting to discover a voice, as well.

Everyone but Della laughed soundlessly, needling the air with vibrations.

The humans had no doubt sensed the brutal mirth digging into their skin, and as if shaking off the swarming prickles, Kristine and Annie both flailed their arms. Their fear tickled the vampires' appetites until it made the juices in their mouths flood and drip.

Caw . . . CAW . . .

Yet Melinda . . . Melinda wasn't trying to scream, although Della could smell her alluring fear. No, Melinda hopped out of bed and darted to Annie, shielding her younger sister with her body as her horrified gaze focused on the screeching birds that were throwing themselves against the window.

None of the humans had noticed the eyes glowing in the room's dark corner yet.

Kristine ran to Annie and Melinda's bed, and they fumbled round, cringing and holding each other.

The other vampires laughed with even more verve, but their gaiety had risen to such heights that they were softly hissing now instead of keeping silent.

As the humans registered the sound, they went still, and Della began to pant, spellbound by their chemical fear, by this proximity to Melinda.

Ready? Violet asked mind-to-mind.

Even Della answered with the crowd this time.

Ready.

She couldn't take her eyes off Melinda in her flannels, her moonbeam hair covering Annie as she hugged her sister. . . .

The most dominant vampires sprang out of their hiding place while Noreen and Della hung back.

Blanche swiped Kristine to the floor.

Polly bowled Annie over and down to the mattress.

Violet—

Violet had chosen Melinda.

Later, Della would recall a blast of possessive anger and that was all, but she found herself flying toward Violet and intercepting her in midair, then pounding her to the ground.

Not this time, Della thought while staring down at Violet. The other vampires froze, most of them poised over their numb prey.

Violet stared at Della for a moment with her blazing eyes, then . . .

Then she began to laugh-hiss.

Anger, shame, fright—all of it rushed Della.

She planted her clawed hand over Violet's face, caging the other girl's laugh to silence.

She could feel Violet's mouth open in shock as Blanche's mind-laugh ripped through their consciousness and mixed with the screams of the ravens.

Haaaaaaaaahhhhhhhssss!

Caaaaawwwww!

But before Della's mind caught up with reality, Noreen yanked her off Violet and bound her in an armlock.

"Don't cause trouble," she frantically whispered into Della's ear while pulling her back to the corner. "Not unless you want to challenge her."

Della's pulse was smacking against her skin, and she panted heavily, her mind a whir.

Confident that Della would offer no more resistance, Violet didn't retaliate. Instead, she went about her business, fixing her gaze on the all-too-human Melinda, who was by now on her own hands and knees, ready to fight.

Yet she was no match for Violet, who easily grasped Melinda's neck and yanked her off of the bed.

The human smacked to the carpet, her body jerking into a grunt that she couldn't voice. Immediately, Violet clamped her claws into Melinda's long hair, pulling her head to the side for a clear shot at her neck.

When she reared back her head, then sank her teeth into Melinda, Della groaned . . .

. . . and then Violet—cruel, taunting Violet—linked her sensations directly to Della, and Della could all but taste the blood, could feel the intoxication of having it flow into her own mouth, even though Violet was the one imbibing.

Enjoy, Violet mind-said.

Blood, thick, hot. The mere link was almost as rich as the liquid itself. From a young, pure girl, it tasted like honey, making the body flush, making the belly warm with a sharp ache.

It made a creature want to gnaw, to have more, to take bites instead of merely drinks—

Overtaken, Della slumped to the floor, listening to the suckling sounds. She hugged her knees to her chest, cradling herself, in a warm place that she never wanted to leave.

One by one, the ravens' banging ceased as they fell away from the window. Outside, their bodies would litter the ground, providing the distraction Violet had promised when the sun rose.

The dominant vampire unlinked from Della, and the room quieted as Violet then detached from her prey's neck. There would still be enough blood left for Della, plus enough for Melinda to recover without an undue amount of concern. She would be sick tomorrow, but Della realized illness wouldn't cause the human to forgo her basketball match since it had already been played today.

Della had missed it. . . .

Violet reached over and grabbed Della to drag her near.

"You wanted her?" Violet whispered roughly. "Then have her."

She shoved Della's face into Melinda's neck, strands of the other girl's long silver hair soaked with blood from her wound.

Della's mind screamed no, but her appetite was much stronger. She sniffed the blood, so fragrant that it made her mind explode with a shower of flower-petal colors.

Unable to fight herself, she molded her mouth to Melinda's wound and sucked, cuddling up to the girl she'd always worshipped from across a classroom. Melinda, perfect, beautiful, everything Della wished she could be—

She devoured her blood, unable to rise above her gluttony.

After what seemed like only a moment, Violet jarred Della away from her meal, fisting Della's shirt while her last gulp trickled down her throat.

"It's as if you've never restricted yourself to a mere drink," Violet said, shoving Della away. "You take too much and there'll be trouble to pay. Haven't you learned a thing from our lessons?"

Head down—Della didn't want to see how off-color Melinda would be, didn't want to see her shivering and stultified—she backed away, low on all fours, into her corner. Like the other girls, she licked the remnants of the blood from her lips, then extended her tongue to lap up every bit from round her mouth before allowing her skin to absorb any lingering drops.

Drinking blood through flesh—it was a gift of their line. A talent to be utilized if they willed it, although Wolfie had taught them to appreciate the primal, oral delight of using their mouths and teeth instead.

By now, Noreen had fed, as well, having divided her time between the two smaller girls so as not to take an excess of blood from either of them. As she finished, Violet went back to Melinda, where the lead vampire touched her prey's neck, then cocked her head in ecstasy while healing her victim. Her energy fused with the human's skin to mend it, creating a red glow where they connected.

Afterward, she touched Melinda's temple, clearing the memory from her mind.

Blanche and Polly did the same to the younger girls, enjoying it just as thoroughly, and Noreen and Della cleaned up the remaining mess, absorbing every spot of blood with a touch.

They returned to humanlike form, then tucked the humans under their duvets, knowing that they would slumber heavily, waking in the morning drained of energy yet never recalling what had transpired.

As Della wobbled on her feet and backed away from Melinda's bed, her stomach turned.

She'd been famished, but the blood wasn't sitting well.

Melinda . . . How could she have?

Della stumbled to the door, opened it. In back of her, the other girls mind-chatted away, chuffed by their meal.

That window suffered quite some damage from the ravens, Noreen thought. *And all those bodies outside? Oooo.*

Violet laughed. *A freak event of nature. The house will be aflutter with the news come morning.*

The fear made those girls even more delicious, Polly added. *Let's go to another room.*

Not for a while, Violet said. *Not for a long while.*

Della clutched her stomach while they padded through the hallways and into their own wing.

But even from twenty meters away, they could hear conversation.

Mrs. Jones and Mademoiselle in the housematron's room.

Calm, Violet thought. *Stay calm and we shan't get caught.*

After checking each other for evidence of their play, the girls rounded the corner to find Mrs. Jones's door open. Their housematron was at the computer, and Mademoiselle was leaning over her shoulder and peering at the screen, which showcased images from a movie—probably the one they had just seen in town.

Mademoiselle glanced up at the girls as they crowded the door. She frowned.

Even the whey-faced housematron knit her brow.

"Looking healthier, Mrs. Jones," Violet said politely. "Hello, Mademoiselle."

"Up late, are we?" Mrs. Jones said in her cold-husky voice.

Violet pushed Della to the front. "This one is feeling under the weather, and we've all been tending to her. We just came from the loo, in fact."

"Rather well-dressed for that sort of activity," the housematron said.

Frowning, Mademoiselle came toward Della, who backed away. Stomach . . . churning . . .

Or perhaps the memory of what she'd done with Melinda was roiling in her belly.

"How are you feeling, dear?" their teacher asked.

Della broke away from the crowd, running for the nearest loo, barging through the main door and then a stall.

There, the blood came up. Bad, bad . . .

When she was finished, she remained on her knees, grasping for lav paper and wiping blood from her skin, refusing to reabsorb it.

After flushing it all away—at least physically—she stayed slumped over the toilet, wishing she wouldn't have to emerge. Yet when she finally did, it was to discover the girls leaning against the tiled wall.

Waste of good blood, Polly mind-said while inspecting her nails.

Violet looked ready to spit. *Della, I know this human habit has carried over, but from now on, tell us if you intend to make pavement pizza and we'll consume more of the meal ourselves.*

Leaning over the hand basin and turning on the tap, Della stared at the porcelain, the white, sterile purity. *I'm sorry. I can't seem to hold it down tonight. . . .*

Binge and purge, binge and purge, Violet singsonged. *We've heard it all before.*

Yes, said everyone except for Blanche, who was gauging Della with something close to concern. *We've heard it alllll before.*

As their words ricocheted inside her head, Della turned off the water, then peered in the looking glass, seeing a pale, bloated face.

Her lip curled, and she pushed away from the image, distancing herself from the thing that was wearing such human clothing.

"There we are," Violet said, opening her arms to her. "There's our Della."

Our Della.

She rested herself in Violet's embrace, and another pair of arms came round her, then two more, causing Della to disappear into the huddle of the only family she knew.

ELEVEN
The Tall, Thin One

Two Days Later

Dawn dropped a fresh newspaper onto the kitchen counter next to her oatmeal, apple, and milk. The Monday headline taunted her.

"BONEYARD ON BILLITER BARES A CLUE! Local Girl Identified."

Across from her, Kiko sat on a stool eating his breakfast. "Why're you cranky? The Friend assigned to the detective inspector was lurking around him when he got this news last night, so it's not like we were left in the dust."

"I just wish we hadn't wasted all that time this weekend interviewing contacts for the other girls who might've been our Kate."

"Take it down a notch, Sparky." Kiko sipped from his mug of tea. He'd tried some chamomile instead of coffee today. "I'm ticked, too, but you don't see me getting all worked up."

"It's not so much the wasted time as . . . Well, okay, yeah, it is the wasted time. But it's also that the paper said Kate Lansing wasn't even reported missing because her stepmom evidently kicked her out of the house and didn't keep in contact with her." Dawn sat down, feeling spent already. "You'd think she also might have friends who noticed she was gone, but no."

"Believe me, I know what you mean, but you can't take it to heart."

She was about to say that she didn't, but it'd be a lie. For a long time, Dawn hadn't had many friends or family, either, and every time she looked at that barely smiling girl named Kate Lansing in the newspaper photo, she saw herself.

Kiko folded the paper in two, covering the picture and head-line. "I'll call Kate Lansing's stepmom when the clock hits seven. That's still early, but I'll take my chances."

"There's probably been hordes of other journalists trying to get through to her since the details went public."

"Sure, but who calls people before a decent hour? I'm not rude like that."

Before Dawn could laugh, Kiko jumped off the stool and mo-seyed toward the exit. But then he glanced back at her.

"I sure do wish I could've envisioned Kate Lansing's name be-fore the cops or the media got a clue," he said. "You're right—we need to speed up this hunt."

He left, and Dawn marveled at how well-adjusted he seemed. After they'd gone to Highgate Cemetery on Saturday, he'd been sky high, but the excitement had thrown him off his game and he'd spent the rest of the weekend shaking and sweating, craving his pills. Dawn had dogged him the entire time because this sort of be-havior usually led to him going back on the meds.

But a Friend or two had lulled him with their voices, and this time he hadn't fought it. He wanted to stay clear in the head, he'd said. He *needed* to so he could keep the one thing he loved most in life—his job.

Dawn couldn't even guess at how long this new hunt addiction would substitute for the pills, but maybe, just maybe, his sobriety would stick this time.

Holding to that hope, she ate the rest of her breakfast, trying not to think about all the hours they'd puttered away these past couple of days. It hadn't been easy securing those Kate interviews, either, what with Remembrance Day on Sunday.

God, if they'd just known Kate Lansing was their girl they might be halfway to the Underground by now. . . .

But at least they'd tracked down Colleen Abberline's son, Justin, discovering that he worked in a borough called Croydon, just south of central London. They were going to surprise the twenty-three-year-old today at his job and try to find out exactly why Kiko had been drawn to him via the Highgate vision.

She abruptly stood to clean the dishes because every time she thought about Highgate she got antsy, mostly because she'd been so paranoid after leaving Kiko's envisioned grave.

While trekking through the empty cemetery lanes in search of Natalia, Dawn had kept a throwing blade primed, imagining red eyes trained on her back. And the gloomy feeling had only continued when she and Kiko had found Natalia sketching her own site in a palm-sized notebook.

The new girl had rendered a decent image of a sign with a circled number five on the grave's right side, plus a brand-new headstone bearing a Celtic cross and the faded name of thirty-two-year-old "Eleanor" scratched into the stone.

Like Kiko, Natalia hadn't seen the detail in her fleeting vision.

After she'd finished and Kiko had gotten his fill of touching objects around the gravestone for a reading that never materialized, Natalia confessed that she was too distracted by the continued "weird hollowness" to hear any clear voices.

That's when they'd headed for the pinkish gatehouse in an attempt to see if they could access information about Colleen's or Eleanor's graves: who kept them, who'd purchased them, etc.

Kiko had taken the reins, pretending he wanted more information about his distant relative Colleen. Natalia had caught on quickly, doing the same with Eleanor.

Unfortunately, the elderly man who'd let them in was a tough nut to crack, and he'd given them only an official address where they could make enquiries. But still spazzed on his success, Kiko had gotten cocky and tried to use some of that hypnosis Costin had been teaching him. It failed, and the man had dismissed him with a buh-bye glance.

Afterward, the team had seen to a few of those useless Kate interviews then returned to headquarters and, when Costin had awakened and fed, he'd managed to use his enigmatic wiles where Kiko hadn't been able to.

Although Costin had weighed using his hypnosis over the phone again, in the end he'd decided that there wouldn't be any major repercussions involving the people who could give him information. Actually, the main thing he had to worry about was any vampires who might be tuned in to his revealed presence aboveground, so he'd shielded himself during the brief calls he made, since shielding was supposed to be tough for any decent vampire to detect.

He'd had to call from an open window, of course, but Dawn had taken up his back because it was just too risky to have their ultimate weapon in the open.

But the contacts had yielded the answers they'd been hoping for, starting with Justin Abberline's name and a few personal details via a calling number that the Highgate enquiry address had led them to. Then, Costin had personally phoned their new lead at the Croydon business hotel where he worked, easing into the hypnosis, hoping to catch Justin before he shielded, if he were a true vampire.

By the end of the brief call, which would leave Justin with the impression that he'd been talking to a run-of-the-mill customer and that was it, Costin hadn't gotten any vamp validation. Yet Kiko had insisted that he'd seen the guy in a vision for a reason, so the next day, Kiko had called the hotel, himself, hoping Justin was working.

He was, and Kiko had finagled an appointment by saying he

was an old acquaintance from America who had known Colleen when she was younger. So he and Justin had arranged to have coffee during a break at work today, when Kiko could maybe get a touch reading from him.

As for the team's other Highgate grave subject, Eleanor, Costin had only found that she'd recently been buried by an elderly cousin, the only surviving relative of the family. After Costin had tested the older woman and decided that she, too, was either shielding or not a vamp at all, the team had scheduled an interview with her for tomorrow.

After all that trouble, Dawn decided, one of these leads would *have* to pay off. If not, she was going to punch a hole in a wall.

She went upstairs to her quarters and tiptoed past Costin's sleeping form to the bathroom for a good toothbrushing. Then she went back down to the computer room, where she saw that Natalia had joined Kiko at a terminal.

"Good morning," the new girl said.

"Top of the day to you, too."

Dawn noticed that Natalia had taken the Remembrance Day poppy out of her black hair and clipped her curls back with a big brown barrette that matched her wool pantsuit.

Dolly Do-Right, Dawn thought. Costin's background search on her had produced no red flags, and he'd taken some pleasure in announcing that to Dawn yesterday.

But . . . big whoop. She still wouldn't shake the feeling that she needed to be on guard.

"Aren't you hungry?" she asked Natalia. "It might be a good idea to eat something before we go to Croydon."

"Oh." Natalia seemed surprised. "I've been doing Eleanor searches, so I forgot."

"Please eat." The last thing they needed was a newbie passing out.

Natalia got out of her seat and headed for the kitchen.

Kiko kept staring at the computer screen, even when his competition was gone. "Thank you. She's like a monkey on my back, hanging over me, watching everything I'm doing."

"She's just trying to learn."

"She's out to make my life sheer bloody 'ell."

Dawn groaned. "Don't do that."

"What? Talk like a local?"

"Kik, no one's going to mistake you for one. Ever."

He chuckled. "Just give me a month, and I'll be saying things like 'Crikey!' or 'That's bloomin' wonderful!'"

"And you'll be such a celebrity that they'll have to invite you on a BBC show like *Strictly Come Dancing*."

"Smashing!"

Dawn made to go out of the room. She could handle a lot of things, but not a Faux-British Kiko.

"Hold up," he said. "I made contact with Kate Lansing's stepmom. Thought you'd want to know."

"Wow." Dawn leaned against the door frame. "I can't believe she's answering the phone with all the press that has to be cramming themselves down her throat."

"I've got a feeling about her, and I'd say that it's because fame whores answer their phones twenty-four-seven."

"Is this an official feeling?" Dawn asked.

"No, but I lived among fame whores, so I should know." Kiko logged out of the computer and stood. "Sounds like she took the day off from work, so she's available this afternoon for some 'journalists' who requested the honor of an interview."

"Great. That'll give me enough time to get back here for Costin's wake-up."

"Don't you still have that bagged blood in your closet fridge?"

"Always."

"Mate."

Huh?

Kiko looked expectantly at her. "You should say, 'Always, mate.' Now that we're settled here in Jolly Ol', you're allowed access to the language."

"I'll work on my Britcabulary." She began to leave, for real this time. "I'm just going to grab some quick target practice with a few weapons down below, then be ready in time to scoot out the door with you and Natalia for Croydon."

"Sounds like a plan."

And, two hours later, after emerging from the subterranean room where they trained, Dawn was shower fresh and ready to roll, wearing her crucifix necklace outside of her long johns and thick henley shirt today. If Justin Abberline had been shielding from Costin on the phone, she wanted to see if he was a vampire who'd react to holy-wear.

A couple of Friends kept their distance as the trio took a near-empty tube train to Victoria Station. All the while, Kiko looked up at the map and chortled at the colorful stop names. It never got old.

"Chalk Farm," he said. "A place where school supplies sprout from the ground like corn in Iowa."

Dawn couldn't resist, either. "Hackney Wick, where a man had best watch for sharp objects around his nethers."

Natalia stared at the map, as if dying to come up with one of her own, but she stayed quiet.

Soon they came to Victoria Station, emerging from the underground and up into the bustling crowds, the aroma from scads of food vendors like bakeries, sandwich shops, and pizza places competing for the taste buds.

They bought a bunch of roses from a flower stand, then used the western tote board to locate the next train stopping in East Croydon. Afterward, they headed for their coach terminal.

In less than a half hour they'd arrived at East Croydon's commuter station, using an online printout to find Drayer's Inn, across from the massive Whitgift Shopping Centre.

Croydon was an urban borough that had evolved from a mar-

ket town, and it was sprinkled with everything from Victorian buildings to high-rises that looked like they'd escaped from the seventies.
Instead of the village feel Dawn had found in the main city, with its
tucked-away alleys, creaky pubs, and the odd Roman structure
parked in the middle of more modern creations, their short walk to
Justin's workplace was all Starbucks and Subway—an America
with dreamier accents.

Drayer's Inn wasn't far at all, and when they walked past the
doors into a warm lobby with potted plants and touches of marble,
Dawn spotted Justin immediately.

Or, rather, the jolt of her adrenaline signaled that it was their
interviewee.

Tall and thin and pale, just as Kiko had said. But he hadn't been
able to say just *how* tall. Almost seven feet worth of it.

Just like the descriptions of the Highgate Vampire.

She ignored the urge to touch her crucifix, to make sure it
gleamed in the light and caught his eye right away.

Kiko tugged his scarf away from his neck as he approached the
desk first, standing a yard or two away so Justin could see him.
Natalia and Dawn posted themselves just behind.

"Hi," he said, his American accent also snagging the attention
of a businessman with a clipped gray beard who was checking
out.

The old guy looked Kiko up and down. So did everyone else
behind the desk, even Justin.

Yeah, Dawn wanted to say. *My friend's a little shorter than
your average bear. Get over it.*

Instead, she nodded to them. With polite smiles, they went back
to their dealings.

Justin also smiled down at the group, his gaze catching on the
flowers they'd brought. His hair was Earl Grey brown with a hank
slumping over his brow, his eyebrows thick and long, emphasizing
green eyes and red lips. His navy blue clerk's suit draped on his
shoulders like they were a wire hanger, and his gaze was soft, like

the guy who sat next to you in chemistry class and offered to share
his homework and never asked you to prom even though you suspected he might if you didn't have such a prickly reputation when
it came to dating.

Or the lack of it.

Dawn kept him in her sights. Was he a cemetery-lurking vampire or just a guy who put flowers on Mum's grave?

"I'm Karl," Kiko lied as he stood on his toes and placed the
bouquet on the counter. "I called you about visiting Colleen's grave
while me and my cousins are here?"

"Ah, yes, thank you." Justin's voice was like the cream these
people often put into their tea.

After scooping up the flowers, he glanced at his gold watch,
which had all the blunt shine of an item he probably hadn't saved
up too much cash for.

"Would you mind waiting for five minutes?" he asked, motioning toward the coffee shop to the team's left.

Kiko unbuttoned his big jacket. He had that luxury today since
he'd ditched the shoulder holster and relocated his revolver to an
inside pocket. "We don't mind at all. Can I get you anything while
we're waiting?"

Justin shook his head and offered another polite smile.

With that, Kiko and Natalia moved toward the shop, but Dawn
loitered, veering closer to the desk with her fingers ready to squeeze
the holy water wrist sack, if needed.

Justin's gaze flicked down to the silver crucifix she wore against
the black of her wardrobe.

Is he . . . ? she thought. *Will he . . . ?*

When he met her gaze again, he showed no signs of fear, freez-
ing, or suspicion. Nope—he only bent over to write something, his
hair slouching over one eye.

Okay. Not affected by a holy item. Maybe these vamps were
immune?

Dawn walked into the oaken coffee nook, where a few customers tapped away at computers and read trade paperback novels. Natalia had taken a circular booth across from the dessert case, and she was eyeing some éclairs. Kiko was at the counter, ordering.

"Want anything?" he asked Dawn as she took a seat.

"Nah, thanks."

Natalia leaned against the table. Her coat was still buttoned up. "Any reaction?"

"None whatsoever."

The other girl reclined against the leather upholstery. "I didn't have any indications of something amiss, either."

Dawn turned that over in her mind. If Justin was the Highgate Vamp—or even a vampire connected to the legend—wouldn't Natalia be getting those hollow vibes, just like at the cemetery?

And if Justin wasn't connected to a Highgate creature, then why had Kiko's vision brought them here?

Kiko came over with a mug of coffee for himself and a bottle of Orangina for Natalia. Under the table, Dawn set her PDA to record just before Justin arrived to drag over a chair and place it at the edge of the booth.

"I hope you don't mind," he said, "but I fear there'll be little leg room with me in the booth."

"No problem." Kiko shook the guy's hand, then motioned to Dawn. "I brought my cousin Georgie with me."

Ugh. Dawn wanted to smack him for the cutesy alias.

"And"—Kiko gestured toward Natalia—"our other cousin, Narda."

The new girl's eyes widened a tad, but she went along with it, poor thing.

"Narda," Kiko continued, "doesn't talk much."

Either he didn't want to explain Natalia's not-so-American accent, or he was just being evil.

Dawn gently kicked Kiko under the table as she shifted position. "Good to meet you, Justin."

"Likewise." The young man folded his large hands on the table, where the face of his watch was visible. "I appreciate your condolences."

How British, Dawn thought. He'd made it clear that this was going to be a quick chat without actually saying it.

"Wow, it's been a whole year since Colleen passed away." Kiko began to draw upon tidbits they'd gotten from her obituary, which had mentioned that she'd enjoyed a holiday on the Algarve Coast every year since she'd been five. "It's been a long time since we saw her ourselves. Our family used to spend summers in Portugal, too, and when she was a teen, she would babysit us while our parents went out. . . ."

Kiko trailed off, cueing Dawn to come in.

"Did Colleen keep visiting Lagos after she got out of school?" she asked, just to encourage Justin to talk.

Natalia, aka "Silent Narda," scooted toward the table, as if she wanted to get in on the questioning, too.

"My mother went every summer for the duration of her life." Justin glimpsed at his watch without making it obvious. But his move didn't quite cover the grief that had overtaken his gaze. "Except when she became ill, of course."

Colleen Abberline had died of breast cancer, and unless these Underground vampires could cause tumors, there probably wouldn't be a connection between them and her death.

"So young," Dawn said, meaning it.

Justin drew in a breath, as if all this sympathy made him uncomfortable.

Probably sensing this, too, Kiko wasted no time in touching Justin's hand for a reading.

And when he risked whispering "vampires" at the same time, Dawn almost flew across the table to shush him.

But the word would get Justin's mind on the subject, and if he knew anything about them, Kiko might be able to see it.

The interviewee hesitated, probably because he was reacting to the psychometric touch. Dawn bunched the bottom of her jacket with one hand.

Please have this work. Please give us something.

When Justin snapped out of it, then icily extricated himself from Kiko, something sank through Dawn.

And when the guy stood to leave, something broke.

Anger and frustration boiled over until it burst outward, and before Dawn could stop it, her mental power clamped under Justin's chin like a hand and whipped his face in her direction until his gaze was meeting hers.

Got your attention now? she thought somewhere in the back of her mind.

Both Kiko and Natalia gasped, but Dawn was too stunned to do anything but carry on.

"We'd like to talk to you a little more," she said.

Panic invaded his eyes, and as the full impact of what she'd done hit her, she released him.

Just as she'd released Jonah from those invisible shackles the other day.

Justin fumbled back a step. Then he left without saying anything else.

No one spoke, and when Dawn looked away from her team and found the other people in the shop glancing quizzically at the disturbance, she adjusted the wrists of her jacket. No one had screamed, so they probably hadn't seen.

She turned back to her coworkers, wondering why, once again, her mental force hadn't come out as a punch or a jab.

Kiko said it all. "What. The. Fuck?"

Dawn tried to act like she didn't know what he was talking about, but Natalia was gaping at her, making her feel like a traveling carnival attraction.

"We'll talk later," Dawn said.

Kiko made a "you betcha" sound. "We'd better."

Subject change. Now. "So on to plan *B*?"

"No need, because, boy, did I get some *stuff*."

In spite of the circumstances, he was as chipper as ever, and she realized that was only because he'd gotten a clear reading off of Justin Abberline.

"I'm so ba-ack," Kiko said.

TWELVE

THE WICKED STEPMOTHER

Justin seems like he's always been a presentable guy," Kiko said as they walked out of the hotel after the interview, "but he hasn't always been that way, and he's trying to make sure no one knows it."

Next to them, the red Tramlink rumbled by on its rails, and a few riders stared out the windows, their gazes lingering on Kiko, the little person, until they'd passed.

He didn't notice, but Natalia did. Dawn saw the new girl giving the gawkers a censuring stare right back.

Yet after the transport slithered around a corner, Natalia made sure Kiko knew she wasn't happy about being silenced back at the coffee shop.

"Care to elaborate on your Justin vision?" she asked him. "Or do you plan on brushing me to the side once again?"

"I'm sorry, was that whole Narda thing not appropriate?" Grinning, Kiko stuck his hands in his jacket pockets.

Dawn poked him. "Spill the vision, okay?"

But Kiko wallowed in his awesomeness a tad longer. "You don't even know how much time and effort I just saved us. I got more info out of Justin than he would've volunteered to any three complete strangers."

Natalia sniffed. "I'm surprised you didn't save us even more work by hypnotizing him. That way, you could have asked him to share anything he knows about 'clients.' Or perhaps you knew hypnosis wouldn't work, just as it didn't on the gatekeeper at Highgate Cemetery?"

Dawn held back a surprised laugh. One for Natalia.

Kiko looked annoyed as they turned the corner, where a row of fast-food places, banks, and storefronts stretched toward the train station. The grimy stench of car exhaust from busy George Street mixed with the autumnal temperature as commuters and urbanites came at them in a rush.

"So how does Justin tie in?" Dawn asked.

Before answering, Kiko glanced around, then waved her and Natalia over to the front of a travel agency, where they stood by the glass door in relative privacy.

The scent of jasmine signaled that a few Friends had circled around them, keeping a lookout for anyone who might get too close.

"First off," Kiko said, "I highly doubt Justin's what we might call a 'client.'"

"How can you be sure if you can't sense our 'clients'?" Dawn asked.

Natalia spoke up. "I have to agree with Kiko. Justin seemed very human. Very different from either Frank or even you, Dawn."

That little black spot Natalia had seen on Dawn charred into her even now.

"Then what *did* you see in Justin, Kik?" Dawn asked.

He lowered his voice and stepped closer, where they huddled over him.

"First, I saw Justin sitting on the floor of what looked like a murky flophouse, with other kids smoking, drinking, bundled up in dingy blankets. It was Justin and two other guys, plus a girl who looked real out of place because she seemed the type who would shop at Harrods instead of hanging around with them. They were all shooting up. I didn't see any of them very good at first—too dark. I need to do a mental replay."

Natalia gave Kiko a sidelong glance. "Those people who were with them . . . Were they 'clients'?"

"Not that I could tell."

"This girl," Dawn asked, "didn't happen to be Kate Lansing, did she?"

"Didn't look like her silhouette," Kiko said. "Kate had longer, reddish hair. And even though I couldn't see an exact color for this girl, I know she had a short, smart, Posh Spice style. If this took place a while ago, maybe Kate could've grown it out. Or maybe it's just a different girl."

"Maybe," Dawn said. "By comparing how Justin is now against how he was then, can we suppose that this did happen a decent amount of time ago? He couldn't have cleaned himself up that quick, holding down a good job in a business hotel and looking as healthy as he does."

Natalia was pensive. "He is rather pale. Perhaps he still goes out at night and indulges?"

"No way," Kiko said. "His eyes. He doesn't have junkie eyes."

He cleared his throat, and Dawn rested a steadying hand at his nape.

"Then perhaps," Natalia said, watching Dawn and Kiko from her side of the circle, "his mother's sickness, then death over a year ago, changed his life for the better."

"It cleaned him up," Kiko added.

Natalia kept on going. "And if that's the case, Kiko's vision would have taken place *over* a year ago."

The newbie was really catching on. "A year wouldn't have allowed the girl's hair to go from Posh Spice to Kate-long, would it? Unless she got extensions."

"Let me get a definitive answer right now." Kiko closed his eyes, using the screen of his mind to expand the vision that'd come to him in such a flash at the hotel. "After Justin and his three buddies shot up, they went out on the town. I can see street signs . . ." He smiled. "They were in Brixton, going in the direction of the railway station."

"There're warnings about that place at night," Dawn said. "Druggies. Bad scene."

"And the girl . . ." Kiko shook his head. "Nope, I can see now that she's not Kate. They passed under a streetlight, so I can see her better. God, she's young, way younger than any of the group. Maybe sixteen?"

"Yikes," Dawn said, thinking that if she had a little sister that age, the older guys would've had a mouthful of fist if they even touched her.

Natalia seemed to understand what Dawn's "yikes" meant. "Here, the age of consent is sixteen."

Dawn had already read that somewhere, but it didn't make her feel any less protective.

Kiko continued. "Before they actually got to the station, there was a dark street, an alley . . . I can't see any signs to ID the exact place, but no one is around. Looks like the back of a restaurant, with empty delivery crates and vegetables dropped on the ground. And then . . ."

He opened his eyes, smug as a thug who knows he's being dug.

"Then . . ." Dawn said.

"Then a crowd of young girls walked up. Seven of them in matching skirts, boots, shirts, and ties. Very swank. One girl—she had long brown hair, blazing eyes that looked purple . . . She just started talking to them, like they were in a bar and not in a deserted, vegetable-rotting alley. She had this clipped, upper-crust accent. Harrods. Know what I mean?"

Dawn nodded. "Sounds like they're the same type of girls as the one Justin was hanging out with—Posh Spice Girl—except this group's got their act together."

"Exactly," Kiko said, clearly thrilled that he was providing good material. "The thing is, the brunette seemed to be focusing on the girl Justin was with, almost like the guys were of secondary interest."

Natalia had gotten out her notebook and was scribbling furiously. "Did this brunette and her group . . . You know. Do what 'clients' do?"

She'd hit the jackpot with Kiko, his eyes lighting up. "I'm just getting to the best part. The brunette invited them to this nearby club, and when she smiled she had . . ."

He pointed to his teeth, then executed a soft, dramatic cackle.

Natalia dropped her pen and then picked it up, flowing right back into note taking.

Dawn nudged Kiko for trying to scare the newbie.

Loving it, he added, "But when Justin looked at her again, the teeth were back to normal. I mean, they were slightly messed up like most of the chompers you see around here, but they were teeth."

"Think the drugs had anything to do with what Justin spied?" Dawn asked. "He could've been tripping and seeing weird tricks of what light there was."

"He could've been." Kiko's expression said he doubted it.

"And then?" Dawn asked.

Although Kiko's grin didn't change, something in his eyes did.

"Anything more?" Natalia asked, her pen still.

He shut his eyes again. "Justin and his buds hung back to pop a couple pills while his female friend went off with the toothy brunette and her crowd. The guys followed them into a club down the street—loud music, strobe lights, confusion. Then one of Justin's pals disappeared with the girls, and . . ." He opened up. "Everything fades out after that."

Natalia and Dawn traded glances, and the new girl put her notebook down.

"It all has to mean something," Kiko said, "because that's what Justin thought about when I whispered the key word."

Vampires. But was Justin's state of mind reliable?

"Your visions can be symbolic and cryptic," Dawn said.

"But my touch readings have been straightforward."

"They weren't so much with Frank."

A muscle jerked at Kiko's jaw. He knew Dawn was right because, last year, when they'd been searching for her dad, the psychic had been able to access Frank by touching his shirts. The readings had been scrambled and painful for Kiko, even throwing him into an intense, altered state of consciousness some nights.

Regretting that she'd put a damper on his success, Dawn said, "I wonder if we can get Frank to contact Justin for some follow-up questions tonight. I sort of alienated our interviewee back there in the coffee shop and I doubt he'd give any of us the time of day again."

"Tell me about it." Kiko had come out of his brooding long enough to comment. "It looked like you went all puppet master on him. Is that mental punch of yours morphing?"

He had no idea how much she'd wondered about that, too. "Who knows."

Natalia kept her peace, taking in everything, as Kiko brightened up a bit.

"Can you imagine the possibilities?" he asked. "You could jerk people around even better, Dawn."

"It was probably just a glitch." Did they have to talk about this?

She turned to Natalia, who raised her notebook and pen again. "Frank doesn't have any kind of PI license, so he can use a fake name while telling Justin he's trying to find a missing niece. He can make a search for Posh Spice sound like a personal mission, and Justin should respond to that."

Natalia was wearing a doubtful look.

"What?" Dawn said. "It'd be a bad idea to march up to Justin and announce that Posh might've partied with 'clients' and we'd like to find her, please. It'll be bad enough that Justin gets two weird personal visits so close together. But Frank can use his silver tongue to explain that away."

Natalia thought that over, then took more notes. But she didn't say she understood, and Dawn wondered if she was altogether on board.

Kiko started to walk off, and they followed, the jasmine scent lifting away while the trio merged with the crowd on the pavement.

"For some reason," Natalia said, "I thought you were real private investigators. That's what I sensed."

Dawn dodged a woman with a massive baby carriage. Faux-British Kiko would've called it a "pram."

"Things are different now," Dawn said. "Back in L.A., after the boss recruited Kiko and Breisi, he made sure they had enough investigative work hours and education to qualify for licenses. Even while they pursued acting careers on the side, it was a part of their training while he homed in on the 'clients.' Thanks to some fancy work by the boss here, Kiko can work as a PI, but even back in California, we sometimes needed to come up with a less freaky reason to interview people than reality provided. It doesn't mean we're not investigators. We just aren't official right now."

"Were you a PI, Dawn?"

"No. I guess I've always been a shadow associate. I never had the time or inclination to fulfill any licensing requirements, so I'm actually more . . . physical aid."

"I see." Natalia fell a step behind Dawn.

Kiko added a comment over his shoulder. "Listen, if you're not comfortable with how we go about it . . ."

She caught back up. "I . . . am."

But she sure didn't seem like it as she hunched into her red coat.

They'd come to the railway station, which wasn't a big one spacewise, even though it saw a lot of traffic. Since it was about lunchtime, they grabbed sandwiches from a small stand and got on a train headed back to Victoria Station.

Their scheduled interview with Kate Lansing's stepmother wasn't until 2:30 PM, so they had time to stop by headquarters, where they grabbed naps. Then they took a quick tube trip up to the old St. Dunstan-in-the-East church ruins, which served as a miniature public park these days.

Mrs. Langley had asked them to meet her here, and Dawn suspected that the request had come about because the woman didn't want to host them in her Tufnell Park flat.

When they arrived at the ruins, a wiry, hatchet-faced man in a gray wool sweater stood with his arms barred over his chest at the entrance near the health clinic that had claimed residence on the old church's premises.

The Friends took up the perimeter as the ugly guy watched the team pass. Nodding civilly—Dawn was totally getting good at that—they found themselves in a serene courtyard with damaged gothic gray walls coated by scraggly ivy and light beards of moss. A burst of scarlet gold trees, flowers, and bushes circled the center, where bricks were laid around a low, raised fountain that burbled over the hustle of the city outside.

A skinny woman with gray hair tucked under a floppy tweed hat sat on one of the wooden benches, a book open on her lap. She wore glasses low on her long nose, and she moved her thin lips while reading.

They were the only ones in the public park, so Dawn made some noise by shuffling through a patch of fallen leaves.

The woman glanced up, folding her book closed with veined hands and keeping her place marked with a long-nailed finger. She was reading spiritual quotes.

"Mrs. Lansing?" Dawn asked, guessing their subject's age to be in the late fifties. The woman hadn't kept herself up that well and, for some reason, Dawn had expected a hipper stepmom judging from Kate's youth.

"Hello," Mrs. Lansing said in an anemic yet refined voice.

She didn't stand, but she did extend her hand as they all introduced themselves, providing false names, of course. Dawn actually had some nicely forged U.S. press credentials on her because she'd used the journalist ruse before, but Mrs. Lansing didn't ask for anything.

And Dawn didn't offer, because if there was a big rule of hunting, it was to never give more info than you had to.

After the interviewee had spent one extra, interested glance on Kiko, they sat on an adjacent bench. Dawn had taken care to have her crucifix necklace in full sight, yet it had no vampy effect when the older woman spied it. She did offer an approving smile though.

Kiko clenched and unclenched his fingers, and Dawn guessed he hadn't gotten any clear readings from shaking Mrs. Lansing's hand. Then, as if to put that behind him, he took a digital camera out of his outer jacket pocket since he was playing "photographer" while Dawn and Natalia would serve as reporters for two different articles.

The man they'd seen at the entrance wandered into the courtyard, leaning against the clinic wall as he stared at Kiko. His chin seemed to fold up disapprovingly to his mouth, making him look like one of those shrunken apple heads.

Mrs. Lansing noticed the direction of their gazes. "My brother. He's been very helpful."

"Is he keeping time for your interviews?" Kiko asked.

"That and making certain that there are no photographs. I'm sorry if I didn't make it clear earlier that I wish to have none taken. They unsettle me, as if I've become a breed of celebrity to be captured. I discovered a swarm of flashbulbs outside my flat this morning after you called."

Kiko put the camera away, even though it would've been nice to get a picture for Costin. "No photos then."

"Thank you."

Dawn held up her PDA. "Do you mind if I record?"

The woman hesitated, so Dawn put that away, too, getting out a pad of paper instead.

"No worries," she said, much to the woman's apparent relief. "I'll do it the old-fashioned way."

Natalia already had her own trusty notebook out, and she was sketching Mrs. Lansing. Dawn measured the woman up, too: the reddened eyes, the pallid skin of someone who still hadn't gotten over a shock, a weak chin that seemed to be thrust out so she wouldn't cry. . . .

Earlier, Kiko had called her a fame whore, but she wasn't striking Dawn that way. And she'd been thinking they would encounter someone meaner, too, based on how Mrs. Lansing had treated Kate.

Still, how many mothers—step or birth—could give interviews so soon after their daughter's unthinkable death?

"We're sorry about your loss," Kiko said, starting the ball rolling. "Thank you for talking to us about Kate."

Mrs. Lansing slid a bookmark between the pages of the spiritual quotations. "I've agreed to interviews because I hope to make other mothers more aware—and not only in Britain or . . ."

She looked to Natalia.

"Romania," the new girl supplied, lifting her chin slightly.

Mrs. Lansing didn't seem to pass the type of Roma judgment Natalia had clearly been expecting. Instead, she kept talking.

"Wherever it may be, all families could certainly benefit from Katherine's story." The woman laid both hands on her book, like she was drawing strength from it. "I cannot bring myself to think of how they found her. She was only eighteen. *Eighteen.* If I had known Katherine might end badly . . . If I could have done anything to prevent it . . ."

Dawn tried to sound reassuring. "You wouldn't believe how much this interview is going to help, Mrs. Lansing."

And that was the absolute truth—just not in the limited way the other woman was referring to. They were going to catch her stepdaughter's murderers and then some.

There was a lull, the chirping of birds and the singing of the fountain hardly covering it.

Natalia had moved on to sketching the park itself, glancing around the courtyard, her smile wide and genuine.

Mrs. Lansing seemed to connect with her appreciation. "I'm thankful you agreed to meet me here. I'm a solicitor in an office nearby, and one of the upsides is being able to spend lunch in this garden. I come here when I need the world to slow itself down because there's always comfort to be had within these walls."

She smiled at the new girl, and Dawn could tell she'd taken to Natalia because of this one little moment of them both loving the park.

"I understand this was once a church." The second psychic was putting Mrs. Lansing at ease whether she knew it or not. "How old is it?"

"Built in eleven hundred," the older woman said, and for an instant, she seemed to be so much less haunted by Kate's death. "Then it survived for over five hundred years only to be severely damaged in the Great Fire of London. They did manage to repair it after that. Christopher Wren even added that steeple." She nodded toward the tower that speared out of the clinic. "Everything you see now was still standing after the bombs struck during World War II."

Then Natalia asked something that almost blew Dawn out of her boots.

"Did you ever bring Katherine here?"

Instead of jarring the conversation, the segue led Mrs. Lansing to take off her glasses, then answer.

"Katherine and I were never close enough for that."

Setting aside her small notebook, Natalia leaned her forearms on her thighs. "Was it because you're her stepmother?"

"Most assuredly." Mrs. Lansing stared down at her spiritual book. "Her natural mother passed on when Katherine was very young—four years old. I didn't meet Adam, Katherine's father, until she was ten. By then, she had come to see the family as consisting of merely her and Adam, and I was the invader. A usurper, in fact, because she had come to believe her mother was a perfect queen."

As Natalia asked another question, Dawn leaned back, going with the flow. Kiko tensed, obviously realizing that he was just as shut out as Natalia had been at the coffee shop earlier.

"How did Katherine . . ." The new girl searched for a delicate way to continue.

"How did Katherine arrive at such a death?" Mrs. Lansing looked up. "It's fine to come right out with it. I've cried all I can cry, and now I'm enraged. I'm doing everything in my power to make certain this doesn't happen to any others."

Natalia nodded, encouraging the woman to continue.

"Katherine was rather rebellious," Mrs. Lansing said, "as you might have guessed. She delighted in vexing me. I tolerated it while Adam was alive, but he lost his life in a construction accident at Canary Wharf two years ago. He was the foreman, and . . ."

She choked off, and they all waited, looking at each other and wondering if they should comfort this stranger.

But then she took the story back up, and her voice was stronger. "Katherine had elected to continue living with me since she was still in school and had no other close family. But I knew she would require a firmer hand than Adam used. He quite indulged her."

"She didn't take to your requirements," Natalia said.

"Not at all. At first, we mourned together. Yet after she finished school, she began staying out later and later, coming home reeling with drunkenness. I knew she was up to no good. I ultimately took a stand one week ago. Secure a job, I said, because I would not suffer a daughter who had strayed so far from what Adam and I had attempted to teach her. I would not suffer a daughter who spent her nights drinking away her youth or who found herself on the dole."

Dawn thumbed through her ever-expanding mental thesaurus. "The dole" was welfare.

As Mrs. Lansing leaned forward, her back arched. "Live by my rules or leave the house, I told her, because young girls should listen. They should mind what is right and proper."

Her vehemence made Dawn straighten up on the bench. Here was the stepmom she'd expected.

Kiko had perked up, too, but Natalia remained cool.

"If Katherine had listened," the new girl said, "she might still be with us."

Mrs. Lansing looked gratefully at Natalia, then wilted. "Yes, but it all ended with Katherine choosing to leave instead. Yet I believed she would return within a day. I truly did."

Natalia paused at the building emotion in the woman's voice, so Dawn asked a question, not knowing whether they were being worked by their interviewee or not. Caution paid.

"Did you keep in contact with Kate at all?"

Mrs. Lansing lifted shaking fingers to her lips, and her brother started walking toward them before she held up her hand.

"I wished to contact her," the woman said. "But, again, I believed Katherine would return soon, and I needed to maintain my stance. But a day passed. Then two. She'd left no indication of where she might have gone, so I finally rang her mobile, yet she didn't answer. I then contacted her friends, but they hadn't seen her since school nearly a year ago." Their interviewee's expression fell even more. "I thought she would be back when she tired of this new life. Katherine's spending habits were rather impetuous, and as soon as she ran out of funds, I would have taken her back. . . ."

"Of course you would have," Natalia said, coming over to Mrs. Lansing's bench to sit near her. "You were only doing what you thought best."

"It wasn't enough." The older woman glanced up at the steeple, her gaze damp.

"Mrs. Lansing," Dawn asked, needing to steer things toward the vamps before it all broke apart. "Were there any friends you remember who could've been a bad influence on Kate?"

The woman was already shaking her head. "I've gone over this question myriad times, and still there's no answer. Her friends from school were model girls and boys. I thought Katherine would assume their disposition at some point, only because they seemed to exert such a positive influence on her during her school days."

Kiko was getting anxious, and Dawn guessed that he wanted to ask about Highgate Cemetery, seeing as that's where his and Natalia's visions had been centered.

But Dawn was getting there. "Were there any particular places where Kate hung out? Odd places where she might've met kids who influenced her negatively?"

"Not that I'm aware of. . . ."

If Kiko hadn't been so hot to keep his mojo going, he probably would've rethought his next comment before it tumbled out.

"In America," he said, "kids find trouble in gathering spots like malls or convenience stores or even graveyards . . ."

Oh, subtle.

"Graveyards?" Mrs. Lansing repeated, as if it conjured the image of Kate's disembodied head buried beneath the dirt.

Her face broke into a perplexed scowl before she raised her hand to cover her expression.

And, as she started to cry, their interview came to a close, leaving them nowhere closer to an Underground than when the day had started.

THIRTEEN
The Takeover

By the time the team got back to headquarters, the sky had changed to a dark grumble of coming precipitation, so they went inside and shed their coats and jackets in the entryway while the Friends who'd guarded them swept off to mingle.

A clock chimed an hour past dusk, ushering Frank into the room. "How'd it go?" He was dressed in his dark sweatshirt and cap like he was ready to charge out the door.

"It wasn't *my* best of days." Kiko brushed a hand through his blond hair.

"Don't be so hard on yourself," Dawn said, " 'cos we do have a new lead or two."

As Natalia took out her notepad to show Frank her scribblings and sketches, they related the details of Justin Abberline's interview and asked Frank to follow up with another one.

He agreed, and they moved on to Mrs. Lansing.

"Anything I can do there?" Frank asked afterward.

"I don't know," Dawn said. "Nobody seems to think she's vampy at all. Might be a good idea to put her on the back burner and concentrate on those possible vampire girls Kiko saw in Justin's vision."

Taking up position in front of a tall, iron-grated heater, Dawn held out her hands, trying to absorb warmth as the wind keened outside. All the way home regret had eaten at her as she'd realized, minute by minute, how removed she'd been during the interview with a woman who'd tragically lost a stepchild.

Couldn't she have stepped outside of her investigative role and shown a little more compassion, just like Natalia?

But every time Dawn quizzed herself, she wondered how else she was supposed to shovel through the facts they needed to find their quarry. How else she could get through hearing stories about dead girls and the agony of their parents.

As Natalia joined her, Dawn leaned closer to take in more from the heater.

The new girl spoke. "Mrs. Lansing does appear to be a normal woman. . . ."

"But?" Frank asked.

Kiko took the notebook Frank was holding and flipped to Natalia's sketch of the stepmom. "This is pretty much what we got from her. She was an odd duck, and not just because she didn't want to be recorded in any way."

Seeing a chance to make up for what she hadn't offered back at the interview, Dawn talked over her shoulder. "There're people who don't like to go on the record, and maybe Mrs. Lansing's just one of them."

"Uh-huh," Kiko said.

"And I don't think she's a fame whore," Dawn added, turning to the heater again.

"For your information," Kiko said, "I take that back. Listening to her changed my mind."

"Then why're you still dwelling on bad vibes?" Dawn asked.

Kiko folded his arms over his chest. "Maybe I'm just like you, Dawn, and I don't feel good about how she treated Kate. Mrs. Lansing seemed like she'd be a hard-ass to live with."

Frank interceded. "What were your impressions, Natalia?"

The new girl pulled away from the heater, seeming shocked to be included.

But when Dawn looked at her expectantly, that seemed to get her talking.

"I know how to listen to myself," Natalia said carefully. "My instincts . . . my own inner voices . . . And my senses have never disappointed me. That's why I don't doubt what Mrs. Lansing presented to us today."

Dawn rubbed her hands. "Maybe we'll have another chance to observe her at the coroner's inquest. It should be open to the public."

"Heck," Kiko said, "we could be knee-deep in vamps *tomorrow*."

"Then," Frank said, "let's ask the boss if we should put a Friend on the woman, just to see what we see."

No one objected. Same with getting surveillance on Justin Abberline. Dawn only wished they had enough Friends to cover all of London.

"The boss awake yet?" she asked her dad.

"Yeah, I talked to him for about a minute. But he sounds kind of off tonight."

Dawn turned away from the heater, stuffing her hands under her armpits. "I should get up there. Maybe he didn't feed himself from a refrigerated bag yet."

"Jeez, Dawn," Kiko said. "You'd pee for him if needed."

Dawn fake laughed.

Yet before she dashed off for the stairs, her dad said, "You want to know about the kid in the freezer?"

Her attention was all his.

"I wouldn't look so hopeful if I was you," Frank added.

"Information about the boy's fingerprints came back. Or, should I say, no information came back."

Kiko made a disgusted sound. "Interpol couldn't make anything of his prints?"

"Right. We've got ourselves a Kid Doe." Frank went to Natalia to give her notebook back, then sent her a smile as a bonus.

The new girl beamed, and Dawn looked away.

But Kiko didn't seem like he suffered from running her through the gauntlet today. "Are we gonna have to give up a DNA sample from the boy now?"

"That might be risky," Dawn said. "I'm sure the boss already has a plan for all this though."

"Darn tootin'." Kiko jutted a thumb in the direction of the kitchen. "Listen, I'm going to grab a bite and then hang with Frank while he arranges that second interview with Justin."

The two guys drifted away, but Natalia stayed in the center of the room where Frank had left her. Dawn could tell she wasn't sure where she belonged.

"Hey," she said to the new girl.

Obviously relieved, Natalia came right over, flipping her notebook to a clean page.

Dawn held out a hand to indicate that the psychic didn't need to fuss. "I just wanted to tell you . . . Good job today."

It was like Dawn had showered Natalia with a handful of freakin' gold dust.

"Thank you," she said. "I'm doing my best, and—"

"Well, just keep on doing it." There was only so much mentor shit Dawn could take. "How about you hit the computers to check into any missing girls in the Brixton area? Maybe you'll get something about Justin's girlfriend if she went MIA."

"Certainly." Natalia took off toward the stairs.

"And remember to eat!"

The new girl changed direction and aimed for the kitchen.

Brother. Not too long ago, Costin had told Dawn that jealousy didn't become her, but she was even more positive that playing Mother Dearest was a worse fit.

She went upstairs and opened the door to her quarters, expecting to find Costin readying himself for the night. "Hey, Frank said you sounded sort of—"

The words died in her throat.

Tall candles—they were electric—breathed a romantic glow around the room while a recording of a cello lulled from the corner stereo. By the bed, a white-linen-covered table waited, flanked by two high-backed velvet chairs. On the table, a glass bottle of sparkling water sweated next to an ice bucket, and domed chafing dishes emanated the aroma of beef cooked in what Dawn guessed to be scallions and mushrooms.

She shut the door behind her, not knowing what to make of this. Costin was more emotional than romantic, and the few times he'd made well-meaning but embarrassing Valentine-type gestures, she'd awkwardly laughed them off.

"Costin?" she asked.

The sheer drapes of the bed stirred as he eased out from the shadows wearing a calf-length black coat over a burgundy shirt and dark trousers. His midnight hair looked like it'd only been finger combed, and at this distance, the candles reflected a colorless, wolfish glint in his eyes.

Outlaw. That was what Dawn thought before she caught herself. Before her belly heated and sent a slow melt down and down until it arrowed to a pierce between her legs.

But when he flashed a tilted grin and came near enough for her to see the true color of his gaze, she took a step back.

Blue. His eyes were a predatory blue.

Anger fisted in her, slamming down. Yet instead of smashing her arousal, her clit only stiffened under the sharp pressure.

It made her angrier, even when she told herself that responding to his body only made sense: she was intimate with him every night, and seeing him *should've* stimulated her.

But she didn't want all that now. Not. Now.

"Jonah," she said, her voice hard as she blocked her mind from him in case he tried to enter. "No wonder Frank said you sounded different."

Surprisingly, she didn't feel him knocking at her consciousness to get in. In fact, all he did was silently pull out a chair for her.

Oh, like she was going to just sit down and have a candlelit night with him. "Listen, I don't find this amusing. Go back to where you came from. We don't have time for your reindeer games."

She sounded tough, but she was still aching from the sight of him coming around the corner of the bed.

Why did her damned body have to be so confused?

Fortunately, when he talked, his American Jonah voice put things into perspective. Or, at least, it helped.

"If you think I'm going to jump on you and have my way," he said, "don't. All I want is a truce talk."

She exaggerated a shrug. "Oh, okay, cool beans. I'll just forget about how you think you need everything Costin has and how you make his existence so much harder than it needs to be. By pulling out a chair for me, you've really won me over, Jonah, so let's sit right down and have ourselves a good palaver."

He chuckled. She hated it when men chuckled.

"Hear me out," he said. "Then, I promise, I'll let Costin come back."

"You'll *let* him come back."

Not answering, he poured water into the crystal flute at her setting.

When she didn't oblige him, he put down the glass bottle, hardly bothered by her vinegar. "If you want to get this over with, you'll sit. Otherwise I can stay around all night and leave Costin buried down where it's deep and dark."

The thought of the alienation, the confinement shook her to a response. "So all I have to do is listen, then you'll leave soon? Super soon?"

He held a hand over his chest. "Promise. But, you know, you should really linger over this food. It smells great, even if I have more of an appetite for you than for it."

Making a gagging sound, she started to leave, but he halted her with a lowered, more sincere tone.

"I really do promise, Dawn."

Taken aback by his new approach, she hesitated. Not that she truly would've left anyway, not with Costin trapped. She would do anything—even go through the hell of talking to Jonah—to retrieve her companion, so she wandered over and dropped into the seat.

"I'm only staying," she said, "because Costin can't afford to handle an Underground *and* you right now."

"I want to make sure life goes smoothly, too."

Her bullshit radar wasn't going off as much as usual, so she decided to see where this led. "I sure hope you got some blood out of the fridge already, because your body can't go long after waking without it. And don't even ask me for a nip, because I'm not going to let you anywhere near me."

"Understood. And I did feed, thank you for the concern."

"Please. Don't labor under the delusion that I'm concerned about anything more than Costin's well-being."

"Then I won't."

He was so . . . Well, she guessed "temporarily tolerable" might be a good phrase. But it wouldn't last.

When he opened the biggest chafing dish, a beef-and-herbs aroma filled her. She almost *mmmm*ed.

As much as she wanted to wolf down the food he'd provided, she couldn't stand him knowing that he'd gotten to her. But that was dumb, because he *would* know. Jonah spent every night seeing what Costin saw, knowing what Costin knew. He'd be an expert in how to read her.

And he proved it now.

"One time," he said, smoothly transferring a slice of beef to her plate, "you told Costin that Frank took you out for your twelfth birthday dinner, and you ordered some fancy beef dish you couldn't remember the name of. It was one of the happiest nights of your life, with your dad sober and attentive."

"If you're going to cue the violins next, forget it. Oh, hold up," she said, cocking her ear to the recorded cellos from the speaker, "you already sort of did."

He spooned the creamed spinach and rosemary sweet potatoes next to the entrée. His vampire grace made her watch before she forced herself not to.

"I have to be honest," he said. "I can cook, but I didn't have enough time, so I ordered in."

In spite of how the food was doing its best to win her over, she glared at him. "Tell me you didn't go to the door to get this from a delivery guy."

"I didn't have to." He smiled at her, confident, easy. So unlike Costin's brooding. "I'd been planning this, so when I briefly overcame Costin the other night while you were gone—"

"You overcame him?"

With a nod, Jonah kept going. "I took the opportunity to preorder online, timing this just right and hoping I'd be able to gain dominance tonight and carry this through. The catering service left the meal for Frank to bring in after I told him that I was treating you to a nice dinner. Your dad's going to make sure the others get their share from the kitchen."

God, why had Costin kept from her that he'd been battling Jonah more than she'd known? How far had their struggles gone?

She saved it for later, when Costin returned. "So you hoodwinked Frank."

"I did what I had to do."

"And when you woke up tonight, was it as Jonah or Costin?"

"Costin. But I fought him down and went ahead with my business pretty quickly. It just gets easier and easier."

Shivers traveled her skin, and she crossed her arms to quell the sensation. Simultaneously, her stomach grumbled at the rich smell of her meal, but she didn't touch it. She wouldn't until Costin came back out.

"Then I guess," she said, "tonight is about showing us that you can get control whenever you want."

"I wouldn't say that. But I've spent a long time studying Costin, finding out ways to push him down so I can emerge. Back before we were turned, Costin used to give me time out of body, but now he doesn't, because this body's trapped him and he doesn't have the option of traveling to another host now, so he has to control his shelter more than ever." He closed the chafing dishes, his hands lingering on them. "It's dark where I live, Dawn. It's not easy to stay there night after night."

He paused and, for a split second, Dawn felt for him. In real-world terms, he didn't deserve to be in any kind of jail.

But here and now, with him being uncooperative and with so much at stake . . . ?

As if her pity was the last thing he wanted, Jonah sat in his chair, adjusting his coat around him like he was some kind of careless bad boy who could handle anything. Costin had always said that vampirism was appealing to Jonah because he thought the condition was romantic. Since he'd spent most of his life as a rich recluse, his perceptions of reality were probably out of the ordinary, so he no doubt thought this was the peak of living, with all these heightened senses and appetites and strengths.

But, hell, hadn't Dawn thought so, too, for that short time when she'd had the same thing?

Needing something to distract her—something besides Jonah—she snatched her folded napkin from the table. "I suppose you could say life with Costin has really brought you out of your shell, huh?"

"Touché." Jonah cocked his head a bit. "Back before Costin came to me, I was too busy to go outside. Too much business to attend to. It got to the point where I didn't even see why it was necessary to ever walk out the door of whichever one of my properties I was currently at." He grinned, almost to himself this time. "I can admit now that maybe I got to be such a hermit that I was afraid of what might happen if I ventured out of my comfort zone. It got to be a compulsion, hiding. Then Costin found me."

He waited a beat, the cellos serenading just as softly as the wind outside.

Then, as if he'd talked too much, Jonah rested his ankle over a knee, languid as can be as he hung his arms over the sides of the chair, tapping the legs.

"So, Dawn," he said, "how do *you* like our time in London so far?"

She stared at him. "Talk about conversational whiplash."

"I'm just wondering. You don't seem as . . . lively . . . here as you did in L.A."

Suddenly, her napkin became very interesting.

"I'd even say," he continued, "that you seem more isolated, overall."

"Isolated?"

She couldn't help it—she glanced up, only to find that hungry glint in his eyes again. But this wasn't an aggressive gaze. It was . . . What?

Was it asking her to recognize that he was isolated, too?

As she tried to reconcile with that, he went on.

"You think no one understands because you don't feel quite human anymore," he said. "But you don't feel like the vampire you were, either. You're somewhere in the middle, not knowing where you should go."

She couldn't respond for a second. Two. Three.

Then she managed something that resembled a cutting laugh, but it wasn't a laugh. It wasn't even close. "You must be really bored if you've decided to puzzle me out."

"No, it's just that you've got a lot going on, and it's . . . Well, slightly fascinating."

God, Jonah.

"Yeah," she said, "I'm the Mona Lisa with a mysterious smile that no one can interpret. I'm a question for the ages."

Jonah's gaze sharpened to a dreamscape blue, vivid in the candlelight. "Costin's so tangled up in his missions that he doesn't think enough about you. He *does* think about you, don't get me wrong, but you're not the priority you should be." He leaned forward. "But I don't agree very often with the way he goes about business and . . . other matters."

Dawn raised a brow at the electric candles, the fancy dinner. Not that she was any prize worth the effort, but he'd obviously set her up for more than just a talk. "Listen, if you're trying to seduce me, you're wasting your time."

"Seduce?" Jonah folded his hands behind his head, reminding her of Costin just before they would fall asleep next to each other.

She tried to shake herself out of the comparison, but she didn't have to do it for very long when a whoosh of air from a vent invaded the room, the scent of jasmine overwhelming the aroma of dinner.

And when that jasmine thudded against her, she knew just who'd entered.

Thank God.

"Aw, look," Dawn said, righting herself in the chair. "Your girlfriend came to join us."

Kalin rushed over to Jonah. *"Not done yet?"*

Sighing, Jonah sat up. "You should be resting." Then he glanced at Dawn. "And for the record, Kalin's not my girlfriend."

Something like an invisible shove made Jonah veer off balance.

"Kalin," he said to the air, "go to your portrait and take a nap or something."

Without any further antics, the jasmine screeched out of the room, leaving them alone again.

Dawn watched as the bed drapes stopped stirring. "What was that about?"

"Whenever I'm out, she wants to hang around. And she doesn't like that I'm spending these precious moments with you."

"How sweet—a Friend crush. Just like middle school."

She realized she was joking around and shut up.

But Jonah had noticed, too, and he was grinning again.

"What do you mean she's not your girlfriend?" Dawn asked, intent on wiping that mirth off his face. "You got her to mess with my mind back in L.A. Remember? It was before Costin stepped out of hiding to reveal your actual form to the team. You came to me in the dark pretending to be Costin and—"

"I remember."

At his tight words, she wondered if he regretted using Kalin to bind Dawn's arms so Jonah could touch her, just as he'd always desired.

But that was only because he was in a twisted competition with Costin.

"Kalin's just bent on making Costin jealous," Jonah said, "so she's latched on to me."

"You sure took advantage of that."

"Oh, she's done her share of using. She started coming to me whenever Costin used to give me free time because she wanted to show him how much he might miss her if she turned her attentions to some other guy. She always thought he should've loved her and only her."

Dawn was still back on the L-word part. Had Jonah just mentioned . . . love?

Was he insinuating Costin might feel that strongly about *her* now?

No way. They didn't live in that kind of world.

"If Kalin's worried about him loving me now," Dawn said, "she can get over it. He doesn't."

But after the words were out, she wondered if she'd blurted them because she wanted a sign that maybe they were true.

Or maybe she wanted to know they *weren't*.

Jonah settled back in his chair again, his enigmatic smile digging into Dawn. But she didn't dare open her mind so she could hear what he was thinking.

Love had nothing to do with anything.

"I think," Jonah said, "that no matter how much you pretend the opposite, you actually do want to know Costin's deepest, darkest stuff. You want to know what he's still keeping back, even if you believe he's started to share so much."

She gathered her defenses tighter around her, keeping in a heart that was hammering to get out. "I don't need to know anything."

"I'll tell you if you want."

Temptation. God, it pulled at her. She couldn't even bring herself to tell Jonah to take a flying leap.

His expression grew serious—so serious that she got a weird feeling he was being absolutely genuine again.

"Last chance to tell me to keep it to myself," he said quietly.

Still, she couldn't tell him no.

"All right then," Jonah said, lowering his voice like someone who was breaking bad news. "For a start, Costin does have strong feelings for you, but he detests that you're his master."

He didn't seem to take any delight while his comment screwed in to her, but she wouldn't give him the pleasure of a reaction anyway.

She tried hard to keep her voice even. "Tell me something I don't know."

"You suspected, but you didn't *know*," he said. "You try not to act like his master, but the truth is that you are, and he will never, ever forget that."

"Jonah." She felt pummeled. Every inch of her. "Costin's used to fighting back in every situation, even this one. I accepted that a long time ago."

"He's your submissive, Dawn. And although he's existed for hundreds of years and has trained himself to adapt to each era, there's still a part of him that won't stand for being below a woman. He was raised to be dominant."

She just looked at him while her emotions scurried around, trying to settle, never slowing down because the hurt would catch up. *She*'d been running to stand still with Costin, and she *had* always known it.

She just hadn't been able to admit it.

Anger built again, and she got to her feet and walked away from the table, relieving the pressure before it exploded in a punch or a kick or . . .

God knew what else she might do to Jonah . . . and Costin.

"I get it," she said. "You're trying to drive a wedge between me and Costin, just so you can have your way."

Jonah didn't confirm or deny. He only stood, too, his coat rustling down to his legs. "You've got to know that he's not right for you. You're going to get really hurt, Dawn, and you can stop it before it gets worse."

"You said this wasn't a seduction."

"It's not."

She almost believed him except for the wild, covetous gleam that had returned to his eyes. There wasn't anything soft or even human about it anymore.

It was just a gaze that devoured her and pumped her body heat on high.

He moved away from his chair. "There're a hundred other reasons you should distance yourself from Costin. He's too old for you, for one thing."

This was a joke, right?

Jonah came closer. "When you look at me, the body who houses him, you see an eternal thirty-three-year-old. Don't let that deceive you because Costin's actually . . . what? Over six hundred years? That's appalling."

Dawn inched away. Even though Jonah was controlling that body right now, she was too used to it, especially when it prowled as it was doing now. Her own jamming heartbeat and shaking legs and light head didn't know the difference because they'd been conditioned to respond to every move that body made.

Jonah came even closer, clearly knowing what he did to her, no matter who was in control.

"Jesus," she whispered, not exactly because she needed help, but . . .

Maybe it *was* a last-ditch plea.

At the oath, Jonah jerked, just like he'd taken a dart to the neck.

She didn't like to see that body in pain, and sympathy jabbed her chest, opening her up for an unfortunate instant.

An instant too long.

Jonah's consciousness flooded into hers, warm and serene. It told her that she wasn't alone anymore and, for the stretch of a second, her mind became his, revealing every reaction she'd been trying to hide.

Why would you even want me? she wondered over and over again.

He eased even closer. *The fact that you have to ask explains it.*

He was so near that her world became the color blue—his gaze, swimming with that agonized plea for understanding.

A ravenous sorrow . . .

He hushed another thought into her head, reaching a hand toward her face. *I'm lonely, too, Dawn.*

So lonely . . .

A burst of caution forced her to tear her gaze away from his, and she shielded her hands over her eyes, closing herself.

"Get *out* of me," she said. "*Stay* out."

Slowly, she sensed his hand lowering, sensed him retreating to the table. When she looked again, he had his back to her, posture bleeding rejection.

Don't get soft on him now, she thought. *Don't say you're sorry. Never fall for anything again.*

He spoke. "I made you a promise earlier."

"Right, a promise," she said, almost shaking with the pent-up emotions he'd dragged out of her. Rage nailed over the top of them all. But she didn't know if it was because of Jonah's deception or if it was because *she'd* allowed him in.

Stupid, stupid, stupid . . .

"I'm not going to hold you to any promise," she said, "because you're not capable."

Yet, when he faced her again, his eyes were topaz.

A wounded shade of gold.

"Nevertheless," Costin said in his deep, accented voice, "he has released me."

In the disturbing silence that followed, all they could do was look at each other because no words could cover what she'd found out about the feelings Costin had hidden so deeply.

Or the fact that Jonah could come back to unearth more of them at any time.

FOURTEEN

Lоndоn Babylоn

The Same Night

Oпce again, Noreen was complaining.

"I can't suffer another night of this," she said, tugging at the rusted iron shackles bolting her to the wall of their underground hideaway.

Della watched her for a moment, then became bored with Noreen and glanced to her other side, where Polly wasn't quite as active. Like Della, the other girl was sitting against the rock and taking their latest punishment in stride, tracing a finger round the hole where a key might've unlocked one of Thomas Gatenby's servants once upon a time.

"Noreen," Polly said, "listening to you has got to be the worst punishment of all."

Next to Polly, Blanche was also calm about their wall-chained lot in life.

But a restless Violet was shackled away from them all, her chains attached to the ceiling far from the rock's face.

With her hands extended over her head, she pouted as if wrongly accused. Never mind that she'd been the one who'd dreamed up the entire raven scenario that had kept the school whispering about "bad omens" throughout Sunday and today. Never mind that she'd attempted to blame the idea on Blanche.

Their superior knew better and had punished them accordingly.

Violet, her brown hair covering most of her face as she swiveled from the ceiling, glared at the other girls. "Stop rabbiting on, you two. I can't bear to hear any more."

With a rattle of chains, Polly shirked away from her friend's harsh command, but she and Noreen did fall quiet.

Yet this was no doubt what they were meant to do, Della thought, leaving her mind open because she didn't care if anyone else heard her. They *should* reflect on their behavior and carelessness. Their superior must have taken great pleasure in knowing that they had spent all of Sunday in Violet's room waiting, then today sitting through classes and wondering when the hammer would fall. For Della, knowing that Melinda Springfield had become ill was the most excruciating punishment of all and, although lingering here in chains for hours wasn't precisely a dream come true, it was fitting.

In fact, throughout their punishment, none of them had dared to shrug out of the shackles, even if the task would've been a simple one. Accepting their due was symbolic—an admission that they were willing to redeem themselves.

But, Della mused while laying her cheek against the rock, if they continued misbehaving after this . . .

Thoughts of Briana and Sharon flooded her. Before both girls had left school, each had been punished for masterminding one misbegotten adventure or another, just as Violet was being punished now.

Yet at one point, both had also challenged Violet. . . .

Della went back to closing her eyes, knowing she might be here all night with the rust scratching into her skin, the shackles rife with a stench that reminded her of tainted blood.

After what seemed like hours, footsteps sounded in the tunnel.

Della didn't breathe. None of them did. They didn't dare stir for fear of seeming naughty again.

But when the footsteps paused, Violet sniffed. Polly sniffed. Then they were all sniffing, attempting to confirm an identity. . . . Yes.

Della's limbs went weak at the scent: sulfur from an oncoming rain clinging to cotton, leather, hair.

The group got to their knees as the tunnel's beaded entrance parted, revealing a man with golden eyes under wild eyebrows and long hair the color of a thorned thicket. He looked like a fallen rock star in his tanned leather boots and pants, which were topped by a dashing jacket that covered an untucked gypsy-loose shirt.

He smiled, gaze gleaming. "Have you been punished enough?"

At the amused hint in his east-European tone, the girls grew hopeful.

Violet spoke. "We're so very sorry, Wolfie. Please, is it time for our release?"

The beads clicked together as he let them go, then reclined against a wall, his shadow warped beside him like a bigger, more unforgiving twin. "Twice this weekend alone you have disobeyed. I'm afraid your straying has grown wearisome, my dears."

Della couldn't look at him anymore, not when she feared that Wolfie might discard them now that they had overstepped their bounds one too many times.

But then she heard her voice bouncing off the walls, even before she realized she'd spoken.

"We were only hungry, Wolfie."

Oh, no. Why? Why had she dared?

Out of the corner of her lowered gaze, she saw his boots step away from the wall.

"Della, sweet?" he asked. "Was that you? I can hardly hear you behind all that lovely hair of yours."

His voice . . . It had been kind, holding no malice, only perhaps a chiding reminder to have a care for their feedings in light of current events.

Still, she wouldn't raise her gaze to see what his eyes might tell her for certain.

His leather boots stopped in front of Violet.

"Will you vow no more shenanigans with ravens or house raids?" he asked.

"Yes," they all said together.

"Well, then." The weight of his gaze pressed on Della, then removed itself. "I suppose you've proven your good intentions. After all, I know you meant no harm—discounting what you did to the human food."

She saw his boots move to the rock wall, to the farthest girl first. To Noreen.

Violet stifled a guttural sound, and Della finally glanced up. The girl was furious, and Wolfie's grin revealed that he knew it.

With a gesture, he unlocked the shackles from Noreen's wrists, and they fell to the ground.

"Wolfie," Violet said, her envy traveling in wave upon wave over all of them, "if we cannot go out or even feed here, then how can we decently survive? How can we *recruit?*"

He took Noreen's wrist and smoothed his long fingers over first one, then the other, healing any raw skin with the glow of his touch. All the while, the redhead gazed upon Wolfie with adoring relief.

He smiled down at her while addressing Violet's question. "You will have ample time to recruit. Truth be told, you have already done very well in that department this year." He'd finished his healing, but remained with Noreen, undoing the shirt button at her wrist, sliding his fingers inside to tickle her. "Hence, it's time for you to see the fruit of your labors."

The girls tensed, holding their breaths.

"That's right, my darlings," he said. "A field trip is in order, just as soon as I can be assured of your manners."

Exhaling, the girls glanced at each other, eyes shining. Ever since being turned, Wolfie had dangled the promise of the main Underground; after all, they had been the ones bringing in more members, growing the community's numbers.

But no matter how proud Wolfie was of their recruiting endeavors, not every choice of candidate had been successful. Consider the last one, Kate, for instance. They had recognized what they thought to be a kindred spirit—fun, pretty, someone Wolfie would have enjoyed in the long term—yet she had ultimately been horrified by their courting, so they'd used her for the short term instead.

Della had always burned to ask Wolfie if they might see Briana and Sharon in the Underground—if they had perhaps returned for his sake especially, knowing how he'd favored them. Yet Della didn't chance it because of what she feared she might see in Violet's reaction—a familiar smugness indicating that the departed girls weren't in the Underground at all and that only Violet, the privileged leader, knew of the girls' true fates.

After all, if Briana and Sharon were Underground, wouldn't Wolfie have told them?

But Della would not challenge him *or* Violet.

By this time, Wolfie had left Noreen and was coming toward Della. Her blood thundered with every step he took, and when he flicked his wrist to undo her restraints, she gasped with the shock of the freedom.

Then, as she drew shallow breaths, he healed her with the play of his fingers, which burned into her with his glow.

Warmth rushed to her chest, her belly, a deluge.

"You've had a trying weekend, haven't you?" he said softly, his power fizzing over her skin.

"Yes," she whispered, looking into his feral eyes and buzzing with the current from the visual connection.

He seemed so mild when he added, "Pity the authorities were able to identify a victim very quickly because her head was buried in the area we've used to hide our prey's remains. Imagine—an entire head."

Confusion gripped Della, mixing with the pleasant ache of his hands caressing her wrists.

"It's my fault," she said, knowing he would know, anyway, even if she had been able to hide what she had done with Kate's head until now from the girls. Wolfie had access to all of them if he wished. "I was saving some of my meal share for private, but then I realized how repulsive that was and I buried it instead."

He put his fingers under her chin and raised her head. "And how could you have known that it would turn out this way?"

She started to apologize once more, but he shook his head. "Don't concern yourself, Della. But this is why you girls are receiving an education—so you might learn from situations such as these and never repeat your mistakes when you move on to the Underground, where you'll be free to feed Above on your own."

Looking at the other girls, he allowed his fingers to slide from Della's chin to her neck, where he rubbed his thumb against her jugular. Her belly strained; her legs quivered.

"I'm afraid we've been overly careless recently," he said. "Freedom is a fine matter, but cleverness goes with it hand in hand."

Then, as if he'd driven home his message and was content, he moved away from Della, his fingers brushing near her breast.

She bit her lip, wanting to touch where he'd just touched.

But she didn't, instead watching him go to Polly, where he released the other girl with another flick of his wrist and then healed her with a glowing touch, as well.

Violet shifted in her chains, as if to remind him she was waiting. But Wolfie would draw her out, if only for sheer entertainment.

The brunette tried to get his attention anyway. "Are you saying we won't be able to nightcrawl anymore? Is that the price we'll have to pay for Della's ridiculous buried head?"

Wolfie laughed, but it was only a rumble in his throat. "You do welcome trouble, Violet, don't you?"

She narrowed her eyes at him, and he chuckled, concentrating on Polly.

"Not to worry, dears. You'll be getting back to your favorite pursuit soon. But tonight, you're scheduled to have another rodent meal to show what's in store if you should be defiant again."

None of them groaned out load, but Della could feel their frustration in the very air.

Yet Wolfie would keep his promise. Della couldn't imagine him remaining hidden, denying himself their nightcrawls. In his assumed "human" identity, he took great joy in parading in the open, especially when it involved spending the fortune he had once wheedled from Thomas Gatenby after the man had donated the land for Queenshill.

And after he had died from such "natural" causes.

Wolfie finished with Polly, tweaking her nose. "We will be more careful in the future, yes?"

"Yes," they all said.

"Excellent." He approached Violet. "Man was born wild, and being a vampire has only allowed us to expand on that pleasure. Certainly, there'll be a time when the rest of the world fully accepts what we are, but we haven't quite arrived at that point yet. And until we do, we must roam more carefully while easing society into one phase, then another."

Violet seemed ecstatic to have his attention now, and she leaned her cheek against her raised arm, sending him a provocative look that seemed more fashioned for a twenty-five-year-old than a schoolgirl.

Intrigued, Wolfie made his slow way toward her. "I have lived hundreds of years, and I have seen society accept what they never thought to *be* acceptable. These days, anything goes and, fairly soon, we will not have to hide during our most joyful experiences. Until then, patience is an asset."

Listening to him was like hearing a familiar bedtime story: a tale of how, once upon a time, he'd infiltrated society bit by bit, a vampire learning and adapting and traveling in human circles until he could be thought of as nothing else *but* human.

At least in public.

The moral of that story also remained the same: in keeping to his wildness, Wolfie had found himself.

Della only wondered if she could find the same ending. . . .

He had come to stand before Violet, and she angled closer to him, causing him to lower his brow, as if sizing her up.

Violet glanced up from under her lashes. "Undo me now?"

They locked gazes, so intensely that Della's pulse took up the thud of Violet's. All the girls' heartbeats joined.

Ba-bump. Ba-bump.

With a rakish chuckle, Wolfie motioned toward Violet's shackles, which opened like jaws releasing prey. She stumbled, catching her balance, but not before he walked off toward Blanche and left Violet to heal herself.

The girl sullenly held a hand over the flesh where the iron had chafed.

The rest of the group tittered, yet Della was still worried about trouble during their next nightcrawl.

As Wolfie released Blanche and glow-kissed the inside of one of her wrists, Della asked, "So we won't have to worry about the authorities watching for us?"

Blanche leaned back against the wall, as awestruck as ever by Wolfie's presence while he stroked her wrist and glanced at Della. His expression should have assured her, but . . .

Anxious, she accidentally slipped into Wolfie's gaze and went so deep that she found herself swirling in his disjointed thoughts.

Depends on where the custode *is . . . Perhaps off chasing ghosts around London? . . . And what if another blood brother is . . . ?*

She tore herself out of him. Always causing the most trouble— What now?—

When she heard Wolfie laugh, Della realized he was . . . amused?

Yet then his gaze lowered, and the other girls stared at her, shocked. None of them had ever, *ever* broached Wolfie.

"You forget yourself, my sweet," he said. "I didn't bring you in for a listen, now, did I?"

Punishment. It would only be a matter of time.

He began to shed his jacket while wandering to a divan, then tossed the leather at the foot of the furniture and slunk down to the cushions. "I should be ashamed for letting down my guard, really. Girls are curious by nature. I know better, and it certainly won't happen again."

That feeling of sweat—the pinching, clammy memory—consumed her in her coolness.

"Della," he said, commanding her to look at him.

When she did, she saw that he had leaned back, his wicked hair spread over a pillow, his limbs splayed in lazy abandon.

"From the day you were turned," he said, "haven't I always said you will be cared for? That you should never fear me?"

"Yes." Dry throat. Hurt. "If we obeyed."

"I daresay," Wolfie continued, "that each of you joined because you *wished* to be cared for."

Della nodded, unable to speak altogether now. Maybe it was because shame kept her silent. Shame in knowing he was right, that they had all wanted to stay young girls—the apples of Wolfie's eye—even when everyone else in the world outside had forgotten them.

And to lose that . . . ? She mustn't think it.

"What heaviness there suddenly is here," he said.

Then a smile appeared on his mouth, starting slowly, growing, widening until his eyes glinted with the unfettered abandon they loved.

"I think," he said, "Della must learn what it is to really play."

Violet had sidled away from her chains, as if unsure of her place with Wolfie now. "Della will never learn."

"Are you sure of that?"

As if to prove that Della *could* learn, his eyes flared, and the other girls jumped back, then giggled. Della only smiled a bit, hoping . . . no, *knowing* she'd been forgiven on his end. Knowing Wolfie was going to make everything better and protect them.

He always did.

While the girls held their collective breaths, he growled again, then sprang off the divan.

Even Della squealed now, especially when he grabbed for Blanche, who laughed and broke away from him, coming to hide behind Della.

"Deny me?" he asked in a dramatic bellow. "Who are you to do that?"

Blanche peeked out from behind Della as Wolfie hunched down to his hands and knees.

He crept toward them. "Who's . . . denying . . . me?"

"Not me!" Polly said, pulling Blanche out from behind Della and tossing her to Wolfie.

He caught the dark-haired girl and pawed her to the floor, the two of them rolling over the rug until he ended up on top. Blanche could hardly breathe, she was laughing so hard, and Della felt it, too—the rush of cleansing gaiety.

At the liberty of it, all the girls sprang on him, piling as he nuzzled Blanche's neck and she squealed some more.

Then Wolfie's back arched, and they all tumbled off, backing away in delighted fear as he began to change into his play shape.

His ears pointing.

His snout lengthening.

His tail emerging.

His skin sprouting hair while he howled at the ceiling.

Gleefully, the girls pounced on each other, still in human form, swiping, laughing, tumbling round.

Forgiven, Della thought. *Free and happy, just as Wolfie says we should be—*

Noreen sent Della sprawling across the carpet to the tunnel entrance, and she sprang to all fours, ready to jump at Noreen and join in again.

But a sight behind the beads iced her.

A pair of eyes glowing through the clacking orange and red strands, then disappearing.

Della's chugging blood eased to a stomp, stomp, stomp.

It had been the cat, but it had left them to continue playing, thanks be.

The ever-watching creature was leaving them to Wolfie.

With a relieved hop, Della darted away from the beads, then jumped on Noreen, forgetting the cat eyes in the giggling chaos.

It wasn't until Blanche failed to show for class the next day that Della even remembered.

FIFTEEN

The Ouija Interview

The Next Day

Bridget O'Connell, Eleanor's older cousin, lived in a wealthy area of Harrow in a Victorian house that sat back on the rain-combed grass, reclining behind elm trees and a low brick wall. The inside was just as mellow and well-appointed, with dark, rose-patterned woodwork smelling of oil soap, plus dark-hued, layered window draperies that reminded Dawn of a dress that a fancy woman might've worn at a ball.

"The house is all a bit much for me now," the seventy-some-year-old Mrs. O'Connell had told them after they'd doffed their coats and sat down to tea in one of three reception rooms. A hint of an Irish lilt painted the elderly woman's tone just as colorfully as the pink tinge on her soft cheeks and the blue of her eyes. "My husband passed on years ago, and now it's me and far too many rooms."

Dawn, Kiko, and Natalia smiled back, their tea in front of them on the low cherry wood table. Mrs. O'Connell had already told them all about her husband: how he used to give music lessons here, how she could occasionally hear the memory of a violin or clarinet in an empty room.

Since they were still in the small-talk stage of the interview, they hadn't asked yet about her much younger cousin Eleanor or found out why Natalia had envisioned her grave at Highgate Cemetery. All they'd really done was offer the story that had gotten them through the door—a cover designed to make their vampire-related questions seem reasonable.

Basically, Dawn had used the old "we're on a personal mission for a friend" approach, just as Frank had done to make his own appointment with Justin Abberline tonight. But for Mrs. O'Connell, Dawn had invented a fictional missing pal named Sara who was "an acquaintance of Eleanor's." According to this cover, they were tracking down this friend since everyone else had given up on finding her and, since they'd "uncovered Eleanor's name in some of Sara's sensitive documents," they were coming to Mrs. O'Connell, hoping she could help them by talking about her cousin and why she might be connected to fictional Sara.

More lies, Dawn thought, glancing at Natalia. But as long as they brought down this Underground, they were damn justified.

"It's not often I have the pleasure of company these days," Mrs. O'Connell said from her petal-upholstered armchair across from them. "Not unless you include the odd long-lost third cousin who comes sniffing around for what money I might leave after I've gone to the great hereafter. Since Ellie passed on, I do miss a conversation over tea. She was always kind enough to indulge whenever she was in town from one of her business trips. But I'm thinking you're not here to chat with a dotty old missus and you'll want to be hearing about Ellie now."

Sprightly for her age, Mrs. O'Connell pushed herself to her feet, scuttling past the upright piano and its contingent of mounted musical instruments, swerving behind a silken dressing screen where they could hear her riffling through a drawer.

Dawn took a sip of tea and absorbed the room's antique warmth. Well, it wasn't *warm* warm—in fact, she had goose bumps in spite of a fire burning behind a low needlepoint-covered screen—but it wouldn't be terrible to stay here an hour longer.

Maybe she didn't mind hanging around because she was tired, Dawn thought as the tea traveled from her throat to her stomach in a cooling stream. Tired of running around. Tired of things always flip-flopping on her, like Jonah taking over Costin last night. At least old places had some consistency to them.

Mrs. O'Connell's voice was muffled behind the dressing screen. "Just one more moment . . ."

Natalia, who was sitting next to Dawn, had her gaze on the flower-molded ceiling, obviously listening for any voices from the dead. On the other side of her, Kiko was cupping his hands around his teacup, a vague smile on his face.

Wasn't *he* chilled out? Last night after Jonah had left, Dawn and Costin hadn't found anything new to say to each other, so she'd left her bedroom and discovered Kiko in the midst of the sweats. But he sure was composed today. Dawn suspected that he'd used some Friends, who were even now waiting outside, to calm him again.

Mrs. O'Connell emerged from behind the screen, her hands full of snapshots and knickknacks. "I fetched all the photos of Ellie I could find. Keep telling myself I'll put them in a scrapbook, but I never seem to come round to it. Perhaps you'll find Sara in a picture with her while we talk of Ellie?"

"Great idea," Dawn said, positioning herself on the edge of the love seat as the elderly woman spread the photos and random objects over the table. If the items had belonged to Eleanor, Kiko would be able to use them. "We really appreciate your help, Mrs. O'Connell."

"Not a mention of it." She stood next to Dawn, smelling like rose oil.

Kiko placed his cup and saucer far away from the photos and

went for a small doll decked out in a green shamrock-printed dress, flame-yarned hair, tiny black button eyes, and a red-thread mouth that made it seem like her lips had been sewn shut.

"Did this belong to Eleanor?" he asked.

"Yes, she hand made dolls, and she also knit Aran jumpers for fairs in what free time she had." The elderly woman bustled off to another part of the house, saying, "I'll bring one of those back for you to see. The craftsmanship is so lovely."

Kiko held the doll, trying to get a reading while Natalia and Dawn scanned the pictures. Most of them featured a freckled, auburn-haired child laughing as she did things like riding a pony or licking an ice cream cone. More recent photos showed a bohemian-looking woman with a wide smile and blue eyes holding up one of those sweaters she must've knitted.

Since Dawn was recording their interview for Costin's sake, she took out her camera phone and snapped away for him, too. The quality of her digital pictures would suck when he saw them, but she wasn't about to steal any of Mrs. O'Connell's keepsakes.

Then she whispered to her coworkers. "You get anything?"

"Not with Mrs. O'Connell," Natalia said. "She sounds and looks human. Yet there is . . . something. . . . A murmuring around us."

Dawn's pulse jammed. "So you're hearing a voice?"

"Not a clear one." She sat back, concentrating.

Not to be outdone, Kiko jumped in with his own findings while laying the Irish doll on the table.

"I saw a few things," he said, "but nothing that pops out as being meaningful right now. I just know that Eleanor was at her happiest when she made these dolls."

A creaking on the stairs told them that their hostess was on her way back. The group zipped their lips as she appeared with a sweater.

Holding the thick, green gray creation up to her slight body, Mrs. O'Connell said, "Lovely, yes?"

She handed it over to Dawn, who fingered the intricate knit. Cozy. Dawn handed it to Natalia, who inspected it with the same diligence.

Mrs. O'Connell added, "I always told Ellie she missed her calling. Yet she said she was doing more with her real job than entertaining folks with dolls and jumpers."

As Kiko got ahold of the sweater, Dawn picked up a larger photo of Eleanor wearing a business suit and posing in a studio setting, obviously for some kind of professional headshot. "And what exactly did Ellie do, Mrs. O'Connell?"

"She was a senior finance manager for a global technology conglomerate."

They'd already known that, but maybe the elderly woman would reveal something more. . . .

"Ambitious," Mrs. O'Connell continued, "and smart enough to have gotten to such a position at thirty-two. Made a fine salary. Ellie was particularly adept at investing her personal funds, so she lived high, that one."

Eleanor's obituary had also said she'd died tragically about a year ago, drowning in a hot tub in her stately Kensington flat. She'd been intoxicated, and Dawn was anxious to ease into that topic.

Mrs. O'Connell bent near Dawn. "Did you find your friend in any photos?"

"Not so far."

Their hostess looked the snapshots over, then clicked her tongue, weeding out a couple of pictures that had been peeking from under the first layer. "You aren't interested in these."

On top, she held a polished, full-length picture of what seemed like a school photo for a young Eleanor. But along with the same freckles and delicate features, there seemed to be something slightly off-kilter with this particular image: maybe the wider-set eyes, maybe the less sincere smile.

And she was wearing a skirt with a white shirt and a red tie.

Hadn't Kiko mentioned that the girls in Justin's vision had been wearing ties?

"Ellie had a uniform for school?" Dawn asked.

"Oh." Mrs. O'Connell gazed at the photo, her blue eyes going cool. "This is her sister, Briana, not Ellie herself."

Kiko scrambled over Natalia to see the picture. Mrs. O'Connell gave it to him, and he settled back into place, Natalia brushing her lap off to straighten her pantsuit.

When he looked back at Dawn, his eyes sparkled, and she knew, just *knew*, that he'd recognized Briana from the group of possible vamp girls in his Justin vision.

Now, if only Justin hadn't been imagining those fangs he'd seen on the leader of those girls while he was in a drug-induced haze. . . .

A vein throbbed in Dawn's neck, the beat echoing in her head.

Mrs. O'Connell considered the picture of Briana. "The older students at Briana's school don't have to wear uniforms, but evidently she and her friends had their own way of dressing. You know how it can be with a crowd of like-minded girls—the same hairstyles, the same jewelry . . . anything to show you're a part of them."

A group of girls with the same clothes, Dawn thought. And maybe the same kind of teeth, too.

Their hostess went on. "Ellie, herself, did wear a uniform in the early years at the Kings High School near Bath. They had a top-notch modern languages program there. However, the girls' parents sent Briana to Queenshill near St. Albans because of their arts courses. She was quite adept at sculpting in particular, and she begged her parents to consider that in their choice of institutions. Where Ellie and Briana were concerned, that's the best their parents ever did, of course, with all their world hopping and leaving their daughters to boarding at school instead of providing a true home. Now that I think of it, it's no wonder the girls had such wanderlust."

One word in particular stuck in Dawn's mind. *Queenshill.*

If Briana was hanging around with schoolgirl vampires, guess where the team's next appointment should be?

Dawn hated to take advantage of Mrs. O'Connell's clear naïveté and willingness to help, yet it was time to bring out the massive fibbing guns. "You know, we did see Briana's name mentioned in our paperwork, but it was just a first name and we weren't sure how to contact her. Did the sisters share friends? I know they don't seem very close in age, but is there a possibility that our Sara could have contacted *Briana* at any time?"

"We want to look into any connections," Kiko said.

Natalia stayed quiet.

But Mrs. O'Connell was all about sharing. "Oh, Ellie and Briana didn't socialize within the same circles. They didn't ever see each *other*."

Her cheerfulness had clouded over, and she went for her chair, fairly sinking into it. "They were sixteen years apart, those two. When their parents died overseas on a small plane flight during yet another holiday, Ellie became Briana's guardian. Ellie's career, which required constant travel, allowed her to cover Briana's schooling fees, so it was a trade-off in many ways—Briana's education at the price of Ellie's absence. So you would think Briana would show interest in visiting with Ellie when she stopped in London, wouldn't you?"

"You'd think," Dawn said.

"Yet," Mrs. O'Connell added, "neither sister went out of her way to see the other. Strangely, though, when Ellie perished, it was a surprise to hear how Briana carried on."

"And how was that?" Kiko asked.

"Why, she ran off, as if she were more upset about her sister's death than anyone ever guessed she might be."

"She . . . ran off?" *To an Underground?* Dawn thought. "You mean she disappeared? Never heard from again?"

"Yes," their hostess said. "Now, I never saw Briana much myself—she preferred school to the company of an old cousin—but

Ellie always said she was a temperamental child. Very much ruled by her emotions."

Next to Dawn, Natalia gasped. When Dawn looked at her, the new girl was staring at the ceiling.

She was hearing something again.

"There are times . . ." Mrs. O'Connell started to say before stopping herself. "My. Here I am, indeed sounding dotty."

"Not at all," Dawn said. "Say anything that comes to mind. We're very interested."

The elderly woman folded her veined hands in her lap, then smiled, as if seeking reassurance. "If I told you that Briana won't allow me to sleep some nights, would you think me daft?"

Dawn glanced at Natalia, who gave her a look in return. She *was* hearing something again.

Kiko slid off the couch. "Mrs. O'Connell, we don't think you're daft. And, actually . . . I'm going to be honest with you."

Oh, oh—Dawn could see some turbo bullshit headed their way.

"I get 'feelings,' too," Kiko said. "What I mean is that our friend Sara came to me in a dream, and she told us that her passing wasn't peaceful, that she needed help to move on. That's why we traveled over here all the way from the States—because we know she isn't resting easy and we have the resources to see that she does." Kiko paused, *acting!* at its finest. "We would've done anything for Sara. We will do anything."

Mrs. O'Connell had her hand to her chest, sympathy lining every wrinkle.

"We didn't tell you," Kiko added, "because we thought you'd think we were crazy and wouldn't let us in the door."

The elderly woman shook her head. "No, not at all. I understand more than you'll ever know." A faint smile lit over her lips. "I still hear my husband's music. I feel it."

Kiko nodded, and Dawn wondered if he or Natalia could see any telltale lights around Mrs. O'Connell—signs that the Mr. might still be with her.

Dawn gestured to the picture their hostess still held. "What do you mean by saying Briana won't let you sleep some nights? Do you think she's trying to communicate with you?"

"Yes, but . . ." Mrs. O'Connell's voice fell to a whisper. "I hear her when the moon is out and all is quiet. She tells me she has no place to go. No place to settle but here. I'm her closest living relative, you see."

Good God. Were a vampy Briana and her group of fangy buddies wandering over to Mrs. O'Connell's some nights, using preternatural mind games on the sweet old lady?

Why would they do that?

"Mrs. O'Connell," Dawn asked, "do you think Briana is still even alive?"

Her color receded, her skin seeming withered now. "I hired a private investigator when Briana first disappeared. He didn't come up with a thing. Not a thing. So I truly don't know where she might be or in what sort of state."

Kiko looked at Natalia, who shook her head and indicated she wasn't getting anything clear. Then he leaned over her to speak to Dawn.

"Know what we could use? A Ouija board."

At the statement, Mrs. O'Connell's eyes widened, her gaze drifting to Dawn's crucifix necklace. She'd seen it earlier but hadn't exhibited any major reaction until now.

Time to fib a little more. "We've used the Ouija before to get ahold of Sara, but she isn't always available for whatever cosmic reason. Would you mind if we improvised and tried with Briana, if she's around?"

Thing was, it was daylight, not nighttime, when Mrs. O'Connell usually heard her young cousin.

Or was the older woman only open to Briana at night, when a person was at their most vulnerable?

"My, oh, my," the elderly woman said, still considering the Ouija option.

"If you want," Kiko said, "we could attempt contact on our own and you wouldn't have to take part in it. We could record the session for you to listen to later."

"A Ouija board," Mrs. O'Connell said, looking at them as if she was just starting to realize there was more to her guests than she'd first thought. But she did seem very interested. "Would we be inviting trouble?"

Dawn's heartbeat was almost deafening. "If you want, we could get a professional to come in here afterward and cleanse the house."

Since this wasn't Kiko's nor Natalia's area of expertise, Costin would know the right place to contact—someone separate from Limpet and Associates altogether.

Kiko was already around the table and at Mrs. O'Connell's side, holding the arm of her chair. This was a trick of his—seeming all innocent and boyish so he could persuade anyone who had a weakness for kids.

Just another rule.

"Please?" he asked. "It's just that Sara . . ."

He let their fake friend's name linger, and Dawn saw Mrs. O'Connell's soft heart beginning to tear away from her doubts.

"I am curious," she said. "When Briana speaks to me, she makes no sense whatsoever. I thought perhaps it was only my mind playing tricks. . . ."

"You'll know for sure now," Kiko added.

Mrs. O'Connell pursed her lips, then nodded.

After that, everything seemed to speed up: Kiko asked their hostess for something like a small, clear dish that they could use for a planchette, then a piece of cardboard or large, stiff paper for the board itself.

Then, as Mrs. O'Connell collected the items, Kiko motioned Natalia and Dawn into a huddle while he held up a cross, just in case it would ward off . . . well, anything. Since they wouldn't attract any suspicious stares here in private, Dawn and Natalia followed suit.

"Whatever Natalia's been hearing in this room, we need to grill it," he whispered. "Even if it's not Briana. But no matter what happens, we've got to keep being these amateur Sara hunters and nothing more. Don't let down your acts."

Natalia lowered her voice, too. "*Would* we be able to contact a vampire through a board? If Briana is undead, what is the state of her soul?"

Dawn already had an answer. "If this is just about Briana standing outside at night and using her mind to communicate with Mrs. O'Connell, then my guess is that we won't get the girl through the board."

One of Benedikte's memories, which he'd given Dawn when she'd exchanged with him, slid to the forefront of her mind, just as if she'd been the one to experience it.

It was that natural. And disturbing.

"What?" Kiko asked, seeing her expression.

Dawn erased it. "When the Master in Hollywood turned someone, he'd take their souls and store them in vials and imbibe them whenever he needed a picker-upper. That means a vampire's soul actually *does* get surrendered when it separates from the body during the exchange. From Costin's notes, we know that this has been at least one constant in every Underground—the forfeiting of a soul in trade for all the glories of vampirism."

Kiko added, "And if *this* Underground doesn't have a master who likes to keep the souls for himself, maybe Briana's soul is wandering free out there."

Natalia didn't look happy. "And Briana's soul is what might be contacting Mrs. O'Connell."

"Unless," Kiko said, "Briana isn't a part of an Underground and we're dealing with a different set of vampires altogether. Anything goes with this stuff."

Dawn groaned.

But Natalia was acting like a downer for a different reason.

"Might Briana's soul be in a sort of limbo?" the new girl asked.

"Or, if vampires are indeed damned, would we be contacting her someplace else?"

You could've heard a fang drop.

They were talking about Hell, here. Talking about contacting an entity from the charred beyond.

But she'd told herself she'd do anything for Costin.

"Sounds like a part of the job description, all right," she said.

Kiko had come to grips, too. He'd seen too much already in his short life to be afraid. "I'm ready."

Yet Natalia didn't commit, even when Mrs. O'Connell returned with the glass dish and a piece of cardboard that could've been used as a backing for printed artwork.

Thanking her, Dawn took a marker and created an on-the-fly Ouija board by writing "Yes" and "No" in opposite upper corners. Then she positioned a curved line of the letters *A* through *M*, and *N* through *Z* below that. Then came the numbers one through nine, plus a zero at the end of the straight line, and finally the word "Farewell" on the very bottom.

Mrs. O'Connell pulled all but one curtain closed, leaving a lighted crack overlooking her garden, as if that one spot of beauty would be their reminder of brightness.

Then she turned on a stained-glass-shaded lamp that cast muddled colors over the walls.

Kiko took the clear dish and placed the makeshift planchette on the board.

But when Natalia breezed right by him and took a seat at the table in front of the Ouija, Dawn gaped.

Boy, when Costin had said that the new girl was totally disturbed by all those voices, he wasn't kidding. She was their champion, for sure.

"Hey," Kiko said.

"You know I'm the best source for channeling what I've already detected in here," Natalia said, pushing up the sleeves of her wool suit.

Kiko got ready to deny that, but Dawn guided him to his spot on the love seat, bending down to whisper in his ear.

"She's been hearing that murmur all this time. If her channeling doesn't work, then it'll be your turn."

He gave her a defensive look as she went to Natalia's other side and sat.

"You sure you're okay with this?" Dawn asked.

Blowing out a breath, Natalia placed her fingers on the board, as if to greet it. "I believe with all my heart that we're doing this for rightful reasons. It will work."

She didn't say she was doing this for Kate, but Dawn knew it all the same.

"Does it begin now?" Mrs. O'Connell asked. Her cheeks were flushed even beyond the regular pink she'd sported before.

Dawn gave their hostess a thumbs-up as Natalia moved her fingertips to the glass planchette, which rested between "Yes" and "No."

Then the group slipped into a silence that was diluted only by the humming air and the protesting creaks from an old house.

Briana, Dawn thought, *come out, come out, wherever you are.*

"Briana," Natalia said, echoing Dawn. But her voice was soothing instead of challenging. "We would like to talk with you, if you please."

They waited, and nothing happened except for the creaks, the wood-beam groans, the taut anticipation of stepping into a dark place.

At the lack of response, Kiko sighed, and Dawn resisted the urge to reach over and twist his ear.

Then Mrs. O'Connell spoke.

"Briana?"

The planchette jerked under Natalia's fingertips, then began to circle the board with such violence that one of the new girl's hands fell from the glass. She caught up with it.

"Is this Briana?" Natalia asked, her accent thicker than usual, maybe because of barely contained fear.

The planchette zigged to the upper left of the board.

YES.

Then it began circling again.

"Welcome, Briana," Natalia said, clearly making an attempt to level out her emotions. "Thank you for joining us."

Mrs. O'Connell was scanning the room, as if expecting to see her younger cousin. Her stiff posture belied the fact that she'd been hoping Briana would stay away.

The planchette was going nuts—it landed on the letter *T*, then *W*.

"What is she telling us?" Mrs. O'Connell asked, her lilt ragged.

The planchette continued its course, stopping on *A*.

Then *T*.

The elderly woman pressed a hand to her opened mouth, then stood. "Perhaps I'll wait in the yard."

Dawn got up, just to lend an arm, but Mrs. O'Connell waved her off as they walked toward the entryway.

"Sometimes," Dawn said, "they get dirty mouths. If it's Briana, she might be trying to scare us, just like she probably tries to scare *you* at night, knowing you're alone in the dark."

"I'm hardly surprised at such language. Young people use that word quite frequently. And I believe Briana might be the type to employ it, especially if she believes I could have done more to prevent her death."

If the girl was dead, Dawn thought. "Is there anything you want us to ask her or tell her?"

"Yes, dear." Their hostess reached out to take Dawn's hand in hers. "If you would, please tell her to leave an old woman in peace."

And, with that, she patted Dawn's hand and wandered toward the rear of the house.

After watching the lady leave, Dawn headed back to the proceedings. Somewhere, she heard a door close and, minutes later, she could see through the crack in the curtain that Mrs. O'Connell had entered her happy garden.

Even though the flower petals around her stayed still, her cottoned hair fluttered, so Dawn knew that the Friends were surrounding Mrs. O'Connell and offering invisible, jasmine-scented solace.

As she went back to her seat, she wondered if the spirits knew just how bad Briana might be, and that's why they were leaving the girl to the team. Once, before becoming a Friend herself, Breisi had told Dawn how spirits tended to "travel in their own realms," so maybe they knew Briana was here, but they weren't able to do much more than the team itself could do.

Or maybe the team could even command Briana to talk whereas the Friends couldn't. Heck, the Friends, themselves, could be ordered around by the team.

Dawn sat down to the tune of the dish scraping circles over the cardboard. "What happened while I was gone?"

"More cussing," Kiko said. "Briana's got a bunch of smut synonyms."

Well then, maybe they could do some communicating.

Dawn focused on the board. "Briana, are you, at this time, a soul that was cast out during a vampire birth exchange?"

The planchette picked up speed, then flew over the letters.

I—W—A—N—T—B—L—O—O—D—A—G—A—I—N—

"Good," Natalia said, "but you didn't quite answer."

You go, Nat, Dawn thought.

Then Briana lashed back.

D—A—W—N—I—S—D—A—R—K—

Dawn's sight went black for a shocked moment—a moment of truth?

She sucked in a breath. And when her vision came back, it seemed to be tinted by red rage.

"She's screwing around," she said between her teeth.

"*Briana's* screwing around?" Kiko asked, out of patience.

He got up, then returned with his scarf that Mrs. O'Connell had hung with their coats on the entry rack.

And when he wrapped it around Natalia's head, covering her eyes, the plachette spiraled out from under Natalia's fingertips as she reared back to pull the scarf off.

"What're you doing?" Dawn asked.

"Briana hasn't told us anything *Natalia* couldn't say herself."

He came back around the couch, obviously intending to take over the board.

"Kiko—" Dawn said.

But Natalia interrupted. "It's no matter."

As she calmly straightened her new blindfold, Dawn asked, "What're you talking about?"

"I'm not manipulating the planchette," she said. "And Briana is eager to start again. I hear her murmurs, and they're louder. She very much wishes to talk."

When Natalia felt around the board, determined to locate that planchette again, Dawn refrained from helping her. Kiko had called her out, and she was proving that she wasn't any gypsy con artist.

Natalia found the planchette and took up position again, but what she didn't know was that Kiko had very, very quietly turned the board upside down.

As he sat, resting his chin in a palm and clearly expecting to expose her, the planchette started to swirl again.

"Briana?" Natalia asked.

The dish swerved down to the "Yes" in its new location at the right-hand bottom of the board.

Dawn did a mental "Yessssss." Unless Natalia had somehow known that Kiko had turned the board, this was for real.

Kiko even shrugged. For now.

"Briana," Natalia continued, "answer truthfully. Are you, or have you ever been, a vampire?"

The lamp in the corner of the room flickered, and the planchette took up even more speed as it spelled out two words.

W—I—C—K—E—D—

Natalia could hardly keep up, her body jerking with the ferocity of the planchette.

The light in the corner sizzled, then began to strobe—on, off, on, off.

M—A—S—T—E—R—

Then the lamp went out, and Natalia passed out, smacking her head on the table.

SIXTEEN

THE BLACK SPOT

Just think," Kiko said as they sat at a table in the Hushed Woman pub. "Natalia might be the only member of a team to get her first injury during an interview and not a brawl."

The new girl didn't look amused while holding an ice pack from Mrs. O'Connell's freezer against her forehead, so Dawn pinched Kiko under the table before they could get into a squabbling match.

But he was so pumped about their new leads that he didn't seem to mind.

Their server arrived to drop off beverages, and Dawn dumped a sugar cube and then some cream into her cuppa tea. She was starting to like the stuff.

The pub, itself, was nearly as silent as "the hushed woman" holding a finger to her lips on the sign outside. It seemed to have once been an old house that'd been separated into different dining areas, and the team had chosen a table in a sub-street-level room, which was decorated like a village cottage with an antique butter churn, a spinning wheel, and a rickety hutch with china balancing on the shelves. Something rich—probably the aroma of chestnuts—lent a thickness to the atmosphere. Or maybe it was just the amber lighting.

Whatever it was, Dawn had chosen a seat against the wall.

Once their server disappeared around the corner to climb back upstairs, the team got comfortable.

"Just you wait until real trouble comes down," Kiko said to Natalia, who was sipping her own tea. "If you black out during a fight, you're dust."

Dawn defended her. "She just got overstressed. Lay off."

"No way," Kiko said. "A peppy interview is nothin' compared to what we've got in store."

"What do you mean, nothin'?" Dawn took care to talk in their "normal code." "Bridget O'Connell's going to get her house cleaned of anything Briana might've left behind. Even though she doesn't know half of what Briana said to us, I don't want that girl hanging around there anymore."

Natalia set down her cup. "Briana *was* rather upset."

"Upset?" Kiko asked. "Briana . . . or whoever we talked to . . . seems to me like one of those *people* that likes to screw around with whoever gets in touch with them."

"You think," Dawn said, "that we were talking to a different . . . *person* . . . who was just toying with us?"

"No," Natalia said, getting both of their attention.

"I believe," she continued, "it was Briana, and she had even more to say. I feel as if she were cut off before she finished her last comment."

Kiko stopped his teacup at his lips. "Who cut her off then? Was 'someone' around who didn't want her to talk?"

"I can't be sure." Natalia rested the ice bag on the rough wooden table, revealing the tender bump near her hairline. "There's also a chance she might have been so upset that she abruptly left us because she couldn't tolerate the strain. Mrs. O'Connell did say her cousin was quite emotional."

"Whatever it is," Kiko said, "I doubt we'll ever know."

"What do you mean?"

"I mean you need to get used to not knowing every answer, Narda. And on the same note, don't think that the most important thing is getting Kate Lansing's mystery tucked away nice and neat. The boss has his agenda, and if it leads away from Kate, that's where we'll go."

The new girl frowned while Kiko went back to his tea.

Dawn stirred hers. Natalia would see that using anyone and everyone—dead or not—got them that much closer to justice.

The good of the many outweighed the good of the few. . . .

As she kept stirring, she watched her teammates. And when she noticed Kiko's gaze lingering on the new girl an instant too long, Dawn *hmmm*ed.

But team dynamics took a distant second to sorting out what'd happened back at Mrs. O'Connell's.

With one hand, she dug around in her jacket, which was hanging on the back of the chair, then came up with her pen and notebook. She turned to a page where she'd written down key phrases after the Ouija had gone inactive, then shielded it with her cupped hand.

Her gaze rested on the first disturbing phrase.

WICKED MASTER.

To her, the inclusion of "master" made the message pretty straightforward, but Kiko had started working with anagrams, so she and Natalia had rearranged some letters, too.

But none of them had come up with anything significant, and Dawn hadn't seen the point in making up new words when they had two perfectly good ones anyway. She just wished that the other phrase Briana had tossed out—DAWN IS DARK—wasn't as clear.

Why the hell had the spirit spelled it out? Because that's what

Briana had sensed and it'd struck her so much that she'd been forced to comment?

Dawn folded the notebook paper over that second batch of words, leaving only the WICKED MASTER part visible.

There. Better. Now she could actually think.

And the questions came—too many of them . . . not enough of them.

Had they misunderstood Briana? Had she actually been trying to warn Natalia about the ruler of her Underground because she'd perceived the new girl to be a sympathetic person who could right some wrongs?

Because maybe, just maybe, Briana had been an unwilling vampire. Even if the L.A. Underground had been careful about drinking from and recruiting those who gave permission, Costin had told the team before that this hadn't always been the case with every single community he'd faced and vanquished.

But the most probable scenario hit Dawn again, just as it'd been hitting her all afternoon: maybe Briana had been trying to scare them away from an Underground.

Dawn wouldn't put *that* past a master—assigning one of his underlings to create mischief and confusion in any way possible. In her experience, vampires used any strategy to survive. . . .

Her train of thought was interrupted by their server, who brought the meals they'd ordered: a "nutloaf," which used chestnuts to give texture to an alternative meatloaf, for Dawn, and fish and chips for both Natalia and Kiko.

The two of them looked at their identical dishes as the server left, but they didn't comment as they stuck their forks into the fried cod. Their silverware clanked against the plates in the otherwise empty room.

Dawn moved around in her seat. Kiko noticed.

"I can see you doing the Impatience Hustle," he said. "You want to get to the school, but even the Friends haven't found diddly there yet."

They'd already sent a squad to Queenshill, but that didn't lessen her restlessness. "Maybe every girl who dresses in Briana's uniform is off campus right now, so that's why our Friends aren't finding them. Those girls could've gone 'you know where' straight after class."

Underground.

She chewed on her nutloaf, barely tasting it. When they'd called the school right after the Ouija session, they'd been too late to make a tour appointment for the day. Still, Dawn had pretended to be interested in sending a family member to Queenshill, an institution that worked off of private funding, so the administration had been happy to accommodate a tour tomorrow. While on campus, the team hoped to locate Kiko's vision girls so Natalia could "hear" if they were vampires.

God, they seemed to finally be getting somewhere. Dawn was going to freakin' explode if this was all another dead end.

Kiko laughed evilly. "Wouldn't it be fun for us to go to the school a little earlier?"

"Oh, no," Natalia said. "Assure me we won't be risking the rancor of the staff by invading the property after hours. If they caught us trespassing, they would hardly be open to giving us a tour and allowing us to interact with the population."

Eating, Dawn held up her hand to Natalia, letting her know that they weren't about to blow this opportunity by Nancy Drewing around in the dark. They needed to talk to people first, and *then* they could snoop.

Patience, she told herself. She had to have it, no matter how much she wanted to sneak onto that campus tonight.

"Hey, it was just a comment," Kiko said to Natalia. "Do you really think I'd waste all my fine work just for a romp on a campus that we can explore tomorrow?"

"*Your* work," Natalia repeated.

Kiko grinned, and Dawn knew that he wasn't being an egomaniac so much as he was being a maniac who enjoyed goading the new girl.

Natalia set down her fork. "Haven't you realized yet that neither of our visions would have yielded anything timely without the other? That if I hadn't led us to Mrs. O'Connell's, you wouldn't have identified Briana in a picture there?"

He didn't have much to say to that, so he took a bite of french fry. Or chip. Whatever the Brits wanted to call it.

At Kiko's lack of response, Natalia went back to eating, too, probably thinking this was over. If only.

But while Dawn waited for the lull to pass, she wondered if Costin had sensed that in order to be at full force again, Kiko would need another half.

He washed down his food with tea, and when he placed the cup back in its saucer a little too slowly, Dawn knew her dalliance in the fields of tranquillity was about to end.

She put her notebook back in her jacket pocket.

"Listen, Narda," Kiko said, "if we're going to start a pissing contest here, I should warn you that I can shoot some long and powerful yellow."

The new girl pursed her lips, as if working out the slang.

Then she turned to Dawn. "Pissing contest?"

Dawn explained: competition of egos. The male belief that everyone wanted to have a penis. Et cetera, et cetera.

Meanwhile, Kiko was busy raising his all-powerful arguing finger, gearing up for a knock down drag out. But Natalia raised hers, too, robbing him of speech because he was obviously thinking she was making fun of him when she probably wasn't.

Dawn wondered if she should just propose a finger-wrestling contest to give them something physical to work out.

"I can tolerate an impressive amount of hardship," Natalia said. "I was raised in a strict household where any deviation from my parents' law—such as innocently remarking upon a voice I might hear—was met with punishment. I learned to keep my tongue, Mr. Kiko, but I know also when to use it.

"I was hired for good reason," she continued, hushing her

voice. "But imagine my surprise when on my first night, I found myself staring at bones and a head. Imagine how my dedication was tested when I saw a deceased person in a freezer. And, frankly, I have learned more than I ever wished to know about 'clients.' Yet most trying of all, I have withstood your arrogance and . . . pissing contests." Her voice went back to regular volume. "All I ask is you recognize that if we don't work together, you and I, we might not accomplish anything at all."

And, with that, she lowered her finger, picked up her ice bag with one hand and her fork with the other, then jammed the utensil into her fish.

Footsteps on the floor above took the place of talk as Dawn battled an impressed smile while chowing down on nutloaf.

Then Kiko started to chuckle.

"Okay," he said, going back to his meal. "Fair enough."

Natalia put the ice bag to her head, like she was hungover.

But Kiko got a second wind. Just not in the way Dawn expected.

"The meds," he said, never looking up from his meal. "They affect my attitude. I want them bad, and it grates on me."

Dawn dabbed her mouth with a napkin, trying to find a referee-like way to say this. "It's not just the pills, Kik. You were kind of cranky when I met you."

"But I warmed up," he said, finally making eye contact.

She smiled at him, her throat closing. "Yes, you did."

As Kiko went on to devour his peas, a draft entered the room, accompanying a man and a woman. They'd emerged from what looked to be a sub-street-level entrance from the other side of the hill on which the building rested. Both patrons wore leather jackets, and they shed them after they claimed a table.

Natalia didn't mark their presence. That meant they weren't emanating vampy hollow vibes.

"Kiko," she asked, testing the waters, "why are you still on this medication?"

Dawn decided to save him the explanation. "Remember when I told you about the 'client' who got rough and broke Kik's back?"

Across the room, the two new customers gave Dawn a casual look, then launched into a murmuring conversation while they scanned their menus.

"As you can imagine," Kiko said, "my back hurt, so I took pills for the pain. But I *kept* taking them. Then I started realizing there might be more to it."

"You wished to numb more than your body?" Natalia asked.

"Who wouldn't in this job?" Kiko swigged his tea. "But it wasn't necessarily because of what we deal with. I love what I do. It gives me a fulfillment that I wasn't finding in acting—even though I would've given my eyeteeth for a good part."

Dawn interjected, "You might've found some satisfaction as a lawyer." She turned to Natalia. "Before Kik graduated from high school, he wanted to fight the bad guys with paper and words instead of . . . well, what we use now."

Natalia seemed to understand that Dawn was referring to the gadgets and weapons Breisi dreamed up.

"And who doesn't want to be Batman?" Kiko added. "Anyway, when I couldn't do this job so well anymore, I used the drugs like a blanket—something to hide under while the sounds and sights were muffled around me. But that blanket felt good when it was on. When it was off? Not so good. So I kept going under it."

Dawn didn't mention her latest concern: that Kiko had found a different colored blanket with his increasing reliance on the Friends' lulling him.

Later. They'd deal later.

Natalia had been listening intently, just as she always did. Dawn didn't know if the new girl would be able to physically fight vamps worth crap, but her gift seemed to be in something not many other people had mastered in life.

"I cannot imagine," Natalia said, "how anyone could remain

unaffected by this job. Perhaps this was a reason the boss switched employees in the past?"

"What do you mean?" Dawn asked.

Kiko paused midchew.

Natalia seemed surprised that they hadn't thought of this.

"Perhaps the boss saw early employees break mentally," she said. "He could have learned to retire the members before they . . ." She made an exploding motion near her head.

Dawn and Kiko just locked gazes. It'd taken a near stranger to see it, maybe because Natalia had been the first intimate member to get a good look at what an Underground hunt had done to a team that was entering an unprecedented Round Two.

But had they already crossed lines and maybe even gone over edges that previous team members had avoided . . . ?

Acrid smoke drifted over to their table, and Dawn cuffed it away from her face.

The guy across the room had lit up a cigarette.

Natalia didn't seem to care, but Kiko muttered, "I thought there was no smoking in pubs anymore."

"There's not," Dawn said, eating the last tasteless bites of her meal. With what Natalia had just pointed out, she only wanted to get out of here.

Yet as the smoke kept coming, she got frustrated—and maybe it wasn't even just because of the stench. Sure, she'd spent a lot of effort keeping healthy for stunt work and now for fighting, but . . .

She just wanted to leave.

Natalia wasn't in as much of a hurry. She was probably used to smoke overseas, where it seemed to be more of a regularity than in California.

Irritated, Dawn waved more smoke away. And, as one second passed, then another, it started to take the very real form of everything else that had been invading her this past year.

Benedikte. Eva. Frank. Costin.

Instead of asking the man across the room to put out his ciggie—Dawn was afraid of what she might do if he said no—her frustration grew.

And that frustration built like more blocks teetering on a crooked pile.

She thought about Kate's head . . . the possibility of team insanity . . . the fact that Costin refused to talk about Jonah taking over his body last night, as if he was such a he-man that it mortified him more than anything—

Fury, always so close to the surface, cold and rumbling, gathered in the center of her chest. It rolled, white sharp, nicking her, growing, pushing, pushing—

As the energy rushed out of her, Dawn pictured the scapegoat smoker.

Then, just like she was watching a fuzzy dream, she saw his hand jerk up to his mouth and yank the cigarette away, then crush it to the table where he smooshed it into the wood.

"Yessss," she heard Kiko say.

His voice tweaked her, but before she fully realized she was doing more than just fantasizing, the rage took her over, reddening her gaze.

Benedikte. Costin. Both liars, both users—

Boom—another pulse of energy joined the first, and in her mind, she saw the smoker get yanked out of his chair by her mental grip, felt her somehow forcing his arm up and down, up and down, in a parody of a person lifting his hand to put a cigarette into his mouth then take it out.

She watched the film in her mind's eye, fascinated. Relieved, because she wasn't being yanked around anymore. Someone else was.

In the back of her consciousness, she heard a chair crash to the ground, a woman yell.

Felt hands shaking her, shaking her, then—

Smack!

Dawn sucked in a breath, gaze clearing on the sight of Natalia, who was drawing back her hand as if horrified at what she'd done.

Cheek stinging, Dawn glanced across the room to where the man had fallen to the ground, shaken up, his girlfriend bending down to him and asking what had happened. She was so afraid for her partner that she didn't seem to have witnessed the slap across the room.

My God. My *God*.

Head fuzzy, Dawn stood, grabbing her jacket and reaching into a pocket for money to settle the bill. After she tossed it on the table, she glanced at Kiko, who was surveying her with a mixture of awe and fright.

Unable to endure either, she looked to Natalia.

"Thank you," she said, the words too calm, too level.

The new girl stayed quiet, and Dawn backed away from the table, then turned around to see the smoker getting to his feet.

She should apologize. But . . .

What could she possibly tell him? *Don't wig out, but that was just me losing it. Sorry.*

Instead, she climbed the stairs, intending to catch their server in order to pay for the smoker's meal, too.

And with every step she took, she packed in the rage so it couldn't possibly get out again. Forced it lower, where it kept stretching like a dark thing that'd just fully woken up from a long, hard nap.

SEVENTEEN

LONDON BABYLON

The Same Night

WHEN the girls had gathered to walk to class this morning, Blanche had not emerged from her room to join them.

When they'd checked her bed, they'd found it empty, the room stripped, save for some padded blue hangers left in the wardrobe and a computer-printed note.

I've been taken out of school. Since I was woken up while the rest of you were resting, there was no time to say my farewells. But here I go to Bali to be with my parents! It's the last scenario I ever expected, yet who knows how long this holiday will last before they grow tired of me. Perhaps we'll return to London soon. Until then, expect e-mails.

And then a smiley face below her name.

It didn't seem fair, with Blanche leaving them so quickly and without even a personal farewell. So Della had spent the school day attempting to mind-contact her, yet to no avail. She should've known her friend would be far out of range.

But why had Blanche's parents taken her out of school now,

during this final year? It made as little sense as when Sharon's parents had taken *her* away.

All day Della had wondered . . . and wondered.

And she had kept wondering while trying not to be distracted by Polly and Noreen scratch wrestling in the underground common room, where the group had fled immediately after completing their school duties.

The weaker girl didn't have a chance with the more athletic one's quickness and strength during the swiping. Hence, three matches into it, Noreen was coated with abrasions she wouldn't heal until Polly counted them up, then added them to her ongoing tally.

It seemed to Della that the two girls were taking out their frustration on each other during this playtime. They missed Blanche, yet they felt betrayed since they'd been such a family themselves for over a year now, banded together after being so set aside. Knowing that Blanche seemed so happy to be claimed by her absentee mum and dad hurt all of them.

Well, almost all.

Violet was gleefully cheering Polly on, swinging her legs on her divan, acting just as unconcerned about Blanche as she had when Briana and Sharon had left.

Casting her a disgusted glance, Della continued pacing the fringes of the room.

It was only later, when Wolfie arrived to fetch them to the main Underground as he'd promised, that she realized she'd forgotten about the treat.

Within an instant, he'd noticed that Della, more than any other, was affected by Blanche's departure.

"You miss her," he said, loitering near the beads of the tunnel entrance. "Believe me, I feel the same, but her parents wanted her, Della."

She didn't wish to cause a disturbance, yet . . . "How could you let Blanche go so easily, Wolife? She wanted to be a part of the main Underground, just as much as the rest of us. She might have told her parents to rot if she'd seen it."

Then she added silently, *How could you let* any *of us go?*

"My sweet girl," he said, "it breaks my heart to see any of you leave. And I agree—if she had witnessed her future home, she might have stayed. You'll find that *everyone* stays once they get there. It's so wonderful that not even a parent can drag a daughter away. However, Blanche was no doubt blinded by the fact that her parents expressed interest in her."

Wolfie crooked his finger for Della to come away from the outskirts and join the rest of them. She inched forward.

"After Blanche gets her fill of her parents," he added, "she might want to return for an even better life with her friends, so don't despair, Della. I, too, very much wish she could come back to us one day."

For a naked instant, Wolfie's gaze showed more than his constant good cheer or hunger. There was . . . sadness?

Yet when Violet slid off the divan, clearly more excited about their Underground excursion than the hope that Blanche might return someday, he assumed his usual Wolfie expression once again—a master, not the mastered.

"*We*'re still here," Violet said to him. "Tell *us* about the Underground. Please?"

He flicked a glance over the girl, and she smiled at him.

"Tonight is all about discovery, my dear," he said. "You shall see for yourself soon."

Violet pouted, and he seemed to enjoy that, as always.

"Ah, how proud I am of this lovely class of girls," he said, gifting them each with a grin. "To the world outside, Queenshill has a reputation for developing women who are fit to guide the lower echelon, whether it's in business or social endeavors. But by being selected for this particular, oh-so-secret class, you and your friends have become *vampires* who will lead in surface feedings and in Underground life. All your instruction will indeed be useful."

Overjoyed, Violet clasped her hands. "We'll be like you, Wolfie? Leading nightcrawls?"

"If you wish. You're our brightest and best in the Underground, and although we are equal in that we're one big happy family, everyone adores the Queenshill girls."

Long-living princesses, Della thought, captured by the notion. In real life, she would've never got the chance to feel like one.

Still, she was worried about her friend, out there in the world, all alone now. "Blanche . . . How will she feed without you and us?"

The other girls were surprised that Della, out of all of them, was asking so many questions of Wolfie.

Yet he was pleased with her emergence from the edge of the room. "I've taught you girls quite well, so she'll be able to hide her true self even as she mingles with humans. Blanche will do fine on her own."

Della wouldn't accept that. "We were a group. She'll be lonely."

"Perhaps she'll find other vampires to associate with," he said. "Girls who must leave us often do find others out of necessity. You know from Sharon's e-mails that she identified another group, and perhaps this is the reason she doesn't contact us anymore. Trust that she will be safe for the rest of her nights."

He was winning Polly and Noreen over—Della could see it in the way they tilted their heads at him.

"Della, I know the real reason for your sorrows," Wolfie said, his voice a caress. "The bottom line is that you cannot believe Blanche or Sharon or even Briana broke their loyalty to you."

She held back tears. Wolfie knew how each girl in the group pretended not to treasure the occasional holiday phone contact their parents deigned to make. How the girls told each other that they would be friends through it all and that they didn't need anyone but their new family. How, by leaving, the other three had betrayed that bond.

He always knew.

"If I suggested," he said, "that this is the reason Blanche chose not to awaken you this morning before she left, would that help? Perhaps she didn't wish to see your faces as she betrayed you, and I'm certain Briana also didn't wish to endure that before she ran off."

Della was beginning to understand. At least Sharon had said good-bye before she'd gone.

He leaned back against the wall, his long, wild hair brambled over the rock. "Think of it this way. If your parents came back for *you*, would you turn down the chance to be with them again? I imagine Blanche is ecstatic at this moment. You wouldn't deny her that because you believe she should have stayed here. That is not the act of a true friend."

At the impossible thought of her parents calling the office to ask that she be sent to them, Della's chest balled into itself. All she'd wanted was a minute of attention from them.

But to have hours? Weeks?

Della felt the same wistful reverberations from Noreen and Polly . . . and even Violet.

Wolfie rose, all grace and lean muscle, but Della thought she detected a flash of that sadness in his eyes again.

He missed Blanche, his recent favorite, just as much as Della, Polly, and Noreen did.

Then, as if he couldn't stand even a second of unhappiness, he clapped his hands, then rubbed them, back to being the one who always turned a bad situation into good.

After so many centuries, he'd once told them, you must allow water to flow under all bridges. That was a reason he didn't like to be the one to punish them.

He went to the beads. "In spite of it all, I still have *you*, my darlings."

Violet clamored to be first out. "Will we stay with you in the Underground tonight? After all, it is a special occasion."

"No, I must have you back just before classes begin tomor-row."

Violet pouted.

Yet with dashing flair, he turned away from her and parted the beads for the rest of them.

And, for the first time since Blanche had left, Della allowed her-self a nudge of excitement.

Maybe someday Blanche truly might join us, she thought, al-lowing the others to hear.

Noreen and Polly sent Della agreeable yet tentative smiles while Violet darted past them, saying, "Can't you even offer a smidge of what to expect, Wolfie? Please, please, please?"

"Such enthusiasm," he teased, allowing Polly, then Noreen, then Della through the beads before letting them slap back to place. Then he led the group through the tunnel. "Perhaps I shouldn't have raised your hopes about this old, stuffy place. I do hope there won't be any postvisit comments about how decrepit your Wolfie is."

In spite of his jesting, they all knew he *was* terribly ancient, and it'd actually been just over a century ago that his own master had instructed him to build an Underground. Yet even as the other blood brothers separated and grew more isolated as they constructed their own communities, Wolfie had been too enamored of using Thomas Gatenby's inheritance while exploring the world to settle down so soon. Hence, like a stubborn playboy, he had only committed to his own Underground in the nineteen thirties, long after Queenshill had been established.

The part of the story that always interested Della the most whenever Wolfie told it concerned those other blood brothers—the master vampires who'd exchanged at the same time as he. Wolfie had told the girls about the hideous rumors from other traveling brothers—more carefree creatures such as he—who had not yet built their own communities way back when.

Some masters, they had told Wolfie, were taking over existing

Undergrounds. This was the reason *they* had bided their time in creating their own.

The news had been no shock, Wolfie had told the girls. The blood brothers had been raised and trained as warriors, and this habit had obviously carried over into vampire life, although when the dragon awakened . . .

Wolfie always trailed off ominously here, making the girls squirm because they could guess there would be awful consequences for the disobedient blood brothers.

When the story continued, Wolfie would always mention how he and his companion had been significantly drawn to London for years, and they had settled here only after he'd sensed the aggressive vibrations from another blood brother depart the area. During one of his roams about town, he had even discovered the remains of a series of burned-out subterranean rooms that had been situated in deserted construction areas for the tube.

Remains from the master who had left London?

Wolfie believed so, yet he had still set down roots in this city with such wonderfully open parks, high living, and mystical anchorings. And even though he ruled an Underground, he'd vowed never to hide down below. After all, he hadn't sensed another master since finding evidence of the departed one.

Yet, most importantly, he had no doubts that this Underground was the strongest of them all, and this was the reason other masters had no doubt stayed away.

Even so, Della couldn't help but recall what she'd accidentally heard in Wolfie's mind last night.

And what if another blood brother is . . . ?

Nearby?

As they arrived at the surface door, she told herself that if a master such as Wolfie wasn't visibly concerned about the possibility, she, the lowest of the low, certainly shouldn't be.

Wolfie made a show of listening for vibrations above, then he winked at them as he crouched, then zinged up to the door and blasted through it, springing into the open.

For a beautiful moment, he was suspended against a brittle night sky until he landed, then hunched over the opening to watch the girls follow.

Beginning with Violet, each of them imitated his exit, bouncing upward, then thudding to the crunchy leaves.

Once Della emerged, she immediately helped Noreen chain the door and cover it with dead leaves just before Wolfie whispered, "Follow me," and gave a howl as he zoomed into the darkness and through the thick, scraggly woods so far from the school.

Pulse spiking, Della and the rest leaped to a gallop, falling into his very steps as they bounded over grass and hills and railway tracks, streaking through the moonlight and leaving only a blur for any human eye that might catch their progress.

Della was never happier. Running in her humanlike form. Wind in her hair. Away from her old life and toward the new.

They shot up more hills, then through branches that grabbed for their hair and clothing but couldn't hold on because they were moving so fast and—

They sensed that Wolfie had stopped at the cusp of a hill, and they did, as well, halting in front of a grass-camouflaged door. They panted softly as he motioned to the entrance, causing it to yawn open in the flowing rise.

"In you go," he said.

Violet, Polly, Noreen, then Della hopped down into a pitch-dark gape, so blinding that Della's heightened gaze had to adjust once she landed in a crouch on the dirt.

Wolfie shut the door behind them, and Della's chest beat with a tattoo that linked with that of her friends'.

But, as she began to see vague shapes in the tunnel, she realized the thuds consisted of more than *their* pulses.

There were . . . drumbeats.

Other bodies punching out a common rhythm.

Wolfie's teeth gleamed into a smile in the dark, and he walked off, leading them down a dank tunnel, which gradually became a brick corridor of arched walls that moaned with captured wind.

"This is my favorite part of teaching," he said as the pounding got louder, bouncing round in all their chests. "I always love to see the looks on the classes' faces when they catch first sight."

Noreen clasped Della's hand. Polly did the same on Della's other side.

But Violet? She was right next to Wolfie as the darkness grew to dimness, as the thumping grew to banging.

Where are we? Violet mind-asked him.

He glanced down at her, hardly seeming surprised that she had left the group behind. *Highgate, just off North Road. Highwaymen used to employ these tunnels for smuggling loot, and when I found them, I couldn't resist. I blocked some of the known ones off, then all it took from that point was a touch more digging and decoration.*

But, as you dears know, I had help.

They halted several meters away from what looked to be a belling banner that covered an entrance. The colors reminded Della of a flag waving over a castle, yet that made sense, seeing as Wolfie had spent his existence in and out of castles and palaces and even the woods where peasants used to hunt predators.

He taunted them, his eyes searing through the dark. *On second consideration, perhaps another night would be a better time for your introduction. . . .*

"Wolfie!" they yelled over the drums, needing to finally partake of the treat they'd been promised for so long.

His laugh tore through them as he turned round and leaped toward the banner, then whipped it aside to welcome them to their future, their home upon finishing school. . . .

They all ran to him, peeking in and sucking in a breath at the cavernous, raucous seventeenth-century inn, with rough-pine drinking bars, overturned tables, and bone-spiked chandeliers.

But they could barely see the furnishings through the throng of girls, the powdered, sugared scent of their clothing taking the place of the ale and smoke that should've seeped past the doorway.

There were girls sporting golden half masks that hid their identity as they tossed back their hair and laughed.

Girls wearing dresses from all eras while they stood on wooden chairs and tore at each other's clothing as if they were the stepsisters in a Cinderella story.

Girls sitting on the floor and beating large drums like overbearing pulses. Girls climbing on the upstairs railings. Girls lying on the bar and drinking the blood spilling from the golden taps.

Senses blooming with all the yelling and carousing, Della longed to see their faces. A clinging hope in the back of her mind made her wonder if, perhaps, she would find Briana, Sharon, and Blanche here, where they had been told by a wickedly plotting Wolfie to reveal no secrets until Della and the rest had been introduced to the real Underground. . . .

But that was ludicrous. Wolfie would never go that far.

So she went on to see if she might recognize former students from previous classes. The group had never been told the identities of earlier Queenshill vampires, so she was dreadfully curious.

All they knew was that every two years, girls like them—of proper European stock, of affluence—were turned, then trained to recruit for the main Underground. Then they were sent here, where they could go to the surface to feed at will, or even to attend another school under another name, as long as they shielded and remained alert for nosy humans.

Della clutched Noreen's and Polly's hands, and they clutched back, taking in the vivacious army Wolfie had been instructed to form so that, one day, his master could rise, gather all the Undergrounds, and dominate the world.

An army of scratching, running, singing, laughing, drinking masked Violets, Pollys, and Noreens, and Blanches, and . . .

And probably even Dellas.

But there were also the girls who had been recruited—the ones who didn't quite have the polish of any Queenshill girl.

Kates. Disaffected girls, runaways, bad daughters who took care to remain missing from wherever they had originally come from. Once accepted by the recruiters, they had all exchanged in a ceremony such as the one Della had undergone with her own classmates.

As Wolfie said, they had all become one, big, happy family.

Even so, Della keenly remembered the raw initiation into it—the blood coming out of her, into her, her soul ripping out of her core to go . . .

Where? Was it roaming about, as free as Wolfie had promised?

Or had it gone to the other place—the inferno that was hinted at in the eyes of the cat who kept watch over the girls?

When Wolfie motioned them farther into the chaos, Della was reminded of the very reason she had welcomed the exchange: as long as she lived—and it would be a long, long time, maybe even forever if she could manage—she would be a part of a home, no matter where her soul might be.

A low, cracking scream claimed Della's attention, and she glanced across the room to where a teen boy ran from a girl who was moving in human-time motion, toying with him instead of pouncing vampire quick. He yelled again when she batted him to the floor.

Then he scrambled back up, darting for a table. She bounded into the air, landing on him, then licked him from bare chest to face.

Polly's mind-voice validated what Della was thinking.

Looks as if the girls bring mice down here to play.

Noreen added, *Wolfie would've eaten him right and proper aboveground.*

All of them squeezed hands, excited, their pulses stabbing.

Near Wolfie, Violet was greedily eyeing the boy as he wiggled out from under the attacking girl. He stumbled up the stairs as the vampire alternately snatched at him and laughed.

Wolfie, in turn, was watching his class, his eyes alight. *They're having a masque in your honor. A good soiree will relieve all kinds of pressure from the drudgeries of life.*

One girl dressed in a primal, fringed ensemble and wearing a gilded fawn's mask pranced by Wolfie, touching his hair, just as if he truly were a rock star. And since he loved to brag that he was quite storied, Della thought that, in the eyes of all these eternal girls, he really might be a leather god.

Right behind the fawn, another female, this one in what looked to be a Spanish gown with the full mask of a panther, followed in hot pursuit.

As she passed Wolfie, she whipped off her facial covering to reveal the hairless cat-wolf appearance they had all earned during the exchange.

She barked lightly at her master in greeting, then masked herself again and pursued the fawn. They disappeared through an arch in a far wall.

As yet another girl swished by—this one in a green cape, wolf half mask, and a chaste, ribboned skirt and bodice—Wolfie scooped her into his arms. She giggled and hugged him.

But then that hug turned into something more when her hand crept between them, hidden by her cape.

Closing his eyes, then opening them to reveal that his irises had gone pale yellow, Wolfie whispered into her ear.

She giggled once more, then scampered off.

A dual paradise, Della thought. For the girls and Wolfie.

Hearing Della's thoughts, he winked at her, his gaze mellowing back to gold as he mind-said, *She was one of the first. Still as lovely as the day she was turned.*

A seventy-plus-year-old vampire who hadn't aged past sixteen. And she would never have to grow up and leave the best friends she would ever make.

None of them would, and this warmed Della's blood.

·Safe.

Wanted.

Violet had tracked the green-caped girl through the arch in the wall, her own eyes a feral purple, showing her excitement at this promise of what they would soon have. Della also felt it, just as she could feel it in the pulsing skins of Noreen and Polly.

After straightening his jacket, Wolfie invited the girls to follow him into that arched exit, where the others had gone.

As they made their way hand in hand through the crowd—oh, the smell of yummy sugar, sweetness, *blood*—the other vampire girls reached out to touch Violet's arm, Noreen's red locks, Polly's cheek. One vampire even swooped down from a swing to skim the frizzy hair Della so despised.

They're welcoming the new class, Della mind-said, smiling shyly at them.

The new us, Noreen added.

They left the masque, the cool, black atmosphere beyond the arch swallowing them. Even before her sight adjusted, Della could tell this second area was just as massive as the first, merely by the way it seemed as if she might fall into a hole if she took another step.

And on we go, Wolfie said.

From the direction of his mind-talk, Della realized that he had taken a turn.

Through and through, he added.

He'd taken another turn.

Were they . . . ?

She could see light objects versus dark by now and . . . Yes. They were in a maze—the walls a towering combination of brick and iron grillwork.

As they moved round another corner, she saw the purpose for the iron.

An ecstatic male had been tied with leather strips to the grill-work. He had stubble on his face, and Della realized that this was no teen—he was a young man.

Below him, a girl in humanlike form and garbed in the skirts of a tavern wench was nuzzling his waist. Thus far, she had used her fangs only to inflict superficial cuts, which she licked as if they were lines of candied syrup.

As they passed the scene, a hunger within Della—one never quite satiated—fisted brutally.

She turned her gaze away, only to notice an enthralled Violet clutching Wolfie's arm.

Della knew Polly and Noreen had felt the same pangs, and she wondered if Wolfie was giving this tour in order to stoke their appetites. It would be just like him to tease like this.

Farther into the maze, they passed more couples.

Then trios who had gone beyond scratching and into gnawing.

Then quartets who were feasting on the males, whose eyes had glazed over even as their skin was peeled away like waxen wrappers.

Food, the girls thought as one. *Always hungry, never full.*

Just as they had all but doubled over from their cravings, a breath of light brought them out of the maze and into another room where blood haunted the air to a lesser degree.

This one was bright and looked as if it belonged in Versailles itself.

As Della slowed her pulse from what she'd seen in the maze, she took in the pastoral scenes lining ceilings and the half-masked girls who reclined in silken, gilt-edged corners. Most of them wore voluminous skirts and powder in their upswept hair.

Yet all of them had razor blades they were whisking along the flesh of blissful males who were, perhaps, in their later twenties.

Witness a favorite pastime for our older recruits, Wolfie mindsaid. *You've probably guessed that these boys aren't getting anything they haven't asked for in the world above.*

The class tilted their heads at Wolfie, and he laughed at their innocence.

We find some of our more special treats in fetish clubs, he said. *And if we determine that they won't be missed, they come down here and never go anywhere else again.*

Oh, Della thought along with Polly and Noreen.

Wolfie had never taken *them* to any such clubs.

Wolfie laughed again. *New experiences, darlings. You will enjoy them.*

Even so, when he turned his attention back to the razor-bearing girls, Della saw his smile lessen from when he'd lavished a gaze on them.

Did he spend so much time with their class *because* of their innocence? And once they moved from school to the Underground, would his interest fade in them, as well?

Would he love the next class better?

Della watched as a girl sliced along the belly of a man, lapping her way down and down his skin while making his flesh glow in delicious reds.

Shivering in anticipation—or perhaps it was in fear of losing Wolfie's affection if she should become as worldly—Della let go of Noreen's and Polly's hands, sidling closer to him.

He tweaked her chin, then walked them round and round more rooms: cottages, pirate ship cabins, castle chambers. . . . Every luscious fantasy a schoolgirl might dream of during a lecture.

As they strolled out of the harem room, Della was so swept away that she said out loud, "You spent time in all these places before you modeled your Underground after them, Wolfie?"

"Most, my darling."

She sighed. "I should love to hear even more stories about your life and times."

Pausing, he looked deep into her eyes, and she saw the adoration she craved there. Appreciation.

He touched her cheek, running a thumb over her skin, and Della leaned into his palm.

Then Violet swept by on her way to the closed door, brushing against Della in a hardly subtle warning.

Wolfie chuckled, shaking his head. *You girls.*

But before he let them out, he said, "Keep up now. Hurry along after me. There's much entertainment and sustenance to be had back at the main masque before you leave, and I know you've been exceptionally hungry recently."

When he opened the door, Violet went first, delivering a glare so ugly to Della that she almost shrank away.

But she didn't.

Not with the afterglow of Wolfie.

Once in the dark hall, she realized that they were so far from the masque that the drums were nothing more than faint blips.

Then Della sensed . . . something.

All of them did.

Energy. Malice. Misery.

It was almost as if damp, shivering bodies were pressed against them, and Noreen and Polly crowded Della, as if this would combat the sensation.

But Wolfie had warned them to keep up, and as he sped away toward the sound of drums, they followed, more than happy to leave the awful awareness behind.

They arrived back at the masque entrance to the cheers of the other girls, and Noreen and Polly trailed Wolfie inside.

But before Della could do the same, Violet thrust the banner curtain in front of her, blocking the entrance. Then she veered close, her nostrils flaring.

As if she'd smelled fear on Della, she pulled back, her eyes aglint. *You're still frightened of me, Della. Good.*

Stand aside, Violet, she said, clinging to the last of Wolfie's touch. Wanting to find him and the others again. *You don't scare much of anyone these days.*

Violet's gaze seemed to click to pale slits, and whip quick, the other girl planted her foot on Della's chest and shoved.

Della flew through the air, darker, darker, the blackness becoming thicker, way, way back past all the rooms—

Slamming into a wall, she heard Violet's echoing giggles, far away, while the pitch-dark wrapped her in what felt like a clammy rag.

Reeling, Della fumbled round her, feeling rock, using it to stand as she swayed to her feet.

Gradually, her head cleared, leaving humiliation.

Now that Blanche had left, Violet would be bored, and she would return her attention to the weakest member.

Della could either take it or—

Out of nowhere, two figures appeared in front of her.

Two pairs of unblinking red eyes accompanied by an electric whining sound that made Della press her hands to her ears and open her mouth in soundless surprise.

But just as quickly as it'd happened, Della felt arms wrap round her and zoom her away, out of the viscous pressure of the darkness and back to the noise of the masque.

The laughing and drums seemed a world away, even though they were right there.

In her blurry gaze, Wolfie, her rescuer, stood in front of her, his hands on her temples as he looked her over, his hair clouding round him in the light.

Della, he said, his mind-voice like thunder.

His pique shook her as the other girls stayed back.

He squeezed her head with just enough strength that she couldn't bring herself to speak.

Violet tells me you got lost, he said.

Behind him, Violet came into view, blocking her thoughts from everyone. But the glare she leveled on Della was open enough.

Don't you dare tell what really happened, it said. *Or else . . .*

Della thought about the upcoming nightcrawl they'd been promised, perhaps tomorrow if they were good. Thought about the wonderful night they could enjoy here.

Food. Delectable food.

She looked away from Wolfie and straight at Violet, making certain the other girl knew just how far she would go for the group.

How much punishment she was willing to take if it led to rewards.

I got confused with my direction, she mind-said. *But I was about to catch up, Wolfie.*

This is no place to ever get confused, he said. *We have others at work around the Underground. They leave me to my business, and I leave them to theirs.*

Della closed her eyes as Wolfie let her go. She wished he would glimpse into Violet's thoughts to see if she was lying, but there was no reason when Della herself had covered for her.

Violet could always manage a lie with almost anyone, except for the one who punished them.

When Della opened her eyes, she found that Wolfie was already back to his careless self, scanning the masque as a starving man would set his sights on a feast. The pull of the festivities was too much for him to resist as he linked arms with Noreen and Polly, leaving Violet alone with Della.

The drums beat in earnest as the other girl circled to Della's back. There, she inhaled, exhaled, causing the hair on Della's neck to part with each breath.

Della turned round, nose to nose with her, finally standing up when, all the time before, she'd remained down.

Violet tried to hide her surprise, acting pleased instead. *You thought of the group before yourself, Della. Bravo.*

Mind your back, Vi. I won't warn you again.

Are you challenging me, you prat?

Della only smiled as she turned round to join the masque.

But that smile withered once she realized she'd just stepped into the spot Blanche, Briana, and Sharon had left vacant.

EIGHTEEN

The School for
Fine Young Girls

The Next Day

Dawn fought the London traffic while driving the team's modified Kia Sedona to Queenshill for a 1:00 PM appointment.

Earlier, just before classes had been scheduled to start, a Friend had come down to headquarters, letting the team know that some girls in what they'd begun to call the Fang High Uniform had been seen sneaking back into the dorms and were now in school.

It was all Dawn could do to keep her foot from stomping down on the gas pedal.

But . . . relax, she told herself. The girls would still be there when the team arrived. *Patience.*

Besides, the team had plenty to get done as they made their way to Queenshill. Since returning to headquarters last night, they'd all worked on individual research projects and slept, so this was the first time they'd been able to catch up as a group.

Right now, Kiko was sitting shotgun on the front-left side of the vehicle, looking at Dawn every once in a while like she might all of a sudden bust out into major puppet-master mayhem again. It'd been his job to dig up background on the school and its nearby city, and he was updating them.

"So here's the scoop. St. Albans was named after the first British Christian martyr in the Middle Ages. A real bloody tale, which is appropriate, I guess. He wasn't a Christian at first, but he gave shelter to a cleric who was running from the Roman authorities, who were themselves persecuting Christians, as we know from a little book called the Bible. Alban was so moved by his guest that he converted, and when the bad dudes came to make an arrest, Alban pretended to be the cleric while the guy escaped. Then Alban wouldn't deny his new faith to the Romans, so it was bye-bye for him with a swing of an executioner's blade—that is, after the first executioner was converted by Alban and then refused to kill him. The poor schmuck who took the first executioner's place was miraculously blinded for putting Alban to death."

Wearing another modest business suit, Natalia scooted forward from her spot in the back. She'd tried to cover the bump on her head with foundation and powder, but the wound still peeked through.

"Vampires in a saint's city?" she asked.

Dawn kept one hand on the wheel. "Queenshill is only on the outskirts, so the irony isn't as delicious."

"Anyway," Kiko said, "pilgrims would come through town to pay their respects to St. Alban at his shrine, so there's been lots of traffic over the ages. But the city has a lot more going for it than that. Down by St. Michael's village, there're actual Roman ruins. Verulamium—that's what it was called way back when. And there's even a haunted old house on Market Place."

Natalia tapped her full lips with a pen, and Dawn noticed that Kiko noticed.

Then the new girl said, "London, in itself, has its share of storied places that might draw a vampire or two. Why would they prefer St. Albans?"

Kiko handed her some color printouts. "I don't have a good answer, but just take a look at Queenshill. Note the chimeras on the building's ledges. They don't call them gargoyles because gargoyles technically spout water, you know? But tell me a vampire wouldn't be into all that. Besides, the school is far enough removed from the city that it might serve as a decent hiding place for gathering vamps."

Natalia made a disgusted sound as she scanned the printouts and their chimeras.

Clearly not a fan of the grotesque.

Taking the papers back, Kiko said, "As for Queenshill, there was this eccentric millionaire named Thomas Gatenby, whose family made its fortune off the slave trade. Near the end of the nineteenth century, he suddenly got a conscience and established this school for girls. Later, his fortunes seemed to just disappear."

"I wonder," Dawn said, "if Thomas Gatenby was a pseudonym for one of our blood brothers."

"You never can tell." Kiko sent her one of those random I-can't-believe-you-made-a-guy-your-marionette looks again, then glanced out the window. "For all we know, based on Frank's follow-up with Justin Abberline, every girl in that school might be a vamp, and that could lead to a master who maybe did donate the land they live on."

Frank's interview was one news item that'd gotten around headquarters last night: while Frank had been asking Justin for help in locating the Posh Spice wannabe who'd gone off with those possible vamp chicks in Kiko's vision, he'd confirmed that the hotel clerk had indeed seen fangs on the head schoolgirl. All Frank had needed to do was look into Justin's eyes to spy the victim in his mind while they'd talked about the night Posh Spice Girl had disappeared.

Frank had also discovered that Justin had never again seen his gal pal or the guy friend who'd also accompanied the schoolgirls. But according to Justin, this wasn't much of a surprise. The kids in that disgusting place where he'd been staying—an abandoned loft in East London—didn't always come back. Everyone was in and out. There and gone.

Dawn tightened her grip on the steering wheel. "Just imagine if every girl in Queenshill does wield fang. Are they all cocky enough to use their powers aboveground? Are they really that flip?"

"I sure as hell hope so," Kiko said.

The roadways had gotten greener, and traffic thinned out.

"Natalia?" Dawn asked. "Did you find out anything about who Posh Spice girl might be?"

The second psychic dove right in, relaying the results of her own assigned task. "As far as any missing girls in the Brixton area who match Kiko's vision parameters, I have nothing to share. I concentrated on the name Justin told Frank—'Andrea,' which Posh Spice used when they first met. However, I suspect it was false. I did widen the search, though, yet I found no results of consequence."

"She'll end up being a runaway who could've been reported missing from someplace miles and miles beyond even that," Kiko said, taking out his handheld cross, then buffing it to a silver shine.

"Justin did tell Frank that 'Andrea' had an American accent," Natalia added, "but it's such a large country that my search there turned up many girls, and I could only look into a fraction of them last night."

Dawn turned onto a stone-walled lane that bypassed the city of St. Albans itself. "We could always collect pictures for the most likely matches and have Frank pay a return visit to Justin so he can take a look at them. But at least we know from Frank's meeting that you nailed the time frame for Kiko's vision. That's pretty good work right there, New Girl."

She glanced in the rearview mirror to see Natalia smiling.

There. Dawn had done her good deed for the day.

It obviously spurred Natalia to offer more. "Later last night, while Frank was showing me how to use a stake in the proper manner, Breisi arrived to tell him that they had news from the desk of Detective Inspector Norton. Kate Lansing was last seen with a young man named Harry Dale. You and Kiko were sleeping at the time, so Frank and I did research before sunrise. We didn't find any contacts yet for Mr. Dale, but it's another lead, yes?"

Kiko stuffed his cross into one of many jacket pockets. "Yes, but we're on the straight track to Discoveryville today, with this lead."

"Did you get a vision about that?" Dawn asked.

"Nah." Kiko grinned. "I'm just chuffed—that means pleased here—about what we already have."

She was chuffed, too. But something was bugging her about the ease of this investigation. Was there a reason for them catching so many clues so relatively quickly?

A master-planned reason?

Or was this possible Underground *really* that careless? If so, how had they survived any length of time?

"I'll bet Harry Dale's just another society dropout," Kiko added. "The world has so many victims to offer."

Dawn turned down a slim, downhill street, which was verdant with overhanging trees over the bush-masked stone walls. According to the GPS system, the school was less than half a mile away.

She quickly updated Kiko and Natalia on one other matter: Friend surveillance. Besides the Queenshill contingent, the two who had been watching over Mrs. Lansing and Justin Abberline hadn't noted any odd activity. There'd also been nothing earth-shattering around Mrs. O'Connell's house, either, except for the spirit sweepers Costin had hired from the comfort of headquarters. Fortunately, they'd declared the house clean of bad energy and left the elderly lady to her tea.

And Dawn hoped it would stay that way as she pulled into the small car park by the Queenshill administration office. After cutting the engine, she saw to it that they were well equipped, then they alighted from their vehicle.

Dawn smoothed out her skirt. She'd forgone the more Joe Blow costumes they stored at headquarters because she needed to look like an affluent relative who wanted to send her little buttercup sister to this school. So she'd visited Eva last night to borrow a decent ensemble. The cashmere length of her outfit was tight, because where Eva was willowy, Dawn was muscle, but it'd do for today.

Visiting her mother had been tough, to tell the truth, because Eva had gotten all bubbly and asked Dawn to take this tour or that tour with her, and Dawn had needed to turn her down.

Eva had understood, of course, but seeing the light dim that much more in her hopeful gaze had stayed with Dawn until she'd finally gotten to sleep hours later.

After passing inspection on herself, Dawn saw to final touches, like making sure Kiko's jacket hid his revolver and Natalia's bruise was covered. Then one of the Friends whooshed by to update them.

"We're staying with the girls. In history class now. We'll lead you to them when your tour allows."

Awesome. Then Natalia could see if she heard any hollow Frank-type sounds from them and confirm or deny their vampire states. It was a way more efficient plan than waiting for the girls to feed in front of the Friends or something—if the possible vamps even dared to act out around school.

Dawn thanked the Friend and let her go while Natalia asked a question.

"What do we do if these subjects truly are 'clients'?"

Kiko made a "seriously?" sound. "We carry on like normal people and alert the boss as soon as we can. If we're lucky enough after school lets out, our girls will lead our unobtrusive Friends to our pot o' gold, if you know what I mean."

Dawn drew Eva's thick camel coat over her expensive sweater. Holy crap, they really might find an Underground by the end of the day.

The team turned toward Queenshill, which waited under a sky of clouds that bunched together, swollen with a baleful gray.

The school reminded Dawn of one of those estates you might see on a BBC period miniseries. Something like a—what was his name from high school lit class . . . Henry James?—place where the characters moped around in fancy mansions during stormy days. Queenshill's buildings were composed of brown stones, towers, and leadwork patterned windows with arches and spaded flourishes. And, best of all, there were the promised chimeras lunging away from precipices, their wings spiny, their mouths spread in pointy-tooth leers.

In L.A., Dawn had seen a lot of fake gothic architecture. She'd worked on many a scary movie set.

But this shit was for real, and there was a good chance some vamps were running around in here.

"I don't like the chimeras," Natalia uttered as they walked toward the admin office.

Dawn wondered if there was another reason for the new girl's discomfort.

"You getting those Highgate chills?" she asked.

"No." Natalia trained her gaze on a chimera near the doorway as Kiko went ahead of them up the stairs. "I only find it less than hospitable."

Hmmm. Maybe Natalia really was tuning into some muffled vamp vibes and she just wasn't seasoned enough to know it.

With an emerging smile, Dawn stared down the chimera as they passed under it and arrived at the doorway. "These decorations are used to scare *off* baddies," she told Natalia. "Don't let them get to you. Just stay alert, okay?"

"Okay."

A raven flew in back of them, cawing, and when Kiko opened the door, Natalia dashed inside, holding her coat around her. Dawn exchanged excited glances with Kik as she entered, too.

After about five minutes, they were greeted with profuse kindness since the privately funded school was, after all, trying to make a sale. The secretary outlined the schedule: they would have a tour with one of the school's top students and then meet with the headmaster.

But as far as Dawn was concerned, contact with a student was the thing.

Soon, a ringlet-haired blonde dressed in a maroon blazer and gray skirt came to greet them, and the secretary introduced her as "Astrid," an upper-sixth-form student, which meant she was in her last year.

Astrid had cherub cheeks and an upturned nose, and right off, Dawn recognized her as a straight-A, associate-student-body, accepted-by-the-best-college-ever wonder.

Everyone, including Kiko, shook the girl's hand.

She didn't react much to Dawn's crucifix necklace, and one look at Kiko and Natalia indicated that Astrid hadn't produced any vamp visions or vibes, either.

Maybe all the Queenshill girls weren't vampires after all.

The student led them out of administration and to the main building, where she quickly proved an articulate, self-possessed guide, while highlighting every reason a girl might love the musty halls of Queenshill.

"I understand," she said as they went upstairs to survey the classes in session, "that your sister is devoted to art studies."

Dawn took over while Kiko snapped photos for their fictional sibling and Natalia recorded notes. It was imperative that they didn't look like walking billboards for vampire hunting.

"Yes, she especially loves sculpting." Dawn had decided to use Briana as a model because Mrs. O'Connell had already detailed what it took to be a Queenshill girl. "Since my cousins and I were visiting overseas, we decided to check out possible schools that would enrich her talents when the family moves here."

"Lovely," Astrid said. "We'll be in the art wing soon. There are exhibits in the hallways that you can photograph for her, and I'm certain you'll be meeting with art staff in addition to our headmaster."

She knocked on a classroom door, then briefly introduced the team to a teacher and students who studied under the watch of laminated Shakespeare posters.

After they listened to the class for a moment, they moved on, with Astrid shutting the door and taking up where she'd left off.

"Our art program is renowned, yet Queenshill also excels in business studies. We're very well-balanced."

The team nodded while she took them down the halls, explaining the showcased pictures of "head girls" and "prefects"—model students chosen so that the younger ones might emulate them; they even shouldered responsibilities in running the school.

All the while, Dawn kept track of Natalia, just to see if she was hearing voices or getting that hollow sound from any day-walking vamps. Kiko, himself, was touching everything in sight, using his reading skills.

When they moved to another wing of the building, it became obvious that they were entering art land. Sculptures created out of "found materials" flanked the halls: abstract tin-can pieces, old brick fountains, even a modern piece constructed out of gum wrappers. But there were also traditional paintings.

They entered a studio classroom, and Astrid introduced them to a group of teen girls decked out in paint-splotched white coats, dabbing at canvases.

After they were done there, Astrid guided them to the empty staircase, where Dawn turned on the approval act.

"Carly would love it here," she said. "We thought she might, because a family friend recommended Queenshill to us."

"Oh?" Astrid said. "May I ask whom?"

The team slowed their steps.

"Briana Williamson," Dawn said. "I'm sure you've heard of her."

The blonde's eyes saucered, but she kept her composure. "Briana. I see."

Kiko moved closer and "accidentally" brushed Astrid's arm. She didn't seem to notice because Dawn was talking again.

"Awkward, isn't it? That's why we didn't mention it first off. We know Briana ran away and hasn't been heard from since, but she and Carly met online, and all we heard from my sister was 'Queenshill this' and 'Queenshill that.' Sometimes I think she'd like to come here just to see if she can find out what happened to Briana."

"No one knows what happened, really." Astrid began walking, her spine as straight as one of the wooden beams decorating the halls. "One day she was here, and the next, she was gone. Her sister passed on, and we think it had something to do with that. But I never knew Briana very well, even though I shared a few classes with her. She had her friends and . . . We weren't social."

Right behind Astrid, Kiko turned back to Dawn, confirming that whatever he'd seen in Astrid matched what she was saying.

But something prodded at Dawn: there'd only been seven possible vampire girls in Kiko's vision.

That was hardly an Underground army.

All the same, Astrid, the little pro, effectively doused the conversation about Briana while going back to her main duty—spotlighting the school.

As they journeyed through another hallway, she asked Dawn if Carly was interested in languages. But before the team answered, she stopped at an opened closet doorway and said, "Why, hello, Mademoiselle. We were just discussing your department."

When Dawn came to the supply room and peered inside, she saw that this "Mademoiselle" was a beautiful starlight blonde standing in front of shelves of paper clips and notebooks. She'd been looking in a mirror and touching up the skin around her eyes with powder.

Dawn almost did a double take, because this Mademoiselle was just as chic as one of the old-time movie stars from Hollywood, and the word "Elite" cometed through her mind.

She glanced at Natalia to see if the other girl was sensing a vamp. Natalia pleasantly smiled back, showing no indication of hearing anything strange.

But Benedikte—"Matt"—had also been hard to read.

Dawn yanked herself out of it. Not every Underground was like the one in L.A. She had to remember that and cut loose enough to see this new one for what it might be.

The teacher clicked shut her compact, snow cool as the student guide introduced them. Mademoiselle clasped their hands in hers.

Cool skin, too, Dawn thought as the teacher brushed an absent gaze over the crucifix pendant.

After Kiko touched the teacher's hand, he only sat there with a dopey grin. All right. No good vamp readings on that front, either.

Students began to trickle into the halls, and Mademoiselle excused herself to greet her class, then disappeared into a room a few doors down.

Astrid said, "She's one of our best. One of my favorites."

She resumed the tour, and Natalia followed while a flood of girls started coming toward them, most in their own tailored clothing, some in sweater-skirt uniforms, all in a passing rush of shampoo scents and pale skin.

Any one of them could be vamps masquerading as human, Dawn thought. Any . . .

Then a wash of jasmine circled her, and she saw it.

A bunch of brown skirts, white shirts, and red ties, just like the uniform in Briana's picture. They moved up the hallway like one body, their books at their sides while the other students hastened out of their way.

At their front—a girl with long, lustrous brown hair. At her side—an athletic-looking strawberry blonde with a bob. Right behind—a grinning redhead. And at the back—a student with frizzy hair who kept an intense gaze trained on the leader of the pack.

Adrenaline spun through Dawn, and she took hold of Kiko's jacket.

He saw them, too, and he casually walked away from Dawn, toward the suspects, while Astrid sharply veered away as she and Natalia passed them.

Their resident vampire-hearer showed no reaction until . . .

Natalia plastered herself against a wall, staring at the departing group in the same way she'd stared at Frank back when she'd first met him.

Vampires.

The girls pivoted toward Mademoiselle's room, but Kiko managed to bump into the strawberry blonde.

"Sorry," he said, holding up his hands and offering a smile.

All the girls stopped, looked him up and down. Then all except for the frizzy-haired one giggled at the little person before they swept into the classroom.

Dawn started after them, but Kiko intercepted her.

"I didn't get any information about the big show," he whispered.

She hadn't expected him to see any visions about an Underground since he'd never been able to read vamps anyway. But when she kept staring at the classroom, dying to follow the pack into it, he grabbed her wrist.

He didn't have to say the rest: *We just know they're vamps, and that's all. We're here to find the bigger part of the picture if there is one, and the boss would kill us if we put a possible Underground on guard by making a scene.*

Damn it. *Damn it,* he was right. They had confirmation that there were day-walking vamps on campus, and chasing after them in public might destroy the surprise Costin required to attack an Underground, inquire about the whereabouts of the dragon, then terminate a master. What they needed to do was continue sleuthing so they could get the most information possible about a lair's location.

That's what a team was for—reconnaissance, not attack—and Dawn knew from what'd happened in Hollywood that she could either make this harder for Costin or easier.

It took all the willpower she had, but she kept herself in check.

"Then let's get on with the rest of it," Dawn whispered to Kiko as they started to walk.

Closer.

Closer to the room the girls had entered.

Striding by on the way to Astrid and Natalia, they glanced inside, catching sight of the four identically dressed girls sitting sweetly in their seats and gazing at Mademoiselle as the teacher gave the visitors a placid smile, then shut the door.

NINETEEN

The Calm Before
the Storming

Once the team got back to headquarters, Dawn started running up the walls.

Literally.

One side of the subterranean room held a rock climbing panel while another boasted a mesh net—both of which improved balance, strength, and agility. But as Dawn got to a three-point stance with a silver-coated stake in hand, she aimed for even more advanced training from a bare wall instead.

Training—her only way to find peace of mind while the team waited for night to deepen enough for good cover. Pure physical bursts of energy that she needed to tame before they went back to Queenshill to sleuth around.

She took off toward the wall, and just as it seemed she was going to crash, she planted one foot on it, then used the other to flip herself over and land in fighting position so she could whip around and impale something with that stake.

But when there was nothing there, she dropped the weapon to her side, pushing back the stray hairs from the sweat on her face.

She controlled her breathing. Her emotions.

The team was so close, she thought. But they were also so far from striking down just one more obstacle that kept Costin in the body she'd damned him to.

Before leaving Queenshill this afternoon, they'd met with both the headmaster and the art department head to finish out the whole touring charade, trying not to attract suspicion as Underground hunters. However, the Friends were still on campus to slyly monitor the four vamp girls, who had gone to their dorms and had been sleeping ever since.

But the team had a plan to supplement and speed up the Friends' efforts.

They would use Frank to, in effect, bloodhound around the premises for any Underground entrances when darkness fully came, when his powers would be at their fullest. Dawn and Kiko would stay to the shadows to back him up, and they'd be sure to keep their distance from the dorms—out of typical vampire scenting range—while the Friends kept watch to make sure the team wasn't caught.

Then there was the backup to *that* plan.

If, by sunrise, Frank's endeavors or the Friends' surveillance didn't yield anything, they'd get him back on campus by arranging another tour so he could hopefully pass the girls in the hallway and read some minds. But, again, the problem with that was Frank's powers weren't as sharp during the daylight and he'd have to cover up his skin to a suspicious extent.

There were actually more than a few reasons Dawn was on edge regarding both team plans. First was that they were risking her dad's detection by fellow vamps—but at least he wouldn't be parading around in front of them tonight.

Still, when it came down to it, they *had* to take calculated risks to get anywhere with these Undergrounds.

And she was more than willing for Costin's sake.

As she toweled herself off, she heard him . . . felt him . . . behind her, just as if thinking his name had summoned him.

She kept her back to him. "You restless, too?"

She only asked because, when the team had returned, it'd already been dusk, and Costin had already been awake for hours.

"Always restless," he said, and his voice reminded Dawn that listening to him was the closest she would ever get to hearing an echo from an abyss.

She put her stake and towel in the weapons bag she intended to bring with her to Queenshill. She couldn't heft the bulk of it around while they were scouting the premises, but she wanted her arsenal close by, even if she left it in their parked vehicle.

"Dawn, you seem to be spending all your strength down here. Won't you be tired by the time you leave?"

"I've got more energy than I know what to do with."

"Then perhaps you should use it to fine-tune your mind rather than a body that's already in shape."

She looked at him over her shoulder.

He stood there in his loose trousers and a long, dark robe left open to show the muscled smoothness of his chest, the ridges of his abs. Even though he'd fed from a refrigerated blood bag already, desire kicked at her gut.

Had he come down here so *she* could feed him, too?

Probably not. Earlier, he'd said that he didn't want to sap Dawn's strength.

But she knew that if the team found an Underground hive and she made it back, he'd drink from her before going in for the final attack himself—if his powers even made that possible—absorbing the extra power she always gave him.

"I see," she said. "Right before I run out the door, you decide to mosey down here to talk about fine-tuning my brain. Are you going to show me how to stop myself from making bystanders into Pinocchios? Because, seriously, after all the time you've spent mind-training me, I don't think it's likely. I'm still a bad student."

He put his hands behind his back, then walked along the opposite wall, still keeping her in his sights. "Once you get ahold of your talents, you'll be formidable. I almost wish we had more time before closing in on this Underground. However," he said, halting in a corner and leaning into it, "it would actually require opening your mind to me again for us to train."

Dawn resisted telling him that she would open hers just as soon as he opened his. But that would go nowhere, as usual.

So she pulled a black sweatshirt over her tank, indicating that she was ready to move on. She wanted to take a brisk shower to revitalize herself and to use the soap Breisi had developed to neutralize body scent.

Costin hadn't moved from his watching corner. "Why would you need to come down here and run around, I wonder. Kiko has been resting, and Frank was sitting with Breisi, using her for inspiration."

"Agitation is my inspiration," she said. But then she got serious. "You didn't see those vamp girls, Costin. I keep remembering how they just strolled down the hall, princesses of the palace. The other students cleared out of the way for them, almost like it was their instinct to be scared. For some reason, common sense tells me I should be shaking in my boots, too. But I'm not. Not like I used to with the first hunt."

"You're more experienced than you were over a year ago."

But Dawn wasn't so sure that was it. Maybe she was just stonier now.

As he felt around the edges of her mind, she diverted her thoughts, bending down to zip her bag closed. The sound was like a split down the center of the room.

"So their arrogance bothers you," he said.

She was almost relieved that he'd latched on to this thought instead of the other. "The vamps didn't seem to be on the lookout like they should be aboveground. In fact, they acted like they had good reason to feel protected. Don't they care if someone like us finds them . . . and so fast?"

He cocked his head at her. "There is something else bothering you besides their attitude and the speed of our apparent success."

"Sure. I've never liked Queen Bees. You don't have to read me to know that."

He prodded farther into her mind, liquid warmth and heat-drenched flows. Her belly tightened, but she resisted his lure.

But then . . .

Tired. She was tired of blocking and dodging and being alone.

So she succumbed to his gentle, numbing attack, and it felt so good, except . . . Well, she missed the days when he could escape Jonah's shell and plunge his full essence into her entire body, consuming her from the inside out and washing her clean each time.

One day, maybe he'd be able to do that again. After they got the rest of the masters and their dragon. . . .

He retreated from her mind.

All right. No use avoiding the deeper issues anymore.

She clamped down on her craving for him, but the strain made her tense, tighter. Needier.

"Costin," she said, gesturing to the chasm between them, "we've been across the room from each other ever since Jonah came out and had his chat with me. We both know it."

"I'm sharply aware of his visit's effect. I only wished to clear the air before you left tonight."

Ah. Now she knew what was happening. He'd played this same card previously, the last time an Underground attack had been looming.

She put her hands on her hips and pushed out a breath. "The night you went into Benedikte's Underground . . . Before you left, you tried to make up for all your missteps with me, just in case you got walloped in the confrontation. And you finally told me most of the secrets you'd been keeping because you thought the hunt was over and it was too late for me to leave you in the lurch by getting angry and deserting the team."

"You believe I'm doing the same now? That I'm about to tell you all the hidden, dark secrets Jonah hinted at because I fear you won't return after tonight? Or that I will never see you again if I should go into this lair, myself, soon afterward?"

"I'm just calling a spade a spade."

"Dawn."

He walked toward her, then stopped far enough away to keep his control. But he was near enough for her to see in the simmering gold of his eyes that the primal tang of her sweat from the workout turned him on.

The yearning for him speared her, too, a thrust of sharp heat every time his ab muscles clenched during a breath.

His body—Jonah's body—still functioned on so many human levels, like breathing and pumping blood. Yet as a vampire, there was a sheen to him that made her stare, made her want.

And it was wrong to want someone who fed on her blood. It was also wrong that she didn't care about dying tonight so much as what might happen if she left Costin to fight without her.

Not that he hadn't done pretty well on his own throughout the centuries, but she was "key" to his endgame.

Or maybe she just wanted more than anything to believe that Dawn Madison, who'd been so unneeded all her life, had finally changed that.

From the look on his face, she could tell he wanted to come into her badly, and in spite of herself, she opened her mind, allowing his deluge of colors and affection to push out all her weak, debilitating thoughts.

After sensing her upheaval, he walked over to her, took her jaw in his cool, cupped palm.

I do need you, he thought.

Too intimate, too close to the target. Scarier than any Underground.

Dawn nudged him out of her, her vision going normal until he reached out with his other hand to bring her back to him.

Back to the red haze of being linked, back to the swirling patterns of a prophecy in motion.

Let me be more than your penance, he added. *Just this one time, Dawn, before you leave.*

His lips were inches away, so near that she could feel each of his breaths on her mouth. Her skin became a field of nerves, sensitive, electric, and when he rubbed a thumb over her cheek, she grabbed at his robe for balance.

But just as she started falling, he scooped her up and eased her back to the wall in one fluid motion. Then, against the climbing net, he raised her hands and slowly inserted the strands through her fingers, so she could stand on her own.

She gripped the mesh, looking into the fires of his gaze, linking to him and seeing how much he hungered for her tonight, even if he'd already taken blood. Seeing how, inside the warrior, there was a seed of doubt that this might be the one Underground that caused him to fail in his mission, that this might be his countdown to Hell.

He leaned forward to nuzzle her temple, and she could hear him suck in a breath at the sweat on her skin. Then he dragged his mouth down, tasting the salt of her.

It felt like someone was plunging heat into Dawn, up and down, up and down, as she clung to the net. She was getting wet, plumped, with every kiss on her jaw, then the vulnerable spot below it.

His arousal was building, too—she could feel it prodding her belly.

He knew how to get to her, knew how to break her down.

She let go of the net with one hand to stroke his cock through the thin material of his trousers.

A tremor wracked him and, just like every other time he started to feed, he waged battle with the vampire. Costin, the monster who had hated what he'd become after his initial blood exchange with the dragon. The creature who'd engaged in a bargain to cleanse his soul before Dawn had forced him to become a monster again.

He buried his face in her neck and pulled at her sweatshirt, and she sensed another force in him, flexing, heaving to get out.

Jonah.

Maybe she could stop *this* at least.

"Keep him in," Dawn whispered. "Stay with me, Costin."

The sound of his name energized him and, with a harsh inhale, he raised his head, his eyes a startling silver.

"*Costin* . . ." she said, easing into his mind at the same time to strengthen him.

With a snarl, he took her sweatshirt and tore at it, then ripped at her tank top, her bra, baring her breasts while her nipples hardened in the cool air.

She worked off the rest of her clothes until there was nothing left but rags around them on the floor. Then he kissed her, hard and hungry, wrapping her braid around his fist and pulling back her head, exposing her neck.

She clasped the net again, knowing she might need every bit of strength she had for tonight's reconnaissance. But she would give him blood if he wanted it. Would give him almost anything.

Almost.

He lapped at her throat, gnawing, sucking, but his fangs hadn't come out yet. He was quaking to keep them back as he kept nibbling, and she kept thinking his name, over and over, delving one hand into his hair and jerking his lips to hers.

Costin, she thought. *Stay with me, Costin. . . .*

She opened her mouth, deepening the play of tongue and teeth. Feasting, pulling hair, arching against him so her skin met his—her breasts on his smooth, taut chest.

He pressed a palm against the small of her back, bringing her hard against his erection, where her bared sex rubbed against the covering cloth. She got the material even wetter by leaning back and grasping at the net again, wrapping a leg around his hips and grinding into him.

His tip jammed against her clit, working her to a stiff pierce of anguish.

She pulled at the net, rocking, riding.

"Bite me," she said on a groan.

He took her by the hips and rammed against her even harder. "No . . ."

Forceful, determined not to lose it to the monster he wouldn't accept.

She grabbed him by the hair again and brought them face-to-face. "*Yes.*"

He stopped driving against her, but his tip was still between her folds, where she was drenched and slick.

All she wanted was to feel the needled pop of his fangs, the moment of entry that always seemed to stun her for a second no matter how many times it happened. A bite gave her courage and purpose, filled her with brutal strength even as it floated her into a darkness that felt right at home.

But every time he bit her, she had another chance to climb out of that blackness, even though she always found herself falling back in. . . .

As he looked at her, he loosened his hold, no doubt seeing that dark spot in her.

A tightened knot of panic made her grip his hair all the harder.

"You want to, Costin," she said, churning against him. "Come on."

His body clutched, wracked with ecstasy, and it forced a streak of unrestrained thoughts from him.

She hasn't changed from when we first met . . . still self-medicates by using another body. My body . . .

But then he spoke out loud, as if his pained voice could make her forget what she'd just heard, make him forget that he knew she'd heard.

"If I lose the last of my control . . . He'll come."

Jonah.

"He won't take advantage of any weakness or openings," she said, her mind still back on what she'd heard in his mind. It was one of those secrets Jonah had been talking about, one of those buried things Costin had been keeping from her. Now she knew it, and she wished she didn't. "He knows I don't want him around."

His body jerked, as if he'd been slammed.

It was Jonah beating against those inner walls that kept him captive.

Damn him. Damn him for putting more distance between her and Costin. Damn him for wanting to do more damage now.

She pictured the darkness inside of that body, pictured Jonah trying to get out during a moment that should've been just between her and Costin.

She pictured her mental fist, which she could pound *in* to that body, not at it.

And she did.

Bam.

Bam!

With each strike, Costin jerked, but she could still feel he—not Jonah—was still with her.

Still.

Costin.

At the force of the assault, he dropped her, but Dawn only fell back against the net, catching at it.

Grimacing, Costin pressed his fists to the center of him, as if to keep Jonah in during one last-ditch effort.

"Costin?" she said.

He doubled over, hand outstretched, hair covering his face.

"Costin!"

He looked up, searching her frantic expression, his own a mask of anguish as he pulled at his robe, then stilled.

Panting, he felt around his torso.

"Silent," Costin said, coming to look at her with edged wonder. "He is silent and accepting that you don't want him to emerge."

Dawn kept breathing hard, her mind shut. The skirmish had excited her, and she wanted to use the sexual energy to drive out the demons, the thoughts she'd heard from Costin.

To show him that becoming her own self-fulfilling prophecy wouldn't hurt her.

In return, Costin looked unbearably drawn to the power she'd exhibited—power that he hungered for, no matter how hard he tried to contain it.

She eased toward him, touched his cock.

His eyes drifted closed as she stroked him, undid his fly, then reached inside to coax him out.

He pulsed in her palm, engorged.

Cupping her hand, she moved up, down. . . . "Costin," she whispered, hoping, needing. . . .

He shuddered, his fangs straining out just past his parted lips.

Bite.

The thought shattered open her mind, blasting into his.

Even in his craving-muddled head, she saw clearly that he couldn't resist, and he slid his hands under her bare ass and pulled her to him. But he didn't target her neck—he went for her mouth, his barely emerged fangs scraping her lips as he consumed her with a raw kiss.

His fingers dug into her cheeks, and Dawn moaned into him, absorbing the scratches and nips as she grappled with the net behind her, trying to get hold of it again. When she did, she gnawed at his lower lip, an animal asking for more.

He obliged her by reaching back between her legs, where she was throbbing, slippery, ready.

As he thrust two fingers into her, she opened her mouth on a gasp. They breathed together, mouth to mouth, his fangs stretching to full length as his body shook.

"Do it," she said, offering her neck.

Instead of giving her what she wanted, he rammed his fingers higher into her, lifting her to her tiptoes.

She grunted, wiggled her hips forward until the tip of his cock was ensconced in her folds again. Then she pulled at the net, flexing, and he growled, his fangs gleaming, his eyes all pale heat, his excitement building until all shared thought bled out to a field of white between them.

As pressure expanded inside of her, she levered forward and latched her mouth to his neck, biting at *him* until he groaned and slipped his fingers out of her, then replaced them with one sliding, rough thrust of his cock.

Choking on a tight moan, Dawn took up his rhythm, matching him drive for drive, white, hot, melting down to coat him.

An endless blank consumed them as they worked toward a climax, swipes of red jabbing through the white of their minds with each hammering pound.

Another slice—

Another cut—

Another—

Then, with a gush, their minds joined in one flowing wound as they slid to the ground, clamoring for breath, sweat connecting their flesh.

Bleeding into each other, out of each other . . .

Bit by bit, they came down from their linked crash, their minds turning white again, his come—as lifeless as cleansed water—dripping down her thighs.

She angled her neck to him one more time.

In what felt like a final swipe, he thought, *Love doesn't hurt like this—*

I think it probably would, Costin.

She'd cut him off before he could injure the peace she'd found in the white. But as he began to pull away, she brought him against her, holding to him even though she knew he wouldn't bite her, wouldn't give her what she'd wanted more than anything.

Darkness over the blankness, a taste of something she shouldn't want at all.

Mostly though, she wrapped her arms around him because she was going out to poke at a vampire nest and see what came out from below the ground tonight, and she wanted to give him as much as she could before she might be gone permanently.

It wasn't much, but she tried.

And when she did go, his eyes were topaz. Sorrowful, maybe even a little angry that the two of them weren't able to function in any other way.

But they were topaz.

She would remember that later when they turned blue again.

TWENTY

. . . You Surely Pay

While night shrouded the outside world, the gray cat licked its paws in a buried room far, far from the girls' regular meeting area, which they had left empty in favor of their house beds for the time being.

Well removed from the other tunnels, the cat's small domain was dotted by lanterns that seethed light over the rock walls, where the bent shadows of hooks and blades hung from the ceiling. Although the cat could see quite nicely in the dark, light bred the abominable silhouettes that made the coming ritual all the more exciting.

The creature rolled to its side, rubbing its face against the porcelain claw-footed bathtub. Lethargically, it gazed across the room at the drowsing Blanche, who rested in the depths of a silken cuddle chair. She had been charmed into sleep for over a day now, her black hair spread like darkness, her skin pale against the pink silk.

So young, the cat thought. So pretty.

Then it recalled the night before last, when Blanche's limbs had entangled with "Wolfie"'s while they'd tumbled over the floor, playing. . . .

And playing.

The cat hissed, bolting to its feet.

Too young. *Too* pretty.

Yet when the creature looked once more at the shadowed blades, it was able to shake the envy off its fur. It arched its back, hissing again in preparation to will itself into a more human shape—the one the cat left behind whenever it came under the ground to watch over the much lovelier girls.

As a cat, the vampire didn't cast such an appallingly drab image in the mirror. As a cat, it could actually fool itself into forgetting the beauty it kept losing month after month.

But the ritual was at hand, and it was finally time to shed this animal appearance. . . .

The creature slipped and slid—elongated bones, elastic skin—into its humanlike form, stretching and adapting to a faded disguise that it used aboveground.

When it caught its reflection in the oval, gilt-edged mirror across the room, it shied away.

Yet then, ever vain, the vampire crept closer to the looking glass.

It turned its face this way and that, then leaned closer, even while the glass announced every imperfection that had settled upon the cat-vampire since the last ritual.

Not even the sustaining blood it took twice weekly from the human schoolgirls could keep it from withering into this dry thing. But that blood was merely for survival, and the cat-vampire required so much more.

Touching its sapless skin, it bemoaned how these modern times, with the pollution and cancerous technology poisoning the air, took more of a toll than in centuries past, thus accelerating the need for rituals. Even constant healing could not battle the aging, and although the cat-vampire used much energy to appear as a young woman during the assumption of this "human" identity, the true destruction of its freshness—so hard earned, so nearly impossible to keep—saddened it. When it had first exchanged blood to become this vampire at twenty-eight years of age, it had been long past the budding beauty these Queenshill students possessed. Even so, the cat-vampire had enthralled many an admirer with its elegant pulchritude.

That is, before that pulchritude inevitably wilted.

Its fingers dragged down a face ravaged by day-to-day existence, by lack of the elixir it had begun to require twice a year.

But as it faced the slumbering Blanche again, blood sighed through its veins.

Skin dewed with youth and smoothness. Body lithe and graceful.

Just what the cat-vampire needed to claim Mihas's attentions again.

"Wolfie"—what a name Mihas loved to be called, "Wolfie"—often delighted in repeating how the cat could never be genuinely young again. He had even accused it of hating these girls because they would be at their freshest for years to come, on the perpetual verge of womanhood, while the cat had been far from it for centuries. Mihas occasionally even mocked the cat-vampire because of how the Underground—his own personal paradise—contained a near army of the cat's biggest rivals for his affection.

Rivals who would not degenerate until centuries had passed . . .

On the other side of the room, Blanche stirred in her sleep, just as Briana and Sharon had once done, as well as others before them.

The cat slipped into a satin robe and then went to her. "Wake up, darling," it said while caressing Blanche's temple.

It would not tell the girl about "Wolfie"'s visit to her careless, absentee parents in Paris. It would not relay the news about their subsequent deaths. All the girls—and the rest of society—would continue believing that Blanche's mum and dad were still traveling the globe, yet with Blanche accompanying them now. They would never even know how their precious Wolfie had posed as her father and seen to the details of removing her from Queenshill.

It would do no good to have parents sniffing around, ambivalent or not, so the Underground did what must be done.

Blanche blinked out of sleep once, twice, smiling when she saw the cat. Her back remained turned on the implements that cast such demented shadows over the far wall.

The cat-vampire helped Blanche to sit, then reached for an empty rounded glass from a nearby table. Slashing its wrist with a long nail, it let blood into the vessel.

Blanche hungrily watched the flow. "Have my parents arrived yet?"

"Not yet," the cat said in a tone that it had adjusted era by era so as not to stand out as an ancient creature. Soft conversation always made the elixir-girls simpler to handle, easing them into the ritual. "They should be along soon. You just drink up, because it might be a night or two before you find a way to take blood without your parents knowing."

The cat healed its wrist while handing the warm glass to Blanche, who took it in her palms like round, ripe fruit.

Still sleepy, Blanche closed her eyes as she drank, her long lashes sweeping over her pale cheeks, her red lips a splash of color against her raven-dark hair.

The cat envied the girl once again, almost tasting her purity upon its tongue because the elixir was so close.

Blanche drank until the glass was empty, her eyelids growing heavy because the creature had charmed its blood so it might put the girl into a deeper sleep than the one before.

A sleep of no pain.

As Blanche drifted off, sweetly dreaming of the reunion with her parents, the cat-vampire rescued the glass from the girl's falling hands and caught her as she dipped backward.

"Thank you," it whispered, easing the girl to the cushions once again, "I do greatly appreciate all that you're about to give me."

It stood, placing the glass on the table and allowing enough time for the blood to infiltrate Blanche's. Then it moved to the hanging blades, a forest of scythes and surgical tools.

It selected the shiniest of them all. A scalpel.

As the creature's pulse pumped, it walked to the bathtub, then tested the ankle harnesses dangling above the porcelain. It also made certain that the icebox behind the tub was at a decent temperature so it might hold all the treats that went along with the blood.

A pure heart, a clean liver, fresh lungs . . . Sweets it would eat at its leisure throughout the night that would restore vitality and youth.

Saliva flooded the cat's mouth as it imagined the delicacies, as it laid the scalpel near the tub and stripped the robe off its body.

Then it went to Blanche, scooping her into its arms.

It brought her to the bathtub, where it peeled the uniform from the girl then shackled her ankles so she hung over the receptacle like something delicious to be plucked off a tree.

Only then did the creature step into the tub, its skin throbbing as it allowed its pores to open like tiny mouths mewling and ready to suck in the blood and beauty.

While lovingly pressing its mouth to the girl's fragrant, warm neck—careful, so careful, not to kill her until it had dined on what it needed while the girl's body fruitlessly self-healed until the cat sliced off her head—it saw the dried-up reflection of itself in the looking glass across the room.

But when it tore out the girl's throat and allowed the freshness to rain down, its mirror image went as red as a poppy blooming in the new sunshine.

TWENTY-ONE

THE EMERGENCE

The Same Night

As Dawn drove Kiko and Frank—the reconnaissance team—to Queenshill, she got her head into the zone.

In the zone, she didn't have to think about Costin. She didn't have to dwell on any worst-case scenarios—only what she needed to do to track these vampires, to determine if they were part of an Underground, and to pack them away if they were.

Then she could move on to the next freakish bloodsucking community.

Kiko and Frank didn't talk, either, maybe because they knew Dawn wasn't up for a chat. Or maybe they were in their own zones.

She steered onto the tiny lane leading to the school. The weather had cleared, and the moon stared down, glowing over the burnished green landscape on the one night it would've been nice to have full darkness. Then again, the illumination would help Dawn and Kiko see without the use of their headlights, so she wouldn't complain.

She pulled the SUV off the road a quarter mile from campus, hiding their vehicle among a nook of foliage. Then, knowing from the Friends that the property was gated at night and Queenshill had surveillance cameras that the spirits could cloud, the trio packed light weapons while getting an update from the Friends about the location of the Queen Bee girls.

Afterward, Dawn relayed the content to Costin since he was back at headquarters and too far away for a Friend to efficiently communicate with, or to fly down there and give him the scoop herself. It was even too far to communicate using his and Dawn's shared Awareness.

"Those Queen Bees haven't moved from the dorms since they finished activities for the day and met with house tutors to do schoolwork," she said. "Sounds like our subjects decided to relax in the dorm's common room after that and, interestingly enough, when they entered, the human students left, just like they couldn't handle being in the same space. Right now, the girls are actually napping in front of the TV."

His voice vibrated Dawn's earpiece. "That common room is on the far side of the dorm, facing away from where you are now." He was obviously using the map the team had drawn up for him so he could follow their progress. "The Friends will have time to warn you if the girls change position. You will need to stay alert once you draw close to those dorms."

"Gotcha." It'd be bad enough to be caught by anyone, but they were being extra careful because, if the vamp girls just happened to recognize them from the school tour today, there'd be some major 'splaining to do.

"Good luck," said Natalia over the earpiece. She was also on the line back at headquarters because, without much physical training, she might have to be watched by the team, and that wouldn't work at all.

It'd been different with Dawn when she'd joined up last year. Because of stunt work, she'd been trained to use a revolver, to dodge and run and jump. Sure, her professional battles had been staged, but she'd been in fighting shape. Besides, she'd been "key" to the investigation, so she'd undergone trial by fire.

They all thanked Natalia for her positive wishes, then walked toward the wall that divided the lane from the campus's football field.

"Luck?" Kiko asked. "We don't need no stinkin' luck."

Dawn motioned for him to start climbing the wall while, in the near distance, dogs barked, sawing at the nerves she'd already calmed.

But she told herself to get in the zone again.

Frosty. Ready.

Knowing the Friends were already looking out for them, the team jogged, keeping their bodies low along the tree line as they aimed for a three-story stone house on the outskirts of the main campus.

As Frank went inside, Dawn and Kiko covered him: her with silver throwing blades plus an ultraviolet flash grenade that Breisi and Frank had built, and Kiko with a revolver loaded with silver bullets dipped in holy water. Since they were trying to move around quickly tonight without being noticed, they'd left bigger attack toys, like the saw-bow, in their vehicle.

The spirits had told them that this building was abandoned, but the team was still vigilant while Frank poked around, using every one of his increased vampire senses to ferret out any sign of an Underground entrance where the Friends couldn't.

Not finding anything on the lower floor of the building, which looked like it was used to store old school furniture, he moved to a higher one.

But all too soon, Dawn's earpiece came alive with her dad's gruff voice. "It's clean here. I'm ready to move on."

So Frank continued his bloodhound act around the football field, sweeping from one end to the other. But he didn't find much besides goal posts and a few cigarette butts near a bunch of trees.

Next.

They headed toward the campus's main buildings, with those chimera silhouettes etched against the night. Jasmine floated around the team on the surprisingly mild air while the Friends moved around, distracting an old security guard and keeping watch.

Again, Frank found nothing.

Nothing near the chapel, either, even though Dawn hadn't ruled out the site for possible vamp activity. The community could very well be immune to holy symbols, just like the higher Hollywood creatures had been.

The team rested against the chapel's wall, eyeing the cluster of dorms in the near distance.

"What's the word?" Dawn asked the Friends, who kept coming and going.

Mary-Margaret, a spirit with a Georgia-peach accent, filled them in. *"The girls are still knocked out in front of the common room TV. But the frizzy-haired girl named Della is stirring every so often."*

The team inspected the particular dorm that the Friends had fingered as the home of those four Queen Bees. Dawn pointed to a gathering of trees about eight hundred feet from the house, and Frank gestured that he wanted to go there next.

Since the vamp girls were secure and the trees were a good distance away, they all moved to the new location, where Frank immediately started combing through the leaves while closely scanning and sniffing.

As dogs still barked off yonder, Dawn and Kiko hunkered down by the tree trunks, fixing their eyes on the dorm windows. Some of them were black, but some were lit up, creating a light-dark jigsaw in the night.

The girls were inside that puzzle, Dawn thought. And, damn it, she wished the team could've thought of a nonconfrontational way to arrange for her dad to look into a few of those vamps' eyes for a mind search tonight instead of puttering around with this slow Frank-hound stuff.

But again . . . what if these vamps were capable of recognizing a related creature like Frank? Would they welcome him or attack?

And would the discovery of him put the girls and their possible Underground on alert?

Dawn's skin prickled just before a Friend whished by. Her voice was too excited for Dawn to identify her.

"Vampire!" she said. *"Della has come back to her room for a book, and she's on this side of the dorm now!"*

Light filled one of the windows and, on a held breath, Dawn retreated back into the trees next to Kiko, putting away her weapons and taking out her small surveillance binoculars. She zoomed in while the Friend took the message to Frank.

He went statue still, too.

They all seemed to freeze their pulses as they watched the dorm, hoping the light would go dark. . . .

But then Della with the frizzy hair appeared in her window, glancing around, wrinkling her nose and bending to the bottom of the frame.

Where it was cracked about an inch.

She sniffed at the opening, then bolted up and scanned outside.

A current of terror zapped around Dawn's chest. This Della's sense of smell couldn't be *that* good, not at over eight hundred feet, right? Dawn and Kiko had even washed with Breisi's neutralizing soap.

The girl opened the window the rest of the way and leaned forward, sniffing some more, then homing in on the trees.

No. Way.

When a second girl—Violet, the leader of the pack—came to the window, Della gestured toward where the team was hiding. Her mouth wasn't moving, so Dawn suspected they were mind-communicating. No wonder Costin had sensed activity in London if these girls were so flagrant about it.

But he'd sensed a blood brother, not just vampires. . . .

Then, at the window, Violet said something out loud to Della and gave her shoulder an annoyed shove, pushing the weaker girl out of the frame.

Arguing?

Dawn's first instinct was to grab the longest-distance weapon they had—Kiko's revolver. If she fired away, plugging both girls, would the silver have the same destructive effect she'd seen on vamps before?

Of course, spazzing like that would ruin everything, but her nerves begged her to do something instead of sit here with her heart gagging her.

A third girl appeared in the window to join in the verbal argument—the one with blondish reddish bobbed hair. The one the Friends called Polly.

Then the fourth came—the redhead named Noreen.

The dogs in the distance started barking louder. It was almost like they'd even come together and gotten . . . closer?

The group of Friends who'd been shadowing the team flew into the woods, flapping the tree branches. Breisi, herself, came over to Dawn and Kiko.

"A pack of dogs," she said on a wind-tunneled yell. "They were summoned . . . We'll slow them down while you go for the car!"

Summoned?

Before Dawn could ask for more information, Breisi shot away with the other Friends.

Frank commandoed his way over, murmuring to Costin at the same time. "We're on our way back."

Shoving her binoculars into a pocket, Dawn stood and glanced at the window again—at the four silhouettes staring right at them. Adrenaline iced her.

Underground vamps had developed different talents over the centuries. Had these little Queens summoned a court of animals to flush out what the girls had sensed in the trees?

Had Della recognized their scents from their school tour?

From this far?

Beyond the dorm buildings, the dogs were barking like possessed beasts, and it sounded like they were gathering in number, in speed. Every once in a while, there'd be a yelp, and Dawn could imagine the Friends crashing against them, pushing and lifting them with their pressure to slow them down.

The spirits wouldn't be able to do away with the creatures—when the former hunters had agreed to stay with Costin after perishing, they'd been promised a continuing state of grace, their souls perpetually redeemed by their deaths. They could fight but they couldn't kill.

But couldn't they at least lull the animals into complacency or cloud their vision?

Wait—preternatural sight could usually cut through a Friend's haze, according to Costin. But what about the lulling . . . ?

Dawn grabbed a handful of Kiko's jacket and took off with him in tow, but Frank snatched the psychic from her and gripped her by the arm as he accelerated, throwing caution to the wind and using his vamp powers.

Her toes dragged on the ground while she tried to keep up, branches snapping under their feet, popping like gunshots, and her lungs sharpened with cold gasps as they approached the speed-fuzzed edge of the woods, where the open grass would reveal them.

But they didn't stop.

Neither did the barking: louder, closer, more ferocious than before.

The pack couldn't have been more than one hundred feet away now, and Dawn was flailing with Frank's speed, unable to get her balance—

Until she felt a Friend taking up her back and pushing her.

"*It's me,*" Breisi said, just as cool as always, while Dawn found her feet and got into a rhythm.

More barks behind them—closer, fifty feet?—but there were more yelps because the Friends were still slowing them down.

Dawn pumped her arms as Breisi pressured her along, her feet barely even skimming the grass.

They were coming upon the stone building where they'd stopped earlier. Beyond it was a wall, trees, their car, which was outfitted to protect them from vampires if they could just get to it—

She heard babbling, Friends talking to each other, then suddenly, she was pushed up at an angle, the stone building rushing toward her face as her feet cycled in the air.

"Breisi!" Dawn yelled, seeing in her peripheral vision that the spirits had also elevated Frank and Kiko.

Just before they all smacked into the building, the Friends pushed them straight up, making it look like the wall was pouring down in a tumble of stone.

"*Climb!*" Breisi said, and Dawn and Frank pedaled their feet, reached out with their hands, connecting with each jutting stone, up and up, supported by the Friends.

The spirits were losing energy—the chase had taken too much out of them—so when Dawn reached the roof, she put all her might into running up its shingled incline, then grabbing the chimney so she wouldn't fall back down. Kiko, propelled forward by Frank, also latched on, followed by Frank, himself.

While one Friend spun away from the team to go down and face the dogs again, Breisi guarded them as the pack—five vicious beasts—rushed the house. Some of them began rolling over, engaged in a seemingly one-sided tussle with Friends, but others were barking, still charging, foaming at the mouth, their eyes pale with crazed obedience to the vampires who were obviously commanding them.

Demon dogs, Dawn thought, catching her breath at the sight of their empty, reflective eyes. There was some Dangerous Dog Act here in the UK, so she wondered if maybe these weren't strays so much as a collection from a rebel owner in the area.

"Breisi," Dawn said, turning away from the chimney while still holding tight. "Why didn't we go to the car?"

Her Friend's voice was reedier than usual, sucked of her usual energy because of the exertion. *"Minutes ago, we found animals there, too, somehow waiting for you. We're clearing them out so you can run to it."*

"Animals?" Kiko held up his revolver, clasping the chimney with his other hand. "Let's have at them. First these hellhounds and then the ones at the car."

Costin had gone silent, giving control to the team and lying low, but Breisi probably spoke for him when she said, *"No, Kik, not while you can still hide our purpose in being here. If we show weapons or special powers, they'll suspect hunters. Besides, the car is being guarded by feral cats and foxes—about thirty altogether, and even a vampire and guns aren't going to get them before they lay teeth to your throats or give you rabies, and we can't afford to risk that before getting a better bead on any community locations."*

"Thanks for the consideration," Kiko said.

Bresisi circled them. *"The vampire girls are even now still at the dorm, letting the dogs chase you off, and they don't know why you're here or even that we Friends have intercepted their animals. They've scented us, but they have no idea what we are. It doesn't even look like the girls can see through their animals' eyes—it's only a command mind-link, so we're still in decent shape as long as they stay in the dorms."*

"You couldn't lull the animals?" Dawn asked.

"No—they're already being commanded."

So much for music soothing the savage beast. "Then we'll just wait here for a few minutes."

"That's right," Breisi said. *"But if Greta, who's watching the girls, sees them leave the dorms, she'll tell us while attempting to divert them. Meanwhile, we'll play it safe since we still have a chance of preserving surprise for the ultimate attack."*

"Breez," Frank asked, "why're animals at the car? How would they know to go there?"

"Greta heard Della say after she caught scent of you in the trees that she instructed the ferals to find any strange vehicles near the

*school. She recognized you and Kiko from the tour today and won-
dered why you might be here. She was afraid for some reason. Violet, the leader, wasn't quite as worried about your presence
outside—more curious, actually—but she definitely wasn't happy
about Della calling the animals."*

As the dogs rolled and barked below, Dawn recalled the argument she'd seen between the girls in the window.

Breisi continued. *"Violet reacted in a way I would have never
predicted. Instead of wondering why you were here, too, she said
that maybe they could have some fun with you before going on
what they called a 'nightcrawl.'"*

Fun? Dawn thought of Kate Lansing and Justin's Posh Spice
girlfriend. Had these dead and missing girls been victims of nightcrawls?

Below, one of the dogs tore free from a Friend and ran toward
the building, scrabbling up the stone before being pulled back down.

Good God, when would their car be ready? Dawn guessed they
might be able to run away from the school without a vehicle, what
with Frank's speed and a few Friends, but how far would they get
before more animals caught up or until Frank and the spirits lost
speed because of the extra load of Dawn and Kiko?

*"Three of the girls were excited about beginning this nightcrawl
early,"* Breisi added, *"and they argued with Della in favor of it. But
Della told them they must 'be good' and they all took that into serious consideration. Then Violet yelled at her for calling the dogs,
and Della told her that she only did it because she wanted to see if
she was right about your identities . . ."*

"Did they actually confirm who we are?" Dawn asked.

*"Friends tried to camouflage the girls' view of you by pushing
nearby branches over their line of sight, making it look like a gust
of wind was moving the trees. I'm hoping that worked."*

Hoping . . .

"You know what?" Kiko said. "I think this Della is way more
cautious than the others. But why?"

Hoping Frank might have something to contribute to the conversation, Dawn turned to him. He was on one knee, looking in the direction of the car, just like he could hear the noises from the standoff there, even over the barking.

Kiko had more to offer. "If we ever get a shot at these girls, Della would be the one to isolate. Frank could look into her mind to see what she knows."

"It might be too chancy for Frank to come back on campus for a mind-reading after this," Dawn said.

Kiko was clinging to the chimney, revolver still in hand. "You think we could ambush them during one of these nightcrawls then? The Friends can tell us when the girls leave the dorm, and maybe Frank can get to Della tonight and then split before she knows what hit her. We might even be able to get locators on their clothes to help the Friends with tracking them."

"*Not bad, Kik,*" Breisi said.

Dawn looked at the ground, where the dogs were head-butting the air—the Friends—and baring their teeth at the spirits.

She glanced back in the direction of the dorm. What if the girls decided to begin that nightcrawl before the team got to the car?

Just as she was about to address it, Costin activated their earpieces, his voice sounding rough.

"Clear or not, I want you to go ahead and use whatever means necessary to get to the car before those girls decide they do want a nightcrawl."

Dawn held a hand to her ear, almost thinking she hadn't heard him right. "You want us to expose our real selves?"

"I want you to return to me, Dawn."

Her body seized. Did he want her back because he . . . ?

No, Costin wouldn't indulge any soft feelings for her right now—not with the fate of his soul at stake. He just wanted his "key," and she knew that. God, she knew that.

The dogs were obviously sick of waiting, too, as they proved by backing up, then running at the building, one by one.

She watched, realizing that maybe, just maybe, she could use a puppet move on them. It'd be silent enough and probably wouldn't give off any weird vibes to a vamp. Maybe.

Costin broke in again. "Return to me and we will consider that ambush Kiko mentioned. At the same time, the Friends will stay on the girls and keep reporting in—"

Then something—a gasp?—filled the earpiece.

Trepidation marched up Dawn's spine. "Hey, are you . . . ?"

"I'm fine . . . Dawn."

No, he wasn't. "Jonah?" she asked.

"*Don't* mention that name."

The team stared at each other as Costin's breathing wavered, strained . . . then evened out again as if he were taking great pains to control it.

Jonah. If he was screwing around again, right now of all times, she was going to kill him.

"Are you there?" Dawn asked Costin when he didn't say anything else.

"Don't concern yourself with me." His voice didn't sound much stronger. "Just . . . concentrate on . . . getting back here."

A new Friend flew by, stirring Breisi up. They chattered, and the other one rocketed off again.

"The last of the animals are being driven away from the car," Breisi said. *"But the girls just left the dorms and Greta hasn't been able to distract them or slow them. They're bleepin' fast. . . ."*

Nerves scratching over her bones, Dawn noticed Kiko looking past her. She followed his gaze.

A streak of white and brown under the moonlight blurred until it materialized into four girls who jogged into normal motion, then slowly walked toward the team from the far end of the football field.

Everything—even the Friends—went still, and Dawn's mind switched to pulse-stamped clarity.

Vampires.

She should've been scared, but she'd waited such a long time for this.

So cowboy the fuck up, she told herself.

Kiko hid his revolver as best as he could while holding to the chimney. Dawn slipped her hand into the jacket pocket nearest the chimney and held the UV grenade against her.

The girls kept coming, cocking their heads as one.

Okay. If the team ran, the girls would probably chase them, then maybe even invade the team's minds if they could. Of course, the team had been trained to shield, but what if the young vamps knew a way around that? They'd find all kinds of damning information about Costin.

But if the team stayed, they might be invaded just as well.

Unless they could find a way out of this.

Dawn glanced at Frank, inviting him to enter her mind for a good read as the girls came to within about sixty feet of them.

If we can't talk our way out of this, she thought to him, *let's go for it and isolate Della to find out for sure if these are Underground vamps or just normal ones. After you read her mind, you can shout the news to the Friends and they can take it to Costin.*

Frank's brows arched. She could tell he was wondering again if she had a death wish, because she was pretty much suggesting that they sacrifice themselves.

But she was willing. She had been for a long time now.

If it comes down to it, she continued, *I'll try to puppet Della into a corner while you and the Friends take out the dogs and the other three vampires. When I get her alone, you can look into her before she raises any shields.*

Now her dad's look was asking if she was crazy to expect total mastery over the mental powers she'd never been able to control before.

She took a deep breath, exhaled. *I can do this.*

He paused, then gave the barest of nods and laid his fingers on Kiko's chimney-clutching hand. It would hopefully transfer the plan to the psychic via a touch reading.

The girls had come within ten feet of the building, and the one with the long brown hair—Violet—motioned toward the dogs. The pack of them immediately sat on their haunches, lips peeled back to reveal gums and teeth as they growled at the team.

"Della," Violet said, her tone so light and crisp that Dawn almost thought they were at some flowered social gathering, "you cornered them with your dogs and forced them to climb the storage building. How rude."

The frizzy-haired girl who brought up the back of the group didn't answer while the rest of her crowd laughed.

Interesting. The vamps weren't attacking outright. Maybe they were fore-playing with their next meal? Starting that nightcrawl?

Violet folded her hands behind her back. "We recognize two of you from school today—the girl and the little one. Your presence here is curious, indeed, especially since you feel . . . odd . . . to us."

Were they referring to any vibes from Frank?

Della targeted a question straight at the team. "Why are you here?"

Violet darted a glare at her, but Della didn't acknowledge it.

Yeah, *very* interesting.

Then the leader turned back to them. "Why are you here?" she repeated as if it hadn't already been asked.

Frank put on his affable, everyone's-best-bar-buddy voice. "Because I'm one of you. I've been looking for my kind ever since I got into the city."

Dawn tried not to react at how he'd just revealed that he was a vampire. This was the way he was going to talk the team out of trouble?

Well, she'd play along because she didn't have a better idea, but . . . *shit*.

He nodded at Dawn and Kiko. "These humans are my servants.

I feed off them, send them on errands that I can't do during the day. That's why they were in your school, because I'd felt vibrations in this area and I wanted them to check it out. I was just getting ready to call to you from the trees, to greet you, but it looks like our plan didn't work so well. I could've taken out these pups, myself, but I thought they might be pets, and harming devil dogs is bad manners where I come from."

The redhead—Noreen—at Violet's left shoulder seemed intrigued. "You're an American vampire?"

"California," Frank said, smiling at her, trying to win her over as he'd been doing to women for years.

When Violet glanced at Noreen, who seemed about ready to ask about Disneyland and the beach, the redhead pursed her lips, refraining.

They sure act young, Dawn thought. Were they new? And was that why all of them except for Della weren't very aggressive or paranoid?

They couldn't be Underground. Not unless this was some act to draw the team in.

Violet had come to narrow her eyes at Dawn, as if measuring her up. And it seemed it was for something other than a fight, too. For some reason, she was assessing her even more than she was Kiko or Frank. . . .

Finally, the girl dragged her gaze away. "We don't associate with male vampires, really."

Della stepped to Violet's side, and the leader watched her in what seemed to be hostile astonishment.

"You have guns," the frizzy-haired one said, pointing at Kiko. "I can smell one."

Dawn clasped her grenade at her side.

The strawberry blonde at Violet's left shoulder—Polly—added, "Guns are terrible."

Kiko tucked his revolver all the way into his jacket, then raised his hands as much as possible while keeping to the chimney. Dawn knew he could draw like a flash if he needed to, and that he had another projectile weapon in a different pocket.

"We never know how we're going to be received by various vampires," he said. "Have to keep defensive tools handy."

Violet glanced at the others, and they all giggled at Kiko.

"Aren't you just the most precious creature?" the leader said. "I believe I'd like to have a servant such as you."

But when Della crossed her arms over her chest, signifying that she wasn't welcoming them so early, Dawn's alert system went off.

She leaned toward Kiko and whispered, "Block your mind just in case they don't need eye contact to see into it."

She didn't care if they heard, because one glimpse into the team's heads and the girls would know they were lying for sure.

Della had caught the comment.

"We need to return to our quarters and tell," she said to Violet. "Immediately."

Tell who? A master?

It was as if a bolt struck Dawn, zapping her emotions into chaos until they danced around the edges of her gut.

What if the team had screwed this up? What if these vampires kept them from saving Costin . . . ?

"*I'll* tell if there's going to be any telling," Violet said, getting in Della's face. "Do you understand? Stop with this mortifying behavior."

Della stood there, fisting her hands while Dawn's fright and rage gathered, too.

Then, as if reflecting the darkness in Dawn, the other girl started to change.

Her body hunching.

Her hair receding into her skull.

Her ears and teeth growing to wolfish points.

Her eyes angling into a cat gaze.

And with each stage, Dawn kept pace: bristling, shaking, responding to the threat of danger with just as much of her own.

She could hear Kiko extracting his gun from his pocket as that ball of white anger kept rolling inside her, growing, rumbling, eating away at the dark even while strengthening it.

Della, who looked like a tailless sphynx cat-wolf by now . . . holy shit . . . turned toward the team, pointed a clawed finger at them, and emitted something between a hiss and a growl.

The razor-over-steel sound told Dawn it was time to cut their losses, to get the information they'd come for because the team might not have a second chance.

Maybe it was a desperate decision, but she closed her eyes and brought her dark energy to the surface, picturing Della in its path—the grotesque monster in girls' clothing.

The type of thing Costin needed to vanquish to become whole again.

Push!—

In Dawn's mind, she saw the girl flying backward, her mouth open to expose needled teeth, her arms outspread until she crashed to the grass.

With another mental thrust, Dawn bound the vamp's hands above her head, just like she'd done to Jonah.

Hell came down as she concentrated everything into restraining Della for Frank's mind reading while she kept aware of what was breaking out around her: Frank jumping off of the roof and fluidly hitting the ground in stride while Kiko braced himself against the chimney and pulled out his revolver to shoot off a round that parted the crowd.

His bullet only caught Violet's hair as she leaped far to the side, turned to her friends, and laughed in absolute glee. The others clapped, just like they'd been invited to the party of the millennium.

Kiko took out another weapon from a second pocket—a gun that held silver holy-water-soaked darts—and prepared to shoot double-time.

Della struggled against Dawn's puppeting as the other girls fell to all fours, going through rapid changes before Kiko could fire again.

Dawn saw everything else in her peripheral vision, which barely registered as she focused on pushing, pushing at Della.

Frank winged a silvered knife at one of the vamps—Dawn couldn't tell the hideous, scrambling, giggling things apart anymore—but the creature dodged it, and the blade *swicked* into the grass in back of them.

Kiko kept firing, and somewhere in the back of Dawn's head, she wondered when the cops would come, when the humans on campus were going to get curious and investigate. . . .

A harried voice came through Dawn's earpiece.

"Dawn? Kiko? Frank?"

It was Natalia.

Dawn's concentration wobbled every time Della jerked against her hold or bit at the air, yipping in a way that made the hair on Dawn's arms stand up straight.

"Natalia?" Dawn whispered, hoping her earpiece would pick up her voice. She couldn't manage to talk any louder.

"Dawn!" Natalia's words shook. "I was monitoring in the computer room, away from the boss's inside shelter. When all the chaos started at your location, I heard him fighting something, just as he was before. Then I thought I heard the front door. I checked, and it was closed, but the headquarters defense system was disarmed. I reset it, but—"

Dawn's focus broke, but when Della took advantage, kicking in an attempt to roll away, Dawn slammed out again to push the girl down.

She tried not to think about what Natalia had just said, the implications.

"Natalia," Dawn said, "say his name. Shout it. It might help. But do it only after you turn off your microphone. Then keep monitoring."

"Yes. All right."

Natalia signed off just as the dogs started going nuts again. One of the vampires had obviously reactivated their command over them.

Shit. *Shit.* All this couldn't be happening.

Thank God the Friends regathered to blast against the canines, chopping them away from attacking Frank as he pursued one of the mobile cat-wolf vampires.

The other two ran toward the house but were blocked by more Friends while Kiko reloaded.

All the while, the vampires laughed like little maniacs who'd never had so much fun.

Frank caught up to one of the girls, and she swiped at him, leaving marks on his face. Then she kicked out, sending him hurtling across the yard before she sprang after him.

The girls were strong and lightning quick, maybe the daughters of a master . . . ?

Was that why they weren't running?

Dawn's mind-control started to quiver. She had to concentrate better, but she was also trying to work up enough energy to move Della toward Frank, so he could take over and she could deal with the remaining vampires herself.

But, God, how was Dawn actually going to move the vamp girl? She was already doing everything she could. . . .

She felt Kiko take the grenade from her hand, yet he was still firing the revolver at the vamps, too, and they'd scattered away from the house to avoid the bullets.

He'd have to reload soon. . . .

Dawn's grip on Della faltered again.

"Frank!" Kiko yelled before the vamps could take another run at the side of the house. "Take cover!"

Her dad had engaged with the vampire girl who'd chased him across the grass, and he swung her off of him, tossing her back to her group, her body bowling the other two over, while he took a dive behind a shack by the football field.

Kiko activated the grenade and chucked it at the three gathered vamp girls. Then he fell behind the chimney as a burst of ultraviolet light washed the air.

Dawn lost her mental hold as Kiko grabbed her jacket and yanked her behind the chimney, where she scrambled for balance.

Reality rushed her. Damn it, Della was free—

As the light diminished, the yelps of the girls and dogs told Dawn that the ultraviolet hadn't killed them. But, duh—they were day-walkers. What had she expected?

But when she scuttled out from behind the chimney to seek out Della again, she found that the vamps *were* rubbing against the grass to counteract their burned skin.

"Still alive," she heard Kiko say for the sake of the earpiece as he reloaded. "The grenade just put them off for the time being. These crazies are too fast for even bullets."

Dawn saw Della whining on the ground, too, and she mentally suctioned to her. Then, with all the energy she had, she mind-pulled the girl a few feet toward the football field before Della dug her boot heels into the grass.

The dogs were already recovering, lunging up to all fours before the rest of the vamp girls could. A Friend responded quickly, butting a hound and sending it flying backward, knocking it into one of the vampires as she moaned and rolled on the ground, pressing her paws against her eyes.

"Shoot them, Kik," Dawn urged.

"Getting to it," he said, still reloading.

Then her earpiece crackled to life.

"Need some help?" a familiar voice said. A voice that should still be at headquarters.

Her hold on Della fractured.

God no. It couldn't be. No, no, no.

She heard Kiko raise his guns, but then . . .

Then . . .

Something came flying out of the trees to their right, so fast it was only a line of black.

It stopped just short of one squirming dog that was battling with a Friend, the streak solidifying, showing a male in a dark coat that settled against his body as he took stock of the activity around him.

Jonah.

Dawn's control over Della snapped for good, leaving the vampire sprawling on her back and staring at the sky.

"No way," Kiko said, lowering his weapons, clearly not wanting to shoot the boss.

Then everything whirred into spliced motion, one thing, then another—

Kiko retargeted the other three cat-wolf vamps as they raised their heads, their burning eyes adjusting from the UV flash. . . .

Frank barreled out from behind the shack and raced to where Della was now struggling to her feet. . . .

Then Jonah sent Dawn a glare that told her he had something to prove after she'd pushed him down, down into the pit of his body earlier tonight.

What're you doing? she thought-yelled to him.

He didn't answer, but she already knew.

What had he said at their dinner a couple nights ago? *I don't agree very often with the way he goes about business and . . . other matters.*

Jonah had taken over for real.

Idiot. Didn't he know what he was risking?

Coiled rage sprang out of Dawn, and she used it to try to puppet Jonah out of the fray.

With one *push*, she knocked him back while Kiko aimed at the recovering girls and Frank sprang on Della, holding the vampire to the ground as she wiggled around.

Dawn sent another punch at Jonah. *Wham—*

His shoulder jerked back, but all he did was give her a disappointed look.

Don't even try, he thought to her.

But then a dog sprang at him, and Dawn lost her rhythm in the complete horror at seeing Costin's body attacked.

It didn't matter though, because Jonah reached out with arrogant grace and caught the snapping beast before it clamped to his shoulder. And when another dog came at him, wielding its teeth, Jonah snatched that one, too.

He looked amazed at his reflexes as he restrained both beasts from ripping into his chest and getting to his heart.

Dawn took out her throwing blades. She had to kill those things before they got to Costin and tore out his neck to the point where even he couldn't heal.

One of the dogs did go for Jonah's throat, but he bared his own teeth, reared both feral animals back, then banged their heads together in a spray of blood.

Shell-shocked, Dawn couldn't move. She was only vaguely aware that the vamp girls were running at the building again while Kiko reloaded what might be the last of his bullets and darts.

She also saw Frank finally overcoming Della and gazing into her eyes. . . .

But Dawn couldn't concentrate on much else because Jonah was staring at the dripping carcasses in his hands as the battle continued around him. He dropped the bodies and stared at his reddened fingers.

But then, as if overtaken by the blood, he leaned back his head, lifting his hands to his mouth.

Tasting the temptation.

Dawn's stomach turned. Jonah had never been in charge during a feeding before—it'd always been Costin imbibing the blood, truly tasting the fulfillment—and when Jonah shuddered, she knew he'd finally been satisfied after all the watching, all the torture.

Another dog attacked him and, just by lifting a hand, he caught this one, too.

She had to do something before Jonah got Costin hurt.

"Breisi!" Dawn yelled, already leaping from the roof.

Her Friend swished over and caught her midway to the ground, where the spirit cradled her to a running start toward Jonah.

At the same time, Della came alive to throw Frank off of her. They sparred while Kiko yelled for Breisi, too.

He had to be out of bullets and darts.

Even in the short time it took Dawn to reach Jonah, he'd terminated the rest of the dogs, one by fast one. She skidded to a halt in front of the discarded bodies while he inspected the blood on his hands again, his gaze blindingly ravenous.

Feet away, one of the girl vampires screeched when she saw that their animal comrades were lying all around Jonah.

Party over, she started running back toward the dorms.

Dawn cocked a throwing blade, then cursed when she realized that the Friends could follow the girls to any Underground, because that's where they might be going after getting their asses whopped.

Jasmine stormed off as another vampire girl fled.

Then another.

When Frank gave a gurgling yell, Dawn whipped around just in time to see Della take off, too, leaving Frank, who was covering his neck with his hands.

He collapsed to the ground as Della chased her group, then caught up to the last vampire galloping past the football field. There, she pounced on her, pinned her, glared at her until the one on the bottom wriggled out and raced off.

Della pursued, disappearing into some trees and leaving the branches shivering in her wake.

A gale of jasmine sped to Frank, and Breisi's voice lulled over the suddenly quiet night as blood seeped through his fingers.

"Frank?" Dawn said, fumbling the throwing blades into her pocket. She was thinking of Kiko's back, Breisi's death. . . .

"*Don't worry—he'll heal, it's not so deep,*" Breisi said. "*But we need to get to the car. The ferals have all run off now since the vampire girls have let them loose.*"

She was so serene, so truly not worried.

But Dawn . . . She wanted to cry like a damned baby, and she told herself to stop being weak. To soldier on.

She took a fistful of Jonah's coat, pulled him away from the dog and forced him to go with her to check on Frank.

Her captive got to his feet, unresisting, only touching his mouth with a blank look, his perception clearly just catching up with his appetite.

She wanted to ask him what the hell had made him come out here, why he thought it was a remotely good idea, but there was too much to deal with.

"Dad?" she asked when they came to him.

Frank made an okay sign, and she breathed easier. He was a vampire, damn it. It wasn't the same as human hurt.

Jonah had already gone to kneel by her dad's side and, for a mind-muddled second, she thought he was going to feed from him. But then he put hands on top of Frank's.

Healing. Jonah had thought to heal him before anything else.

Her dad tried to talk through it all.

"Started to ask Della . . . about Kate and vampire home . . ." he rasped. "Only made it past . . . 'Kate Lansing' and 'vampire' . . . before she . . ."

"Don't talk, Dad," Dawn said, guessing that he'd gotten at least some kind of reading from the other words before Della clawed his neck.

Couldn't he hurry up and heal?

"Saw victims . . ." Frank added, just as if he were carrying on a regular conversation during a bout of laryngitis. "Kate . . . so many other Kates . . ."

"*Shhhh,*" Breisi said. Then she sang to him again, and he focused his gaze on the air, as if he could see her. He smiled like he was just getting a freakin' haircut.

Dawn thought she heard sirens in the distance. "We've got to go, especially if those girls decide to come back."

"They won't," Jonah said.

"And how the fuck do you know?" Dawn said. She wanted to kick his ass, his face. "What were you even doing out here *to* know?"

"I literally ran right over because you sounded like you needed help. This body can go like the wind now, but Costin never lets it loose. He knows it can do so much more than he—"

"Are you sure it's not because you wanted to show that you could be free at any time, and you could endanger Costin while you're at it?"

He didn't say anything, and she knew she'd hit a button.

God damn it, if he wasn't so busy healing Frank and if Costin wouldn't feel any part of a beat down, she'd shove her fist down Jonah's throat in an attempt to yank Costin back out right now. She wouldn't even think about how Frank might not be healed this quickly if Jonah weren't here.

He didn't deserve the benefit of any doubt.

Frank started to get up, and Breisi and Dawn helped him while Jonah kept his hands on her dad's neck. They began walking as fast as they could toward the wall, then the car.

In the background, Kiko's voice called out from the roof. "Hey! Someone want to get me down from here?"

Dawn took the brunt of Frank's weight as Breisi whizzed up to Kik, then lifted him down.

When they got to the wall, Jonah helped her dad to climb it, keeping one hand over Frank's wound the entire time.

They arrived at the Sedona, which was marred with jagged scratches. Those, plus the disturbed dirt, testified to the recent ferals versus Friends battle.

As Frank waved Jonah off and got into the back of the vehicle, Jonah turned to Dawn.

"Why is his existence so much more important than mine?" he asked, just like the question had been eating at him this entire time. "Why is he more important than any of us?"

The question struck her. "Because he's saving the world while saving himself?"

"And I can't save the world just as well as he can?"

She almost laughed at that. Jonah, the savior.

But then she recalled that he had volunteered his body to Costin's cause in the first place—that he was one of those justice seekers who populated the teams.

Jonah had just taken a wrong turn somewhere.

As Frank lay down, she saw that most of his neck wounds had already been closed, but he kept healing it while he closed his eyes.

"Get your balls in there, Jonah," she said, motioning toward the car while Breisi helped Kiko to tumble over the wall.

Jonah only stared at her, those blue eyes deep and oddly emotional. "Have you ever considered that being buried inside my new body will shelter him just as well as hiding inside that house will? It's crossed *his* mind, Dawn. But that'd just be another thing he hasn't mentioned."

The words banged at her, trying to get in, but she wasn't allowing them to.

Still, the adrenaline ebbed and left her feeling ill. Costin had always likened his state to being caved in, and he'd told the team previously that buried earth tended to hide a vampire's powers from anything outside.

Was it the same for him?

Could he go outside headquarters if he was sheltered by Jonah's body?

Then why would he hesitate?

She knew. Costin's situation was too dangerous to dick around with.

Jonah lowered his voice. "I liked it, Dawn."

He meant the blood and the fight and the freedom of it all. Dawn shook her head and started to walk away.

"I'd just need a few hours to test the theory that he's safer than you think," he added. "I'll prove he doesn't need to stay behind walls, and we can strengthen all our attacks, speed them up, vanquish all the communities so he can be saved that much quicker. Because that's what you want, isn't it? To save him? Or would that mean letting too much go?"

Before her mind even tapped into that, he took a step away, and she should've known that he meant to leave with or without her blessing.

But then he smiled—an all-too-understanding gesture that took her off guard—and he zinged away in a blur that was gone before she could even react.

"Get him, Breisi!" Kiko yelled from behind Dawn.

Their Friend took off after Jonah.

Costin . . . their ultimate weapon . . .

Her ultimate . . . Something.

As sirens called in the distance, Frank sat up in the backseat, still holding his throat. "FUBAR," he rasped.

She held back all fear, because saying that their situation was Fucked Up Beyond All Recognition was the biggest understatement ever.

TWENTY-TWO

LONDON BABYLON

As the girls tore through the trees where the intruders had been hiding earlier, Della leaped on Violet again, finally catching her for good.

They spun over the dirt and leaves, roots jamming into them while they clawed at each other's skin and bit at each other's arms, rolling, rolling, until Della pinned Violet's legs with her shins and planted her hands on her arms.

Violet still tried to bite, but Della didn't even flinch as she kept restraining the other girl.

From behind the thick tree where Polly and Noreen were hiding, they whined.

"Della, stop!"

"*Della!*"

They kept peering round the trunk with their cat-wolf mouths opened, their skin reddened from the flash of the bomb the little man had thrown. As Della glared at them, her own eyes stung because the explosion had almost felt like looking straight into the sun, which had contained the power to hurt them only when they exposed themselves for too long.

"Quiet, you clots," she said.

The other girls clamped their thin lips together and retreated behind the trunk.

Violet had gone motionless, her slanted gaze malicious as Della listened for sounds of pursuit from the football field.

But there was nothing aside from the sirens that were approaching Queenshill.

Had the intruders failed to give chase because Della had injured the vampire whom the little man had called "Frank"—the one who had trespassed into her mind?

Or perhaps the violent second vampire, who had killed the dogs, was troubling the group now . . . ?

Della didn't know since the battlefield was too distant for her to catch scents or hear any clues.

Polly spoke from behind the tree. "I think they're gone."

"Cowards," Della hissed. "Every one of you ran away from them."

"They had weapons!" Polly said. "No one on other nightcrawls has ever carried weapons. Right, Vi?"

Violet snarled, growling until Della gripped her wrists tighter, making the other girl hiss because of the pressure on her burned skin.

"We shouldn't have begun our nightcrawl early at all," Noreen added.

"We didn't realize those servants had vampires with them because we were concentrating on the humans' scents," Polly said. "It was all brilliant until the dog-killer vampire appeared."

"Not even the bullets scared me." Noreen had ventured away from the trunk a tad. "Neither did Frank the vampire. And if we had got his little servant man back to our underground room, he would have been such a treat. Wolfie might have even liked the girl if she weren't so old."

Della recalled the female with the braid winding down her back. How could she forget when the woman had put Della into a strange freeze merely with an intense stare? Did she have some manner of servant powers from her master vampire that allowed her to mentally captivate others?

And was she the reason the dogs had been flying round—because her mind willed it?

Perhaps Frank the vampire had somehow given her those powers, seeing as he'd come into Della's own mind after saying the words "Kate Lansing" and "vampire." Della didn't know how he knew about Kate, but it had caused her to think about that particular nightcrawl, then others. And by the time Della had banished him from her thoughts and sprung at him, Noreen, then Polly, then Violet had fled, their playtime turned into a nightmare they'd never expected.

"We should have never left the house," Della said, remembering how she had made just such an error in judgment when she'd buried Kate Lansing's head. She'd promised never to disappoint Wolfie again, yet the others hadn't listened to her warnings. "Have we been so coddled by Wolfie that we don't know how to make good decisions when we're on our own?"

Polly got saucy, coming out from behind the tree. "He's always taught us to enjoy what we are, and that's all we were trying to do."

Della bared her teeth at her, and Polly shrank back.

"We're too used to his protected nightcrawls," Della said through those teeth. "We're well versed in choosing recruits, yet we have no notion about how to handle anything beyond that. I know we have nearly a year of education left, and Wolfie will no doubt teach us how to fight for the dragon in the proper manner, but I sincerely doubt he'll be proud of how we responded to our first test tonight."

As she thought of the punishment that would come their way, her burned skin flashed with more pain.

It wasn't fair. She alone had known of a possible blood brother in the area because Wolfie had never given her permission to share the information she had obtained by breaking into his mind. Yet she had done everything within her power to stop the group from this particular nightcrawl without breaking Wolfie's confidence.

Even so, punishment or not, he would have to be told that Frank the vampire could be a blood brother or even a scout for one. And she would have already contacted Wolfie or the cat if they hadn't been out of range at the sub-Underground common room, waiting for them to report for the scheduled nightcrawl.

As the sirens clamored even closer to the property, making them cringe, Della noticed that human students were gathered at all the glowing boarding houses' windows.

Violet took advantage of the distraction by rearing up and aiming her teeth at Della's arm.

Taken by surprise, Della did something she'd never, ever thought to do before.

She spit on Violet.

The other girl jerked back, her eyes saucering as the expectoration bubbled on her bare brow, then trickled down her hairless skull and past her wolflike ear.

Della braced herself, but when Violet remained still—she was afraid? She was afraid!—Della's pulse began to chug.

She leaned closer to the other girl, done with the fear, done with always being the lowly one.

"You should have paid mind to me when I told you I had identified the scent from those trees," she said to Violet. Then she gazed at Polly and Noreen, who were hiding again. "Yet none of you thought this was significant. Not coming from me. And you even seemed to take pleasure in proving that I was wrong. What fun you would have with a little man like the one from school, you said. How delightful it would be to bat him round while we waited for Wolfie. Afterward, we could always charm the intruders into forgetfulness, no harm done." Della's tone had risen in pitch, competing with the sharpness of the sirens, but now her voice snarled in resentment.

"We could charm them just as we did to Melinda Springfield after the raven attack."

None of the others responded, making it obvious that the sirens had abruptly stopped. Bobbies, who'd no doubt been summoned by a report of gunfire near the far football field, were probably at the school's gates.

Polly and Noreen came out, sniffing at the air.

Jasmine, Della thought. They had been detecting the scent since this morning, and it had caused them to wonder whether it was coming from flowers or too much new perfume on a student.

It was stronger than ever now.

As a matter of fact, it'd been stronger during the confrontation.

Violet remained unmoving, and Della could feel how the other girl's muscles were tensed, as if in retracted humiliation.

Della gazed down at their fallen leader, and for the first time, confidence flooded her.

I'm not afraid anymore, she thought, her mind open for all of them to hear. *Not afraid of you, not afraid of answers.*

"Do you even care that you led us into danger tonight?" she asked Violet.

The other girl laughed—a weak sound compared to all her other laughs—and Della dug in harder with her claws.

"Before we sneak back inside, you're going to tell me what you know about Blanche," Della said. "And Sharon and Briana."

Before Violet could laugh more, Della choked her off by wrapping a claw round her throat.

There was fear in Violet's eyes . . . absolute fear, because she knew Della was beyond caring now, that she had taken the last of any abuse.

Flash fast, Della used her other paw to whisk at Violet's face. A warning.

Blood beaded out of the gashes on the girl's red-burned skin as she refused to speak.

"One more opportunity, Vi," Della said. "Something has been happening with our group, and I've had the sneaking suspicion you might be responsible."

Violet tried to shake her head, a last-ditch effort to cling to her dominance as her wounds began self-healing.

But this was the "leader" who'd broken Della down, encouraged her to feed off Melinda, had made her feel like compost that only existed to allow the others to grow.

All Della's bottled resentment exploded, and she leaped to her feet while still gripping Violet by the neck. She swung the other girl round, released her, sent her flying toward a tree.

Violet slammed into it, slipping to the ground while Della stood, hunched, waiting.

The trunk vibrated in an aftershock, heaving leaves to the ground as Violet bared her teeth and growl-hissed.

Della needed no more invitation.

She sprang at her, grabbing her ankle and spinning her body once again over her head then letting her career into another tree, which shed more leaves as Violet stayed on the ground, scrabbling at the dirt.

Coming to stand over her, Della kept her arms arced at her sides, her back bent. "What do you know about our old friends?"

Polly and Noreen were behind their tree again, but Della could hear their thoughts opening, stretching for answers.

Violet wrestled to breathe, then glared up at Della while struggling to all fours. "Wouldn't you like to—"

Della kicked with all of her might, with all the hurt that had collected and waited for a moment such as this.

Violet screeched up through the air, and in what seemed to take hours instead of seconds, she crashed against another tree. But this time . . .

This time a branch speared out of her left shoulder, flaring blood as she shaped her mouth into a silent scream.

A scream that ripped through all of their minds.

Polly and Noreen winced as Violet shuddered, then gaped at the red sprout of branch at her shoulder.

Della's breath scraped in, scraped out.

Power. Was this what it felt like?

Whatever this was, she had finally grown into it, was accepting it, just as Wolfie had accepted himself so long ago.

Her ears perked as the mad shuffle of running footsteps came into range. Bobbies, headed for the football field.

Time to leave. But first . . .

"Violet," Della said, believing now that her voice *could* be so solid, so resonant with command. "Tell me about Blanche, Sharon, and Briana."

The hanging girl opened her mouth, but nothing came out. And when Della looked into her mind, it was nothing more than a jumble of yelps and cries.

Violet—the consummate liar. The one who normally seemed to pin consequences on anyone else if she could manage.

She wasn't going to escape this time.

Della growl-hissed, and Violet's mouth finally worked round the thoughts coming to the surface.

I have no idea what happened to them, she said. *I wanted you to think I knew, but I didn't. . . .*

Della suspected the truth in her words but didn't believe the purity act.

You were happy to have them gone, she said. *Why?*

Please, Della . . .

Why? Did you ever care about where they went? Or were you content as long as Wolfie turned his gaze upon you in their stead?

Della . . .

Tell us!

All right, I wanted them gone. A tear ran down Violet's creature face. *I swear to you, this is the entire truth. Please, heal me. I hurt.*

But Della's frustration had only been stoked. *You rejoiced when each one of them left because you had that much more of Wolfie's affections. Even worse, you blocked the rest of us out of your head and made us believe that you* did *know their fates. This gave you power, didn't it, Vi? It made you think you were so much better when, all along, you knew you weren't. You were frightened to death that we would discover it someday.*

Violet's hair began to flow out of her skull. Her pain wasn't allowing her to hold the vampire form. *You've made your point. I promise, I'll never say a harsh word to you again.* She turned all the way back into her human shape. *Please, Della.*

Violet took hold of the branch jutting out of her shoulder, as if that would somehow dissolve it and set her free. Yet if anyone deserved pain, Violet did, especially since she couldn't even bring herself to apologize for the bullying. It wasn't often that the world offered justice—not in Della's experience—so who was she to put a halt to it?

But then Polly and Noreen crept up behind her, pawing at her legs in a plea.

For a moment, Della didn't understand. . . .

Then she did.

She saw another tear fall from Violet's eye and knew this was her decision to make.

Della's gaze cleared, the flashing glare from the bomb finally abating.

Power. Violet had mauled it. If Della did the same, would that put her on the same base level?

She shook her head, wondering if she would regret this. *You'll never actually heal where it counts, Vi,* she mind-said before scampering up the tree.

She extracted Violet, the branch sucking out of her shoulder, making the other girl moan. Then Della brought her down, handing her over to Polly, who cradled Vi as they started back toward the house.

At the edge of the trees, Della willed herself to change into humanlike form again, just as Polly and Noreen were doing.

We'll heal Violet at the house, she said from her position at the front of the group.

Noreen trailed at the rear. *We won't tell anyone what happened? Let's not tell.*

Della thought of the eyes of the cat and how its gaze would flicker in bruising disappointment once it heard everything.

But there was no other choice.

We have to tell, Della said, drawing on more courage than she'd ever known herself to possess.

Before she lost any of it, she ran toward the house. The others followed, whining at what was surely to come once they reported in.

When they arrived, they sniffed round the door to discern if the path would be clear of humans before they entered. No danger. Yet they found themselves locked out nonetheless, having left their card keys in their rooms.

Thus, Della covertly led them crawling up the wall, pulling Violet with them, to her second-level quarters. The window had been left slightly ajar, so accessing it was a simple matter.

Polly and Noreen laid Violet on the bed while Della headed straight for the door.

Put a chair under the knob after I leave, she mind-told Polly. *It's the best lock we'll find to block any room checks that are sure to be occurring. While I'm gone, heal Violet.*

Polly stood away from the reclining Violet, who was beyond pale as Noreen pressed her hands over her wound. A glow suffused the dim room.

Must we? Polly asked.

Della swallowed. *It'll be worse if they find out on their own.*

With that, she went through the door, shut it behind her, and listened for Polly to jam the chair under the knob. When she did, Della dug her nails into her palms then began her trek down the hall.

Not afraid. I'm not afraid now.

That strange jasmine smell—what *was* it?—hovered while she walked, careful to look human lest any normal students see her.

Minutes later, she was knocking on a familiar door before entering, knowing no one would be inside anyway. Then, drawing in a quivering breath, she called on her vampire powers just this once and darted into the room, quickly shutting and securing the door behind her.

No more jasmine, she vaguely thought.

She moved to a wardrobe, opened it, focused on feeling round the back panel for the spring that she knew would release a door that hid a tunnel to the sub-Underground common room.

A private tunnel not belonging to the girls at all that they would've been severely punished for using in any case but this.

MUCH earlier, after the ritual, the cat had stayed for hours more in its buried, faraway room, absorbed with the sight in the mirror.

Beautiful again!

In the oval reflection, the creature preened, worshipped, celebrated the blush of its revitalized future. Such rosy, tight skin. Such red lips, glossy hair, and refreshed eyes . . .

Pity it would have to use cosmetics when it went back to work aboveground. It was always a shame to cover the rituals' effects until aging took over again.

Even so, it couldn't take its gaze off of itself while caressing the length of its bare body, cupping its firmed breasts and sliding its palms over its smooth stomach.

I don't look a day over my late twenties. Not a moment past the age when it had exchanged blood and become a vampire.

Then it stopped its celebration for a moment, its gaze connecting with the one in the mirror.

Its eyes. There was still the wisdom of ages there. . . .

Yet the pause didn't last long as it continued on to all the other wonderful improvements again.

When it felt a tingle licking at the back of its mind, it knew Mihas had finally entered through the ground door from the forest. He'd arrived from the main Underground, where he had spent last night and today, and had come to meet the girls in the sub-Underground for their nightcrawl.

Excitement raced like tiny bites under the cat's taut skin.

But, through Awareness, it knew Mihas was preoccupied. He was no doubt musing about that event from nearly a week past when one of the *custodes*, keepers who worked for the Underground on a consulting basis, had disappeared from duty. The unit possessed backups, yet the head *custode*'s absence still crossed Mihas's thoughts every so often.

Naturally, the cat had attempted to assuage him; the creature had been his constant, his consort, his calming balm throughout the centuries. If there were a blood brother behind the *custode*'s disappearance, there was no reason to fret. Mihas and the cat had so many resources at their fingertips that falling to one of those storied, scheming blood brothers was laughable.

And he always believed the cat, just as much as it believed.

The creature took one last look at its naked mirror self then dressed in a silken gown that recalled the old days when Mihas had loved the cat more than he did now. It spent its time aboveground in a relatively drab disguise, mainly because it didn't look young and gorgeous enough to assume this form—Mihas's favorite.

But now . . .

Now it couldn't wait to show Mihas its rejuvenated look before the students arrived. It couldn't wait to win him back.

Anxious to see the desire in Mihas's eyes—when was the last time it had seen that from him?—the creature moved past the newly cleaned blades hanging from the ceiling, then exited the room. It took care to charm the rock door so no one else would enter if they ever found the hideaway.

It rushed through the tunnels, the hem of its heavy gown barely dusting the floor. In the final tunnel leading to the girls' common room, its Awareness doubled in vein-quaking force.

Mihas. Companion. Beloved.

When it ultimately came to the beads that decorated the entrance, the Awareness tripled.

It bit its lip to hold back the overwhelming yearning for him while peeking through the rounded plastic baubles.

There he was, sprawled on a divan while paging through a manga book one of his "darlings" had brought down here to read.

The cat touched the beads, creating a mysterious prelude to its entrance, playing with Mihas as much as he played with everyone else.

Yet he still paged through the book.

Anticipation gnawed under the creature's skin now, and it rattled the beads once more.

Another turn of the page.

The cat wouldn't rush in. It wouldn't *give* in.

Yet then Mihas glanced up, a wide grin curving his mouth as he tossed the book aside.

The cat pressed its hand to its chest, which drummed with hollow vibrations.

"I can see your outline through those beads, Claudia, and I scented those clothes of yours long before that." Mihas cocked his head. "No more cat form?"

He sounded excited, even under the teasing tone.

Long, long ago, the cat had trained its voice to a husky, smooth timbre—a tone that fooled the world above, and even itself sometimes.

"Why look like a cat when there's no need now?" it said. "Not after what Blanche gave to me tonight."

At the mention of the girl's name, Mihas leaned forward, his forearms on his thighs. He hated it whenever one of the students was sacrificed.

Perhaps a reminder of what their nubile bodies yielded would return some perspective to him. . . .

He spoke, casting a pall on the cat's well-planned ceremony of revelation.

"In case you're wondering," he said, "the girls are becoming suspicious about yet another disappearance, but they're more affected and lonely than anything. The remaining members of the class always seem to get that way after three of their own have left with little explanation."

"I cover the absences. Sharon was allowed to say her farewells before she departed. Plus, I took up her identity while e-mailing the rest of the class, just as I'll do with Blanche. I'm also sure you managed to distract the girls with your Underground tour. Every time the third one leaves, your enthusiasm for your home seems to make them forget until the next student's departure."

And, make no mistake, the cat was watching to see which girl would come next. Which lovely girl threatened it the most.

Wolfie stood. "It's a hard time for them, Claudia. After the third girl, it always becomes more difficult to disguise these rituals of yours. There are only so many times one of them can run away or be claimed by their parents before the rest begin to concoct nefarious explanations."

"I shouldn't need but one more ritual before the school year ends and the remainder of this class moves on to the main Underground." The cat brushed against the beads in a bid to regain Mihas's attention. "Then I'll have a crop of new girls who won't know any better."

The restless clack of the strands had indeed snatched his focus, just as Claudia had hoped.

"Show yourself, my love," he said, his tone gritty, as it always was when the cat became a new woman again.

Yet Claudia knew this wouldn't last. Not with his darlings near and dear to keep him satisfied—a situation the cat allowed only because Mihas always returned to it in the end.

Still, at this wonderful moment, Claudia knew he was keen to see the results, even though sorrow also colored his voice.

But he would forget about Blanche soon, just after Claudia stepped through the beads.

The creature savored this moment of utter control. It was going to make him suffer for turning his affections elsewhere while Claudia's beauty had shriveled.

Although he was forbidden to consummate his lust or actually feed from the fresh, sweet, finely raised Queenshill class, he did everything but poach them from the cat. Yet he would realize, once again, that these were not his girls at all—they belonged to Claudia, just as *he* belonged to her.

It had always been thus, even before the cat had secured a job on campus fifteen years ago in order to make the harvesting for its rituals easier. The sub-Underground was Claudia's own paradise, and every two years it carefully chose seven girls for the class, which consisted of students who believed they were only being primed for the Highgate Underground.

There was much work involved, mainly because the girls had to fit the profile of a neglected daughter who wouldn't be monitored by parents—a candidate who was too afraid to leave what the community offered, even if they began to suspect strange doings. The girls were always the type who never wished to reach womanhood, with all its gnarled, snatching thorns and terrifying dark places.

Claudia was even now weeding out younger candidates for the next class of seven—a safe number that would carry the cat through its rituals and then some.

Mihas ran a hand along the wall on his way toward the entrance.

"Yes, come," Claudia said, feeling those tiny bites of stimulation eating through its skin to make their way to the top, where its flesh ached. "I thought you had perhaps grown overly fond of Blanche and you might not enjoy what her sacrifice has brought about. Show me I was wrong."

"How can you say that when you've always been the fairest of the fair?" Mihas eased to the other side of the beads, his hungry voice filtering through them. "You have forever owned my heart, even if my attentions have occasionally wandered."

"Oh, the charm," Claudia said. "How it slays me."

Mihas smiled, his teeth gleaming.

But the cat would not allow him such an easy escape, even if all it wished to do was part those beads and see the blossoming of renewed adoration in his gaze.

So long. Too long . . .

"I have always owned your heart?" Claudia asked. "Even, centuries ago, when I first grew ugly and you left me so you could wander the surface world while I remained below? You had your entertainments, while I played the good companion, minding our responsibilities. Remember, it was only a little over a year ago that you took those trips to the States—Los Angeles, Chicago, New York—all to see that band you like. Then it was off to Ireland, then Scotland—"

"I have always returned to you, my love."

"You stay once I restore myself with young blood—the kind you, too, believe gives you such power."

When Mihas lent more wattage to his pointed smile, Claudia's blood rushed south. He had such sway.

"Whether it was in Persia," he said, "or in South America or anywhere in France—you knew I would end up by your side. Yet, here in London, I have settled, except for my holidays. I believe that should merit some appreciation."

"The dragon commanded the creation of Undergrounds, Mihas. Not I."

"Ah, details, details." His charisma traveled like strokes from a reaching hand. "Does it not mean anything that we have created all these children together—little girls we outfitted to communicate with each other as one true class? Fearless, hungry, vicious things who are half me, half you?"

He could talk Claudia into his graces every time, but he was forgetting that their progeny—part of the wolf that defined his vampire form and part of the cat that defined Claudia's—didn't touch any emotional chords within.

Yet that wasn't true of Mihas. Rumors from traveling blood brothers testified that other master vampires had developed cravings for the souls of the children they created. Would his affection for their progeny follow the same pattern? At the moment, he loved his girls for their flushed skin and dimpled smiles, but he didn't have an appetite for anything so meaningful as a soul connection.

And if that ever happened, Claudia might not be able to compete anymore.

The creature teased the right side of the beads, pushing only a few strands back. "You talk of children, Mihas, but all I've ever wanted was you."

He looked at Claudia's exposed hand—the fruit-soft skin—and his eyes got that lost and hungry glaze for which the cat had been wishing. He was all Claudia's now.

"Mihas," the cat-vampire said, nearly purring as it finally parted the fall of red and orange.

His expression deepened to stricken male worship, and he fell to his knees.

"My Claudia," he whispered, strangled by his passion as his teeth lengthened in uncontrolled lust. "Oh, my Claudia."

The cat smiled, leaning toward him to claim its reward for enduring his faults, his naughtiness.

As it touched its mouth to his, the prick of his teeth pierced the new softness of its lips, dragging Claudia into a dreamy reawakening of love.

DELLA had bounded through the tunnel where she knew help—and punishment—would be waiting. There had been sharp roots along the way, digging into her skin, but she was already healing from the cuts.

Yet she was hardly even thinking of them anyway.

Telling the truth was more important than anything, and she was willing to stand up to the consequences. Unfortunately, she would be doing it face-to-face since she had not been able to reach Wolfie or the cat with her thoughts from the boarding house. As usual, a layer of earth had blocked a mind-reach from the surface to below, so here she was, running, running. . . .

When she came to a cavern, she sensed both of her superiors. She picked up speed and, within a second, arrived at the beads dangling before the common room's entrance, winging them aside while stumbling in.

The sight before her stopped her cold.

Anguish gripping her, Della spun away to avert her eyes, mostly because she hadn't expected to see Wolfie kissing . . .

Who?

She heard the kiss end, heard Wolfie say, "Della?" like a man under a wicked spell.

She hedged her gaze back to them, almost apologizing before her words collapsed to nothing.

The woman he was with . . . She had a face so colorful, so striking, so *changed* that Della didn't know what to say.

"Della," the woman repeated, and her normally haggard voice even sounded polished, as if years had been washed off like a crust of dirt over something buried and forgotten until now.

Della couldn't stop looking at her, mainly because she'd never seen the woman in this guise—only as a cat and as the much less stunning authority figure the girls knew from school.

As the surprise wore off, Della took in the nuances: The glistening brown hair let out of its bun to tumble down her back. The flushed skin showcasing high, imperious cheekbones and scarlet lips. Her rose silk gown only added to the handsome, regal effect, its collar high, its skirt a rustling, full bloom.

So breathtaking, Della thought, that she understood the reason Wolfie had been kissing her.

But when she noticed how the woman's mouth was turned downward in obvious displeasure at being caught, Della's pulse suspended. If she had felt like a meal at any time during one of Violet's devastating glares, this put those to shame.

She felt as if she was about to be sliced apart and then bitten to pieces.

The woman stood away from Wolfie, who groped to keep ahold of her slim waist.

Knowing flattery would only aid her, Della said, "You . . . You look so lovely. Beyond lovely."

And . . . phew.

"Well." The woman held a hand to a pink cheek, pleased. "I'm afraid you've caught me shifting to a form I don't often use. It takes too much energy to seem this young." She smiled at Wolfie. "Energy I should be using to stave off any weakness we vampires can experience during a long day."

Mihas rose up, still staring at his companion. "The cost is always worth the results."

They exchanged long glances and, somehow, Della thought the comment contained more than she was meant to know.

She might have thought further on it if tonight's disaster wasn't making her so anxious.

When Wolfie brought himself to acknowledge Della again, he frowned, his teeth receding from their aroused state. "What has happened to you? Your . . . skin?"

Della touched her bomb-burned, root-scratched face, which had already begun healing on its own.

The woman followed up with another question. "Where are the others, Della?"

Fear resurfaced, trembles overtaking her belly. She had to tell them. No choice.

She opened her mind like the pages of a book she'd hidden

under a pillow, and they expertly thumbed through every detail: the intruders, Violet's idea to start their nightcrawl by capturing the little man, the resulting disaster.

They even saw what Della had done to Violet afterward.

When she finished, Della couldn't even swallow, could hardly breathe. Time to pay . . .

Wolfie lifted his thick brows and connected gazes with the woman once more, clearly communicating with her. Then he glanced at Della, and smiled with what she thought to be a touch of sadness.

"You really are a fighter," he said. "Impressive judgment. A fine addition to the main Underground. Once you mature—"

"She *has* matured," the woman said sharply.

Wolfie sighed, and Della wished she knew the reason for it. Had she already begun to resemble the less pure girls in the main Underground? Had she already lost Wolfie's interest?

Yet from the way the woman was assessing her with that feline gaze, Della thought perhaps this was more about Wolfie liking her too much.

A chill overtook her.

"A wee person shooting bullets," the woman said, as if musing aloud about the intruders. "And a female who uses her mind to such an extent. Fascinating traits for the servants of a vampire such as this 'Frank.' "

Wolfie folded his hands behind his back, a gesture that wasn't so much relaxed as concerned. "None of our girls perished in the altercation."

"They didn't precisely come out smelling like English roses, either," the woman said. "I've told you—your training has always been too lax. Intruders appear, and the students think it's time to flit about. Certainly, you've taught the girls hunger, Mihas, and that is vital in creating a fearsome soldier. Yet while flippancy suits you, it will not aid *them* when the dragon summons us."

"There's still time to polish their skills."

"Make it the present time, if you please."

Della was near to bursting. "And Frank the vampire? He wanted to know about Kate Lansing. You saw that he went into my mind to find information about her."

"A preternatural detective, perhaps?" Wolfie asked. "In this day, everyone is an entrepreneur."

The woman tilted her head. "He didn't ask about an Underground?"

"No," Della said. "At least, not before I silenced him."

She laughed, as if admiring Della, and the sound raised her hackles.

"From what you showed us, Della," she said, "'Frank' wasn't a blood brother. Yet I'm rather curious about this motley group. We've encountered many a vampire before who wasn't affiliated with an Underground, and they've never proven a problem. I'm always interested in the study of them."

"Claudia," Wolfie asked, "you don't find it interesting that—"

"Yes, yes, that the chief *custode* has gone missing, as well," she said. "We've experienced stranger coincidences in the past. Besides, we've been informed that the *custode* has already been replaced with another, and the unit is surely investigating even as we speak. They'll take care of the matter if these intruders should be a threat."

Wolfie shot a glance at Della, and the woman laughed again.

"Did you not reveal to me," she said, "that your *darling* here had the tenacity to poke into your mind and she's heard the word '*custode*' before? Of course, you didn't punish her, Mihas, so it would seem to be of little importance."

"I was careless," Wolfie said. "So kill me."

He grinned at her before she smiled indulgently—embarrassingly so, to Della—and addressed her charge again.

"You're going to be taught about *custode*s soon enough, but I see no reason to put off the lesson now, especially since you met them in the Underground when you visited. Remember those red-eyed beings who greeted you in the dark?"

Della wished not to recall them at all.

"These days," the woman continued, "you might say they are 'contractors' because they work on their own and leave us to our business, which is the way Mihas and I have liked it. They haven't failed us yet."

"They do always manage to cover our tracks," Wolfie said.

"*Your* tracks."

Della tried to tell herself that the Underground had faced situations even more serious than this before, and they had flourished. Why else would they be taking this news so well?

Wolfie came to Della, ruffled her hair. "But my darlings should never have to worry. So don't."

Even as he said it, his attention strayed back to the woman in her silken gown, her glowing beauty. But she was watching Della with that monstrous and destructive gaze again, plucking her apart with only a look.

Was she . . . jealous? Why, when *she* had been the one kissing Wolfie only a short time ago?

"Mihas," she said, still watching Della. "Why don't I take the girls to a neutral, safe place away from here while the *custode*s investigate? Meanwhile, you can travel the tunnels and emerge from an exit far away from Highgate. We might as well be cautious until the *custode*s inform us otherwise."

"Tunnels," he said, as if disgusted. And why wouldn't he be when he so loved to run free?

"Until then," the woman added, "you should stay in one of your city flats. Don't pay visits to the Underground yet. I'll keep watch for those intruders, although I suspect the *custode*s will be taking them in hand soon enough."

Wolfie looked upon her as if she were the most brilliant woman in mind and body—his queen.

Something also changed in the woman's eyes—heating like a steady candle's flame in a dark room.

"Della," she said, her voice lowering to an intimate hush, "off with you now. Wait for me out of the room."

Blood rushed to Della's face as she ducked toward the beaded exit. They were going to kiss again. . . .

"Yes, Mrs. Jones," she said, obeying before her housematron decided to punish her after all.

TWENTY-THREE

The Return

THE team had gathered in Frank's room at headquarters while an ominous silence ticked down to the moment when Breisi might return with news of Jonah's whereabouts.

At Frank's weapons table, Dawn and Kiko were laying out their best-loved tools so Natalia could select which ones she preferred to carry after she was ready to stand with the rest of the team outside these walls. As for Frank—he'd been coerced into sitting on his bed, even though he was basically healed.

No one talked at all, but it wasn't because they were worried about Jonah. Well, they *were*, but the awkward lack of conversation had more to do with the fact that Eva was also present, dabbing at the fused wounds on her ex-husband's neck with healing gel as he kept trying to tell her that he was okay, that the wounds hadn't gone all that deep.

As Eva ignored his protests, Dawn tried not to be bothered by her mother's gentleness with him. Since Breisi wasn't around, Eva was able to play nurse, so there weren't really consequences to finally being able to touch Frank after all these months of keeping a near distance from him. Watching it made Dawn so sad for her.

She thumped a holy water bracelet to the table with more force than she needed to use.

Kalin, she thought. The Friend had set up this situation with Eva and Frank, and Dawn had no doubt that it was out of pure vindictive pettiness.

The spirit had been charged with watching over headquarters tonight, and after hearing about Frank's injuries, Kalin had shot right over to Eva's and brought her back here, where they'd been waiting for Frank when the team had returned. Of course, Kalin had explained that she'd thought Frank might need some human attention while the rest of them were busy battening down the hatches, checking the motion-sensored outside UV lights and arming the automated silver-arrow mechanisms by the door.

But Dawn knew better.

Kiko had his back to Eva and Frank as he set a holy water vial next to his dart gun. His movements were tight, not only because he was anxious about Jonah, but he was also ticked that he hadn't been able to hit any of the Queenshill girls with his bullets or darts. Yet that only made him want to go out again, to prove himself ten times over.

"All right, all right," Frank said to Eva from across the room. "I've got enough gel on now."

"Just a little more . . ." Eva said.

Dawn and Kiko connected gazes, on the same mental page.

"What a troublemaker," he said softly enough to keep Eva from hearing.

Natalia was scanning the dart gun. "Who's making trouble? Not Eva."

"No, not Eva," Kiko said. "Kalin. She found a roundabout way to irk Dawn, even during what has to be the most inappropriate time ever, with Jonah running around. See, Kalin knows that Breisi, who's always defending Dawn, won't be too stoked about Eva playing nicey-nice with Frank like this. I don't know why Costin keeps her around, especially when she's got a thing for Jonah, who's a bad frakkin' apple, himself."

At the bed, Dawn saw that Frank had heard every word, and he gave her a warning look, as if Eva might hear and get her feelings hurt. Or that Kalin, who was roaming the house, might take offense.

Natalia poked at the dart gun, then took her finger away, as if the thing might bite. "Speaking of Jonah—"

"Breisi and the others who joined her will get him," Dawn said, trying to persuade herself more than anything as she carefully set a mini flamethrower next to a full-sized one. "And maybe she'll even talk some sense into him."

"I don't understand," Natalia said. "Why hasn't Breisi been able to catch him yet?"

"Because," Kiko answered, "the Friends are quick, but they're no match for any vamps. Also, I'm pretty sure they're all worn out from everything else they went through tonight."

Dawn nodded. The team had discovered that the spirits had done even more than wrestling devil animals and shepherding Dawn, Kiko, and Frank around; the Friends had diverted curious humans from the area until the team had departed the campus and the police had arrived. They'd also kept tabs on the Queenshill vampires, reporting that the girls had engaged in a scuffle and then retreated to the dorms. Apparently, Della had really injured Violet, who was being healed by Polly and Noreen while Della had disappeared into the housematron's room, shutting Friend Greta outside before she could follow her in. And it didn't help that the vents were closed in Mrs. Jones's room.

Their surveillance had been cut, yet this wasn't necessarily bad news. Not if this room led to an Underground entrance, as they suspected.

Dawn's hopes picked up speed, pumping through her, but she was brought back to reality right quick. Searching for a vamp community would be useless until Jonah returned with Costin, their ultimate Underground weapon.

Good God. Was that all she could say about Costin? That he was an ultimate weapon? Why was that the first thing she always thought to call him?

Natalia broke in. "What if Breisi never finds Jonah?"

Dawn wouldn't even consider it. "She will."

"But what if—"

"No what-ifs."

Natalia didn't press on. Thank God, because Dawn wasn't going to mull over what she might have to do if Jonah decided that he wanted to keep Costin suppressed.

But what if—jeez, the dreaded words—Costin *couldn't* even get out of that body altogether when push came to shove and it was time for the final attack? He hadn't been successful in leaving Jonah before, so what even made her think he'd be able to do it when it counted the most?

Spurred by the questions, she left the weapons table and headed for the door. "I'm going to try again to get in touch with that jerk on the earpiece. He might've had his fill of adventure by now."

Kiko stopped her. "Contacting Jonah won't do any good. He's gonna do what he's gonna do. Besides, there's always a chance Costin might overcome him and force him to return."

"No, he'd never take the risk of exposing himself out there, no matter what ridiculous theories about being protected have crossed his mind. Jonah's in total control right now."

She realized that everyone in the room was looking at her with sympathetic expressions, just like they understood the extent of her frustration, her worry.

But they didn't. How could they unless they'd been the ones who'd seen how Costin fought himself night after night? How he longed to be rid of the body she'd locked him into with that exchange over a year ago?

Eva's motherly perusal especially got to Dawn. Or maybe it was just the sight of her parents both sitting there, side by side, as Eva paused in the middle of capping the healing gel, her knee against Frank's thigh.

Once upon a time, Dawn thought, *there were two people who loved each other. . . .*

Ending the tale right there, she went for the door. If she could raise Jonah on the earpiece, maybe she could save Costin from any harm that his host might inflict on them.

She walked down the hall, sensing Kiko and Natalia right behind her. She headed for the stairway, which would lead her to the bedroom window where she had a good view of the street.

"I can't stop thinking that maybe Della summoned an Underground to go after us," she said to them. "And that this Underground might get to Jonah before Breisi does."

"Those girls might not be a part of any bigger group," Kiko said, "especially an Underground that's been around for any length of time. Remember—Frank only saw the murdered girls in Della's mind before she shielded."

They had stopped at the stairs. Kiko rubbed his back, and Dawn knew he would need to rest it, knew he might even ask a Friend to lull him so he wouldn't have to take a pill.

Natalia watched him, too, and Dawn decided she would privately ask the new girl to keep an eye on the situation.

But Kiko read them perfectly, the perceptive fool, and he folded his arms over his chest.

"So?" he asked, a fighter all the way. "What do you think we should be doing beyond contacting Jonah to get him back here?"

He was asking her?

Dawn almost laughed, but then she saw Natalia watching her with the same question in her gaze.

That's when she realized it: as Costin's right-hand gal, she was basically in charge now. Her. Dawn.

They were FUBAR, all right.

But now wasn't the time for thinking about how she'd never committed to a damned thing in her life, how she wasn't capable of more than temporary gigs or relationships.

Act! like you know what you're doing, she told herself. *Costin would want that.*

"Kik," she said, "maybe you can acquaint Natalia with more of our arsenal later and take her down to the entry now so you can catch the Friends as they exit and enter the trapdoor. At the same time, the two of you can brainstorm ideas for getting into that housematron's room."

After things returned to normal, of course.

Both of them seemed relieved to have direction, and they went downstairs, leaving Dawn to go up to her room so she could wait at the window, where she'd tried to reach Jonah on the earpiece before.

Once there, she parted the heavy curtains, revealing the cemented, gated, ribbon-strewn Cross Bones Graveyard across the street and the buildings loitering behind it like disinterested guardians.

"Jonah?" she said, schooling her voice so that it didn't reflect how pins and needles she felt. "Jonah, if you're not answering because you think I'm angry with you, come on. Talk to me. I'm not mad."

Silence.

All right, more *acting!* "I know you want to be a hero as much as anyone. You were during the Hollywood attack." She paused because it was the truth. "You were *real* brave."

That night, Jonah had fought Benedikte just as courageously as Costin himself had. *That* night when the world had turned even more upside down than before . . .

Dawn's throat heated, making the words tough to get out. "Please, Jonah. We need your help as much now as we did then."

More silence.

Hopelessness weighed her forward, and she barred her arms over the window, resting the crown of her head against the cold glass.

What were they going to do now?

What was *she* going to do?

When her skin prickled, just like it had back at Queenshill when Della had come to the dorm window—no, wait, just like on Billiter when she'd first seen the red-eye boy watching them—Dawn raised her head. She scanned the graveyard, the low rooftops beyond it.

A movement in her peripheral vision sent ice ricocheting through her, but when she focused on it, there was nothing.

Spooked, she shut the curtains, inching away from the window, her heart stretched in a trembling line from her chest to her throat.

Someone—some *thing*—had been out there.

Vampires?

Or . . . ?

She tore out of the room, down the stairs, through the entry where Kiko and Natalia were arguing over a pen and a pad of paper.

"Any word from the Friends?" Dawn asked as she dashed by. "Anything outside we should know about?"

"No," they both said.

Leaving them behind, Dawn busted through the heavy wooden door that served as the entrance to the lab, then descended to unlock the main door itself.

Once in the sterile room, which was filled with everything from weapons in progress to crates containing equipment they still hadn't unpacked, she went for the freezer, opened it up.

A huff of iced air obscured her vision, making her stomach drop until the image of the frozen boy—the one who'd sported that night vision—cut through the haze.

He hadn't gone anywhere.

No, his skin was still rosy compared to its layer of frost, and the incisions in his head and chest, plus the tears in his neck from Frank, were still stitched shut. His underwear was iced, his limbs spread as he reclined against the board he was strapped to. And his face was still so young—almost pretty with full lips and a cleft in his chin.

A strange laugh burbled out of her throat.

God, what had she expected? For him to be resurrected and leaping around on rooftops again?

She shut the door, feeling better until she wondered what *was* outside if it wasn't him.

Or . . . Damn it, maybe she was being paranoid. That was a distinct possibility, too.

She rubbed her arms, remembering what Natalia had said about Costin retiring his former teams before they went insane. . . .

Her earpiece crackled, then went dead.

"Jonah?" she asked.

Waiting. Waiting. Wait—

"Dawn."

Relief—a wave of it—slammed her. Then came affection, until she realized this wasn't Costin, only his host. His enemy, for all intents and purposes tonight.

"How is he?" she asked levelly, trying to avoid any references to gutting Jonah or pulling the hairs out of his head one by one.

He sounded resigned. "Our beloved pal is safe. Nothing to worry about."

Anger rolled inside her, but she told herself to cool it, to get him back here no matter what.

"Jonah, I think something's outside headquarters either waiting for you to get back or waiting for us to come out. Where are you?"

"Ah, you saw movement outside. Was it from the rooftops near Cross Bones? That's just me, Dawn."

Once again, relief hit her. Then frustration. Then she looped back to anger.

"I was just going from surface to surface," he added, "taking in each view. It's a lot different than looking through any kind of window in that house . . . or in this body."

"Is that where you've been the whole time? Dorking around nearby?"

"No, I arrived maybe five minutes ago. Breisi and some Friends just caught up and they're here nattering at me to get inside. I'm afraid I led them on a merry chase tonight, going from one place to the next. They'd catch up with me and, before any of us knew it, I'd be gone to the next thing. Couldn't stop myself, but you know how it is. Don't tell me you don't remember."

She did know, even from that one black spark of a moment after Benedikte's exchange. Damn Jonah, she did know.

Cool. She had to stay cool. "Jonah, do you know how worried sick we've been?"

"I had everything under control. You might not believe this, but part of Costin is grateful that I took us for a test-drive out here. Then again, part of him wants to maim me, but that'd be a little masochistic."

Dawn's patience was winding down. "Jonah . . ."

"How about disarming the outside defense system, and I'll get in there so you can read me the riot act in person? I'm all set if you are."

He sounded so . . . cooperative?

But she'd take it.

She sprinted, banging out the lab door. A thump of pain burst through her arm but she didn't care—adrenaline numbed it as she tripped up the stairs, into the entry where Natalia and Kiko backed away from her when she emerged and slammed the door behind her. They had their earpieces on so they knew the deal.

She ran to the control panel on the far end of the fireplace, avoiding Kalin's empty portrait.

"Just give me the word," Jonah said, "and we'll zoom right in as soon as you open the door."

"No games? You're not messing with me?"

That's when his voice got that sincere tone that always confused the hell out of her.

"You think I might've gone turncoat because my tender feelings were hurt by you and your enthusiasm for using your mind powers?"

"No," she said too quickly, because she truly hadn't thought he might do that. It stunned her that she trusted Jonah at all. "You disagree with Costin sometimes. You told me already, but I never thought you'd—"

"That's good enough for me," he said. He sounded as if she'd uttered the magic words. "Let me in?"

Jonah had the most precious thing to the team . . . and to her.

So, wasting no more time, she addressed Natalia, who'd come to stand with Kiko near the door. "When I count down to zero, open up. Kik, cover Jonah's entrance."

Dawn opened the weapons storage panel near the door, taking out a stake and a dart gun like the one Kiko had used earlier. He got the gun from her, then targeted the entrance.

She went to the other side of the fireplace, to the control panel. "Five," she said, punching a button with every number. "Four. Three. Two. One—"

On zero, Natalia flung open the door, diving out of the way while a rip of blackness flashed in and heaved itself against the wood to shut it as his body solidified. Jasmine from the Friends joined him, swirling around the room in agitation. More jasmine whooshed down the stairs behind Dawn, then banged into Jonah in welcome.

Kalin.

Breisi's voice swished around Dawn. *"Before we debrief, give him what for."*

"Oh, I will." Dawn armed the defense system again while he brushed off his coat and offered a wary smile while Kiko pulled back his weapon.

Then, as Breisi and the other Friends forced Kalin away from him and out of the room, Dawn saw a hint of blood around Jonah's mouth.

Her stomach dropped. Had he fed?

My God. Costin would be screaming, wanting to get out, far away from the wildness, the hunger of an appetite so out of control. Even though she couldn't sense what he was feeling from his buried place inside Jonah, she knew that feeding on anyone but her—indulging the monster in him—was the last thing he'd ever want to do, and Jonah had made him watch, helpless in the cell of that body.

Seeing the direction of her livid gaze, Jonah touched the smudge by his lower lip, his eyes darkening.

"It's what I am," he said. "What we are—Costin and I. I'm not afraid of what I want, and I can't withstand the torture of being so close to what satiates my appetites while knowing I can't have any of it." He wiped the blood away. "Do you know who Tantalus was?"

It sounded familiar—like the word "tantalize."

He continued. "He angered the gods, and as punishment, he was forced to stand in a pool of water below a tree that bore fruit. Whenever he reached out to satisfy his appetite, the branches inched back. Whenever he bent to drink the water, it ebbed away from him. That's what it's like for me, Dawn. Do you understand?"

She didn't want to, so she shut out the fingers of sympathy that pulled and tugged at her conscience.

He obviously saw an opening. "If Costin and I are going to share this body, I won't stand for that torture anymore. I can't."

He was chipping away at her, damn it. "Thing is, Jonah, we've got some special circumstances going on, and if you want to be any kind of hero, you'll take that torture. You'll help Costin clean out the Undergrounds, and when you're both done, you'll be free of him. This body will be all yours."

"And what will you do then, Dawn? When Costin's gone and if you're still alive, what's going to take the place of him—of your purpose?"

That dark, empty spot in her furled, and she went to the weapons stash, putting the stake away. Then she headed for the stairs,
with Kiko and Natalia watching her go.

Jonah was the only one who followed. "You didn't answer me."

"You've got a lot to account for first." Yeah, like she was going
to have a real heart-to-heart with him. *Ever.* "Who did you feed on
tonight, Jonah? Do we have to worry about any fallout from your
rampage?"

"I wouldn't call it that. There was a woman in Bloomsbury—very
willing, disease free—and she won't remember a thing. I was careful, even though I wonder if this body is strong enough to ward off
any diseases. Notice we've never even been sick before."

"Don't you dare experiment anymore with Costin."

God, Costin . . .

She got to her bedroom, wanting to shut Jonah out until he allowed Costin back, but as she closed the door, he reached out a
hand to block it.

He stood there, just over the threshold, his eyes a piercing blue,
his hair ruffled from a wild night.

Her stomach flipped, especially when she thought of how Jonah had tried to get out when she and Costin had screwed earlier.
How he'd been . . . tantalized.

Warped. This was bent and all she wanted was to wake up in
the life she used to have before vampires.

"Hey," he said, bracing his hands against the door frames.
"You've got your ultimate weapon back for the team, and you might
be *this* close to an Underground."

"You put Costin in the middle of a bunch of possible Underground vampires and you didn't give a fig about using your powers
in the open. Am I tickled? No."

His gaze went dark again as he leaned into the room. "I can
take Costin places that he's never been able to go during a hunt.
His hosts have never been as strong as you made me with that

exchange of our blood, Dawn. He's been wondering for a while whether or not I would be enough to shield him outside of head-quarters' walls. He'd never say it, because Costin doesn't take risks with himself until the final attack, but he wondered, and *I* acted when he wouldn't do it himself."

Then why the hell hadn't Costin shared this with her? They could connect minds, but there'd always be secrets. He was too good at hiding them.

They both were.

"I hope you're not questioning his courage," Dawn said. "He's got more than any of us."

"He's got a lion's share," Jonah said, leaning back out of the room and dropping his hands from the door frame. "But with this vampire's body, he's not sure of much right now. And for Costin to admit that is to admit weakness."

Costin, the warrior. Of course he'd never admit to it.

"Let me help, Dawn," Jonah said softly. "I want to."

Anger, helplessness . . . She pushed it all down so it joined that dark spot within her, making it grow like a stain that wouldn't stop spreading.

But she cinched it shut, stopped the flow of it, knowing what she had to do. Hating that Jonah always forced her to bargain with him for Costin's sake.

"You want to help us more actively," she said.

"I do. And before you have to ask—yes, if you consider me as an option for the team, that would buy my cooperation. If you meant it."

There was nothing else to do, especially if Jonah could act as a shield for Costin. They couldn't continue *this* way.

It was a devil's bargain, but what else could she do right now?

Swearing to get Jonah back, she locked gazes with him until she opened herself up enough for him to flood her.

I promise, Jonah. Now release him.

He stayed inside her an instant more than she wanted him to, brushing against her mind, causing red, tingling friction to gasp through her before he eased out.

"I'm holding you to it," he said, his eyes changing color, the ebb of an ocean pulling away to reveal the sun-washed sand.

And just as the last slant of blue turned topaz, he whispered, "Remember."

When the change was complete, Costin trudged one step forward before she went to him, catching him before he fell from exhaustion, from what Jonah had put him through. She supported him as they slumped to the floor, his arms around her as he buried his face against her neck.

She smelled the night on his coat, in his hair, smelled a hint of blood from Jonah's last meal. When his fingers tightened on her, she wondered if he'd fully tasted the exquisite trace of it in his mouth just now. She wanted to see into his mind to get an answer, but she stayed out, content to be with him, happy just to have him back.

Because there was time for a few minutes of peace, wasn't there? Time before they went to Queenshill to find out what was behind the housematron's door.

Time before Jonah demanded that Dawn honor her end of the bargain she'd been forced to make.

"Costin," she whispered, as if saying his name over and over would keep him here for at least the rest of the night.

"I won't allow him back," he said, his voice thick. And she knew it was because of the feeding, the blood. The self-disgust of having to give in when he'd always been a knight who'd never compromised, never surrendered.

"Everything's going to work," she said. "We're going to find out if those girl vamps will lead us to that Underground, and then we're going to take on whatever comes our way. Together. Got it? *Together.*"

But he'd already passed out into an undead rest, even though sunrise was a couple hours off.

Dawn pulled him closer, grasping his coat as if her fingers were stitches holding them together, binding them, doubling their strength for what would be coming with just one of the Undergrounds that could free Costin.

And maybe even the rest of them, too.

Dear Reader,

I hope you enjoyed *A Drop of Red*, the book that starts off the London Underground portion of the series. You know that this series, as with the Hollywood Underground trilogy (Books One through Three), is structured a little differently than most, and by the time you get to Book Six, the mystery, character, and mythology arcs introduced in this installment will be resolved.

This means that, in August 2009, Dawn and the team's hunt for the London Underground is going to continue in *The Path of Razors*, and I hope that you'll enjoy what's to come as Limpet and Associates soldiers on in its endeavors. . . .

Until that time, happy hunting, and thank you for all your support. You're the ones who keep the Undergrounds going.

All the best,
Chris Marie Green